C0-AAV-993

He was irritating, out of control, and downright frustrating . . . and that was only the beginning of the list.

"It seems our paths are destined to cross, Mademoiselle Lavoisier."

She cast about for a retort that would put him in his place, when she saw his glance drop to her shoeless foot. She groped beneath the bench for her discarded slipper. To her horror, Tark, with a single, fluid move, retrieved the satin slipper and favored her with a sardonic smile.

"You seem to have a propensity for loosing your footwear, Isabeau. It calls to mind a story I once heard from my grandmother."

Mom Dieu, did he think she had cast him in the role of a fairy-tale prince? "I'll thank you to return my shoe at once," she managed to say, as she made an undignified grab for her footwear.

Tark dangled the slipper just beyond her reach. "You should be more careful of your belongings, my sweet Isabeau. Who knows what price you might find yourself paying to reclaim them?"

The sight of the rugged man twirling her slipper by one bright ribbon should have amused her, but Isabeau didn't laugh. Tark had some reason for seeking her out tonight. He unnerved her. "Give me back my shoe, *m'sieur.*"

Tark crossed his arms, tucking the sea-green slipper in to the crook of his elbow. "I must warn you, I drive a hard bargain."

Righteous indignation overcame her apprehension as she tugged off her other slipper and brandished it before him.

Since you're so enamored of that shoe, you should have its mate." She hurled the slipper at him. It landed at his feet, like a bright-plumed dovefelled by a hunter's shot. She looked up to meet Tark's gaze. He was as she was by her action.

"Alexa Smart has a fresh new voice that sizzles with excitement. *Masquerade* is guaranteed to keep you reading until dawn."
—Judith French, author of *This Fierce Loving*

FOR THE VERY BEST IN ROMANCE — DENISE LITTLE PRESENTS!

AMBER, SING SOFTLY (0038, $4.99)
by Joan Elliott Pickart

Astonished to find a wounded gun-slinger on her doorstep, Amber Prescott can't decide whether to take him in or put him out of his misery. Since this lonely frontierswoman can't deny her longing to have a man of her own, she nurses him back to health, while savoring the glorious possibilities of the situation. But what Amber doesn't realize is that this strong, handsome man is full of surprises!

A DEEPER MAGIC (0039, $4.99)
by Jillian Hunter

From the moment wealthy Margaret Rose and struggling physician Ian MacNeill meet, they are swept away in an adventure that takes them from the haunted land of Aberdeen to a primitive, faraway island — and into a world of danger and irresistible desire. Amid the clash of ancient magic and new science Margaret and Ian find themselves falling helplessly in love.

SWEET AMY JANE (0050, $4.99)
by Anna Eberhardt

Her horoscope warned her she'd be dealing with the wrong sort of man. And private eye Amy Jane Chadwick was used to dealing with the wrong kind of man. But nothing prepared her for the gorgeous, stubborn Max, a former professional athlete who is being stalked by an obsessive fan. From the moment they meet, sparks fly and danger follows!

MORE THAN MAGIC (0049, $4.99)
by Olga Bicos

This classic romance is a thrilling tale of two adventurers who set out for the wilds of the Arizona territory in the year 1878. Seeking treasure, an archaeologist and an astronomer find the greatest prize of all — love.

Available wherever paperbacks are sold, or order direct from the Publisher. Send cover price plus 50¢ per copy for mailing and handling to Penguin USA, P.O. Box 999, c/o Dept. 17109, Bergenfield, NJ 07621. Residents of New York and Tennessee must include sales tax. DO NOT SEND CASH.

ALEXA SMART
MASQUERADE

PINNACLE BOOKS
WINDSOR PUBLISHING CORP.

PINNACLE BOOKS are published by

Windsor Publishing Corp.
850 Third Avenue
New York, NY 10022

Copyright © 1994 by Diane A. S. Stuckert

All rights reserved. No part of this book may be reproduced in any form or by any means without the prior written consent of the Publisher, excepting brief quotes used in reviews.

If you purchased this book without a cover, you should be aware that this book is stolen property. It was reported as "unsold and destroyed" to the Publisher and neither the Author nor the Publisher has received any payment for this "stripped book."

The P logo Reg. U.S. Pat. & TM off. Pinnacle is a trademark of Windsor Publishing Corp.

First Pinnacle Printing: December, 1994

Printed in the United States of America

This is for Gerry,
who never said if, *but always* when.

Thanks to my fellow writers,
Carol Caldwell and Kathryn Young,
who don't let me get away with anything,

and special appreciation to
Denise Little,
a good friend and one heck of an editor.

One

Tark Parrish spent a few moments praying for death.

When it was not forthcoming, he opened his eyes. He wished he hadn't. Above him hovered a Dantesque creature . . . naked, with bared teeth and red-rimmed eyes baleful. He squinted up at the figure, wondering if he'd died in the night and been transported to some mythical nether region. Then his vision cleared. He realized that the loathsome being was his own image, reflected in the gilt-edged mirror suspended over the bed.

Careful not to jar his pounding head, Tark dragged himself upright against a jumble of white satin pillows. The pale glow of a midwinter sun seeped past the heavy velvet drapes. Beside him, Elisabeth stirred restlessly beneath the pearly sheets. Her red hair twisted across the pillow like a nest of bright snakes. He edged away from her and clutched at the bedpost to steady himself.

"Where in the hell are my clothes?" More importantly, where in the hell was he?

Given the decor, they must have spent last night at the brothel owned by the quadroon procuress, Ophelia.

The room boasted gold-veined red wallpaper that complemented the draperies. The carpet continued the same tasteless color theme with an army of fat yellow Cupids cavorting on a field of scarlet pile.

Nothing, though, could compare with the bed. It frothed around him like some monstrous confection, white-flounced, with gold Cupids serving as bedposts. Tark removed his hand from one cherub's dimpled buttocks. He groaned. The garish red and gold seemed to pulsate, and did little to soothe his aching head and queasy stomach.

He reached for the bottle of whiskey on the bedside table and finished off its contents. As the liquor spread through him, bits of his memory drifted back. He'd left his favorite waterfront tavern, the Gilded Albatross, and met Elisabeth around midnight. What happened afterwards was lost in a haze of disjointed images. Tark frowned as he studied his now-empty whiskey bottle. To end up in such a state he must have drunk the whole damn thing himself. That, or . . .

A sudden suspicion took hold. He swapped the bottle for the crystal tumbler abandoned on the same table. He peered into it, then ran a finger along its inner surface. As he expected, traces of fine crystalline powder clung to his skin.

Damn Elisabeth and her voodoo potions.

His grip on the glass tightened as he remembered how she'd solicitously poured him whiskey from a small silver flask. Last night had been the first time he'd seen her in several weeks. Impatient as he'd been, he had downed the drink without question. Now, he realized he'd been drugged, and the alcohol had heightened the powder's aphrodisiac but mind-dulling effects.

He cursed, then viciously hurled the glass. Even the petulance of the musically accented voice beside him couldn't diminish his satisfaction with the resulting crash.

"Really, *cher,* must you make so much noise?"

Elisabeth yawned and stretched like a disgruntled cat rousted from a hearthside perch. "Lie back down." She turned so that her lush form molded against him. "It's too early for civilized people to be up and about. Besides, I can think of more enjoyable ways to spend the morning."

"Then why don't you show me?"

His half-ironic suggestion proved unnecessary. Her nimble fingers were already expertly exploring him. Tark gave himself up to her ministrations. Vain and demanding she might be, but the beautiful Elisabeth Tremaine had proved herself the most accomplished lover—Creole, or otherwise—that he'd ever taken.

Through half-closed eyes, he watched their images in the mirror above him. Her ivory skin and fiery hair contrasted sharply with his own tanned flesh as she moved down the long length of his body. Sprawled naked amid a tangle of satin, performing intimate acts upon him, Elisabeth bore little resemblance to the refined New Orleans belle who held sway over the Creole society he despised. The sight afforded him a measure of bitter satisfaction far greater than that of mere sexual gratification.

Her skilled mouth soon brought him to the brink of climax. But even as he pulled her up to straddle him, intent on the relief that waited between her welcoming thighs, it occurred to him just what day it was.

"Son of a bitch," he groaned. His desire was doused as effectively as if he'd been tossed into the muddy Mississippi. How in the hell could he have forgotten his appointment with Aloysius Burnett?

Ignoring Elisabeth's indignant protest, he disentangled himself from her grasp and sat up. The action sent a blade of agony through him. He was getting too damned old to spend his nights in drunken abandon.

"What time is it?" The pain subsided enough for him to drag himself up from the bed. Not waiting for an answer, he grabbed the washstand pitcher and dumped its contents over his head. The cold water hit with a vengeance, plastering his dark hair to his skull and streaming in icy rivulets down his bare chest. He gritted his teeth and reminded himself that this kind of mortification was supposed to be good for the flesh.

The remedy, though crude, proved effective. Oblivious to the puddle beneath his feet, he toweled off and began the search for his clothes. He finally located them draped across the plaster arms of the life-sized Cupid near the door. He pulled on his trousers and boots, then shrugged on his shirt and fumbled for the buttons.

"It's inside out, *cher*," Elisabeth observed in a silky tone that didn't quite mask a glimmer of spite. Convinced now that he did not intend to rejoin her, she gave a peevish tug at the tasseled cord beside the bed. "If you insist on waking me at this ungodly hour, I simply must have my coffee."

She settled against the pillows and draped the sheets about her. Her pale, full breasts were exposed to his gaze. Tark ignored her blatant attempt at distraction and tucked in his unbuttoned shirt, then reached around for his jacket. He withdrew the revolver nestled deep in its pocket and shoved the weapon into the rear waistband of his trousers. Once he pulled on the jacket, the revolver would be concealed, yet within easy reach—a precaution he deemed prudent in light of his current situation.

Behind him, he heard the rustle of satin just before a pair of slim white arms wrapped around his waist. Elisabeth pressed herself to him, her nipples taut against his back. Her hands slid beneath his shirt and moved along his bare chest in soft, seductive strokes.

"Tell me, *cher*," she asked, "what could be more important than staying here with me?"

"I've got a business to run."

Not that too damn much of the company remained to look after, he amended with silent bitterness. His mistress had no idea of his precarious financial situation, and he had no plans to enlighten her to the fact that Parrish Company, Ltd. tottered on the verge of bankruptcy. Though Elisabeth might deign to consort with a wealthy American, she would draw the line at bedding a penniless one. His silence would spare her the painful dilemma of choosing between her twin vices of avarice and sexual lust.

"I'm not at your beck and call." He pulled from her embrace and turned to face her. "If you want someone to crawl between the sheets with you, I'm sure one of Ophelia's employees can accommodate."

"I don't want someone else, *cher*. I want you, heartless *américain* bastard that you are."

She stalked back to the bed and flung herself among the rumpled sheets. Then, with one of her typical abrupt mood shifts, she favored him with an arch smile. "You can at least agree to join me at Clarisse Dumas's cotillion next week."

"What about your reputation?" he pointed out, all too familiar with the animosity that still lingered between Creole society and its brash American counterpart. "Are you willing to risk being seen in public with me?"

"Of course not, *cher*. But just because we won't dance together doesn't mean we can't arrange a *tête-à-tête*—in Madame's own bedchamber, perhaps."

Despite his worries, Tark reluctantly grinned at her brazen suggestion. He'd promised Clarisse he would make an effort to attend her next function. A lifelong friend of his family's, the old dowager wouldn't hesitate to flay him verbally if he went back on his word.

"I'll be there."

He was spared further discussion on the subject by a discreet knock on the door. He stepped aside for the Negro maid who entered, bearing Elisabeth's coffee. Though in dire need of a quick cup himself—Ophelia's potent chicory brew was strong enough to revive even the dead—he headed out into the hallway. His final glimpse of his mistress revealed her berating the luckless servant for some transgression.

With a shake of his head, he made his way below and headed out the front door of the house. He stopped on the stately gallery that spanned the building's facade to reach for his pocket watch. *Nine forty-five.* Barely a quarter of an hour to make his appointment with Burnett.

He strode to the gate of the elaborate cast-iron railing

that surrounded the property. Reaching the wooden *banquette*—the New Orleans equivalent of a sidewalk—he hailed a passing carriage for his trip to the waterfront. Once inside, he settled back against the torn leather seat and bleakly contemplated the interview that lay ahead.

The banker's terse letter requesting this meeting was no surprise. It had been preceded by months of similar correspondence from other creditors and investors questioning the financial stability of Parrish Company, Ltd.

Our board of directors has voiced concerns . . .

. . . regret that we are unable to consider your firm for any future contracts . . .

Tark sighed wearily. He had met all objections with repeated reassurances that the situation was under control. His words had begun to echo with the hollow ring of stubborn bravado as events proved otherwise.

He had gone from wealth to the brink of ruin in what seemed weeks, though in fact he could trace the beginning of his company's decline to a point little more than a year earlier. At first, he had passed off the various mishaps, revoked contracts, and soured investments as part of a run of bad luck—frustrating, but beyond his control.

As time passed and the incidents escalated, it dawned on him that some force other than coincidence was at work. Then, three months ago, someone had ransacked his office. Though the intruder stole nothing, he *had* combed through Tark's records. This overt ploy led Tark to conclude that someone was waging a campaign to undermine Parrish Company, Ltd.

Faced with imminent bankruptcy, he had liquidated his remaining assets and invested in one final shipment, a cargo bound from Ecuador aboard the steamer *Esmeralda*. He had also taken steps to discover who was trying to ruin him. He'd enlisted the aid of his old friend, Tom Sullivan, a member of the metropolitan police force, who had extensive criminal contacts and a decided bent for intrigue.

Tark drew his jacket more tightly against the January wind that knifed into the coach. The action failed to banish the cold despair that gripped him. Once the *Esmeralda* docked in New Orleans, he would be in the black again and no longer at this shadow enemy's mercy. But if his gamble didn't pay off . . .

So caught up was he in his thoughts that it took him a moment to realize the carriage had reached the docks. He signaled the driver to halt. He'd make better time on foot.

As he climbed from the coach, the familiar muddy scent of the Mississippi hit him, tinged with the pungent scent of decayed fish and overripe fruit. Carts and carriages maneuvered through workers and onlookers. The clomp of hooves offered a rhythmic accompaniment to the hollow rumble of wooden wheels on the wharf. Snatches of conversation drifted by, an odd medley of English, French, and Creole patois that was unique to New Orleans. The frenetic bustle held none of its usual lure for him. He focused on the line of foreign vessels that had docked since last night.

A flash of color against the dull grey of a steamer caught his eye. Passengers filtered from that ship, among them a raven-haired young woman in a shimmering gown. *Some wealthy man's mistress,* he thought, for neither husband nor chaperone accompanied her. No family of means would allow a female relative to travel unescorted. Judging from her trunks, borne by a contingent of stevedores, he could guarantee she was no poor immigrant journeying to the New World in search of employment.

Perhaps it was the color of the dress she wore—*emerald* green—that held his attention. Whatever the reason, he watched the girl make her way down the rickety gangplank. He couldn't distinguish her features; still, she possessed the supple grace that often accompanied youthful beauty. All the more reason to assume he'd not been mistaken in his original assessment of her character.

Not that he held her profession against her. He considered the straightforward exchange of sexual favors for money a refreshing change from the coy bartering of the same for marriage and social standing. At least the first way, both parties knew in advance what to expect. Marriage was a different story. He had cause to know.

A shout from the dock interrupted Tark's memories of wedlock's darker side. The young Negro who led the girl's procession stumbled on a loose board of the gangplank. He swayed with dizzying grace, but despite a chorus of encouragement from his fellow laborers the trunk he carried slipped from his grasp.

With the boy in pursuit, the luggage tumbled wildly down the wooden walkway. The crowd around him realized its danger and parted with undignified haste. With a final bound, the trunk flew from the gangplank and hit the pier, landing a few yards from his feet. Its heavy clasps burst apart noisily. Then, like an exhausted animal, the trunk rolled onto its side and disgorged a froth of white undergarments onto the wharf.

While the hapless boy struggled to right the battered chest, the girl made her own way down to the pier. Amid the sea of lace, under the disapproving stares of her fellow travelers, she gathered her scattered clothes. Reminding himself that Burnett still awaited him, Tark started back down the wharf. He paused when he heard the dockworker's voice.

"Hey, girlie, I reckon you'd look right fine in that there frippery." That drew guffaws from the other stevedores.

A second man took up the cry. "Yeah, darlin', why don't we take a look an' see if what yer wearin' right now is just as purty?"

The men's comments grew progressively lewder, and Tark hesitated. The chit would find herself in an unpleasant situation unless someone intervened. Lady or whore, she didn't deserve the men's abuse. As he debated turning back—hell, he didn't have the time for charitable gestures—a breeze swept through the tangle of spilled clothes and whisked a gauzy scrap of cloth in his direction. A second gust caught the garment and wrapped it raffishly around his boot.

The incongruous sight reminded him of nothing so much as a medieval lady's favor tied for luck around her knight's arm. He freed the gossamer fabric—a silk stocking, he realized with amusement—and started toward her. When his shadow fell over her, the girl, startled from her task, glanced up to meet his gaze.

He halted, silk banner in hand, and stared down at her wide-set eyes—eyes the black velvet of a Louisiana night—peering up at him beneath a slash of dark brows. Her full red lips held a hint of childish curve, and he decided that she was younger than he'd first judged. Her forthright gaze had none of the brittle boldness common to those women driven by choice or circumstance to barter their bodies. Instead, he saw in her eyes the innocent wariness of a woman unaccustomed to a man's scrutiny. He revised his conclusions.

Alone she might be, but some man's mistress, she most definitely is not.

He assessed the rest of her appearance. Though not beautiful in the conventional sense, she possessed an aristocratic elegance that would make a woman like Elisabeth appear tawdry by comparison. Her tightly laced bodice confined but couldn't quite contain a swell of alabaster flesh that hinted at a lush figure corseted beneath the modest gown. In stark contrast to her pale complexion, raven hair that had been swept back demurely spilled in wind-raked black tendrils down her slender neck.

Desire flared within him, spreading with an almost painful heat from his belly down through his loins. He found himself wondering how it would feel to thread his fingers through those silken tresses as he eased his body over hers and penetrated the hot, secret core of her womanhood. She'd wrap slim, white legs around his waist and move beneath him, until he expended his need in a final shuddering stroke that—

Sweet Jesus, what in the hell am I thinking?

Tark glanced down at the stocking in his clenched fist and exhaled, shaken by his reaction. He'd never made a habit of ravishing innocents, preferring instead the skillful embraces of an experienced lover. Still, something about this girl struck a sharp chord within him—a chord that demanded an answering refrain.

Praying his embarrassingly physical reaction to her hadn't been obvious, he gallantly proffered the crumpled stocking. "I presume this is yours?"

The girl rose to her feet, her expression reflecting swiftly veiled distaste. In a tone that was polite to the point of curtness, she replied, *"Merci, m'sieur."*

Creole.

The word reverberated through his mind. The French-tinged accent was unmistakable, as was her contempt for all things non-Creole, himself included. Tark choked back a laugh. Sweet Jesus, a moment ago he'd been ready to bed her. Now, knowing what she was, he'd be damned if he'd take her, even if she offered herself to him right here on the dock.

"If you please, *m'sieur* . . ."

Her low, musical voice held a note of impatience, and he realized they were engaged in an undignified tug-of-war over the stocking. He let it slide from his grasp.

"Do yourself a favor, *mademoiselle,"* he said. "Pick up your clothes, find yourself a carriage, and get the hell out of here before one of your friends"—he gestured at the dockworkers—"decides to get better acquainted."

He didn't wait for her reply but turned toward his warehouse. He didn't know or care if the chit took his advice. A mocking voice within him said that he was behaving like a fool. Hell, he knew that this girl had nothing to do with his past . . . nothing to do with another sweet-faced *mademoiselle* whose innocent demeanor had hidden a treacherous heart. Why had he reacted so violently upon learning she was a Creole?

He quickened his steps, covering the short distance to his wharfside office. By the time he strode through his office door, his wall clock was striking the quarter hour. Aloysius Burnett was already there, impatience stamped across his narrow features. He favored Tark with a sour look.

Two

"My apologies, Mr. Burnett," Tark said. He hurriedly took his own chair behind the desk and reached for a stack of ledgers. "I was delayed by an earlier . . . appointment."

As he spoke, he glimpsed his reflection in the banker's spectacles and winced. *You're making one damn fine impression,* he thought. *A quarter of an hour late, only half-dressed, and thoroughly hung over.* Hell, Burnett might even come away from this meeting prepared to offer him a job sweeping floors in one of his banks.

The man withdrew a sheaf of papers from his portfolio. "Your housekeeper was good enough to show me inside. And now, if you can spare a moment, perhaps we might review the current contract terms between Parrish Company, Ltd., and my organization."

At Tark's nod, the banker arranged his papers in neat piles across the desk. Balding and unprepossessing, Aloysius Burnett favored sober black suits and a starched demeanor that more befitted an undertaker than the foremost representative of an investment group with ties to the sugar and cotton exchanges of New Orleans. Tark knew that, the man's sartorial shortcomings notwithstanding, he was one of the city's shrewdest financiers.

"Our board of directors has reviewed at length your company's past performance," the banker began in a precise tone. "For the past five years, you have served our investors as a buyer, shipper, and broker, fulfilling these roles in a manner that proved profitable for all parties. You have also handled, with a fair measure of success, numerous independent consignments that fell outside our scope of interest. The board additionally examined reports of certain . . . incidents that have plagued your firm over the past twelve months. On three separate occasions, the dock authorities have seized your records. Charges concerning altered bills of lading were levied—"

"—and dismissed. You know my operation is strictly legitimate. I haven't smuggled so much as a bottle of whiskey in almost seven years," Tark protested.

"We realize that fact," Burnett primly reassured him. "Your wartime activities, while duly noted, have no bearing on this situation. Still, we see other areas of concern."

The man consulted another page, and Tark braced himself. Burnett did not disappoint him.

"In March of last year—and then again in June—fire broke out in your warehouses, resulting in the combined loss of half-a-dozen cotton consignments. July and August saw dockworker strikes on an almost weekly basis. Pilfering of goods is not an uncommon occurrence on the wharf, however, in the final six months of our previous fiscal year, we noted a marked increase in such activities—solely in connection with the shipments you handled for us." He paused in his recitation and glanced over his spectacles at Tark. "Need I continue?"

Tark shook his head. He could relate another half

dozen similar episodes, himself. More than once, he'd been forced to strip off his jacket and unload shipments alongside his crew to assure the cargo reached its destination intact. "So, what is the board's recommendation?"

"To a man, they expressed serious doubts concerning continued association with your firm."

Tark grimly digested this. He'd anticipated it, but that did nothing to ease the tightening in his gut. Still, if he could convince Burnett to forestall his final decision, at least until the *Esmeralda* made port, the contract might not yet be lost.

He flipped through the top ledger and stabbed a finger at one page of entries. "In the five years you've been dealing with me, your investors' yearly profits— and your own—have increased on an average of fifteen percent," he asserted. "Last year, gross profits exceeded six figures. As for those incidents you mentioned, all investors involved recouped their losses. No one was out a single cent—"

"—except for you, who made up the difference from your own pocket." Burnett gave a tight smile at Tark's look of surprise. "Yes, Mr. Parrish, I am well aware that every reputable underwriter in the city has ceased to do business with you. My best estimate puts it at three months since any shipment you have handled has been insured. I also understand that your personal finances are now strained to their limits."

Tark scowled and slammed the ledger shut. "Since you know so much about my business affairs, why don't you tell me why I'm suddenly a *persona non grata* in this city?"

"I have been wondering that very thing." The banker

plucked off his spectacles and polished them as he considered his answer. "Unfortunately, I can make only the most general of assumptions. My guess is that you've made a powerful enemy who, in turn, has taken it upon himself to systematically divest you of your assets. I can offer you nothing more, save for my personal observation that this man now has you by the proverbial short hairs."

At Tark's sardonic nod of assent, Burnett slid his glasses back on and revealed his first hint of humanity. "Perhaps if I might compare our figures against yours once more . . ."

While the banker busied himself with the ledgers, Tark prowled the room. His first impulse was to put his fist through the nearest wall. Barring that, he could use the bottle of whiskey he had stashed in his desk to dull his headache, which had returned with a vengeance. He contented himself instead with reviewing his encounter with the raven-haired Creole girl.

Despite the antipathy he had thrown up as a defense against her, he found himself lingering with an odd pleasure on the memory of her full, soft lips—lips that could capture a man's soul with one whispered endearment and sear his flesh with a single kiss. In her dark eyes, he had glimpsed the embers of desire that glowed beneath the ashes of her innocence. He knew that, stoked by the right man, her girlish yearnings would readily flare into a blaze of womanly desire—

". . . must understand our position."

Burnett's voice, which Tark realized had been droning on for some moments, took on a sharp edge. Putting aside all thoughts of the girl, Tark faced the man.

"Just what are you trying to tell me?"

"Believe me, I find the situation as distressing as you do," the banker replied as he returned the documents to his satchel. "Your capital is all but depleted, you own nothing of value for use as collateral, and your credit is nonexistent."

"So what's the problem?"

Burnett shot him a sour look as he tied shut the leather case and stood. "I assure you, Mr. Parrish, this is no matter for jest. Even taking into consideration my personal admiration for your abilities, until you return your operation to a firm footing, I simply cannot advise the board to renew your contracts."

"Just give me until next month, and I'll have the money," Tark urged as he strode back toward the desk. Sweet Jesus, he couldn't afford to lose Burnett. If word spread that the banker's group had pulled out, his few remaining clients would immediately follow suit. He'd be left with nothing to show for almost seven years of hard work but a drawerful of past due bills and a year's remaining lease on this converted warehouse that served as both home and office.

The banker shook his head in polite disbelief. "You are indeed an optimist if you anticipate that Central American venture of yours will yield a profit. And even assuming you do raise the funds to stave off bankruptcy, you still face other problems that cannot be resolved with an infusion of cash."

"If you're referring to those 'accidents' . . ."

"I am." Burnett drew himself up to his full five-foot-six height, which was a good head shorter than Tark. "While this unknown person continues to sabotage your activities, those who deal with you will face risks no sane investor can afford to take. Perhaps six months from now, if your situation improves . . ."

The man's voice trailed off into doubtful silence as he moved toward the door. Tark put out a restraining hand. *Don't do this to me, Aloysius.* The plea formed in his mind, but he left the words unspoken when the banker spared him a look of outright pity and disengaged his arm from Tark's grip.

"Good day, Mr. Parrish . . . and good luck."

Tark summoned what remained of his pride and stepped aside to let the man pass. He watched through the open window as Burnett picked his way along the wharf, dodging the laborers who rolled immense kegs of molasses toward the sugar sheds. He remained at his post even after the banker vanished from sight. He might have continued the vigil indefinitely had he not been distracted by the pain that ripped through his right hand.

Puzzled, he flexed his swelling fingers and saw that his knuckles had been scraped raw. The mystery came clear when he noticed the shoulder-high section of splintered wainscot within arm's length. He'd finally put his fist through the wall.

Tark sucked at his torn flesh. He felt better for having succumbed to impulse. The pain of his battered hand served as a catharsis, diluting the despair that had threatened to overwhelm him. Now that he knew what Burnett's people planned, he could devote his energies to uncovering his unknown foe.

But as he turned from the window he thought not of his current desperate straits, but of the girl in green who had captured his imagination. With a pang of regret he realized he might have been the man to kindle that fiery passion within her, had she not been a Creole.

With a sigh, Isabeau Lavoisier settled against the thinly padded seat of the hired coach. Her fashionable slippers pinched her feet so that she barely noticed the way the bench's sharp edge bit into her thighs. As the carriage jerked forward, she eased the shoes off and wriggled her toes.

Cheered, she flashed a smile at her brother seated across from her. Philippe ignored her gesture and feigned rapt interest in the scenery. Isabeau sighed in exasperation.

"Stop sulking, Titi," she cajoled, using her childhood nickname for him. "Little as you deserve it, I have forgiven you for leaving me alone so long on that wretched wharf."

Philippe assumed an air of injured dignity. "It's Lucie's fault I was delayed. First, the wretched girl scorched my favorite shirt; then she all but poisoned me with her cooking. You know what a delicate constitution I have. Once I tasted the unspeakable mess she tried to serve me for breakfast, I felt it prudent to dine elsewhere. And then—"

"*Assez!* Enough, *mon frère!*" Isabeau raised her slim, white hands in surrender. "You've convinced me that your suffering far outweighed mine. So now that we have settled that, why don't you tell me everything that has happened since your last letter?"

Mollified, Philippe launched into an account of his latest doings. How much Isabeau had missed her brother's exuberant, frivolous companionship. If not for his regular letters to her over the past two years, she might well have succumbed to incurable homesickness during her stay with Grandmère in Paris. Philippe had kept her abreast of the latest news and gossip, so that she felt that she had never left New Orleans.

As the coach rumbled along, however, she found that even her brother's amusing anecdotes couldn't dispel the sense of uneasiness that weighed on her like an unfamiliar cloak. She tried to attribute that emotion to excitement over returning home. Honesty compelled her to admit that her uneasiness stemmed from her encounter with the *américain*.

It all had started with her green gown. She had donned the silk in hopes of bolstering her spirits. It had been a relief to put aside the drab mourning gowns she had worn since her cousin's death six months earlier. But the bright color had made her stand out from her older, more soberly-attired fellow passengers.

The mortifying scene repeated itself in her mind. The two elderly spinsters who had served as her chaperones for the voyage from Paris had parted company with her several miles downriver, leaving her to fend for herself. Had she anticipated what would happen, she would have been less enthusiastic in bidding the stern sisters *adieu*.

Within minutes of docking, she'd been kneeling on the sodden wharf trying frantically to gather her wind-tossed undergarments. Adding to her dismay had been the lewd comments of the dockworkers . . . who doubtless would have paid her scant notice had she been more demurely garbed! After her two years in France, their English words had rung oddly in her ears. Still, she had little difficulty understanding their meaning.

Then *he*'d appeared before her, a dark, threatening male who towered over her crouched form. She judged him to be a decade older than her own nineteen years, though his air of weary detachment made him appear older still. He wore his black hair long, disdaining the fragrant pomade that most men of means affected. In contrast to his dark coloring, his eyes were the blue of a midsummer sky. His features were aristocratic, but his tanned complexion and unshaven state better suited a laborer than a gentleman.

And a gentleman, he most certainly was not.

Isabeau blushed. No gentleman would dream of striding about a public wharf in such a state of undress—no doubt the result of the previous night's overindulgence in women, strong drink, or both. The puzzling fact that he wore his shirt inside out had concerned her less than the way that garment gaped open to reveal his tanned flesh and well-defined muscle. She had been unable to look away, fascinated by the way a thatch of crisp, black hair fanned from the base of his throat and narrowed down the length of his flat stomach. She'd not dared let her gaze drop any lower.

In those first few unnerving moments, she had thought the man a buccaneer—like Jean Lafitte, she'd told herself, though the *américain* had proved that he lacked that French pirate's legendary gallantry. Not only had he subjected her to a bold scrutiny that held her speechless, he'd then dismissed her with a few contemptuous words. As he had stalked off to wherever it was that buccaneers spent their days, she told herself it was relief, not regret, she felt at the fact she'd never likely see him again. Unwilling to dwell on that memory, Isabeau turned her attention back to her brother.

"Tell me," she asked as she gestured at the coach's dilapidated interior, "did your maid also lose our carriage? Or did you decide you preferred driving about the city in a hired rig?"

It was not an idle question, for her family prided itself on its equipage, descended as they were from a long line of equestrians. The fact that most Creole families preferred to rent their carriages had not stopped the Lavoisiers from keeping a select stable.

Philippe's exuberance dissolved into chagrin as he met her gaze. "We don't exactly own a carriage anymore, Isette."

"I see." Her calm tone surprised her, though the months of living with Grandmère had no doubt inured her to such announcements. "Did someone steal it, then, or did you lose it to one of your friends in some wager?"

"Neither."

Philippe donned an offended expression at the implied lack of moral fortitude on his part that her question raised. "It's just that I owed my tailor a small sum, and he was reluctant to extend my credit. Since I could hardly attend this year's balls in last season's clothes, he accepted the carriage and horses as downpayment on a modest wardrobe." He glanced up at her in uncertainty. "You do understand, don't you?"

Isabeau didn't trust herself to answer. Grandmère Emelie's favorite maxim flashed through her mind.

Appearances, chère, *appearances. Above all else, one must keep up appearances.*

Grandmère adhered to that stratagem with a single-mindedness that bordered on fanaticism. The fashionable lower level of her *maison* boasted watered silk, intricately patterned rugs, and marble floors. Isabeau had been overwhelmed by it all upon her first arrival. Though accustomed to wealth, to her seventeen-year-old sensibilities the manor's opulence bordered on the decadent.

Her astonishment grew when Grandmère's maid led her to a cramped second-story alcove and announced it would be her quarters for the duration of her stay. That floor and the one above were both bare of furniture, save for the battered bed and wardrobe in Isabeau's own tiny room.

She soon learned that her grandmother was an inveterate gambler who had long since depleted her late husband's fortune. Though reduced to pawning the furniture and bibelots Grandpère Lavoisier had collected throughout his diplomatic career, Grandmère ingeniously preserved an illusion of wealth—which extended to providing her marriageable granddaughter with the proper gowns for every occasion. Only Emelie's few remaining servants and Isabeau knew the old woman spent her nights on the parlor *chaise longue,* having long since sold her elegant bedroom suite. With such a grandmother as an example, she should be grateful that Philippe had merely bartered their carriage.

"Don't worry, Titi," she reassured him. "I know you will find a way to return our coach to us."

They continued the drive in companionable conversation, though it wasn't until they reached home that Isabeau allowed herself a sigh of relief. As the carriage rolled up to the courtyard gate, she saw that their home reflected no outward signs of her brother's financial

woes. The narrow *port-cochère* town house stood three
stories tall. Its arched carriageway entrance featured a
series of iron bars above the pair of heavy paneled
doors. Louvered shutters, open to let in the winter sun,
framed each window. The red brick facade was similar
to that of the other houses along the street, enlivened
by elaborate wrought-iron on the windows and balconies. The ironwork always reminded Isabeau of black
lace on a gown.

The inner courtyard was a different story. Brick walls
on three sides supported a tapestry of vines grown wild
from neglect. A few blooms still dangled from the
shrubs like forgotten Chinese lanterns, their delicate
scents mingling to form a seductive perfume. The dying
greenery all but hid the former slave quarters.

With a critical glance at the courtyard—it would take
weeks to return the garden to its former glory—Isabeau
hurried into the house. She made her way through the
well-loved rooms, spending a moment in each. Here, in
the study, Papa had spent much of the day. She fancied
that a lingering hint of his tobacco hung in the air. In
the parlor, Maman's sewing box still occupied one corner. A skein of yarn peeped from beneath its lid as if
moments, rather than years, had passed since her mother
last put aside her work.

Isabeau swallowed against the sudden tightness in her
throat. She had been fifteen and Philippe, barely twenty,
when Jean-Paul and Thérèse Lavoisier had fallen victim
to "Bronze John," as the Orleanians called yellow fever.
Time had dulled her grief, but hadn't filled the emptiness their loss left within her heart.

Putting aside her memories, Isabeau made her way

up to her old bedroom. She gasped in delight. Gone
were the narrow cot and tiny wardrobe of her childhood.
In their place, were graceful mahogany furnishings
cushioned in delicate hues. Subtle beige silk replaced
her once-cherished cabbage rose wallpaper, and a Per-
sian rug covered the floor.

"Do you like it, *chère?*" Philippe joined her at the
doorway. "I engaged M'sieur Devereau to redecorate it
for your return." He stepped past the pile of Isabeau's
trunks and walked over to the dressing table. He picked
up a miniature and studied it, then fixed Isabeau with
a look of appraisal. "I can't believe how much you have
grown, *mon enfant.* You look much like Maman now."

"Do you truly think so?"

Isabeau took the tiny portrait from him. As a child,
she had never dared compare her own gamine looks to
Thérèse's aristocratic beauty. Now she realized Philippe
was right.

Her mother's complexion was the same rose-tinged
ivory as her own, their finely chiseled features almost
identical. Thérèse had the same dark unruly hair, though
styled in a fashion popular twenty years before. Her
wide-set eyes were the color of a midnight sky, and
Isabeau, as well as Philippe, had inherited that distinc-
tive feature.

Still clutching the portrait, Isabeau gave her brother
an impulsive hug. "I have missed you, Titi." She admired the room once more. "Your M'sieur Devereau is
quite the artist. I am curious, though, how you could
afford his services when you cannot even pay your tailor's bill."

"Don't concern yourself," he replied with a dismissive wave. "We've merely suffered a slight financial set-back—temporary, of course. I have the situation well in hand."

Isabeau arched an eyebrow in disbelief. She knew her brother well enough to guess his reply fell short of the truth. Once she saw for herself how Philippe ran the household, she would demand some answers.

"Why wasn't Oncle Henri with you to meet me?" she asked instead, broaching a subject that had nagged at her since her return. Their uncle had served as a father to them since their parents' deaths, and she had been surprised that he was not with Philippe to greet her that morning.

Philippe frowned. "At the last minute, he claimed to have important business out of town . . . some appointment or another that would keep him busy until next week. One would think he might be more considerate, since we're the only family he has left."

"We are, now that Lili is dead."

Her brother looked contrite. "I didn't mean to upset you, Isette. I know how close the two of you once were."

"She was your cousin, too, *mon frère*. Why am I the only one concerned about her death? In your last letter to me, you took five pages to describe the functions you had attended, but barely two lines to explain how Lili had died of yellow fever. As for Oncle Henri, his letter was dated a week later, yet he never mentioned that his only daughter was dead."

Philippe summoned an uncertain smile. "You know I hate to talk about such matters," he defended himself, "but that doesn't mean I'm a heartless cad. In fact, sev-

eral people mentioned how touched they were when
wept at her funeral."

"Indeed? And did Oncle also express himself in so
public a fashion?"

Philippe shook his head. "I am afraid, *ma petite,* tha
Henri had a falling out of sorts with Lili shortly before
she died. If anything, he seemed more angered than
grief-stricken."

"A falling out?" Isabeau replaced the miniature in its
original spot. "He doted upon Lili, and I cannot believe
she would have done anything to hurt him. Why, from
what she wrote me, he even was content with her decision to join the convent."

Philippe turned away as she spoke, but not before
she glimpsed his expression. "You know something
you haven't told me," she exclaimed. When he gave a
shrug, she grasped his arm and shook it. "What happened? Why was Oncle angry with her?"

"That's something you should ask Henri to tell you,'
Philippe answered. "We're invited to join him for supper
as soon as he returns. For now, Lucie will help you
with your trunks."

His gesture toward the doorway forestalled her protests. A plump, chocolate-skinned mulattress had padded
into the room.

The girl kept her head bowed, so that her features
were hidden beneath a bright red *tignon,* the wide scar
she wore tied about her wiry curls. Around the girl's
neck, partially hidden by her voluminous shift, was a
worn leather thong.

An odd sort of necklace, Isabeau thought, until she
glimpsed the red flannel that hung from it. Then she

realized that tied to the cord must be a *gris-gris,* a voodoo charm consisting of a small cloth bag stuffed with herbs and bits of bone or brick or even graveyard soil. Isabeau suppressed a shiver of distaste. Apparently, the dark religion that had long been a part of the city's culture still held sway.

"You may unpack the *mademoiselle*'s clothes," Philippe instructed the girl as he started for the door. He paused on the threshold long enough to notice the newly battered steamer trunk.

"Surely Grandmère might have provided you with decent luggage," he remarked. "This chest looks as if it's been dropped onto the docks."

With those words, he hurried from the room. Isabeau didn't follow him, for she knew her brother could be as stubborn as she. She'd do better to speak with her uncle. Still, the question of Lili lingered. She could not imagine what her gentle cousin might have done to so displease Oncle Henri.

Three

"It seems Georges suggested his own mare might have won the race had it not thrown a shoe. Monsieur Labreche was outraged and demanded satisfaction."

Philippe paused in his story to glance at his uncle and Isabeau seated across from him at the sumptuous supper table. "Georges could hardly refuse so public a challenge, but he took exception to facing a man old enough to be his *grandpère*. Since the choice of weapons fell to him, being in a biblical frame of mind that day, he proposed they settle the matter with ass jawbones."

Philippe grinned. "When Labreche heard that, he fell into a fit and had to be carried home by his seconds. To this day, any mention of Philistines still sets the old fellow off."

Oncle Henri chuckled in appreciation, and for a moment Isabeau was reminded of her father. The two men had closely resembled one another, with their ascetic features and dark hair. In the past two years, however, Henri had changed. His face was now bloated and stamped with signs of dissipation, while his manner had grown abrupt to the point of secretiveness.

Unable to continue a pretense of enjoying her meal, she gestured for the servant to remove her plate. Her brother's clowning did little to cheer her, for she had spent the past several days in an unsettled state. Her first sad duty had been to visit the St. Louis cemetery where her cousin was interred. Later had begun the ritual of receiving calls from old friends come to welcome her back. She had hoped to learn something more about Lili's death, but her careful questions brought no answers. Though the girls freely shared gossip about other Creole families, their chatter shed no light on Lili's fate.

Isabeau leaned back in her chair. She had hoped to speak with her uncle tonight, instead, but each time she tried to introduce the subject of Lili, Philippe interrupted with another story he had overheard at his club. She had reached the end of her patience. Since experience had taught her that her brother would not run dry of gossip before the meal's end, she asked without preamble, "Oncle, why have you not mentioned Lili's name once this night?"

Silence greeted her question, followed by the clink of a spoon against crystal and an unintelligible curse. She glanced over at her brother to see him dab furiously at an amber stain on his blue waistcoat. Despite her concern, she suppressed a smile. She wondered which upset Philippe more, Lili's name or the fact he'd spattered caramel sauce all over himself.

Her smile faded as she turned back to her uncle. Henri reached for the wine decanter. "May I offer you more, *ma chère?*" he asked.

Taking her silence as assent, he poured the ruby liquid and favored Isabeau with a benevolent smile. "I hope you won't mind that I accepted an invitation for you. Clarisse Dumas has planned a Carnival cotillion and insisted—"

"I'm not interested in Madame Dumas or her invitation right now, Oncle."

Ignoring Philippe's warning look and his kick under the table, she persisted, "You can't brush aside my questions about Lili as if nothing happened. She is dead, and we must accept that fact. Please, tell me why you turned against her."

As she spoke, Henri's expression hardened into a pale, emotionless mask.

"You are mistaken if you think I have not accepted my daughter's fate," he told her. "She was dead to me long before she departed this life, so do not mention her name in my presence again."

"But, Oncle—"

Henri cut her off with a gesture and abruptly pushed back his chair. "I fear I am fatigued," he said. "I trust you will not mind if we end the evening early." He kissed Isabeau's cheek, then headed for the hallway.

Isabeau stared in stunned silence as the heavy mahogany door closed behind him. Philippe refolded his napkin and set it beside his crystal dish.

"It would seem, *ma petite,* that we are dismissed," he observed when Henri's servant entered with their wraps. "I only wish you'd waited until after supper to provoke him," he added. "I'm sure Oncle had the usual bottle of brandy waiting in the parlor for me."

Isabeau followed the servant and her brother through the dim hallway. Her uncle's harsh response had taken her aback. She had expected outrage, perhaps, but not icy indifference.

"This is absurd," she declared, her shock thawing into anger by the time they reached the front door. "Why does he so resent Lili? André," she told the servant, "tell M'sieur Lavoisier I will speak with him once more before he retires."

"Never mind, André," Philippe said, as distress flashed across the Negro's face. "My sister will talk with her uncle another time."

Isabeau's protest died as she glanced from him to the old servant. *"Eh bien,* another time," she agreed. But she held her tongue only until they settled in the coach before turning to her brother again.

"This has gone far enough," she said as the carriage rumbled down the darkened avenue. "I am no longer a child to be kept ignorant of painful truths. Since Oncle refuses to talk, tell me what happened between him and Lili."

Philippe shifted in his seat and stared out the window. "You're blowing the situation entirely out of proportion. Why can't you just let the matter rest?"

"Tell me what you know, Titi."

"Yes, well, you see—"

Philippe paused, and by the faint light from a nearby street lamp she saw him blush. "To be honest, I don't actually know what set Henri off."

"Then why pretend otherwise?"

He shrugged. "I'd hoped you would do better than I in wresting the truth from him. I thought if you knew he refused to confide in me, you might not want to pursue the matter. I *had* expected you to go about it in a more subtle manner."

"And what would you have me do—skulk about On-

cle's study in search of an incriminating document?"
she asked with a touch of asperity. "Or should I bribe
André into telling us what *he* knows?"

"I tried that already," Philippe admitted. "André is
not a man to be swayed by money. We'll have to think
of something else."

They rode in silence, and Isabeau tried to sort through
what she had learned. Philippe snapped his fingers and
gave a muffled exclamation.

"Why didn't I think of it before? If you want to learn
anything, you should talk to the Mother Superior at the
Ursuline convent. That's where Lili died, you know."

"I didn't know," Isabeau responded, surprised. "I had
assumed she went home once she took ill. You are right.
We must see the Mother Superior tomorrow."

"You must see her," her brother corrected. "The old
nun never had much use for me. *Mon Dieu,* don't you
remember how she ranted the time I spirited you away
from school for Mardi gras and brought you back
dressed like a gypsy princess? Besides, I have a pressing
engagement tomorrow afternoon."

The carriage jerked to a stop outside their courtyard
doorway. Once inside their home, Isabeau forgot her
concern about Lili long enough to seize upon Philippe's
last statement.

"What do you mean a 'pressing engagement'?" she
asked. In the weeks following their father's death, those
words had meant meeting with yet another creditor to
plead for more time to repay a debt. "If we are short
of funds, I still have some of the jewelry Maman left
me. We could sell—"

"Non!" Philippe rounded on her. "I can handle our

finances. I don't want to hear your offering to sell your baubles again!"

"If you do not care to discuss the matter, then I think I will retire." Little good her jewelry would do them tucked away while they starved to death.

He sullenly waved her on, and she started for the door. She glanced back in time to see Philippe pour himself a snifter of brandy. She left him staring moodily into the glass. No doubt he would drink himself into a stupor and then sleep until midday, just like Grandmère . . . not that he would be of use to her tomorrow. The Mother Superior did not suffer fools gladly, and by his own admission the nun had long since consigned him to that class. Without Philippe in tow, she would stand a better chance of learning something.

Still, Isabeau frowned as she started up the stairs. Now that she had bruised his feelings, he might dismiss out of hand anything the Ursulines told her. She wouldn't allow that to happen, she vowed. She couldn't. From what she'd so far gleaned, unraveling the truth behind Lili's death could prove a task better handled by two than by one.

By the time the sun's pale morning rays threaded past her bedroom shutters, Isabeau already had pulled on a simple two-piece walking ensemble of grey cashmere over a pleated plum silk skirt. She hurried downstairs, intent on a private word with young Lucie. At that unfashionable hour, it was unlikely that Philippe would intrude upon them.

As she expected, Philippe had not yet made his way

downstairs. Her conversation with Lucie, however, proved fruitless. Whether the maid knew nothing about Lili or whether she simply had been schooled not to gossip with her employers, Isabeau could not say.

Faced with another stumbling block, it occurred to her that perhaps Philippe was right. Perhaps she had merely imagined intrigue where none existed. She wasn't discouraged enough to abandon her visit to the Ursulines, however. By mid morning, she had made her way to the convent, a sprawling estate that consisted of an imposing collection of buildings overlooking the river.

Nothing about the place had changed, she thought as she fondly glanced over the familiar, sparsely furnished parlor where she awaited the Mother Superior. Sunlight wove through the shuttered windows and played about whitewashed walls, bare save for a rough-hewn cross upon which an anguished Christ hung as a reminder of mankind's sinful ways. Beneath her feet, dark wooden floors gleamed, a tribute to the countless hours novices had spent on their knees, scrubbing. Here, the Mother Superior conducted the convent's worldly business and here, too, she met with the occasional intractable student.

Isabeau was no stranger to this parlor. While she was a student at the Ursuline school, her headstrong ways often put her at odds with the nuns. Daily, the good sisters had shaken their heads over her, declaring it impossible to transform the independent Lavoisier girl into a proper Creole *mademoiselle.*

The parlor door opened just then. A familiar, black-robed figure stood in the entryway.

"You look well, *mon enfant,*" the Mother Superior said, closer to smiling than Isabeau could remember ever seeing her. The nun seated herself behind a polished table and motioned Isabeau toward the room's only other chair. The wooden rosary that encircled her frail frame echoed the gesture with a muted click. "It seems that, despite our fears, you have grown into a fine young woman," the nun continued. "Perhaps our years of instruction were not in vain."

"Grandmère was most pleased with my accomplishments," she ruefully replied, recalling how much of that "instruction" had consisted of penance for one transgression or another. Honesty compelled her to add, "She did despair at my lack of humility."

"Humility is a virtue all women should cultivate, *mon enfant*," the nun answered with the same glimmer of a smile before her expression darkened. "I can guess why you have come here. What a pity your return home has been marred by the death of your *cousine* . . . *la pauvre fille*."

Isabeau leaned forward, encouraged by the woman's show of sympathy. "Will you help me, Mother? I want to know how Lili died."

The nun's pale eyes glowed against the wrinkled parchment of her face. "Your *oncle* told you nothing?"

"Non. Philippe wrote me just before I left Paris to say that Lili had taken ill quite suddenly and died—of the fever, he said . . . just like Maman and Papa. When I tried to question Oncle Henri yesterday, he forbade me even to mention her name."

The old woman sat silent for a moment. "I am sure that, in time, he would have told you everything," she replied. "He took Lili's disappearance hard."

"Disappearance?" Isabeau echoed in confusion.

Philippe had not mentioned this. "Do you mean she had left the convent before her death?"

The Mother Superior nodded. "It began almost six months before her death. Lili was absent from prayers. I notified Monsieur Lavoisier when she did not return by nightfall."

"But surely Oncle searched for her."

"He did not." The nun shrugged, her rosary answering the gesture with a dull clatter. "Monsieur Lavoisier seemed convinced that some unscrupulous young man had enticed away your *cousine,* and he was content to let the matter rest. The sisters informed the other students that Lili had returned home temporarily because of an ill relative."

"But I do not understand. Did you also believe my *oncle's* explanation?"

The Mother Superior shrugged again. "Alas, who can say? For myself, I fear she was . . ."

The nun hesitated, as if weighing the possible effect of her words. When she spoke again, Isabeau couldn't suppress the suspicion that the woman had intended at first to say something quite different. "I fear she was unsuited to life within these walls, despite her professed vocation."

The nun sat forward and fixed her with a keen look. "Lili wrote to you, *ma fille,* until the time she left us. Perhaps her letters mentioned a man?"

The letters, Isabeau thought with a pang. They had linked her with her cousin for two years. Through them she had seen the unmistakable change in Lili. The girl's bright accounts of dances and shopping had given way to speculations on sin and damnation, while she rejected marriage as frivolous. Finally, Lili wrote of her intention to join the Ursuline order.

Isabeau stared at the sun-streaked wall as she recalled Lili's declaration. At the time, she had seen her cousin's decision as a betrayal of their happy times. For once, Grandmère agreed with her opinion, dismissing Lili's vocation as folly.

"Every well-bred girl has a duty to marry a wealthy and titled gentleman," the dowager had proclaimed with a pointed look at her other granddaughter.

Knowing the old woman referred to a proposed match with the Marquis du Sansluce, Isabeau prudently had remained silent. Her brother and uncle had sent her to Paris with the hope of her finding a husband. Yet she had yet to find a gentleman who suited her. Despite Grandmère's pressure, she certainly did not intend to consent to this betrothal. She knew that neither this nor the fact the prospective bridegroom was thirty years Isabeau's senior, and rumored to be pox-stricken, concerned her relative in the least.

Faced with such a dilemma, she had decided that Lili's resolution was not without merit. Since she could hardly picture her fragile cousin in a man's embrace, let alone a marriage bed, she penned her approval of the decision. Lili's correspondence afterwards grew sporadic. Finally, her cousin ceased to write.

By then, Isabeau remembered, she herself was betrothed to the marquis. Wrapped in her own misery, she never noticed Lili's continued silence. It had been within days of her planned return to New Orleans that Philippe's letter recounting their cousin's death reached her.

"The letters, Isabeau," the Mother Superior repeated

more urgently. "Did they give any hint why she would leave?"

Isabeau shook her head. "The last one arrived in early summer, but she wrote nothing out of the ordinary."

"Pray God I was wrong," the nun muttered. Then, as if recalling Isabeau's presence, she continued, "I saw no more of Lili until that night six months ago. She refused to say where she had been and asked only to stay the night. By dawn, she was dead."

"And was it the fever?"

The Mother Superior hesitated. "The symptoms were much the same," she admitted. "The physician claimed that several people had died of it—though the outbreak had been a mild one."

The Mother Superior fell silent, and the only sound was the breeze beyond the window. Isabeau drew a breath and struggled to retain her composure. She had not believed until this moment that her beloved cousin was dead. Lili had suffered through some terrible trial without a word to anyone.

Anguish ripped through her like a knife. If she had left Paris sooner, she might have arrived to comfort her dying cousin. If she had stood firm against Philippe two years ago and stayed in New Orleans, Lili might have turned to her instead of running away. If only—

"Isabeau."

The Mother Superior's voice pierced the wave of regret that threatened to engulf her. "Yes, Mother?"

The nun drew a worn carpetbag from the small cabinet beside her. "I found this after Lili disappeared. She must have meant to take it with her. Since your uncle wanted none of her possessions, I thought you should have them."

With those words, the Mother Superior stood, indicating the painful interview was at an end. Isabeau clutched Lili's bag and turned to leave. "God go with you, *mon enfant*," she heard the nun murmur in a voice trembling with emotion.

It was well past midmorning by the time Isabeau was seated at her dressing-table mirror, gazing into its silvery depths. Now, she could not but recall the countless times when she and her cousin had sat before the same glass.

Rippling black tresses and frothy golden curls would tangle together as they leaned against each other and giggled at some childish fancy. Then, she and the motherless Lili had been as close as sisters, though they had differed in temperament and appearance. Friends and family had shaken their heads over Isabeau's headstrong ways, even as they exclaimed over the charm of the blond, blue-eyed Lili. Everyone had loved the girl, Isabeau thought with a pang, yet it seemed Lili's death had left no void in her own family.

"And why is that, *cousine?*"

No answer followed her whispered question. Willing back the tears, she glanced at the envelope and battered missal. She had found both items amid a tangle of clothes stuffed into the carpetbag. The prayer book had belonged to Lili's long-dead mother, Aurore, for it bore the woman's name in faded ink on its flyleaf. The envelope had been tucked within its pages, apparently forgotten.

She skimmed through the missal first, looking for a marked passage or other clue. When nothing caught her eye, she put it aside and searched the unsealed envelope. From it, she withdrew two letters—one written on cheap yellowed paper, the other penned on heavy ivory bond that matched the envelope. She unfolded the latter and read the message inscribed in an ornate yet masculine hand.

"Tonight at eleven. Ophelia will come for you. F."

Frowning, she set that note on the dressing table and picked up the second sheet. As she smoothed the creases from the page, her own name leapt out at her from the jumble of pen strokes. It was a letter from Lili to her, she realized in amazement. If not for the signature, however, she would have been hard-pressed to recognize her cousin as its author, for the words were scrawled across the page in a manner unlike Lili's usual neat script.

Isabeau scanned the page. The missive had been written in haste and, judging from its date, within days of her cousin's disappearance.

My dearest Isabeau, the letter began. *I hope you will excuse my prolonged silence. For weeks I dared say nothing of the evil that has happened here, much less commit such things to paper. I realize now I can remain silent no longer, but must confess my sins in the hope God will forgive me. My penance will be harsh, but no less than I deserve for my transgressions.*

It is said that Lucifer was the most beautiful of the angels, and I know now that is true. I pray you will believe I struggled against temptation, and I pray, too, that you will never succumb to evil as I have. My shame is such that I must leave the convent, never to return.

I will write you at length once I have settled elsewhere. As always, you are in my thoughts and prayers. Your miserable cousine, Lili.

Isabeau sat in silence for a moment. The anguished tone of Lili's missive would confirm Oncle Henri's explanation for the girl's disappearance, she thought in no little dismay.

Her cousin had indeed been involved with a man, perhaps the same "F" who had sent the message. But had Lili left the convent to join her lover? Or had she fled to avoid the censure of her family and the Ursulines? And why had she never mailed the letter or written again?

"Questions, always more questions," she muttered, crushing the envelope as if to squeeze an answer from it.

The letters told her everything and nothing about Lili's fate. Ophelia was an unfamiliar name to her, for she had known all her cousin's friends. If this woman had been an acquaintance, she would have made herself known to the family by now. As for the man . . .

Isabeau shook her head. Lili's lover must have been married, she reasoned, or perhaps long gone from the city. Why else would he not have stood by her? Either way, she doubted he would step forward now to admit his involvement and explain where Lili had been during those months.

"Why didn't you confide in me, Lili?" she wondered aloud, staring at the crumpled paper. An instant later, she gave a surprised cry at the sight of a penciled smudge on the back of the envelope. She leapt from her chair and threw open the shutters, holding up the paper to the window, to make out Lili's handwriting.

The faded words read, *Twelve Rue de Fleur.*

Four

Daylight had melted into dusk when Isabeau heard her brother at the door. "Tell me, *mon frère,*" she began, "have you neglected to mention anything else concerning our cousin—other than the fact she mysteriously disappeared from the convent several months before her death?"

"Mon Dieu, I knew there was something more I needed to tell you," he exclaimed on the way to the parlor. There, he tossed his jacket on a chair and poured himself a brandy, then stood against the mantel.

"Don't just stand there with a disapproving expression upon your lovely face, *ma petite,*" he complained, not making any apology for his omission. "Tell me what you learned from the nuns."

"The Mother Superior could only tell me that Oncle Henri claims Lili ran off with a man."

"So that's why Henri wouldn't discuss the matter." Philippe took a pensive sip of brandy. "I take it you have another explanation for what happened?"

"I'm sure this is a clue as to why she left," Isabeau answered as she held out the crumpled envelope and its contents.

Philippe perused both letters. Distaste thinned his

finely chiseled features. "I'd say Oncle was right. From this,"—he gingerly held the letters at arm's length—"it would appear that our sainted cousin was not averse to the occasional assignation."

"And why would this so-called assignation include another woman?" she demanded and snatched the pages from his hand. "Besides, that is not all I wanted you to see."

She gestured at the envelope he held. "There, on the back . . . it is an address in Lili's handwriting."

"And you intend to locate this place to learn more, don't you?" Philippe squinted at the envelope, then clapped a hand to his forehead. *"Mon Dieu,* it grows worse," he gasped out. "Do you know what this Rue de Fleur is?"

When Isabeau shook her head, he replied, "To put it quite bluntly, that street is a picturesque spot off Basin Street, where the city's finest whores ply their trade."

"And what does this have to do with Lili?"

"I think it's quite obvious, *chère,"* he answered, as a blush darkened his skin. "Our cousin must have found herself in an unsavory situation once she left the convent. Better let the matter rest before someone learns what you've told me."

Isabeau gasped and opened her mouth to protest, but he cut her short. "Listen to me. If Lili had been living there in unfortunate circumstances, we wouldn't want the entire city to know. Since she can hardly defend her reputation now, people will assume the worst."

"The worst?" Isabeau echoed in shock. "Here we have a chance to learn the truth, and all you can do is worry about what people will say."

Philippe drew himself up to his slender height. "Hasn't Henri suffered enough tragedy in his life—first losing his wife in a terrible accident, then his only brother, and now, his daughter. Besides, my concern is also for you, *ma petite.*"

In a tone of reproof he continued, "How do you expect to find yourself a husband, if word gets out our cousin did God-knows-what after she fled the convent? It's bad enough that whispers are beginning to spread about the fact you broke off a respectable match for no better reason than you didn't care for the man. You are nineteen, after all . . . almost past marriageable age."

"But I could not—"

Isabeau broke off at the look on his face, feeling compelled to defend herself yet unable to tell her brother the story behind her engagement. Still, her anger abated as she considered the truth of her brother's argument. "Perhaps certain secrets are better left alone," she admitted, "but I will not believe that Lili would vanish without a word, no matter the circumstances. I simply cannot let the matter rest, as you say, even if it means that people will talk."

Philippe rolled his eyes. "Do as you please, then," he wearily replied. "Just don't expect me to help you dredge up any scandals."

Isabeau suppressed a sigh of relief as her brother tossed down his brandy in a gulp and headed for the door. At least he hadn't forbidden her to pursue the mystery.

Her victory proved short-lived, though, when he paused to glance back at her. "One last thing, *chère.* Whatever else you may do, don't even think of setting foot near that brothel. That part of town can be a dangerous enough place for a man, let alone a woman."

The grey sky blushed with a hint of dawn as Isabeau leaned from her carriage window and gazed at the unfamiliar streets. She couldn't shove aside the worry that Philippe's words of yesterday had planted in her mind.

That part of town can be a dangerous enough place for a man, let alone a woman.

Perhaps she should have brought Lucie with her. Still, she had not forgotten how gossip spread through the city via the Negro grapevine. Had her maid accompanied her, anything she might learn about Lili's fate would be common knowledge by nightfall.

Better that she risk Philippe's wrath by herself, she decided. He'd never even miss her, since he rarely rose before noon.

"And besides, *mon frère,*" she muttered aloud, "what you do not know will not hurt you."

Clinging to those last words, she focused instead on the scenery, savoring the color that painted the horizon. The pink glow lent the city a special charm. Even the lanes of broken cobble looked picturesque, despite the dust cloud that followed in the carriage's wake.

At least it hadn't rained recently, or chances were she would be standing up to her ankles in filth while the driver dragged horses and coach from mudhole to mudhole. That was the one thing she hadn't missed about New Orleans. On such days, she recalled, it was easier to walk—dress held high above the *banquette,* and shoes and stockings carried by a servant.

The empty streets slowly gave way to the usual morning procession of dark-skinned *vendeuses* bound for market. Isabeau watched as the bright-kerchiefed women strutted down the road, balancing upon their heads baskets laden with fresh fruits and vegetables ultimately destined for that evening's supper tables.

In their wake followed the Negro workmen, soberly clad and carrying the accoutrements of their trades. The sound of their musical patois as they called to each other drifted through the hushed avenues.

As her carriage continued on, however, Isabeau frowned. The buildings were shabbier and more gaudily painted, their balconies strewn with broken crockery rather than the usual bright flowers. Laundry stretched in rows between houses and flapped in the breeze, like ragged carrion-eaters awaiting the neighborhood's demise. Several structures appeared long abandoned. Their boarded windows reminded her of blind eyes unable to see the tawdriness that surrounded them.

When the carriage left that slum behind them, Isabeau leaned back against her seat to regret the changes in her beloved Vieux Carré. Even before she left New Orleans, Creole families had begun to abandon what outsiders called the French Quarter for more modern parts of the city. Now, entire neighborhoods were falling into decay.

"And all because of the *américains*," she exclaimed bitterly.

Not content with wartime occupation, the Yankee soldiers had remained for years after, to inflict their brutal rule upon the populace. Isabeau shivered at the thought. Though she'd been no more than a child at the war's end, she could remember the insults and cruelty the Orleanians had endured from Northerners.

The carriage crossed the furthermost boundary of the Vieux Carré—Rampart Street—and turned down Basin Street. The action put an end to her reflections. A moment later, the vehicle halted on a side street. The driver glanced down at her, with disapproval on his craggy features.

"This here's the place," he sourly confirmed. "You sure you know what you're doing?"

His tone suggested that she did not. Brushing aside the thinly veiled insult, Isabeau climbed from the carriage. She paid little heed as she counted out a few coins in payment, for her attention was held by the impressive structure she saw before her.

She had never seen a brothel and had expected to find a tasteless cottage with scantily-clad women hawking their wares from every window. Instead, she stood before a formidable cast-iron gate opened to reveal an elegant Italianate home that would rival the finest of the city's Garden District. Only the brass placard mounted beside her on the gatepost offered a clue as to the establishment's nature.

"Madame Ophelia's House of Discreet Entertainment for Refined Gentlemen and Ladies," she read aloud—to the coach driver's consternation, for he snatched the coins and whipped up his team. Isabeau stared after him as he clattered down the avenue. She had planned to ask the man to wait, but she could hail another hack once her business here was concluded.

Taking a deep breath, she slipped through the gate and made her way up the steps of Number Twelve. How, she wondered, did one gain entrance to such a place? Did a person knock first, or boldly walk past the front door? After a moment's debate, she took the first course, availing herself of the doorknocker in the shape of a leering Cupid.

When her summons brought no response, she stepped back off the gallery and glanced uncertainly at the upper story. Perhaps the brothel's occupants were still abed; even *prostituées* had to sleep sometime. Then a flicker at one curtained window caught her attention. She hurried back to the door, vowing to remain until someone answered.

Her persistence was rewarded when the door cracked open, and a portly Negress peered around its edge. Isabeau swallowed back her nervousness to ask, "Are you Ophelia?"

"Not hardly, chile," the woman replied. Her stern mien relaxed into a brilliant grin as she opened the door a few inches wider.

Isabeau immediately recognized her mistake, for the woman sported a crisp blue *tignon* over grizzled curls, and wore the sober black gown and starched white apron of a housekeeper. The Negress propped her bulky weight against the door frame—effectively blocking Isabeau's view of the foyer beyond—and stared down at her in kindly concern.

"Now, what does you want with Madame Ophelia? She don't just see anybody who comes apoundin' on her door, 'specially not at this time o' day."

"But it's important that I speak with her," Isabeau insisted. "It has to do with a young girl—"

"You ain't from one of them ladies' organizations, is

you? Lands, don't you fancy white folks got better things to do than worry yourselves over other folks' business?" The Negress proceeded to shut the heavy door in Isabeau's face.

"Wait!"

Isabeau flung herself at the door and blocked it with her shoulder, forestalling the woman's move. "I'm not from any ladies' society," she hastily explained. "All I want is some information about my cousin. I heard she . . . stayed here not long ago. Her name was Lili Lavoisier, and she—"

"I don't know nothin' 'bout no Lili," the housekeeper interrupted, her dark features resuming their stern lines. "Now be on your way, chile, before you finds yourself in a heap o' trouble. This street ain't no place for the likes o' you."

With surprising agility for one so large, she shoved Isabeau and slammed the door. The key clicked as it turned in the lock.

Stunned at the woman's response, Isabeau stared at the door that remained resolutely shut. Anger flooded her, and she reached again for the doorknocker. How could she return home, when she had learned nothing of her cousin?

Maybe Philippe was right.

The unbidden thought gave her pause. By now, the day had ripened, and with the sun's bright rays returned a measure of practicality. Likely Lili had never even set foot there, and the Negress feared their conversation might wake her mistress. Such an explanation would certainly be in keeping with her abrupt behavior. And even if Lili *had* been there . . .

Isabeau let the knocker drop quietly back into place. Since the girl had chosen to keep her whereabouts secret once she left the convent, who was Isabeau to pry into her cousin's affairs? Lili had made her own choices, as she herself should. Isabeau started back toward the *banquette*. Her first choice would be to find another carriage and return home. Now that her resolve had wavered, it occurred to her that she was alone in an unsavory neighborhood.

Philippe's warning rang in her ears as she surveyed the empty street and spared a glance at her fragile footwear. The black kid slippers were suited for dancing along polished ballroom floors, not traversing the uneven wooden walk. Still, with no carriage in sight, she had little choice but to walk.

She shrugged with as much nonchalance as she could summon and started down the street. Still, she could not banish a sudden feeling of being conspicuous, dressed as she was. In her haste to leave home without waking anyone, she had pulled on the first gown at hand, an elegant creation of velvet-trimmed burgundy wool piped in black braid. While the heavy fabric readily countered the chill of a New Orleans winter, its rich tone and low neckline made for less-than-appropriate attire for an early morning stroll.

She halted when three disheveled rivermen staggered around the corner across from her. Intent on the whiskey bottle they shared, the trio appeared oblivious to her presence. She prayed the men would stumble on by without noticing her. Once she reached Rampart Street, she might find a coach or even a night patroller on his way home. But she had taken no more than a few steps when they spotted her.

"What's ye hurry, sweet thing?" one called out.

Isabeau feigned deafness as his companions guffawed. She was concentrating on picking her way rapidly along the splintered walkway. *Mon Dieu,* why had she not listened to Philippe? She had survived one brush with such men that first day on the wharf. But there she had been surrounded by other people. This area's inhabitants would be still abed or not inclined to interfere.

She glanced back only to see that the men had crossed to her side of the street. Only a few steps to the corner, she reassured herself, just before the heel of her slipper wedged between the splintered planks of the *banquette.*

She caught herself and avoided sprawling to the ground, though this delay sent anxiety surging through her. With a smothered cry, she slid her foot from the trapped shoe and leaned over to free it. She had just managed to dislodge the slipper, when a pair of beefy arms dragged her upright.

"Now, what's a purty thing like you doing all alone?" the largest of the rivermen exclaimed, and spun her around to face him.

Isabeau shrank in his embrace as he pressed his unshaven face close to hers, exhaling a fetid odor of garlic and whiskey. Before she could reply, he wet his lips with the tip of a blunt tongue and added, "Looks like you could use a man to take care of you."

"Yeah, darlin', why don't we be friends?" the shortest man leeringly suggested.

Checking her impulse to scream, Isabeau took a breath and managed a smile. *"Merci, m'sieur.* Thank you for your concern, but I am on my way to meet my brother. He will worry if I am late."

With a quick move, she extricated herself from the first man's grasp and took a step back, the wayward slipper still clutched in one hand. Before she could pull on the shoe and turn to run, however, the short man caught her arm and gave a nasal laugh.

"Hey, not so fast, girlie," he demanded, with a grin at his companions. "Looks like we done got us one of them fancy Frenchy gals. How's about we show the mam'zelle what a good time she could have with us."

"Yeah, honey, we're lots more fun than any relative," the first man exclaimed and roughly pulled her to him.

Isabeau shrieked in fear and outrage. Her trepidation grew when he ground his pelvis against her so that she could feel his lust. She slapped at him with the soft-soled slipper until, with a coarse laugh, the riverman grabbed it and flung it away. She instinctively resorted to her only other means of defense—clawing at his arms until her nails left crimson trails along his sweaty flesh.

"Bitch," he sputtered and shoved her to arm's length with one beefy hand. She flailed at his face, drawing bloody marks across his unshaven cheek.

Her captor bellowed and struck her across the temple with his fist, momentarily stunning her. As Isabeau sagged, the third man, who had remained silent until then, tugged drunkenly at her arm.

"Lemme 'ave 'er," he slurred as he pulled her from the first man's clutches.

At his touch, she screamed again and broke free. When he stumbled after her, she swung about and, though hampered by layers of skirts and petticoats, landed a kick squarely in his crotch.

"Slut!" he gasped and dropped to his knees.

Isabeau turned to run, but now the short man caught her skirts and tumbled her to the ground. Even as he fumbled with his trouser buttons, the first man shoved him aside and dragged her upright. He pinned her arms and hauled her, kicking and screaming, toward an open gateway alongside one of the silent houses.

"Let her go."

The sound of a man's voice, accompanied by the click of a revolver, stopped Isabeau's attackers. She twisted to see her rescuer, but her hair had slipped from its pins and hung in a heavy curtain over her eyes, obscuring her view.

"We was only havin' some fun," the one who held her whined. "We didn't know she was yer gal. C'mon, honey, tell yer fancy man we didn't hurt you none."

Isabeau shook her head and tried to catch her breath, but all she could manage was a gasp. She had to fight back a hysterical laugh. *Mon Dieu,* not only did the rivermen believe she was a woman of the streets, they also thought that this newcomer was her protector.

From beneath her veil of hair, she glimpsed a pair of expensive black boots moving closer at the same moment one of the men chuckled nervously. "Now don't get all riled up, mister. We was gonna pay for it, wasn't we, boys?"

"Let her go," she heard her rescuer repeat, with menace in his voice.

The sweaty hands released her, and Isabeau hit the ground with a thud. By the time she pushed her hair from her eyes, the rivermen had fled. The half-formed words of thanks froze on her lips, however, as she stared at the man. Her first thought was that she knew him. Relief coursed through her. Just as quickly, she determined he was a stranger, although he did look somehow familiar.

Then she choked back a horrified gasp. *Sainte Cécile,* he was the same *américain* who had treated her with such contempt upon her arrival home—the very man she had dubbed a buccaneer!

Five

When the *américain* made no move to assist her, Isabeau scrambled to her feet, then smoothed her crumpled gown. Venturing another look at her rescuer, she saw that in one tanned hand he gripped a lethal-looking revolver, while in the other, he held her missing slipper. His expression of contempt forestalled any thought of humor at the incongruity.

He thrust the shoe toward her with a careless gesture, such as he might use to discard an oft-used rag, demanding as he did so, "Yours?"

"Merci, m'sieur," she softly replied and reached for the shoe.

Her hand brushed his, the brief contact sending a shiver through her, as if her fingers had closed on cold steel instead of warm flesh. She tugged the slipper from his grasp and pulled it on again, all too aware of the *américain*'s continued scrutiny.

What kind of man was he? she asked herself, unable to understand the resentment he seemingly bore toward her. Here, she had been accosted by crude ruffians, yet he acted as if *she* were at fault. Surely he didn't believe she had encouraged the rivermen's attentions!

Once she could trust herself to speak, Isabeau lifted

her chin and fixed him with a cold look of her own. "Please do not trouble yourself, *m'sieur.* I am unharmed and no longer require your assistance."

"That's just fine by me, lady," he retorted, tucking the revolver beneath his jacket. "Believe me, I've got better things to do than look after some simpering *mademoiselle* who doesn't have sense enough to avoid a street like this."

Refusing to dignify that insult with a reply, Isabeau started back down the *banquette.* A voice within warned her against venturing the streets alone again, but she ignored it. Better to risk another encounter with the rivermen, she decided, than to spend another instant under this buccaneer's insolent stare.

She had taken only a few steps when she heard the welcome rumble of a hired carriage as it rolled to a stop beside her. Without a glance back, she told the driver her destination and clambered inside. A smile curved her lips as she pictured the man's probable chagrin at being left behind.

Let him walk, she thought. That emotion was promptly replaced by a prickle of unease, however, when the hack remained motionless on the street. Anxiety sharpened her impatience, and she rapped on the ceiling to urge on the driver. She heard a quick exchange of voices just before the carriage door flew open. Before she could protest, the *américain* had settled on the seat across from her. He stretched his long legs across the coach's narrow length and leaned back, arms folded across his chest, as he surveyed her with a look of triumph. Her reaction was instinctive. Even as the carriage jerked smartly forward, she lunged for the door.

The *américain,* with a fluid move, reached forward and shoved her back against the seat. Isabeau struggled upright again and shot him a look of fright and fury. *Sainte Cécile,* it was bad enough that she almost had fallen victim to the rivermen. To be accosted by predatory males twice in one morning was intolerable!

Summoning a burst of bravado—for she hadn't forgotten that this man carried a pistol, and was not averse to using it—she demanded, "Stop this carriage immediately!"

The man scowled and promptly signaled the driver to halt. "Suit yourself," he replied, his tone hostile as he reached past her to unlatch the door. "I didn't intend to hold you against your will. All I wanted to do was keep you from leaping out of a moving coach and being crushed beneath its wheels. Not that I'm overly concerned about your precious Creole hide," he clarified at her look of disbelief. "I just don't think I could stand the sight of blood this early in the day."

"How unfortunate for you, *m'sieur,*" she managed in what she prayed was a level tone and gestured toward the door. "Now, will you please get out?"

The *américain* gave an inelegant snort. "It so happens *I* was the one who hired this coach. If you don't like my company, you're more than welcome to find your own way home, but I'd suggest you stay put. As you'll recall, a woman alone is none too safe on these back streets."

A chill swept her at the thought of her fate at the rivermen's hands had this man not intervened. She blinked away tears and took a shaky breath. "And am I safe with you, *m'sieur?*"

His gaze swept over her, and he favored her with a slow smile. "You didn't think I rescued you from that scum to ravish you, myself, did you?"

At Isabeau's reluctant nod, his smile faded. "Take my word for it, *mademoiselle,* I don't have the slightest interest in anything you've got to offer."

With that insult, he pulled the door shut and signaled the driver to proceed. She scarcely took heed of his last words. She shut her eyes and wrapped her arms around herself, trying to control the trembling that racked her slender frame.

But the men did not hurt you, after all, she frantically reminded herself, to no avail. It was as if her struggle with them had sapped blood and left fear. With that chill came a tightening of her chest, so that each breath was an effort. *Mon Dieu,* if the *américain* hadn't happened upon them when he did—

"Drink this," came a harsh command that penetrated her turbulent thoughts. She opened her eyes to see that the man had thrust a silver flask beneath her nose. The alcoholic fumes left no doubt as to its contents.

When she made no move to take the flagon, he held it to her mouth. "Drink this," he repeated in a softly dangerous tone. "I'm not in the mood to cope with a swooning female right now."

A glance at the implacable expression in his cold blue eyes cut short any thought of protest. He tipped the flask against her lips, and she obediently swallowed the liquid that poured from it.

Tears sprang to her eyes, and she gasped as the liquor burned her throat. *Sainte Cécile,* was the man trying to poison her? Though she had grown up in homes where wine flowed more plentifully than water, never once had she tasted anything like this liquid fire. She shot him an accusing glance.

"Better?" he asked, a hint of amusement coloring his tone.

Isabeau's scathing retort died on her lips. Oddly enough, now that the first shock had passed, she did feel much recovered. A comforting warmth suffused her, and her trembling, though not quite stilled, was no longer the palsied shaking of a moment before. She nodded and managed a tremulous smile. "I am much better, *m'sieur.*"

"Then to our respective healths, *mademoiselle,*" he said and raised the flask in a mock salute before draining its contents in a single long swallow.

While he replaced the cap and returned the container to his pocket, Isabeau reached a hand to her disarrayed hair. A few pins still clung to the tresses, and with unsteady fingers she gathered her curls into a haphazard twist—not that it mattered if she presented a disheveled appearance before this barbarian!

She spared another glance in his direction, relieved to see he had turned his attention to the scenery beyond the window. As she studied his strongly chiseled profile, she realized why she had not recognized him at first.

Shaven and dressed as he was this morning, he looked less the buccaneer and more the gentleman. She noted in grudging approval that he eschewed extremes of fashion, wearing instead a well-tailored dark suit and buff waistcoat, of simple but impeccable design. The expensive fabric was cut to emphasize his muscular physique. A neat cravat devoid of garish stickpins topped his crisp white linen shirt. Only the restless air of danger he projected seemed out of place.

The carriage hit a deep rut just then, putting a halt to her contemplation of the man's appearance. She glanced up to find his blue gaze upon her. Color flooded her cheeks, and she looked away, but not before she glimpsed awareness that defied his earlier claim of disinterest.

They sat almost knee-to-knee within the coach's narrow confines, so close she could breathe the lingering hint of soap and freshly pressed linen that clung to him and mingled with the faint musky scent of his flesh. She preferred that bold and wholly masculine smell to the cloying fragrances most men of her acquaintance affected.

The coach struggled through another series of ruts, and with the vehicle's sway her skirts brushed the taut fabric that covered the man's well-muscled calf. She shivered, as if she had raked his bare flesh, and edged away from him, then scolded herself for her missish behavior. Something about the man's presence acted upon her as the whiskey had, heating her from within and leaving her breathless. She took refuge in polite conversation.

"My name is Isabeau Lavoisier," she began. "I suppose I should thank you for saving my life, M'sieur—"

"—Tark Parrish," he supplied in an ironic tone that mocked her attempt at civility. "As for saving your life, I dare say those men were most interested in divesting you of your virtue."

She blushed at the truth of his statement, but before she could reply, he demanded, "Just what in the hell did you think you were doing, wandering the waterfront alone?"

"I was looking for someone, that is, I . . ."

She broke off, stung by his tone of condemnation, yet reluctant to discuss with him the circumstances of Lili's death. Barbarian that he was, he likely would find the situation a matter for jest.

"I had my reasons, *m'sieur,*" she curtly informed him. "They are none of your concern."

She waited for another caustic reply, but he shrugged and lapsed into his reverie. Relieved, she settled against her seat, though she kept a wary eye on her companion. Her limited experience with *américains* had taught her they were not to be trusted, and she suspected Monsieur Tark Parrish would prove no exception.

Not until the carriage halted beside her courtyard gate did the *américain* stir again, to assist her from the coach. Even as she accepted the calloused hand he extended, he roughly closed his fingers over hers and all but dragged her onto the *banquette.*

His move left her pinned between him and the carriage, so that he effectively blocked her passage. She started to demand he step aside, but the words died upon her lips as she met the intensity of his cold gaze.

His hand gripped hers, and she could feel his pulse throbbing against her flesh in a way that sent her own heart thudding. He'd pulled her so close that she could feel the heat of his body. What frightened her most was the way that he stared at her—like a dying man given a glimpse of both salvation and damnation, yet unable to choose between the two.

She must have made some protest, for his strange

expression faded. "Take care in the future where you walk alone," he warned as he let her step away. "Next time, I might not be there to rescue you." Then he climbed into the coach and signaled it on, leaving her to stare after him.

Barely had that vehicle rounded the corner, when the wrought-iron gate behind her clicked open. Startled, Isabeau swung about, certain her brother waited ready to demand an explanation. Instead, it was the mulattress, Lucie, who stood behind the intricate twist of bars. Isabeau's initial relief faded, however, when the dark-skinned girl murmured, "It is well you have returned, *mam'selle*. M'sieur Philippe is already awake."

"Awake?" Isabeau echoed in dismay. "Does he know that I've been gone?"

"No, *mam'selle*, not unless I tell him so."

The girl's words seemed to hold a subtle threat, and Isabeau caught her breath. *Mon Dieu*, could Lucie have witnessed her taking leave of Monsieur Parrish? The thought sent a blade of unease through her, for she could picture Philippe's outrage should he learn she had gone alone to the brothel after he had warned her not to. His response if he heard of her return in the company of an *américain* did not bear thinking upon.

But when the mulattress kept her gaze fixed on the brick walkway, her demeanor properly respectful, Isabeau decided she had misjudged the girl. Even so, she cast about for an excuse to justify her being abroad so early in the day.

"Grandmère and I often attended morning Mass," she offered by way of explanation, avoiding a lie as she left Lucie to draw her own conclusions. She prayed the girl wouldn't notice her disarrayed hair, or the fact her gown bore creases that even an hour spent kneeling in prayer could not have produced.

If Lucie found the story implausible, she gave no sign, but silently held open the gate and stepped aside. Isabeau exhaled relief and made her way past the girl into the courtyard. Once inside the house, she paused outside her brother's bedroom. Off-key snatches of the whimsical new ballad made popular by Lydia Thompson, the musical-comedy star, floated from behind the closed door. Despite the harrowing events of the past half hour, Isabeau found herself smiling. Philippe always performed his morning ablutions to the accompaniment of some tune or another. She moved in the direction of her own room, her smile broadening as she silently repeated the nonsensical chorus of the ditty.

. . . *may the fish grow legs and the cows lay eggs, if ever I cease to love* . . .

Once inside her bedroom, however, her amusement faded when she glanced in her mirror. She looked little worse for her encounter with the dockworkers, save for her crumpled gown and the faint bruises on her wrists. She examined those red splotches where the riverman roughly had grasped her, then put a hand to her temple. It throbbed where the man had struck her, leaving another telltale mark on her ivory skin.

She stripped off her gown, unable to bear the sight of its vibrant wine color. She pulled on a sober blue day dress and settled at her dressing table. She took down her hair and repinned it, careful to arrange a few curls so that they covered the bruise on her forehead.

But even as she pushed aside thoughts of the rivermen's assault, she found her mind turning to the *améri-cain*. The memory of his disdain rekindled her anger, and she seized upon that emotion, unwilling for the moment to examine any other feelings he might have sparked in her. Why, he had never even apologized for the rough way he had handled her, she told herself in outrage. No *gentleman* would have dared treat her in such a manner.

But only a man of his sort could have dispatched those dockworkers with such ease.

The thought was sobering, and she realized that she owed Monsieur Parrish a debt of gratitude. Why, then, could she only dwell upon his lack of manners? Had he been a Creole rather than a hated *américain,* she would have made him a pretty speech of thanks. Instead, she had let prejudice overrule courtesy, using him as badly as he had used her.

She should admit to him as much, she decided—if she ever encountered the man again. Few outsiders set foot in Creole homes, let alone won introductions to unmarried young women like herself. Chances were, this meeting had been their last.

With that realization came a sense of regret, an emotion she dismissed as ludicrous. Far better that she contemplate her family's future. Despite Philippe's attempts to hide the truth from her, she knew their financial situation was precarious. Her brother's fondest hope in sending her to Paris was that she return with a wealthy husband. Had she heeded Grandmère's wishes and married the Marquis du Sansluce, her family would now be provided for.

The fact that she detested the man and his mincing

manner should not have mattered, she realized with a nagging sense of shame. After all, in every other respect the match was advantageous. She had known since childhood that love-matches were rare. Why, then, had she been unable to face her duty and make such a sacrifice?

Isabeau studied her reflection, remembering how, soon after her arrival at the convent school, she had come upon a group of older girls as they discussed marriage. So intent were they in their conversation that they didn't bother to send her away. Her curiosity had turned to dismay as she listened to stories of friends and sisters married off to virtual strangers.

"I shall marry whomever I please," she had blurted out in the midst of their discussion.

The other girls had stared in disapproval. One young lady gave a contemptuous laugh. "What do you know of marriage? Why, you're only a child. You'll marry whomever your *papa* chooses for you, just as the rest of us shall."

"I won't," Isabeau had insisted. "I shall marry a handsome gentleman who rides a grey stallion and loves me with all his heart."

The other girls laughed and turned their backs on her. Isabeau felt tears in her eyes. "I *shall* marry him," she whispered, though she had no idea where she had gotten such a notion. She would never wed a man she did not love.

Now reality replaced childish fancies. She *had* to marry well this season, she reminded herself, or else she and Philippe would find themselves out on the streets. Or they would be condemned to the same life as Grandmère, hiding their poverty behind a bold facade and a houseful of empty rooms.

Isabeau managed a smile and reached for the stack of gaily colored pasteboard cards at her elbow. The Lavoisier name still carried enough influence that she had received more invitations to Carnival balls than she could accept. Why, if her brother and uncle had any say in the matter, the house would soon overflow with wealthy suitors anxious to marry into a socially prominent family, regardless of its financial state.

She let the gilt-edged invitations filter like so many bright leaves through her fingers and back onto the dressing table. She'd shine this season, and by Carnival's end would have her choice of wealthy husbands. Too bad a certain dark-haired buccaneer wouldn't be present to see her surrounded by *real* gentlemen.

Dusk had long since fallen by the time Tark paid the coach driver and made his way back into his office. He locked the outer door and lit the lamp, then strode to his desk. With a snort, he shoved aside the ledgers, not caring when one slid to the floor. Instead, he flung himself into the chair and, running a hand through his dark hair, reviewed the day's events.

His discussions with his few remaining clients had all ended badly. As he'd feared, news of Burnett's defection had traveled through the business community. Now, no one dared to trust a firm deemed a poor risk by one of the city's most respected financiers.

Equally disheartening had been his conversation with Tom Sullivan. Despite his network of criminal contacts, the night patroller had yet to discover the identity of Tark's enemy. And, finally, word had come that the *Esmeralda* was not due to make port for another two weeks . . . two weeks that he could not afford to wait.

With a disgusted shake of his head, Tark dug through the bottom desk drawer, intent on continuing what he had begun at the Albatross earlier in the afternoon. Finally, he unearthed the whiskey bottle he kept stashed there for emergencies. More searching produced a chipped but serviceable tumbler. He set both items on the scarred desktop and leaned back in his chair, admiring the way the lamp's dull yellow glow played off the full bottle and set the amber liquid afire.

It had been years since he had turned to alcohol for solace, yet in recent weeks he found himself seeking the sweet oblivion of her embrace. She was a fickle mistress, though no more so than other past lovers. Some nights, she offered the blessed respite of sleep, only to torment him with painful memories on others. But as she slowly insinuated herself back into his life, he found he was inclined to forget the cruel price she previously had exacted for her companionship.

A rap at the inner door cut short his contemplations. His housekeeper, Alma, clomped into the room with the stride of an avenging angel, although she brandished a dustrag rather than a flaming sword.

"I suppose you'll be wanting your supper." She addressed him with the abrupt informality of a long-time employee. "Lord knows how I'm supposed to keep this household running on schedule, given the hours you keep."

"Don't worry about me, Alma," he replied and indicated the bottle before him. "My plans for the evening are already set—unless you have any objections?"

Though the last was said with more than a touch of irony, he noted that Alma was not amused. She planted her fists on her hips and met his gaze. "As a matter of fact, Mister Parrish, I do. If I let you drink yourself into an early grave, I'll never get my money—or have you forgotten that you owe me three months' back wages?"

He hadn't forgotten. When business took its final turn for the worse, the housekeeper had offered to stay on for room and board until times got better. Now it occurred to him that she might decide to throw in her lot with someone else.

His expression must have reflected his concern, for Alma's frown dissolved into sympathy. "Now, don't be worrying yourself. We've been through too much together over the years for me to up and leave when you're having such a time of it. Besides which," she leveled a pointed glance at the unopened bottle before him, "I'd be neglecting my Christian duty if I left you to fend for yourself."

"You're a jewel," Tark answered. "I can't think why Ned Deaton hasn't snatched you out from under my nose yet."

"Now, go along with you," she scoffed, though pleasure pinked her sallow cheeks at his mention of the Gilded Albatross's portly owner. "What respectable woman would want to saddle herself with the likes of him?"

"Plenty, I'd wager." When Alma merely harrumphed, he warmed to the subject. "You should see the crowds the Albatross draws every Saturday night. Why, I'll bet there's not a riverman on the Mississippi who doesn't make his way there come payday. With the kind of money Ned's making, he could keep a woman in style."

"Style, you say! Why, when he took me out driving last week . . ."

She trailed off at Tark's grin and favored him with a disapproving look. "There you go, distracting me while I should be scolding you for your sins. To my mind, what you need is a wife to help you mend your heathen ways."

Tark's grin faded. "If you'll recall, I tried marriage once before. It didn't work out."

His reply was an understatement, but he could tell that Alma remembered those hellish months all too clearly. "It was a black day for us all when that hussy became mistress of Belle Terre," she muttered, giving her dustrag an agitated twist. Then, recovering herself, she went on in a more normal tone, "If you won't be needing me, I'll retire to my room and do some mending."

She clomped out and pulled the door shut. Her heavy tread echoed down the hallway. Satisfied he was alone now for the night, Tark turned his attention back to the bottle and finally admitted to himself the true reason for his unsettled state: a certain Creole *mademoiselle* by the name of Isabeau Lavoisier.

More of a surprise than seeing her again was the fact she had been standing on the steps of Ophelia's brothel. Several explanations sprung to mind but, given what he knew of the chit, none left him satisfied. As for his rescue of her from the drunken rivermen, he soon had reason to regret that deed.

Her assumption that he'd intervened to slake his own lust had redoubled his contempt for her ilk. Still, he had glimpsed in those eyes an awareness of him that belied her indifference. He told himself she was no different from any other woman he had bedded.

Now, however, he realized that his treatment of her had been spurred by something deeper. Beneath his disdain lay fear that he might be tempted to listen to his heart.

Tark toyed with the empty glass. Here he was, letting her get under his skin, when chances were he'd never set eyes on her again. As the *mademoiselle* would no doubt be the first to point out, they didn't exactly move in the same social circles.

He reached for the bottle, determined to exorcise her from his thoughts with a dose of whiskey, when a better cure occurred to him. He set down the bottle and shoved back from the desk.

Tonight, Clarisse Dumas was holding her cotillion, an annual event which in previous years included nearly every Creole in the city. With any luck, Isabeau would be in attendance, as well. Once he saw her preening with the rest, he'd lose all interest in her. And if by chance she wasn't there . . .

Tark allowed himself a smile of anticipation as he recalled Elisabeth's suggestion of the week before. No matter how events transpired, tonight's gathering promised to provide him some entertainment.

Six

"Madame Dumas gives the finest cotillions, don't you think?" Isabeau exclaimed as she entered the ballroom on Philippe's arm.

Her brother halted just inside the doorway, and she gazed about her in delight. Clarisse Dumas's elegant salon had been transformed into a veritable Eden. Garlanded trellises and potted palm trees sprouted in artful disarray along every wall, even spilling past the two pairs of French doors that opened onto a gallery overlooking the courtyard beyond.

Above her, light blazed from a trio of chandeliers that cascaded from the high ceiling like crystalline waterfalls. Beneath their flashing brilliance, elegantly dressed couples waltzed to the strains of a small orchestra discreetly tucked behind yet another cluster of palms. The atmosphere reverberated with gaiety, for each guest knew the carefree Carnival season must soon draw to a close, to be replaced by the solemnity of the Lenten observance.

Philippe met Isabeau's smile of anticipation with a grin of his own as he echoed that sentiment. "Enjoy yourself while you can, *petite*. Remember, you have barely two weeks of dancing and parties before Ash Wednesday puts an end to your frivolity."

And to my chances for finding a husband this season, she silently finished for him. Her spirits flagged as she thought back to their noon meal. Between bites of Lucie's execrable cooking, Philippe had reviewed the social and economic status of virtually every Creole family in the city.

The discussion continued into the afternoon, until he narrowed the list to the dozen or so gentlemen whose bank balances deemed them worthy of her consideration. According to his timetable, she should be engaged by Easter and married by early summer—with the final choice of a bridegroom to be all hers, he declared.

Even as she contemplated this prospect, Philippe's grip on her arm tightened. "See, what did I tell you?" he crowed, nodding toward the boisterous dandies headed in their direction. "All of the city's eligible gentlemen are in attendance—"

"—as are all the unmarried women in the parish."

She gestured at the numerous debutantes who lined the ballroom. Tonight, even the plainest *mademoiselles* blossomed beneath the lights, their eyes aglow and cheeks pink with excitement. Clad in the white gowns appropriate for girls of their age, they reminded Isabeau of flowers plucked from a winter garden.

She gave her gown a glance. Though she had refrained from wearing those bright colors traditionally reserved for older, married women, her amber silk with its fashionably pouffed skirts and lace-trimmed décolletage seemed out of place amid this sea of virginal white.

Philippe didn't notice her dismay. He gave her hand

a squeeze as his friends crowded around them, anxious for an introduction.

"Remember what I told you," he murmured. "Save most of your dances for René, Jules, and Antoine. They're the wealthiest of the lot. And forget about Armand. I just learned that his father has disinherited him again."

"Don't worry, *mon frère*," she answered in an ironic undertone. "I promise not to dance with any penniless dandies, no matter how they may plead."

With an effort, she summoned a smile for the gentlemen. *Mon Dieu,* but she found it distasteful, this calculated approach to matrimony. The thought of the chits and bills she had accidentally discovered beneath Philippe's desk blotter earlier that day kept her from abandoning his scheme. His insistence that all was well did not change the fact that, unless she made a successful match—and quickly—it would be only a matter of weeks before they found themselves on the streets.

Urgency spurred her, and she accepted one young man's invitation to dance. Freed from brotherly duties, Philippe made his excuses and started toward a pert blonde. Isabeau gave a thoughtful frown as she watched him. He had arranged for her to return home from the cotillion in the company of his friends, Marcel and Camille St. John. His obligations, he claimed, would take him away well before midnight.

Just meeting with an old acquaintance. Earlier, she had accepted this evasive reply without question. Now, noting his buoyant mood, she wondered if this mysterious rendezvous meant he had made progress toward resolving their financial difficulties. Or, just as likely, maybe he had planned an assignation with some unsuitable woman, she thought with an uncharitable half smile. But thoughts of her brother faded when, several dances and as many partners later, she finally pleaded fatigue.

Sending her escort in search of champagne, she joined a group of debutantes who lined the far wall. The evening was proceeding much as she had feared, she realized with a sigh. Thus far, the only emotion that any gentleman in attendance had stirred in her was boredom. Not that they were not all perfectly respectable young men of good families and impeccable breeding, she amended. But they all treated her as if she were a delicate creature incapable of rational thought.

And just what kind of man would you prefer? a sly voice within her wanted to know. *An ill-mannered buccaneer whose sole redeeming quality is the ease with which he can dispatch other undesirables?*

"Mon Dieu, non," she exclaimed aloud, and blushed when the other girls turned to stare. *Non,* she silently repeated. She preferred refined gentlemen who—dull though they might be—behaved with a decorum and treated women with respect. But before her inner voice could mock that sentiment, a familiar whine interrupted.

"Isabeau, I've been looking everywhere for you."

Wearing a frilly white gown whose color and cut did nothing for her sallow complexion and underdeveloped figure, Camille St. John plopped onto the chair beside her and assumed a martyred air. "Philippe has not yet sought me out tonight. You did tell him I would be here, didn't you?"

"Of course I told him, Cammi," Isabeau assured her. "Perhaps he's just not seen you in this crush."

She was tempted to add that his reaction had been a groan of dismay, a sentiment little removed from her own opinion of the girl. Cammi had been among the first to renew acquaintance upon her return home, though a few minutes' conversation had confirmed Isabeau's suspicions that friendship had little to do with the girl's enthusiastic welcome.

She knew that Cammi had long been enamored of Philippe, who in turn tolerated her simply because she was the sister of his best friend Marcel. With Cammi finally of marriageable age, however, he found himself torn between discouraging her attentions and not offending his friend.

Unaware of Philippe's feelings, the girl had made clear her intentions to ingratiate herself with Isabeau to gain an ally—and, eventually, a sister-in-law. Placated now by Isabeau's explanation, Cammi gave her beribboned blond curls a shake.

"Then I shall wait for him here," she announced with a conspiratorial smile, then gave Isabeau's bright gown an approving glance. "It's fortunate for you that Lili was only your cousin," she prattled on, "or else you would have been in mourning all through Carnival, and missed every ball and cotillion."

Not giving Isabeau a chance to reply to this tactless reference to Lili's death, the girl continued in an excited stage whisper, "Isn't that Elise Baudier?"

She indicated a plump, pretty debutante whom Isabeau recognized from convent days. "I heard that Etienne Renaud called on her three times in a single month," Cammi went on. "When her *papa* demanded he make his intentions known, Etienne fainted on the spot and had to be carried from the house."

"And what of Elise?" Isabeau's concern for her one-time acquaintance was genuine.

Cammi rolled her eyes knowingly. "Why, her reputation is ruined, of course—even though she swears nothing lay behind young Renaud's reaction."

Isabeau frowned at the relish the girl took in repeating that tale, recalling, too, Cammi's reputation as a gossip. Before she could quash the girl, an imperious voice broke in on their conversation.

"If you must indulge in rumor and innuendo, Camille, kindly confine yourself to tales of those persons who are not my guests."

Madame Dumas herself, clad in her habitual black, stood before them. Her reproving gaze fixed upon Cammi. Then the dowager turned to Isabeau, and her expression softened.

"Ah, *chérie,* you have indeed grown up since last I saw you," she exclaimed in the lilting tone that belied her eighty-odd years. "I am sorry that I have not called at your brother's house to welcome you back, but I do not go about the city much these days. The damp, it is bad for my old bones."

"But it is I who should apologize," Isabeau protested with a fond smile as she stood and dutifully kissed the old woman's powdered cheek. "I have been meaning to visit you, but Philippe has kept me busy every moment since my return."

"Ah, that is to be expected. But now that you are here, it is time we discuss your plans for the future."

So saying, Madame beckoned with an imperious air and, leaning heavily on her silver-tipped cane, led the way to the outer salon. With a parting glance back at Cammi, who stood staring after her, Isabeau followed.

She, at least, had nothing to fear from the dowager, Isabeau thought as she threaded through the crowd. Madame's tongue intimidated the fainthearted, but Isabeau had long ago learned that a generous heart lay beneath the woman's thorny exterior. Still, Madame's approval was sparingly bestowed. Isabeau felt fortunate to have earned her regard.

When they paused beside a garlanded column, Isabeau turned to her companion. The dowager had changed little, though her softly wrinkled skin now stretched more tautly over her aristocratic features. Her braided coronet of silver hair gave her a regal air, and her blue eyes, while faded almost to white, snapped with ageless authority.

That authority was evident in Madame's voice when, after a few moments of polite exchange, she peremptorily said, "We must find you a husband, *chérie.* After all, most girls your age, they are long since married with a brood of children clinging to their skirts, *n'est ce pas?*"

"*Oui,* Madame," Isabeau replied, though she felt her smile stiffen. "I see you have been talking with Oncle Henri and Philippe."

"Indeed, I have."

Madame gave her a smile and patted her cheek. "Let me speak frankly, for you have been like a granddaughter to me in these years that I have known your family. All is not as it should be with your brother and *oncle.* Philippe, he has once again fallen in with bad company and gambled away every cent, just like your dear, late *papa*. As for Henri . . ."

The dowager shook her head and clucked her tongue in disapproval. "Your *oncle,* he is as clever as he is handsome, and that is his downfall. I know something of his affairs, *ma chère,* and I fear he has dared to bargain with the devil. He will do what he must to save himself, with no thought at all for your happiness."

"But, Madame, how can you think such a thing?" Isabeau protested. She could admit that the man she called her uncle bore little resemblance to the carefree relative she remembered from her childhood.

The woman must have sensed her dismay, for she grasped Isabeau's hand in her fragile white fingers. "Do not worry, I will see to it myself that we find you a suitable husband." Then her pale gaze bored into Isabeau's own. "What is wrong, *ma petite?* Don't you wish to wed?"

"Of course. It's just that—"

"Ah, say no more," the dowager interrupted. "I have heard the tales. You left behind in Paris a young man— this Marquis du Sansluce—and now you regret your hasty decision, *non?"*

"No," Isabeau exclaimed in horror. "I left Paris because Grandmère insisted I should marry him, and I just could not. He was older than Oncle Henri and afflicted with some terrible pox that everyone said he caught from his Italian mistress. He had a pale flabby face and red lips, like a woman's, and . . ."

She stopped and clamped her mouth shut, unable to meet Madame's gaze. She'd been about to say that the marquis once cornered her in a dark hall of her grandmother's *maison*, pinning her against the wall as he fumbled with the laces of her bodice. She had escaped the man's embrace by landing an unladylike blow to his ample midsection. Afterwards, she took care never to be alone with him, though it had been days before she could forget the feel of his pudgy hands, cold yet slick with sweat, against her warm flesh. How could she explain something like that to Madame?

But when Isabeau glanced back up at her, the old woman wore an expression of gentle understanding. "I see now, *petite*. But if we found the right gentleman— young, handsome, and strong—you might feel differently, *n'est ce pas?*"

Isabeau nodded.

"Bon!" the dowager exclaimed. "Then I have found such a gentleman for you. In fact," and she gestured dramatically, "he is here even now."

Curious, Isabeau turned, as her gaze came to rest on a tall, dark-haired man who stood slightly apart from the others, intent on the colorful whirl of dancers. His back was to her, and she admired the way his well-tailored jacket emphasized the breadth of his shoulders. Though his pose was casual, she sensed about him a haughty disdain, different from the coy preening of the other men.

As if feeling her scrutiny, the man turned to meet her appraising glance. She gasped and almost dropped her fan when she found herself staring at a familiar, piratelike visage.

"Sainte Cécile," she whispered in disbelief, snapping open the fan to conceal her face.

Her move came too late, however, for the man favored her with a nod and started toward them. Isabeau watched his approach with dread. Dressed as he was in black, the color unrelieved save for the white splash of his shirtfront, he reminded her of some dark demon bent on mischief.

Madame shot her a triumphant glance. "Did I not tell you he was handsome, *chérie?*"

Isabeau willed herself to stay calm. What was this *américain*—an outsider—doing at a Carnival ball? Surely he could not be the same man Madame proposed as a possible husband for her. The evening must be a nightmare, she promptly decided, wrapped in the glitter of an elegant dance.

All too soon, Tark Parrish stood before them, his face a mask of polite concern as he favored them with a bow and glanced in Isabeau's direction.

"You look pale, Mademoiselle Lavoisier. Allow me to escort you outside for a breath of fresh air."

"No!" she blurted without thinking. Then, seeing the stunned look on Madame's face, she quickly amended, "That is, I'm quite well, M'sieur Parrish. Please don't trouble yourself on my account."

Madame glanced from her to the *américain* and gave a *moue* of mock displeasure. "But the two of you know one another. Indeed, you have spoiled my little surprise." She turned toward Monsieur Parrish and gave him a playful tap on the arm with her black ostrich-feather fan. "I was afraid you would decline my invitation, as usual, *cher.* What changed your mind?"

"I decided it had been too long since I'd paid court to my favorite lady," he replied as he gently raised the old woman's hand to his lips.

Pink washed over Madame's pale cheeks, and she favored the man with a coy smile even as she addressed Isabeau.

"Ah, but this one, I sometimes forget he is an *américain,*" she exclaimed with a dramatic sigh. "Did you know, *chérie,* that our M'sieur Parrish is of a respected and wealthy St. Louis family? How unfortunate that with the war—"

"I don't think Mademoiselle Lavoisier wants to hear my family history, Clarisse," he mildly interrupted. "The past is the past."

Isabeau glimpsed the look of discomfort that flashed across his features. She hoped Madame would give Monsieur Parrish a taste of his own medicine.

Instead, Madame withdrew her hand and changed the subject. "I will forgive your neglect, *cher,* if you will tell me how it is you already know my young friend, when she has only just arrived home."

Isabeau's breath caught, and she forgot her interest in the man's background. *Mon Dieu,* what if he mentioned their riverfront encounter to Madame? Not only would her own reputation suffer, but rumors might surface about Lili, as well.

But surely even a barbarian such as he possesses a modicum of decency.

She shot the *américain* a look of anguished appeal—a look he either didn't notice or else chose to ignore. "Ours was quite a dramatic meeting," he began instead, his blue eyes glinting. "I had occasion to be abroad early this morning, as did Mademoiselle Lavoisier, and by lucky chance I heard her cry of distress. Of course, I promptly came to her aid."

"But what is this? Were you in some danger, *ma chère?*" Madame exclaimed with a startled look at Isabeau.

With an effort, she choked back denials and smiled at the dowager as she replied, "He is exaggerating, Madame."

He is a loutish buccaneer, Madame—a rogue, a villain.

"On the contrary, I fear the *mademoiselle* was in dire straits, indeed," Parrish countered, slanting a glance in Isabeau's direction while she gnawed her lip in frustration. "I found her on the street embroiled in a most terrible struggle."

Though he addressed the dowager, his gaze never left Isabeau as he continued, "Our lovely lady was clutching two bolts of silk in her arms and couldn't decide between them. The shopkeeper was partial to the turquoise, but I convinced her that only the emerald silk could do justice to her beauty."

As he concluded his fanciful version of the morning's events, Madame gave a chortle of laughter. "But you are quite droll, *cher,*" the old woman exclaimed. "I thought you perhaps had rescued her from a band of brigands. That would make for a romantic first meeting, *non?*"

"It would, at that," Parrish agreed, the gleam in his blue eyes unfathomable.

Isabeau met his gaze with a chill look of her own. Her initial relief that he had not betrayed her, gave way to anger at his enjoyment of her discomfiture. But she couldn't ignore the breathless sensation that gripped her—not that she had any intention of succumbing to Monsieur Tark Parrish's doubtful charms! Why, he was nothing more than a blackguard who could assume a gentleman's facade at will.

If Madame sensed the tension between them, she gave no indication. She beamed at them both before flicking her fingers in dismissal. "We have spent enough time talking, *non?* Now dance, you two, while I attend to my other guests."

Once the dowager took her leave with majestic dignity, the *américain* offered Isabeau his arm. "Her ladyship commands."

"You cannot be serious, *m'sieur,*" she exclaimed, ready to do battle now that she no longer was forced to guard her words for Madame's sake.

His smile faded, replaced by a look of cool appraisal. "I am quite serious, *mademoiselle.* Surely you can suffer a single waltz with me to please an old woman."

It was on the tip of her tongue to inform him that she would rather cavort naked through the streets than dance with him, but something in his expression forestalled her.

"Very well," she agreed, "but rest assured that I tolerate your company only because I do not wish to offend our hostess."

"I have no doubt on that score, *mademoiselle,*" he replied and led her out as the orchestra began its opening strains.

She placed her hand on his arm, trying not to dwell on the hard muscle beneath the smooth fabric of his jacket. Though he held her no more closely than was proper, the sensation of his hand against her back took on an intimacy. Unlike the soft white digits of the pampered Creole men, the fingers that grasped hers were tanned and calloused—the hands of a man who took what he wanted from life. And what he wanted now, she sensed with foreboding, was her.

She shoved aside that realization and focused her attention beyond his shoulder. Never mind this barbarian's wants, or the glances upon them. She would see this obligation through, and then dismiss the man. She might even convince him to abandon the burden of her company.

As they started off across the floor, she seized upon the first banal comment that came to mind. "The weather is quite mild for this time of year, isn't it?"

"Quite mild," he concurred.

After a turn about the floor, she dutifully observed, "And the orchestra is exceptional tonight, don't you agree?"

"Exceptional."

She counted the palm trees that ringed the dance floor and then continued, "And perhaps you've heard that the Russian Grand Duke will be in New Orleans for Mardi gras this year?"

"So I've been told."

She bit her lip in frustration. *Mon Dieu,* was the man immune to tedium? His expression didn't conceal the amusement in his eyes, an indication that her attempts to bore him were having just the opposite effect. Equally disconcerting, given their proximity, she noticed certain details of his appearance.

Minus their usual scowl, his firm lips had a sensuous curve that sent her pulse thudding to an uneven beat. A small white scar scored the rough-cut angle of his jaw, and she found herself wondering how he'd come to be injured.

Probably in some back-alley brawl, a voice within her declared. Suddenly aware of the turn her thoughts had taken, she gave herself a sharp mental shake. She'd consented to this dance only for Madame's sake, she reminded herself, and made a final attempt at polite exchange. "They say the weather will continue pleasant for the Grand Duke's stay."

"Undoubtedly."

Tark drew out that last word with deliberate casualness as he coolly met her gaze. *You'll never make a poker player, my sweet Isabeau,* he decided with satisfaction. Conflicting emotions played across her features, yet he sensed that she wielded her anger more as a shield than as a weapon. Now she conceded this battle of words to him, and he accepted her defeat as his due.

But who will win the war?

The question played through his mind as they moved across the dance floor. He took pleasure in baiting her, watching those midnight eyes flash with anger while she clung to her Creole pride. He had noticed, as well, that softening of her manner—a softness that faded when she recalled just who and what he was.

He, on the other hand, had no trouble remembering who she was. Upon arrival, he had searched for her, eventually spotting her in the company of a young dandy whose similarity in features marked him a relative. Tark had watched her from afar, like a hunter.

She didn't simper and preen, as he had predicted. Neither did she confine her attentions to one man. She danced with any number of partners, who appeared cut from the same expensive cloth. Watching her smile and flatter them, he'd been seized by an unexpected emotion he finally recognized as jealousy.

On the heels of that realization followed the determination to prove himself wrong. He had made his way through the crowded ballroom in search of Clarisse, intent on a formal introduction to legitimize his acquaintance with the girl. However, he turned to find both women watching him from halfway across the room. From there, everything had fallen into place, with Clarisse an accomplice as she insisted that he dance with the chit.

Seizing the opportunity to vindicate himself, he immediately acquiesced. Unfortunately, the spark of attraction he'd vowed to quash flared into desire the moment they set foot on the dance floor and he took Isabeau into his arms.

So you were wrong, a rational voice within him conceded. *Admit it, finish the dance, and get the hell out of here before you make a total jackass of yourself.*

He silently repeated that advice as the music ceased and he continued to hold her, ignoring the stares of the dancers who had begun to filter past.

"M'sieur, our dance is over," she protested when he made no move to release her. "I would like to return to my friends now."

"And I would like you to stay," he countered, though he cursed himself for his folly.

Sweet Jesus, you've already got Elisabeth willing to fall into bed with you anytime you want her. Why complicate things?

"Please, M'sieur Parrish," she said more sharply, and this time he heard trepidation in her voice.

"All I'm asking for is another dance, *mademoiselle.*" *Let her go.* "Call it my price for rescuing you this morning."

Color flooded her cheeks, but she met his gaze with a proud look of her own. "If you require repayment," she stiffly answered, "then I will send around my maid with an appropriate sum on the morrow. As for the next dance, I have already promised it to another gentleman."

Before he could react, she quit the dance floor, leaving him to stare after her in silence. Around him, the other dancers took their positions, their glances more eloquent than any barbed whispers. Meeting their gazes, he felt a warmth rise up his neck.

You did it, Tark, my boy. You let her make a damn fool of you before God and every Creole in the city.

His embarrassment ignited into anger, and he shoved his way through the crowd. His first impulse was to track down the impertinent chit and turn her over his knee. Then he reminded himself of the inconvenience of facing down every gentleman who would demand satisfaction on her behalf.

Uttering an imprecation that drew a gasp from female guests within earshot, Tark headed for the linen-draped table in a far corner. Behind it stood a natty, middle-aged Negro pouring champagne into glass after fluted glass. He glanced up at Tark's approach and abruptly set down his bottle.

"Why, Mister Parrish," he exclaimed with a welcoming smile, "it's been an age since we've seen—"

"Do you have any whiskey back there, Robert?" Tark

interrupted, even as he acknowledged the man's greeting with a curt nod.

Robert's smile broadened into a conspiratorial grin. "I've just the thing, sir."

He reached beneath the trailing edges of the crisp white cloth and produced an unopened bottle of bourbon, which he set on the table with a flourish. "Kentucky's finest, guaranteed smooth and easy as a good woman's loving."

"That'll do fine."

Tark waved away the crystal tumbler the man proffered, and caught up the bottle, then hesitated. He and Robert had exchanged more than one confidence over a glass of brandy during the years when he had visited Clarisse on a regular basis. Now, he felt an urge to ask the older man's advice.

Robert, old friend, I am obsessed by a beautiful, feisty young woman who feels nothing but contempt for me. So what do I do now?

His fingers tightened around the bottle. "Give my best to Sarah and all those grandchildren," he managed instead, deciding he'd have to handle this on his own.

The man nodded. "I'll do that, sir. Enjoy the cotillion."

Too damn late for that, Tark grimly thought. He strode toward the nearest of two pairs of French doors, which led out onto a balcony that overlooked a courtyard. Once past the threshold, he halted on the white-columned gallery and took a deep breath. The evening air proved a welcome change from the smoky warmth of the ballroom.

He leaned against the railing and from the second level surveyed the square below. Outbuildings combined with the main house and a stuccoed wall to his right to form the courtyard's perimeter. Against that wall and almost at the foot of the stair sat an oversized wrought-iron arbor. Threaded though it was with heavy vines, bare spots in the arbor gave evidence of the season. A generous sliver of moon illuminated the wide, brick-paved walks that enclosed raised beds of fronds and rows of neatly trimmed low hedges. Beyond the splashing fountain in the courtyard's center, shadows spilled in careless abandon across the brick.

Tightening his grip on the bottle, Tark headed for the closest of the two L-shaped stairways that led down to ground level. There, he bypassed the arbor and headed for the shadowed recesses beyond. In the darkness, he sprawled upon a wrought-iron chair and began contemplating how to salvage his wounded pride.

His anger had eased somewhat, though the sting of humiliation had yet to abate. Little matter that, as an American in a city of Creoles, he'd been the recipient of more snubs and cuts than he could count. What stung was the fact that, never had he suffered the ignominy of having a woman abandon him on a crowded dance floor.

The memory spurred him to action, and he cracked the seal on the whiskey bottle. Raising it to his lips, he took a swallow, savoring the bourbon's sharp warmth. Finally, he blotted away the drops that had trickled down his chin.

" 'Smooth and easy as a good woman's loving,' " he softly repeated the Negro's words, then gave a disgusted laugh. "I'll have to take your word on that, Robert, since good women have been conspicuously absent in my life."

He took a second swallow and shut his eyes, tempted

for a moment to spend the remainder of the evening as
he'd first intended—thoroughly drunk. Somehow, the
prospect wasn't appealing now. Neither was the thought
of marching back through that crowd of scandal-hungry
Creoles.

*So you're going to skulk out the back way like a dog
with its tail between its legs, all because some little chit
wounded your pride.*

At that inner voice, his eyes flew open and he straightened. But it was not just about pride, he thought as another explanation occurred to him.

It was about control—or rather, the lack of it.

He took another quick swallow of whiskey, as a realization began to crystallize. How long had it been
since he'd had control of his own destiny? A year?
More? He had spent the time dancing like a marionette
every time his unknown enemy tugged the strings. Had
the habit become so ingrained that he was willing to
accede to everyone's whims but his own?

Not likely.

Music drifted to him as he took another slow sip of
whiskey. He might not be able to do anything about his
foe, but he'd be damned if he would leave this place
letting a slip of a girl get the best of him.

Seven

Philippe Lavoisier sat at a corner table in the Orleans Club and admired the jewel-like shimmer of his claret. He had been forced to leave the cotillion with undue haste to keep this appointment. If all went as Henri had assured him, he would soon possess the means to live in the style his aristocratic nature demanded!

He bitterly contemplated the reversals in fortune that had led to his suffering these past years. The Lavoisier family had been wealthy once. But then, four years ago, the life of ease he had taken for granted came to an end.

As did other Orleanians of means, the Lavoisiers always had spent the summer visiting friends north of the city. Removed from the threat of yellow fever, a usually fatal disease whose appearance was tied to the sultry summer months, the family would spend the days in careless leisure, ticking off the time until their return to the bustle of New Orleans society. That year Philippe's parents had sent him and Isabeau ahead, intending to join them a few days later. The delay had cost Jean-Paul and Thérèse their lives.

Still, that season's fever epidemic had been mild, taking few victims in addition to Philippe and Isabeau's parents. Orphaned, the pair encountered disaster of another sort upon their return home. Creditors had swarmed into the house, seeking repayment for debts that, unbeknownst to his family, Jean-Paul had accrued. When Philippe finally settled accounts, little remained of his father's once-substantial estate.

They had managed for a time on their own—Isabeau, at the convent school and he, juggling funds to carve out a life of leisure from their paltry inheritance. At Henri's suggestion, he finally sent Isabeau to Paris in hopes that Grandmère Emelie might find his sister a wealthy husband. Then he had taken the ignominious step of closing the house and striking out on his own.

He found himself forced to take rooms in the less-fashionable section of town, unable even to afford his tailor. As time passed, however, the assets he had invested yielded a small profit. He reopened the old house and once more indulged in the refined way of life that was his due as a Creole gentleman. But within a year his investments soured, and he faced unpleasant alternatives: curtail his extravagant lifestyle, or borrow.

He chose to borrow.

The loans were small, at first, and only for a week or so, he assured his friends as he pocketed their cash. Slowly, the amounts grew. Acquaintances avoided him, while bill collectors hounded him. Even Marcel made excuses to shun his company. Philippe feared he was doomed to repeat his father's mistakes. And then he met Rivard.

The man gave no other name. One evening, the stocky, middle-aged gentleman joined Philippe at the table where he sat drinking, using up his last few coins.

"I have heard of your troubles, *mon ami,*" Rivard had

murmured with an engaging smile. "Your *papa* was a dear friend of mine, so how can I let his son lack for anything? Whatever you want—money, fine clothes, women—is yours for the asking."

"You are very . . . kind, *m'sieur*," Philippe had slurred as he toyed with the stem of his wineglass. "Unfortunately, I cannot accept . . . your generous offer."

"But why not?"

Philippe drew himself up with as much dignity as he could muster, given his intoxicated state. "I do not know you, *m'sieur,* and no . . . honorable man can accept charity . . . from a stranger."

"But you insult me, *mon ami*," Rivard countered, his dark eyes sorrowful. "As I told you, your *papa* and I were great friends, so how can I be a stranger?" With those words, his new acquaintance produced a bulging pouch and spilled a flood of coins onto the table.

Philippe swallowed hard, mesmerized by the gold winking up at him with a brilliance that mocked and enticed. He glanced blearily up at the man across from him. Rivard's smile, bright against his olive skin, held a comforting hint of paternal indulgence. The offer was too good to resist. Philippe accepted a staggering sum and promptly went on to toast his new-found benefactor with another bottle of claret.

With the money, his friends returned, while his creditors departed satisfied. A month passed, then two, and still he heard nothing from his benefactor, who vanished as mysteriously as he had appeared. He resumed his former lifestyle, with fine clothes, expensive women, and gambling. The days passed in a leisurely fashion, the only change a triumphant letter from Grandmère to inform him that Isabeau was engaged to a marquis. Even as he celebrated this good fortune, a second letter arrived from his sister requesting that he arrange for her return to New Orleans, alone. He had swallowed his disappointment and paid a first-class passage.

Then, ten days ago, Rivard had returned. Once again, he seated himself at Philippe's table, but this time he produced a contract that bore Philippe's signature.

"This is your handwriting, *mon ami,* is it not?" the man amiably inquired as he pointed to the bottom of the page.

Philippe snatched the paper from him and studied in horror a document he could not remember signing but which clearly stated his intention to repay the borrowed sum within one year and at an exorbitant rate of interest.

"But I cannot raise this sum," he choked out, thrusting away the damning document and reaching for his wineglass.

Rivard's expression never changed, though his dark eyes took on a hard glint. "That is the same thing other gentlemen have claimed, *mon ami.* Sadly, they no longer have need of their money."

"You don't mean . . ."

Philippe's voice trailed off when Rivard smiled in a gesture like feral baring of teeth.

"You have two weeks, *mon ami,*" the man finished in a jovial tone. "Use them wisely."

That night, Philippe had taken stock of his remaining assets, which totaled maybe one quarter of the original sum. His attempts to secure a second loan to cover the first were quickly rebuffed. Even Henri claimed he could not lay hands on such an amount in so little time. Finally, he carried every cent to the gaming tables.

For several nights, he played with desperation born of fear, winning small pots only to lose three times the sum on the next roll of the dice or turn of the cards. Publicly, he laughed off his misfortune as a matter of no consequence. Privately, as he stumbled home each night with less money than the evening before, he found it harder to believe that fate might intervene with a windfall of cash. Then, the day after Isabeau's return, he received word from his uncle that Henri had set up tonight's meeting with Franchot Calvé for him.

Philippe finished the last swallow of wine with a satisfied smack of his lips. With midnight tomorrow his deadline for repaying Rivard, the rendezvous with Calvé came none too late, he reflected with a return of his usual cockiness. He set down the glass and signaled for another bottle, then leaned back in his chair and mentally sorted through what he knew of the wealthy recluse.

Though rich and influential, Calvé was said by some to have sprung from a less-than-humble background and to have fled France after killing an aristocrat in a duel. Another rumor had it that Calvé was himself of noble blood but had renounced his title for reasons unknown. Other gossip recounted his activities during the Crimean War where, as the son of a French aristocrat and a Russian noblewoman, he had fought with equal zeal for both sides.

Despite Calvé's seemingly unorthodox background, the enigma of the man tantalized Creole society. His presence at any affair bestowed immediate status upon the host. Not that Philippe had ever been linked socially with Calvé. The closest he had ever come to conversation with the man was a mumbled apology for jostling him in a crowded salon during one of the man's infrequent public appearances. He only prayed Calvé had forgotten the incident.

As those thoughts occupied his mind, a tall, well-dressed gentleman approached his table. "Monsieur Lavoisier?" The man's voice was smooth and cultivated, with lingering traces of a Parisian accent. "I am Franchot Calvé."

Returning the greeting, Philippe rose to his feet and gestured to the chair beside him. Calvé took the seat across from him as a waiter appeared with a bottle of wine and another glass.

"Your uncle told me about your unfortunate situation," Calvé announced after the waiter had retreated. "He suggested you and I might come to a satisfactory arrangement."

Philippe nodded as he studied the man through wine-fogged eyes. Calvé was younger than he'd remembered him and possessed a leonine grace similar to the *maîtres d'armes*—the fencing masters—he had admired as a boy. His golden eyes and mane of bronze hair enhanced the feline image. A pale scar sliced across his cheek—doubtless the result of some long-ago duel, Philippe thought with envy—but this mark did not detract from the man's aristocratic good looks.

Satisfied with his appraisal, Philippe reached for his glass. Though the man seemed affable, something dangerous was lurking beneath those jungle-cat eyes. Calvé, he judged, was not a man to cross. On the other hand, such a powerful foe might also make a valuable ally. "I'd like to hear your proposition."

"It concerns the merchandise in which I deal," the Frenchman began, withdrawing a slim cigar from his jacket pocket. "I require someone to act as my liaison and handle certain delicate . . . transactions for me. Unfortunately, the last man to hold that position proved to be, shall we say, unsuitable."

He paused to light the cigar, then glanced at Philippe through a cloud of blue smoke. "His replacement must be loyal and willing to take risks, but above all he must be discreet. Do you understand me?"

Philippe met his gaze and nodded. He had suspected even before they met that Calvé's business involved some illegal venture—smuggling, perhaps. Whatever his occupation, it was obviously profitable, Philippe decided with a covetous glance at the other man's expensive clothes. Still, he would do well to learn more about the man's affairs.

"And what is this merchandise you mentioned, m'sieur?"

Calvé smiled slightly. "I would rather not say yet. Let me assure you, however, that your pay will compensate for any unpleasantness. I will even advance you the funds to cover your current debts."

At those words, a wild struggle began in Philippe's mind. How could he accept a potentially illegal job with no notion of what he'd be doing, and why? That would be folly. He might end his days in prison. He didn't care to speculate on worse possibilities. But if he didn't repay Rivard, he would wind up dead.

Philippe took a deep breath. To repay Rivard and still

have the means to live in style was surely worth any risk. After all, he could always leave Calvé's employ should the situation become dangerous. "I accept your offer, *m'sieur.*"

Calvé smiled again, but the look in his eyes was unfathomable. *"Bon.* I will contact you again tomorrow."

"As you wish. My address—"

"—is already known to me." Calvé put out the cigar and stood. "Until tomorrow, Monsieur Lavoisier."

"Wait." Philippe half rose in his chair, blushing at the desperation he could hear in his tone. "What about the money I owe?"

Calvé fixed him with his golden gaze, and Philippe glimpsed again the savagery that lurked beneath the man's civilized facade. "Your debts were settled this morning."

Philippe fell back into his chair and watched Calvé vanish into the crowd. Perhaps he'd been hasty in joining with the man. But Rivard posed the more immediate threat, and by paying him off he could start afresh.

Philippe managed a smile and raised his glass in silent toast to himself. Then a thought struck him, and he put down the glass. Why, he wondered, had his predecessor been found unsuitable?

"Are you certain that you don't want me to ch-challenge that mannerless *américain* to a duel?" Marcel St. John asked for the third time in the past quarter hour. "Since Philippe has already left, I w-would be glad to do so in his stead."

"I am quite certain, Marcel," Isabeau assured the young gentleman beside her. Though concern was evident in his eyes, his tone was uncertain, and she knew Philippe's peace-loving friend no more cared to face the *américain* than did she.

"I am only thinking of your reputation," she hastened to set him at ease. "You know it would not be proper for a Creole gentleman to challenge a barbarian such as Monsieur Parrish."

"Y-you are right, of course," Marcel agreed, managing a shrug that didn't quite mask his relief.

Isabeau gave him a fond smile. Unlike his younger sister, Marcel St. John was reserved to the point of shyness, more comfortable with philosophical debate than physical confrontation. Even so, he had witnessed her dance with the *américain* and had taken offense at the man's behavior. Had she wished it, Marcel would have made good on his offer—and would have been injured or killed for his efforts.

"Let's not bother ourselves any longer over Monsieur Parrish's lack of manners," she proposed. "I would rather dance, instead."

She summoned a carefree smile as they stepped onto the dance floor, though turmoil raged within her. She had been looking over her shoulder, fearful lest the *américain* should claim the dance she had denied him. She had seen no further sign of the man, and she wondered if he might have quit the cotillion in disgust following that undignified scene.

And good riddance, she thought with a toss of her head. Now, if only she were spared the embarrassment of explaining to Madame why she had humiliated her guest, the evening might be termed a success.

The orchestra commenced a bright air, and she fell into step. How different it was to dance with a gentleman like Marcel, she mused. With him, she needn't be concerned with veiled insults or unwelcome advances. Even so, she had begun to suspect that Marcel harbored an affection for her that went beyond friendship . . not that she had encouraged him.

Isabeau frowned slightly. Philippe had confided to her that Marcel had been enamored of their cousin, Lili, though his shyness prevented him from pressing his suit. Isabeau had not witnessed Marcel's reaction when the girl made clear her intention to join the Ursulines. Still, from what Philippe had written her, his friend had taken the news with equanimity. But what if Marcel had turned to *her* as a substitute for Lili?

As if reading her thoughts, Marcel tightened his grip on her and blurted, "I-I have already spoken with your b-brother . . . that is, he is agreeable . . . w-what I mean to say is, w-would you consider m-marrying me?"

"Marry you?" she echoed almost in dismay. *"Mon Dieu,* Marcel, can you truly be serious?"

"I-I am quite s-serious. I-I always have admired you . . . y-you don't have to give me your answer n-now."

He glanced miserably around them, as if to seek assistance. The music ended on a flourish just then, a provident bit of timing, since they both had come to a halt in midstep. Isabeau let the young gentleman lead her off the dance floor, struggling for a suitable reply. How could she refuse him without wounding his sensitive soul?

But maybe marriage to Marcel was the answer.

The thought took her aback. Her first impulse had been to dismiss the notion, since she felt sisterly love for him. But she realized that in a marriage of convenience, why not align herself with someone whom she considered a friend, whom she both liked and respected?

As they wended their way through the crowd, Isabeau spared Marcel a glance, trying to picture him as a suitor. Beneath his light brown hair, his even-featured countenance was unremarkable, save for the shy sweetness of his smile. He was a few years younger than Philippe, but he exhibited far more maturity than her brother's other friends. The St. John family was wealthy and influential, enjoying a respect that many did not. As a suitor, Marcel was eminently acceptable.

But could I be happy with him as a husband?

She continued to grapple with the question even as she turned again to face him. "I am most flattered by your offer, Marcel, but, as you said, I do need time to consider it. Perhaps I can give you my answer by Shrove Tuesday . . ."

She managed an encouraging smile. Marcel's mild features were alight with pleasure. "At the Comus ball, then," he agreed and pressed her hand with brotherly affection.

Isabeau returned the fond gesture. "What I need now is a breath of fresh air," she said with a nod toward the open French doors. "I think I will step out into the courtyard for a few minutes."

"Let me accompany you," he offered, and then blushed. "T-that is, if you would like me to."

"You would be my first choice of a companion," she

replied, "but with all that has happened tonight, I need a few moments to myself."

She started toward the ballroom's far wall, where two pairs of French doors stood ajar. They led, she knew, to a broad gallery that overlooked the courtyard where she had played many times as a child. Tonight, that courtyard served as a cool refuge from the warmth of the ballroom—or as a discreet meeting place for lovers eager to steal a kiss.

She hesitated at the nearest of the lace-curtained casements. If she had allowed Marcel to accompany her, would he have kissed her? Did she want him to? Somehow, she suspected that the transition from friends to lovers might be more difficult than she had thought.

She stepped out into the night. Light from the ballroom illuminated the wooden gallery, while a slender silver moon cast a faint glow onto the open square below. She saw in relief that the courtyard appeared temporarily deserted.

She gathered up her skirts and made her way down the nearest wooden stairway. The train of her gown came lightly rustling behind her. A moment later, she had dismounted the final step, feeling through the thin soles of her kid slippers the cool brick of the courtyard. Within the square's confines, however, she stood protected from the chill night air, so that only a whisper of breeze caressed her.

She went to the wrought-iron arbor and settled upon the stone bench beneath it. Beside that seat stood a life-sized stone rendition of the huntress-goddess, Diana, offering symbolic protection. With a sigh at that image, she closed her eyes and listened to the babble of the nearby fountain. It proved a soothing contrast to the music filtering from the ballroom, and she relaxed for the first time that evening.

The fountain's murmur had almost lulled her into drowsiness, when she heard the rustle of fallen leaves along the bricks. *Footsteps?* Her eyes flew open, and she scanned the square. Shadows obscured its corners, making it impossible to determine whether anyone lurked within the courtyard's walls. The sound did not repeat itself. Still, she couldn't shake the feeling that she was no longer alone. Not that she should have expected more than a moment's privacy before some other guest sought the same haven, she reminded herself. But the sound she had heard was almost furtive in nature.

She gathered up her skirts and stood to leave, when a fragment of conversation drifted above the orchestra's soft strains. She saw three fashionably dressed women standing on the gallery above. Light spilled out from the ballroom and wrapped them in its glow, so that Isabeau could make out every detail of their elaborate gowns. But she had the advantage, she realized, for they could not see her in the half-light of the courtyard.

Loath to eavesdrop, she started to make her presence known, when a lilting word caught her attention. Cloaked by shadows and vines, Isabeau forgot her good intentions. She peered around the arbor and tried to hear more.

"Tark is alone tonight," the plump blonde said with a giggle.

The curvaceous redhead favored her companions with an arch smile. "Yes, but he won't leave that way. To be sure, he would never do for a public escort, but he is more than acceptable in a private capacity."

The blonde giggled again and toyed with the tassel of her gold-plumed fan. "It sounds as if you're rather well acquainted with the man."

"You might say that we are . . . intimate friends."

Using the open French door as a mirror, the woman adjusted the neckline of her turquoise gown so that her breasts were shown to advantage, then tilted her head to admire the effect. Isabeau studied the woman with interest.

Intimate friends, indeed! It took little imagination to guess why the *américain* might have taken such a woman as his mistress, she thought with disdain. With her ripe figure and painted face, the redhead exuded a lush sensuality that few men could resist—and that she, herself, would never possess, Isabeau ruefully admitted.

Unaware of her scrutiny, the woman turned back to her companions. "You must admit that he's handsome in a fierce sort of way, and quite well-bred for an *américain*," she continued in a purr. "After all, he was once married to a Creole girl."

"Yes, but remember what happened to her," the brunette spoke up.

So Monsieur Parrish had once been wed. Isabeau waited to learn of this bride's fate. But no explanation was forthcoming.

"I can't believe that Clarisse Dumas allows a man like him in her home," she heard the brunette say. "Why, I understand that he once showed up at a formal ball in a shocking state of intoxication."

"But he is quite wealthy, *chérie*," the redhead replied with a laugh. "Surely you know that money excuses any number of faults, even in an *américain*."

"Who was the pretty child he was dancing with earlier?" the blonde wanted to know. "La, but it was amusing to see her stalk off in a huff, leaving the poor man standing there alone."

"Why, she's Henri Lavoisier's niece," the brunette informed her with a smirk.

"You mean—"

"—the very one, just returned from Paris. I heard tell of a scandal with a marquis—but then isn't it always the innocent-looking ones . . ."

The dark-haired woman trailed off with a knowing look, and Isabeau was mortified by the brunette's glib dismissal of her. However, she was stunned even more by the woman's next comment.

"Your Monsieur Parrish seemed quite taken with the chit, at least until she abandoned him," the brunette added with a glance at her red-haired companion. "Perhaps he's set his sights on another Creole bride."

"Perhaps she thinks an *américain* would be less choosy," the blonde chimed in.

"Believe me, *chérie*," the redhead interjected, "the man has no interest in marriage."

Despite the woman's tone, Isabeau sensed a possessiveness that made her wonder at the nature of the redhead's relationship with the *américain*. She almost missed the next comment.

"No doubt the girl was too young at the time to know about the scandal," the blonde decided. "Still, a touch of danger makes it all the more exciting, so perhaps we should tell her."

"But of course," the brunette dryly agreed. "Imagine

the thrill of making love to a man and knowing all the while that he murdered his first wife."

The music ended, and the women melded back into the ballroom crowd amid a flurry of satin and perfume. Isabeau barely noticed their departure as she tried to sort out her wildly racing thoughts.

M'sieur Parrish, a murderer? Mon Dieu, *could it be true?*

She had sensed within his personality a thread of violence. She had seen how he used a pistol to disperse the drunken dockworkers.

Then common sense reasserted itself. Surely Madame would not treat him as a favored son if he were guilty of such a heinous crime. She reminded herself that the gossip about her that the women had repeated was grossly distorted, so why should their tales of the *américain* not be exaggerated? She steeled herself to return to the ballroom, when she heard a sound behind her. This time, it was the echo of a man's firm tread.

Startled, she swung around and nearly fell into the waiting arms of the *américain*.

Eight

"Eavesdropping is a lamentable habit, *mademoiselle,*" Tark Parrish said and reached out to steady her. "I can assure you, one rarely overhears anything pleasant spoken of himself . . . or herself."

"I was not eavesdropping," Isabeau protested. "I merely stepped outside for a breath of fresh air."

"I see." He eyed the arbor with its screen of vines, then glanced at the gallery above. "You just happened to be close enough to overhear everything said by anyone who chanced to step outside. The fact that you have a few stray leaves clinging to you doesn't necessarily mean you had your ear pressed up against the arbor," he ironically observed as he plucked them from her hair.

Isabeau felt heat rise in her cheeks and was grateful for the shadows. Why, of all the people present tonight, did he have to witness her lapse of propriety? Still, she took a measure of comfort in the fact that he apparently had not overheard the women's conversation, since he had made no reference to it. But after their confrontation on the dance floor, she would be a fool to further provoke him.

"Very well, *m'sieur,* I will admit that my manners are

not what they should be. And now, if you will excuse me, I must return to my friends."

When she tried to step around him, the *américain* blocked her way. He propped his half-empty whiskey bottle in the crook of the stone goddess's arm and fixed Isabeau with a look of appraisal. Isabeau met his gaze with a calm she did not feel, all too aware of the way the moonlight played across his face and lent harshness to his features.

Even had she not seen the bottle, she would have guessed from his speech and his eyes—like rough-cut gems beneath hooded lids—that he had dulled his wits with whiskey. She knew the effects alcohol could produce in a man: anything from good humor and temporary courage to maudlin tears and blind fury. The *américain,* she judged, had imbibed enough to make him unpredictable, like a dog that might allow itself to be taunted a dozen times—or only once—before turning on its attacker.

"You cannot leave yet," he insisted in the soft tone he had used that morning. "If you'll recall, my sweet Isabeau, you still owe me the honor of another dance."

As if on cue, threads of melody drifted to them, and Tark indicated the courtyard. "And since the orchestra has kindly cooperated, I see no reason to postpone that pleasure."

"Don't be absurd," she retorted, praying that the tremor in her voice wasn't noticeable. "I will not dance with you here, or anywhere else. Now let me pass, or I shall . . ."

"Or you'll scream? Or will you simply swoon?"

He shook his head in exaggerated reproach. "You disappoint me, *mademoiselle.* I expected more spirit from a young woman bold enough to wander Basin Street alone."

At this last jibe, she had to suppress the urge to vent her angry confusion in a shriek. *Mon Dieu,* what did he want? Why did he pursue her, when she had made clear her feelings for him? They seemed to be engaged in a contest of wills. She didn't know the rules or the prize that lay at stake, but she did not want him to best her at the game.

"If I consent to one more dance, M'sieur Parrish, do I have your promise it will be our last?"

"You have my word, Mademoiselle Lavoisier . . . as a gentleman."

Surely no harm can come of a single waltz, she told herself as she placed her hand on his arm. He swept her into the dance, so that they circled beneath the starlit canopy of sky.

They danced in silence, with only the click of his bootheels to echo the whisper of her fragile slippers on the brick. In the distance, the orchestra played, its sprightly notes dulled by the rustle of fallen leaves as her gown swirled, and swept the square.

What does he want of me?

This time, her thought held a note of longing. She glanced up to find his gaze upon her, and the hunger that burned within those blue eyes set her pulse thudding. While they had waltzed beneath the ballroom's bright lights, she had been able to distance herself from the unwelcome attraction his presence stirred within her. Here in the moonlight, the familiar ritual seemed charged with intimacy, and she realized she could not deny her heart.

A chill had settled over the courtyard, yet the heat of

his body all but seared her flesh when he drew her closer still. She released a tremulous sigh, and she leaned her head against his shoulder. It was madness, she told herself . . . but then, was not madness an integral part of the Carnival season?

She gave herself to the night's seductive spell, half expecting, half dreading what must come next: familiar, meaningless words of love freely given and so quickly forgotten. When they didn't come, she chided herself for her folly, though an absurd stab of disappointment still swept her.

Sainte Cécile, what was she thinking?

Intent on proving that she was unaffected by this man, she hadn't considered the consequences. Should someone see her alone with the *américain,* Philippe or Oncle Henri would feel obliged to duel with the man to satisfy the family honor. Though Henri was an indifferent marksman, Philippe could hold his own with a pistol against any opponent. How could she live with either man's death on her conscience?

With a cry of dismay, she halted even as the music ended on a flourish.

"What is wrong, my sweet Isabeau?" Tark murmured, his fingertips brushing the curve of her throat.

She shuddered at his touch and broke from his grasp. "I . . . I must leave now, *m'sieur.* The dance is over."

"Not quite yet, *mademoiselle.*"

He caught her wrist and drew her within the arbor, pinning her between him and the statue. "Did you truly think that all I wanted from you was another dance?" he demanded, his voice rough with whiskey and desire.

"I know that's not all you wanted, or you never would have followed me out here."

"But I didn't follow—"

Her words broke off in a gasp as he slid one hand down her bare shoulders and along the curve of her back. "Tell me again," he harshly urged. "Tell me that you didn't come looking for me, to finish what we'd only started."

"Leave me be!"

She tried to shove past him, but succeeded only in entangling herself in the train of her gown. *Mon Dieu,* what ever had possessed her to dance with this drunken barbarian? Worse, how could she have imagined that she harbored any feeling but contempt for him?

She heard the orchestra resume and realized that, even should she cry out, the sound would be lost. Desperate, she tried to reason with him.

"Your attentions are quite unwelcome, M'sieur Parrish, and—"

"Tark," he corrected in the same husky voice. "If we're to become better acquainted, I would prefer that you call me Tark."

"I have no intention of continuing our acquaintance, *M'sieur Parrish . . .*"

Her voice faltered as he traced the swell of her breasts above her low-cut gown. *How can you let him do this to you?* she raged in silent desperation, but to no avail. Her flesh burned beneath his touch, the heat went spreading through her limbs, leaving her incapable of movement. When she didn't protest, his caresses grew bolder. Now, his strong fingers cupped her breast, and his thumb lightly teased the taut nipple that strained against the silk fabric of her gown.

"Please." The word escaped her in a moan that was as much a plea as a protest. "Oh, please."

"I will please you," he hoarsely murmured, his breath hot against her cheek as his lips moved down its soft curve and along her throat. "I'll stroke your flesh until you tremble with desire and beg me to love you. That's what you want from me, my sweet Isabeau, is it not?"

It *was* what she wanted, she realized with a shameful thrill—had been what she'd wanted from their first meeting. It didn't matter that he was one of the hated *américains,* that he had treated her with contempt from the moment they first met. She gave herself up to his intimate exploration.

His mouth seemed to possess her flesh, nuzzling and licking her bare skin until she thought she'd swoon with delight. An odd shiver built within her, radiating from between her thighs even as she felt a hot, unfamiliar moistness there. Instinctively, her arms linked around his waist. Her hands moved with tentative strokes upward beneath his jacket and across his back.

She felt the play of muscle beneath fine-spun linen when he pulled her closer and groaned out, "Sweet Jesus, but I want you."

Before she could protest, he pressed her against the statue, the hard outline of his erection unmistakable as he moved his body against hers. The stone folds of the goddess's tunic caught at her gown and bruised the flesh beneath, yet that discomfort was lost amid the sensations that spiraled within her.

He shifted slightly and thrust his knee between hers,

parting her legs so that she straddled his muscular thigh. She gasped at this sudden, intimate pressure, and his mouth found hers.

His kiss was no token of affection, but was demanding. The taste of whiskey mingled with desire, and it overwhelmed her as his tongue probed the recesses of her mouth. After the first shock of this invasion, she tentatively parried his thrusts, growing bolder as she sensed the building urgency in his response.

He pressed his thigh more insistently between hers, and she moved against him—slowly at first, and then with a wanton eagerness. What she waited for, she wasn't sure, yet when those spirals of pleasure began to spread into an all-consuming need, she knew that he alone could fulfill it.

"What a charming tableau," interrupted a cool feminine voice, just as the forgotten whiskey bottle slipped from the statue's frozen embrace and shattered against the bricks.

"What in the hell—"

Tark's muffled curse echoed Isabeau's own cry of dismay. She hurriedly pulled from the embrace. She recognized the speaker as the same red-haired woman whose conversation she had overheard.

"The old man told me you were here in the courtyard," the redhead addressed Tark in a brittle tone. "Unfortunately, he neglected to mention that you weren't alone." Then she turned to Isabeau, and her words took on a spiteful glee. "Let me offer you a bit of advice, *chérie*. The next time you set your sights on a man, be very certain he's not already spoken for."

Isabeau opened her mouth to protest, but the explanation caught in her throat. She shot Tark a glance, praying he would convince the woman that it had been a mistake. When he appeared more concerned with the broken bottle at his feet, her dignity fell away. She gathered up her skirts, pushed toward the stairway, and stumbled up its wooden steps toward the sanctuary of the ballroom above.

Tark watched her flight in silence, then gathered his whiskey-dulled wits to round on Elisabeth. "And just what in the hell were you trying to accomplish with that little performance?"

She smiled and drew closer with a whispered rustle of satin, her cool white fingers coyly plucking at his shirtfront. "You might show a bit more gratitude, *cher,* considering that I just saved you from an unpleasant fate."

"What are you talking about?"

"Why, the Lavoisier family, of course. Between the brother and uncle, they've lost or gambled away every cent. Their only hope of staving off ruination lies in the girl making a wealthy match."

"And what does that have to do with me?" he rasped out, though dawning comprehension began to penetrate his alcoholic fog.

She ran her hand down the bulge in his trousers and gave a laugh. "The fortune-hunting little chit had you hard and ready, didn't she, *cher?* In another minute, you would have been under her skirts and she would have been screaming rape. No doubt her uncle or brother was waiting nearby, ready to storm out with a dozen witnesses in tow in time to catch you with your trousers down around your ankles."

Her tone took on a malicious note. "By morning, you'd have found yourself leg-shackled to the little slut, not that I'd dream of letting a little thing like marriage come between us," she finished with an arch smile.

Sweet Jesus, it had all been a set-up.

Tark laughed at his gullibility. It made sense, the way their paths continued to cross. The chit had seen him as ripe for the plucking from that first moment on the dock. Hell, he wouldn't be surprised to learn that her visit to Ophelia's brothel was somehow connected to this scheme, though how she might have learned that he frequented that establishment was something he couldn't guess. And as for her performance tonight . . .

Tark shook his head. He'd seen affronted innocence played this skillfully once before. If he hadn't been so damned drunk, he would have realized the parallel. He was unmoved by the seductive promise in Elisabeth's tone when, with a final intimate caress, she suggested that he wait a discreet interval and then follow her out to her carriage. Instead, he sank down on the stone bench and gave himself up to the bitterness of recalling that long-ago summer night soon after the war's end.

The pleasure of your company is requested . . .

. . . a cotillion honoring the brave defenders of our beloved city.

The invitation from his neighbor arrived soon after he had taken up residence at Belle Terre. On the appointed night, he strode past the door of Claude Blanchard's ostentatious home and learned how entrenched was the Creole disdain for Americans—himself included. The fact that, as a former blockade runner, he might be numbered among those brave honorees proved of little comfort in the face of his cold reception. The guests made clear that, invitation or not, M'sieur Tark Parrish was not welcome.

After fruitless attempts to pierce their collective reserve, he had quit the place in disgust and made his way to the solitude of his host's sprawling estate. Drunk as he was by then on bourbon and indignation, he didn't realize that his departure had not gone unnoticed.

Our gardens, they are magnifique, *m'sieur. You must let me show you.*

Seventeen years old, with the face of a Botticelli angel and the morals of a Basin Street strumpet, Delphine Marie-Louise Blanchard had proved a welcome balm for his pride. In the privacy of the garden gazebo, she proceeded to offer her own apology for his treatment at the hands of her father's guests. By the time she finally spread her thighs for him, he no longer cared that bedding his host's only daughter might not improve his standing among the locals.

Tark gave a shake of his head at the memory. Hell, he'd wanted her so badly that he hadn't even thought it odd when she ripped open the bodice of her expensive ball gown, so that her ample breasts gleamed in the moonlight. But even as he fumbled past her petticoats to thrust into the waiting warmth of her—confirming his suspicions that she was no virgin—lamplight flooded the garden.

But he forced himself on me, Papa. *I tried to stop him, but he wouldn't listen.*

He recalled fragments of what happened next, though Delphine's cries of rape had echoed in his mind for days. His last impression was of repeating his vows before a hastily summoned priest. When he finally awoke the next afternoon, he found himself possessed of a hangover and a brand-new wife.

In the weeks that followed, he learned the extent of the Blanchards' treachery. The fact that he was an American was of little importance to them, since he fulfilled every other important requirement—he was single, wealthy, and likely the only adult male within a fifty-mile radius who hadn't already sampled what Delphine was eager to share. Not only had she and her father orchestrated every move leading up to the so-called rape, they also managed to get his drunken signature on a prenuptial agreement that stated that he would assume responsibility for Claude's staggering war debts.

Now, the realization that he'd almost fallen victim to a similar plot had a sobering effect on him. Not that being wedded to him would solve the chit's problems, he reminded himself. In fact, he might have enjoyed watching the Lavoisiers scramble to cry off once he'd informed them of his true financial state. In case they had it in mind to try this stunt again, discussion with his would-be future bride seemed in order.

And then, my sweet Isabeau, we'll see just how far you're willing to carry this little charade.

He roughly pushed aside thoughts of the Lavoisiers and stood. The remains of the whiskey bottle crunched beneath his boots as he started across the courtyard. A small wooden gate in the wall opened onto the street beyond, where Elisabeth's coach waited in the shadows. With a glance around him, he climbed inside and settled against the cool leather seat.

As always, she was ready for him, her skirts tucked up with careless haste. Waiting only long enough for him to unbutton his trousers, she straddled him amid a crush of flame-colored satin and proceeded to ride him with an eagerness that quickly brought him to the brink of climax.

But even as he matched her frenzied bucking, driving into her with a ferocity born as much of anger as desire, he found himself imagining another woman—a raven-haired beauty with ivory skin and eyes like black velvet.

Beauty. Treachery. Could the one exist separately from the other?

The question echoed in his mind as he spent himself in a surge of passion that temporarily erased Isabeau's image from his mind. The answer continued to elude him.

Nine

A dark man astride a grey stallion pursued her through the twilight streets of the ramparts. Shadows obscured his features; still, she had recognized him from the moment she'd first glimpsed him silhouetted against the auburn sky. Though she was afoot, the horseman never gained ground but remained always in sight each time she glanced around.

The only sound to break the silence was the clash of shod hooves against the cobbled street. Soon they neared the river, and she could feel the sodden wood of the docks beneath her bare feet as she ran faster still.

With a hollow rumble, the stallion galloped onto the wharf behind her. Its labored breathing ripped through the still night in a harsh rhythm that matched her own anguished gasps. Then the stallion was beside her, never breaking stride as the dark man leaned forward.

She cried out at the sudden cruel pressure of his arm around her waist as he dragged her up onto the saddle before him. Her hair tumbled from its pins and whipped wildly about her shoulders, as the wind-raked tresses like silken cords bound them together.

They moved as one to the jarring beat of a mindless

gallop in a headlong flight through the red-streaked darkness. The stallion thundered on toward the water's edge, and she realized in sudden fear that the man had given it its head. Her cry of warning tore into a ragged scream as the great silvery beast reached the wharf's edge and heaved itself toward the water.

For a long moment, they hung suspended in the night, and she heard the man whisper an anguished demand— forgive me. Then the dark waters of the Mississippi rushed up to meet them, and her answer was lost in the cold, heaving silence of the river.

Isabeau struggled out of darkness into a ripe morning where the songs of birds had long since given way to the bustle of the streets. She stumbled from her bed and pulled open the shutters, squinting against the light of a late-winter sun. The air bathed her in a caress, though her nightgown clung to her body as if she had awakened from some fevered illness.

As well she might have, she thought, for the dream's images rivaled any delirium. She leaned against the sill and attempted to recapture the dream before it shattered under daylight's scrutiny. All she could recall was that the *américain* had pushed his way into her sleeping thoughts like some malevolent night demon. That intrusion seemed a more intimate violation than even his bold demands of her the evening of the cotillion.

"Leave me be, M'sieur Parrish," she heatedly muttered, more unnerved than she cared to admit. But she could not keep her thoughts from returning to that ill-fated night a week ago.

Within minutes of that mortifying scene in the courtyard, she found herself huddled within the darkened confines of the St. Johns' carriage as it rumbled down the silent avenues. With an effort, she had satisfied Cammi's eager questions over her urge to depart the cotillion, pleading faintness from too much night air. Marcel's delicately phrased concern proved no less trying, though she took comfort from his stolid presence. *He,* at least, was a gentleman—unlike a certain *américain!*

A blush heated her cheeks at the memory of his bold caresses. *Mon Dieu,* she actually had submitted to—no, encouraged—his advances, behaving with the abandon of a strumpet. How could she blame him for failing to come to her defense, when she herself could think of no excuse for her actions? Not that a man like Monsieur Parrish would be concerned for her reputation, she decided. No doubt he had forgotten their encounter . . . had gone on to indulge his lust with his red-haired mistress.

Her comfort lay in the fact that she had not seen the man since. The days that followed had flown by in a blur of parties and cotillions. Some had been informal gatherings—just a few young people gathered for cakes and *café au lait* in the hostess's courtyard—while others had been splendid affairs based upon Carnival themes.

Isabeau gave a sigh that was half rueful, half amused. In a single evening, she had attended one ball dressed in an outlandish creation of multihued ruffles to represent her favorite flower, the pansy. In another dance she was garbed from head to toe in shades of green, purple and gold, the official new colors chosen for Carnival. The days to come promised more of the same.

Her amusement faded, however, when she glanced about her. Last night's ball gown lay across the chair where she had draped it in the early hours of the morning before falling into troubled sleep. Once again, Lucie had neglected to perform even the most basic of her tasks.

She jerked the bell pull to summon the mulattress. When she failed to appear, Isabeau completed a hasty toilette by herself and pulled on a simple dark day dress, vowing to have a word with the girl about her duties. Despite her brother's claims to have the domestic situation under control, she suspected that Lucie, as the household's sole servant, had done as she pleased.

Isabeau frowned, confronted with the uneasiness that assailed her when she thought of the young mulattress. The girl exuded a sly air that poorly suited her surface humility. Even more unnerving, she moved so quietly through the house that Isabeau was seldom aware of her presence until she all but stumbled over the girl.

Fastening the final hook on her gown, Isabeau started downstairs toward the library. She was anxious to put this morning's interview with Philippe behind her. Last night, her brother had proposed that they compare notes about the past days' events so he could gauge the success of his plans concerning her hoped-for engagement.

"Your marriage campaign," as he referred to it, approaching the situation with the zeal of a newly commissioned military officer given his first taste of battle.

His list of suitors had undergone revisions, for he had obtained invitations to events more exclusive than their social position warranted. Could she show him anything less than gratitude? But she had not told her brother of Marcel's proposal.

That omission she could not explain. No doubt

Philippe would be pleased, since Marcel was his best friend. Still, an entire week remained before she was to give the young man his answer—time enough for her to weigh the decision. Until then, she would indulge her brother's wishes.

She reached the library and found the door ajar. A quick glance showed that Lucie had neglected this room, as well. To her rumbling stomach's dismay, no coffee and pastries awaited her. Last night's coals lay dying in the grate, while the shuttered windows barred all but a hint of morning sunlight. Isabeau made a mental note to add this room's disorder to her list of complaints to discuss with the servant.

When she reached the window she glimpsed a shadowed figure seated at the desk. At the sight, Isabeau suppressed a smile. Trust Philippe to wait for a servant to ready the room for him, rather than sully the aristocratic image he had of himself by performing such a task on his own.

She flung open the shutters, allowing a subdued noon sun to bathe the room in hazy light. "Really, Titi," she exclaimed as she snatched up the poker and stirred the coals before turning to face him, "are you so helpless that you must sit in the dark, rather than . . ."

Her playful rebuke broke off with a gasp as she realized that the man at the desk was not her brother. She brandished the poker like a rapier and took an uncertain step forward. "Who are you?"

"I assure you, *mademoiselle,* you have nothing to fear." The stranger gracefully rose and raised a hand. "Your brother is expecting me. You must be his sister—Mademoiselle Isabeau, is it not? I am Franchot Calvé."

Franchot Calvé. The name drew a spark of recognition, though she knew she had never before met the man. He stepped toward her, and a ray of sunlight touched his burnished hair, momentarily suffusing him in a golden haze. Unbidden, a phrase from Lili's last letter flashed through her mind.

Lucifer was the most beautiful of all the angels.

If such were true, then this man must be the devil incarnate, she thought. She put aside the poker, feeling foolish at her missish behavior. She offered him a hesitant smile.

"My apologies, *m'sieur.* My brother neglected to mention your visit. Please do be seated, and I will ring for some coffee and find out what is keeping Philippe."

"As you wish."

The man returned her smile, and Isabeau felt a blush warm her cheeks. Now, she recalled where she had learned his name. At more than one cotillion she had heard whispered tales of the Frenchman—concerning his parentage, the source of his money, and the reasons behind his reclusive nature. He seemed a man of immense wealth and influence—whose successes were greeted with envy and fear. Now, he was in her own library. Isabeau took a moment to study him.

The crescent-shaped scar on his right cheek served to temper what otherwise would have been a face too perfect for a mortal. He was tall—as tall as Monseiur Parrish, she thought—and she had to look up to meet his gaze. She had guessed the color of his eyes to be hazel. Now, she saw they were an unusual shade of amber.

No, not amber, she decided. *Gold.* His eyes were lion-gold and held her own with a predator's hypnotic gaze.

She could see herself mirrored in their depths, and a superstitious chill raced down her spine at the thought that he had captured a piece of her soul with one glance.

She reached for the bell pull and perched on a nearby chair while Calvé resumed his own seat. "Do tell me how it is you and Philippe are acquainted," she asked in a forced if bright tone. "I recently returned from a stay in Paris, and I do not yet know all his friends."

"Actually, it is your Oncle Henri with whom I've been acquainted for some years now." His voice was comforting yet disquieting, like the smooth purr of a lion that has chosen to lie down among the lambs. "In fact, our . . . friendship is why I have given your brother a position in one of my companies."

"Philippe has taken a job?"

Isabeau was shocked. A Creole gentleman might conceivably run a plantation, but work for a living? *Mon Dieu,* never! And Philippe was not one to flout convention.

"Tell me," she asked, "exactly what does he do for you?"

"Your brother assists me in my import and export ventures—quite a respectable enterprise, I assure you." Isabeau knew from his smile that he had guessed her thoughts. "In fact, he will soon be handling an important . . . diplomatic transaction for me."

"I see."

The job did sound respectable, and the fact that a man of Monsieur Calvé's stature was involved would remove any stigma which might be associated with such an endeavor. Her misgivings faded, replaced by a surge of feminine interest.

Indeed, he is an attractive man, she decided, grimacing as she wondered whether Philippe had added him to her suitors. Piqued by the prospect, she returned the man's smile with a warm one of her own just as the door flew open and her brother hurtled into the library.

"My apologies, M'sieur Calvé," Philippe exclaimed, ignoring Isabeau as he gestured at Lucie, who followed him with a heavily laden tray, and directed her to a table.

"I didn't mean to keep you waiting," he continued and ran a hand through his hair. "I fear I oversle— . . . that is, I lost track of time . . ."

"Do not distress yourself, Monsieur Lavoisier," the Frenchman interjected. "Your charming sister kept me quite entertained."

"Isabeau?" Philippe glanced up and started, as if noticing her for the first time. "Ah, yes, my sister. Then the two of you have already introduced yourselves?"

Not waiting for an answer, he snatched a milk-laced cup of coffee from Lucie and presented it to the man, who accepted it with easy grace. Watching them, Isabeau compared Philippe's rumpled air with Monsieur Calvé's understated elegance. From the way her brother fawned over him, he apparently joined the rest of the city in its awe of the man. She didn't know whether to be amused or disturbed.

Instead, she rose and favored both men with a smile. "I am sure you gentlemen have business to discuss. It was a pleasure to meet you, M'sieur Calvé. I hope we will see each other again soon."

"I will look forward to it," the Frenchman replied as

he stood and offered her a slight bow. "At your service, *mademoiselle."*

"I'll be with you in a few minutes, Isette," Philippe chimed in and stepped aside to let her pass.

As she started from the room, with Lucie at her heels, she spared a glance at a mahogany table near the door. A marble chessboard was spread across it, with the white and black pieces at the ready for the next conflict.

All the pieces save one, she noticed with a frown. A single white ivory pawn was missing, leaving a gap in the neat rows. Yet another example of poor housekeeping to lay at Lucie's feet, she thought in irritation.

She determined to settle the subject once and for all when, a quarter of an hour later, Philippe joined her in the dining salon.

"How much longer must we endure this?" she demanded once she had enlightened her brother as to her grievances.

Philippe shrugged. "I'd say we're fortunate to keep the girl for as little as we can pay."

"Fortunate?" she echoed in disbelief as she took a sip of coffee. "Tell me, *mon frère,* how long has Lucie been working here?"

"A little more than a year. Why?"

She stirred her *café au lait.* "It is more than her housekeeping, Titi. Something about her bothers me. I'm not certain why, but I don't trust her."

Philippe paused in the midst of devouring a *beignet* and gave her a quizzical look. "Has she done some-

thing, absconded with one of your baubles, perhaps? If
you insist, I can dismiss her."

"She has not stolen anything—at least, not to my
knowledge." She hesitated, trying to pinpoint just what
her concern was. How did one explain a vague feeling
of unease? "Doesn't it seem as if she watches us? Every
time I turn around, she's there behind me."

Philippe shook his head. "You get the strangest notions in that pretty head of yours, *ma petite*. If that's
your only complaint, I don't understand the problem."
He took a sip of his own coffee and grimaced. "I will
admit she's not much in the way of a cook or housekeeper, but she is the daughter—or niece, or something—of Henri's manservant. André is honest, so I'm
certain the girl can be trusted."

"I'm sure you are right. It is just that—"

"It's just what?"

Isabeau shook her head and gave a rueful smile. "Do
not worry, Titi. I am sure I am just being fanciful."

She reminded herself that Lucie hadn't done anything
to inspire distrust. Her demeanor was appropriate for a
servant and, as Philippe had pointed out, they were fortunate to retain her.

She reached again for her coffee cup, then noticed
the folded slip of narrow paper Philippe had set beside
his plate. Curious, she caught it up and asked, "What
is this?"

Philippe snatched the slip of paper back, but not before she had the chance to scan it.

"A bank draft," she answered her own question in a
stunned voice. *"Mon Dieu,* Philippe, why is M'sieur
Calvé paying you five thousand dollars?"

"It's not for me," he replied, as he avoided her gaze. "We have an arrangement to transact a business deal. It's not your concern."

Another time, she might have bristled at this dismissal. Now, however, a greater concern assailed her. Though Philippe had allowed her only a glimpse at the check, that had been enough to convince her that Monsieur Calvé's handwriting was uncannily familiar. But why hadn't Philippe noticed it?

She took a deep breath, fearful that her brother would again declare her fears unfounded, yet unable to ignore her suspicions. Still, it was better to risk Philippe's derision, she decided, than to remain silent.

"Titi, do you think M'sieur Calvé might have been the man who wrote the note to Lili that I found?"

"A man like M'sieur Calvé, involved with our *cousine?" he gasped, once his fit of amusement subsided. "How did you ever come to such an absurd conclusion?"*

"It is not absurd," Isabeau retorted. "The handwriting on this bank draft resembles the writing on that note of Lili's I showed you—a note signed by someone with the initial F—"

"—which could as easily be short for a dozen other names." So saying, Philippe gave the check a cursory look, then stuffed it into his pocket. "I'll admit, I can see some similarity between the two hands, but that's flimsy evidence to convict the man of ruining Lili, wouldn't you say?"

"He knows Oncle Henri," she persisted, "so isn't it conceivable that he might have become acquainted with Lili—"

"—while she was safely in the Ursulines' care?"

"I suppose you are right," she admitted. The idea did seem implausible. As Philippe had pointed out, what interest could a wealthy, sophisticated man have had in an Ursuline novice?

Philippe paused in the act of spearing a peach slice and gave her a calculating look. "I've heard that most women find Calvé irresistible. In fact, he's considered one of the city's most eligible bachelors, not that I understand why . . ."

"Are you perhaps wondering, *mon frère,* if I am among those women who are overwhelmed by his charms?" she asked with a twinge of irritation.

"Let's be realistic, *petite.* You need a husband, and I need money. Calvé is rich, unattached, and handsome—and he did seem to take more than a polite interest when the two of you met earlier. What could be simpler?"

What could be simpler, indeed?

Isabeau shook her head, but honesty compelled her to admit that the prospect of being seen in public with Monsieur Calvé was not unappealing. Besides which, her practical side determined, time spent in other gentlemen's company would help her make a decision regarding Marcel's proposal.

"Very well," she agreed and pushed back from the table. "If he does wish to call on me, I would not object."

"Does that also mean you won't mind that I've already accepted an invitation for us to attend the opera with him tomorrow night?" Philippe asked, his expression a study in contrived innocence.

"Mon frère, you would try the patience of St. Rita."

"As would you, *ma petite,"* he said with an answering

grin. He stood and gave the remains of his meal a withering glance. "I believe I'll dine elsewhere this evening, so don't wait on me if you choose to subject yourself to such torture twice in one day."

With an exaggerated bow in Isabeau's direction, he strode toward the doorway and nearly ran into Lucie. Isabeau gestured the girl into the room. "You may clear the table," she told her, "and M'sieur Philippe will be dining out tonight."

"Very good, *mam'selle*." The girl reached into her apron pocket and withdrew an envelope. "This came while you and M'sieur Philippe were eating."

It was inscribed with Isabeau's name but bore no mark of its sender. "Do you know who sent it?"

"No, *mam'selle*. Someone rang the bell and left it tucked in the front gate."

Another invitation, she decided, opening the envelope to extract a folded sheet of paper. The single sentence was written in a delicate yet elaborate hand on familiar ivory bond. *If you wish to learn the fate of your cousin's child, you will attend a voodoo ceremony at the sugar sheds tonight at midnight.* Isabeau read the note a second time before its meaning penetrated her stunned senses; then she swung about to face Lucie. "Who brought this?"

"As I said, *mam'selle*, I saw no one."

"Then tell me what you know about a voodoo ceremony held on the ramparts," Isabeau swiftly countered.

Lucie looked up from the stack of dishes she held. Her dark countenance was expressionless. "I know nothing about voodoo, *mam'selle*."

"But what about the *gris-gris* you wear around your neck?" she demanded.

The mulattress set down her dishes and reached beneath the gown's neckline, withdrawing the object that hung from the leather strip. "Do you mean this, *mam'selle?*"

Instead of the expected tiny bag of red cloth, a tiny wooden crucifix dangled from the thong. Isabeau stared at it, puzzled. "But the other morning . . ."

She trailed off when she met the girl's gaze. Though Lucie's features remained impassive, her eyes held a flicker of hostility that sent a shiver through Isabeau.

"I must have been wrong," she told the girl, "but I do expect you to notify me should another such message appear at our gate."

"Certainly, *mam'selle.*" The girl padded from the room, leaving Isabeau alone with her thoughts.

She paced about the room and tried to sort out all she had learned about Lili's fate over the past weeks. The idea that her cousin was with child when she had disappeared had never occurred to her. Yet suddenly it seemed the most likely explanation. Why else would Lili not have contacted the family after leaving the convent . . . and why else would Oncle Henri have been so anxious to bury his daughter's memory?

Isabeau carefully folded the letter. While she could hardly wander about the docks at midnight attending voodoo ceremonies, she had to do something. And the best thing to do, she told herself, was speak with Oncle Henri. Even though he had hardened his heart against Lili, surely he could not ignore the plight of a helpless babe.

Ten

"Why do you persist in such folly?"

Henri slammed his snifter of brandy onto the mantel. His gaze was accusing. Isabeau suppressed a twinge of guilt. The afternoon sun flooded his library and illuminated his autocratic features. He was no longer a young man. She could see how the years of careless living had begun to take their toll.

"But Oncle," she went on in a reasonable tone, "I only want—"

"What do you want, niece?" he interjected, his usually pallid complexion now purple. "Despite my express wishes, you continue to bandy about my daughter's name, and now you come to me with some ludicrous story about babies and voodoo. I sent you to Paris in the hope your Grandmère might instill some sense into you, but obviously I erred."

Isabeau was stung by his words but determined not to swerve from her purpose. "Do you deny that Lili left the convent because she was with child?"

"That is a vile accusation," Henri sputtered. "How can you cast such aspersions on a member of your own family?"

"But Oncle, even if Lili did run off with a man, who

is to say that she had not already married him in some private ceremony? If so, the babe would be your legitimate grandchild."

She showed the note she had received that morning, along with the letter from Lili to her and the one from the mysterious F. "You cannot brush aside all I have told you, when the proof is right here."

"I see no proof," Henri exclaimed and snatched the pages from her. "You've shown me nothing more than the scribblings of a hysterical girl and two anonymous notes from people bent on destroying our good name."

Before Isabeau could protest, her uncle tossed the notes onto the grate, then stirred the embers with a poker. The coals flared and reduced the pages to ash.

"There," he said as he turned toward her. "Let's hear no more talk of voodoo ceremonies, eh, *ma petite?*"

Isabeau stared in silence at the cinders, unable to believe that her uncle had just destroyed her only clues in the mystery. Finally, she raised her gaze.

"If that is what you wish, Oncle," she replied, though her thoughts were in turmoil. Didn't he care that his daughter might have left a child? The uncle she remembered would never have been so callous. She gathered up her cloak and managed a wan smile. "I must leave now, for I promised Philippe I would be home tonight when he returned."

"I am sorry you cannot stay longer, *petite.*" His tone was affable, as if they had not argued only moments before, and he drew a gold coin from his waistcoat. "Here, buy some new frippery for yourself."

At her protest, Henri pressed the coin into her palm

and gave her a pat on the cheek. "I insist. Now, you and Philippe must join me for supper later this week."

Isabeau started home on foot, glad of the bustle of the streets that reflected her own unsettled mood. Even if Lili's baby *had* been conceived out of wedlock, the Lavoisier reputation was such that no one would question Henri's word should he claim otherwise. Why, then, was he opposed to learning if this baby did exist?

Could it be because he knew the identity of the father?

The question sent an uneasy chill through her, and she halted on the *banquette*. Even if Lili's lover had been an influential man, Henri would have had no compunction about obtaining satisfaction on his daughter's behalf—a hurried wedding, if the man were unattached, or a generous settlement and a nine-month European tour for Lili, if he were not. No, she told herself, her uncle couldn't have known the man and still have left his daughter to her fate.

Isabeau made her decision. She would attend the voodoo ceremony and learn if the child existed . . . or if the note was a cruel hoax.

"She's gone," Henri said and threw open the doors that separated the library from the parlor. "I suppose you heard everything that was said?"

"I found it very . . . enlightening," his guest replied as he accepted a snifter of brandy. "It is fortunate, isn't it, that your niece confides in you."

"I must warn you that Isabeau is a headstrong girl." Henri glanced over the rim of his glass. "I have no doubt she'll attend this ceremony, despite my wishes."

"But that is precisely what I want. Her presence will help put into effect the plan I mentioned. Shall I assume, *mon ami,* that I will have your cooperation, as usual?"

Henri shot him a hunted look. "Will I never be free of you? Have I not paid for my actions many times over? It not my fault, you know. If she had not deceived me that one last time and sullied the family honor . . ." He gripped his glass more tightly, and his voice rose to an anguished shout. *"Mon Dieu,* when will you be satisfied?"

"Never."

With that pronouncement, the man set aside his snifter and rose. "If you prefer, *mon ami,* you may take your chances with the local constabulary, although those fine gentlemen might prove less . . . understanding than I concerning matters of honor. But it is not just your own crime that interests me. Do you not recall that bit of biblical wisdom concerning the sins of the fathers?"

He started for the door, not bothering to glance back at Henri as he added in parting, "This debt will never be repaid—not in your lifetime. And do not worry about your lovely niece. I assure you, tonight she will be in good company."

Henri's brandy snifter slipped to crash onto the marble tile beneath his feet. The sound of his guest's laughter drifted back to him.

Calvé's instructions had been short. *Be at the Orleans Club tonight at ten-thirty. A gentleman will contact you there.*

Philippe sipped his glass of claret. Twenty minutes had passed and his impatience was growing. While he didn't want to give his benefactor the impression that he was not grateful, a measure of promptness did seem in order.

He was debating whether to abandon the scheme and risk Calvé's displeasure, when a backslap brought him to his feet. He swung around, ready to take a glove to the ruffian. He found himself facing a stocky, middle-aged *américain* who towered over him by a good six inches.

The newcomer stuck out his hand and grinned. "Evenin', Mr. Lavoisier," he boomed in a jovial voice. "The name's Josiah Grubb. Mr. Calvé sent me."

Philippe clasped the man's outstretched hand, grimacing as Grubb pumped his arm with excessive vigor. When the man released him, Philippe resumed his seat and wiped his palm on his trouser leg.

This Grubb was no gentleman, he thought. While the man's clothing was impeccable—no doubt Calvé's doing—he had a common air about him evident from the fact he ordered an ale, and from the way he proceeded to pare his grimy nails with an oversized knife. Philippe frowned and prayed the rest of Calvé's staff was not so boorish. Philippe's reputation might suffer should he be seen in the company of such men.

When the drinks arrived, Grubb downed his in a series of gulps, followed by a belch. "Ready for the night's work?" he asked, wiping his greying mustache.

Philippe summoned an enthusiastic air. "But of course, *m'sieur*. Perhaps you'll tell me first just what it is we'll be doing."

"Nothin' difficult, boy," Grubb answered. "We're just goin' to pick up some cargo from the docks."

The man tossed a few coins onto the table and stood. Philippe followed him to a hired coach and clambered in. The vehicle jerked forward, all but tossing him into Grubb's lap.

Philippe scrambled to regain his seat, as Grubb said, "I shore hope Mr. Calvé knows what he's doin', foistin' a dandified fella like you off on me and Bandy."

"Don't worry, *m'sieur.*" He straightened his jacket. "I'm well able to keep up my end of this bargain."

Grubb lifted a shaggy brow but made no reply. Neither man spoke for the remainder of the drive, though Grubb kept up a tuneless whistle that set Philippe's teeth on edge. After what seemed an eternity—though doubtless it was little more than half an hour later—they reached the waterfront.

The river's fishy smell hit him with almost palpable force. He put a scented handkerchief to his nose and climbed from the coach to survey his surroundings. The wisp of moon that clung to the charcoal sky chose that moment to take refuge behind the clouds. Its sudden absence blanketed the wharf in darkness. The snap and jingle of reins signaled the coach's departure, but Philippe could barely make out its retreating shape.

With a muttered "Stay put, boy," Grubb disappeared into the night. A few seconds later, Philippe heard what sounded like water streaming rapidly against some nearby object. An inordinately long time later, the sound ceased. Grubb soon rejoined him and, fumbling with the buttons of his trousers, gestured for Philippe to follow.

Philippe complied. The lapping of the river against

pilings, combined with the blanketed night, made him feel as if he were suspended in time. He had never been to the waterfront under such circumstances, and his vulnerability made him edgy. Grubb, on the other hand, appeared unperturbed by the lack of light, as he made his way through the shadows.

Like a river rat, Philippe thought, at home with the sodden wood and the night. He thought to check whether the man's eyes shone red in the light like those of other nocturnal creatures.

Grubb halted, and Philippe strained to see what held his attention. Grubb clutched his arm, indicating he should not move. After a moment, a tiny light flared in the distance, vanished, and then reappeared.

"That's the signal, boy," Grubb muttered in his face. The man's breath smelled like the river, and Philippe struggled not to gag as he followed in the direction of the swaying light. A moment later, a low voice stopped them.

"Here."

The voice and the flickering light originated from a small building a few yards beyond them. The moon broke through the clouds, and Philippe saw that the speaker was a bewhiskered man of indeterminable age.

"You're late," the man growled as he approached them.

Grubb chuckled quietly. "Bandy, this here's young Philip. We're supposed to learn him the business." He turned to Philippe and gave him a familiar nudge in the ribs. "There's work waitin' to be done. C'mon, boy."

Philippe gritted his teeth. That appellation was getting on his nerves, but Grubb outweighed him by a good fifty pounds. He fell in step, following the glow of Bandy's lantern off the dock and down the muddy bank to the river's edge.

They trudged along the darkened shoreline for a good quarter hour, and Philippe resigned himself to the fact his imported kidskin shoes would not survive the ordeal. Several times, he trod on something that seemed to squirm under foot. Suppressing thoughts of snakes and river rats, he concentrated on keeping up.

His eyes were accustomed to the dark by now, and several yards away he made out a small, flat-bottomed boat bobbing against the shore. Once they reached it, Bandy hopped aboard and pulled back a tarpaulin to reveal half-a-dozen long, narrow crates.

"What is inside?" Philippe wanted to know. In the lamp's yellow light, he made out the faint imprint of official lettering which someone had tried, with marginal success, to obliterate.

Grubb hauled him back. "Ain't nothin' you need to know 'bout, boy. Now lend a hand."

The trio heaved the boxes onto the beach. Once the last had been unloaded, Philippe paused to wipe his brow and prayed the ripping sound he'd heard had been the splitting of someone else's pants seam.

Bandy, meanwhile, had disappeared. He returned leading a pair of sturdy mules hitched to a battered, two-wheeled cart. They lifted the crates onto its splintered bed, and Bandy coaxed the beasts up the slight incline of the riverbank.

The cart made slow progress over the soggy ground. Once, when its wheels became mired, Philippe was forced to take up position alongside Grubb and push from behind. They reached flat ground, finally, and Philippe flopped onto the damp earth, heedless now of any possible damage to his clothes.

Grubb nudged him with the toe of his muddy boot. "Now ain't no time to rest, boy. We still have us a delivery to make."

Philippe groaned and climbed onto the cart, perching uncomfortably atop the crates. Bandy whipped the mules into motion, and the wagon rolled along a grassy stretch before bumping back onto the dock and creaking toward the streets.

Once they reached a narrow side road, Grubb shoved a jar of water at Philippe. As he raised the container to his lips, Grubb gave his arm a shake.

"Don't you have any brains, boy?" he asked in disgust. "That water's not for drinkin'. It's for the wheels."

When Philippe stared at him blankly, the man gave a contemptuous snort. "Just watch." He dipped water from a bucket at his feet into a second jar, then trickled the water onto the axle near one wheel. "Now, do the same with yours."

Philippe complied, and the creaking sound that accompanied them ceased. "I learned that trick from my granddaddy," Grubb explained. "Back in the old days, if the authorities caught you with greased axles, they figured you for a smuggler. No one pays much mind to that kinda thing anymore, but squeakin' wheels draw attention. This way, we can travel real quietlike, but if anyone stops us, we can pass for honest deliverymen."

Philippe frowned at that assurance but made no reply. They drove silently now except for the clomp of the mules' hooves against the cobble streets. Reaching to fill his jar, he ventured, "Where are we going, M'sieur Grubb?"

"No need to be so formal, boy," the man replied. "Grubb'll do fine. You'll see soon enough."

A few minutes later, the streets did begin to look familiar. Finally, they turned down a narrow avenue and halted alongside a high stone wall. Philippe glanced at the familiar wrought-iron gate and shot Grubb a puzzled look. "Why, it's the archbishop's residence," he softly exclaimed, recognizing the collection of whitewashed structures that once had been home to the Ursuline nuns but which were now owned by the Archdiocese of New Orleans.

Grubb made no acknowledgement, but simply said, "You just wait here, boy. Me an' Bandy'll be right back." With those words, two climbed from the cart and made their way past the gate, leaving Philippe alone outside the walls.

Uncertain what was expected of him, Philippe scrambled down and patted the nearest mule's grey muzzle. The beast flattened its ears and rolled a wicked black eye in Philippe's direction, while its mate snapped at him with long yellow teeth. He yelped and took a prudent step back, then gave a guilty glance around him.

The moon now shone brightly, and he realized that anyone who glanced down the street could notice him standing there. What reason could he give for his presence? Delivery to the good fathers?

Grubb's assurances to the contrary, he doubted anyone would believe such a tale, given that it was almost midnight.

Giving the mules wide berth, he leaned against the

wall and buffed his nails on his lapel in studied non-chalance. When he finally heard a step, he straightened in relief, ready to demand of Grubb just what he meant by leaving him alone for so long. But the words died on his lips as he found himself facing one of the biggest men he'd ever seen, one of the city's night patrollers.

Philippe nervously noted the large cudgel. He swallowed uneasily as his gaze dropped from the cudgel to the pair of oversized pistols strapped about the man's bulky waist.

Grubb, where are you? he wondered in desperation, even as the night patroller moved closer and bared his teeth in a smile that was no less menacing for its many gaps.

"How about telling me why you're standing here alone with a cart in the middle of the night," the man demanded.

Philippe tugged his jacket into place, praying the man wouldn't notice his mud-splattered clothing. He donned his haughtiest expression. "I am afraid, *m'sieur,* that is my concern," he replied in a voice that only shook slightly.

The night patroller's grin widened. "And *I'm* afraid, mon-soo-war, that everything that happens on this street is *my* concern," he replied in crude imitation of Philippe's Creole accent. He tucked the cudgel back into his belt and rested his palm on the butt of one pistol. "I think we need to have us a talk, don't you?"

Philippe shot a glance behind him, for the situation was getting out of hand. The last thing he needed was for some uncouth *américain* night patroller to haul him off to prison. He summoned a confident smile and tried again. "There's no need to upset yourself over this, *m'sieur.* I have a perfectly logical explanation for being here. You see, I . . . that is, I was just—"

He realized his words were having no effect on the man. He was ready to abandon the cart and run, when he heard the wooden gate creak.

"Is there a problem, *m'sieur?"* came a crisp voice behind him. He turned to see a black-robed woman whom he recognized in surprise as the Ursuline convent's Mother Superior step briskly through the gateway. The wooden beads of her rosary clicked to match the knocking of Philippe's knees.

The night patroller dropped his blustering manner and tipped his cap. "I'm sorry, Sister. I didn't realize the gentleman was here on Church business." He glanced over at Philippe. "My apologies, sir."

Philippe managed a stiff nod, hoping his relief was not too apparent. "No harm done, *m'sieur,* but you would do well in the future not to harass honest men."

The night patroller gave the nun a respectful salute and walked into the darkness. The gate creaked a second time, and Grubb and Bandy eased past the narrow entry. Once the echo of the night patroller's footsteps had faded, the nun turned to the pair.

"Make haste."

Though puzzled as to the Mother Superior's role in all this, Philippe helped carry the crates toward a small outbuilding. The nun fitted a large brass key into a padlock.

The heavy door swung open. Moonlight poured into the building, and Philippe could see that the dirt-floored room was already filled with crates and barrels of various sizes. He helped settle their cargo alongside several other boxes and then filed out with the rest.

"I trust I will not see you again until next week, Monsieur Grubb," the nun said as she locked the door. "And tell Monsieur Calvé that I cannot guarantee secrecy if he does not inform me of deliveries in advance."

She glance at Philippe, who pretended interest in the flowerbed beside him. "Who is this young man?"

"That's young Philip. He'll be workin' with us for a while," Grubb answered. "C'mon, boys. Our job's done for the night."

Philippe glanced over his shoulder one last time as the cart started down the street. Had the nun recognized him from his visits to see Isabeau years before? Probably not, he decided after a moment. More troubling was the fact that the Mother Superior was involved with a man like Calvé.

"How long have you been using the archbishop's residence to store these, er, goods?" he asked Grubb.

"Several months, now. I don't know what Mr. Calvé's got on the sister, but it must be somethin' pretty good for her to agree to this arrangement."

Then he shot Philippe a sharp look. "Best keep that in mind, boy, if you ever get to thinkin' about crossin' the man. If he can blackmail a holy lady, there's no tellin' what he's capable of doin'."

Eleven

A sliver of moon clung to the black sky. Its chill glow split the wharf into light and shadow. The creak of timbers melded with the rhythmic lapping of water to break the night's stillness. Here on this levee, the breeze was filled with the smell of molasses, a cloying scent which masked even that of the river.

Isabeau climbed from her hired coach and stepped toward the sugar sheds. She recognized the rambling structure from her wait on the docks the morning she had arrived home. Then, brokers and merchants crowded its open storage area, while the nearby weighers gestured and shouted as they operated their scales. A procession of Negro laborers had rolled barrels of sugar and molasses from the adjacent steamers, until those goods overflowed the enclosure and its wharf. While those casks and hogsheads still remained where they painstakingly had been stacked, tonight the huge sheds appeared deserted.

A gust off the river billowed Isabeau's cloak. She shivered, but not from the cold. Philippe might somehow learn of her plan—from Henri, perhaps, or else Lucie—and forbid her to attend the ceremony.

Her luck had held. Philippe had quit the house even

earlier than usual, leaving her free to slip away. Now she began to question the wisdom of her expedition. Perhaps Oncle Henri was right, and the note was nothing more than a blackmail ploy.

But what if it wasn't? What if Lili had indeed borne a child, a child that belonged with its rightful family?

The question steeled her resolve. She spared a glance behind her at the coach. Despite the late hour, the driver had made no comment as to her choice of destination or the fact she was a woman traveling alone. His reaction puzzled her, until it occurred to her that he had made this trip before. The promise of double his usual fee had convinced the weatherbeaten driver to wait for her. She prayed the man wouldn't abandon her the moment she left his sight.

Isabeau reached the head-high maze of barrels. Beneath the enclosure, two separate stairways led to the upper story of the peak-roofed sheds. At the head of one stairwell, faint yellow light seeped from beneath a closed door—a door which no doubt led to the ceremony. To reach it she had to transverse the casks and hogsheads. She gave that darkened labyrinth a doubtful look. Anyone—or anything—might be lurking within it.

For a moment, her courage failed her. With Philippe or Marcel by her side, she would plunge fearlessly into that maze. *Mon Dieu,* right now she would even welcome Monsieur Parrish's doubtful company, for he at least had experience in fending off attackers.

Isabeau gripped her reticule, reassured by the hard outline of her borrowed pistol beneath its soft velvet. Her memory of the *américain's* pistol-wielding rescue had given her the idea to arm herself tonight, though she had never handled such a weapon.

She had despaired of finding anything more lethal than Maman's knitting needles lying about the house, when she finally discovered the old-fashioned pepperbox tucked away on a shelf in the library. Philippe must have overlooked it, she realized, when he sold Papa's gun collection. Though hardly on a par with Monsieur Parrish's oversized revolver, surely the little pistol could slow an attacker.

Now, she started toward the lit doorway. The aroma of molasses threatened to overwhelm her as she wove through the barrels. She fancied she also smelled a faint hint of decay. Perhaps some previous nighttime wanderer had lost his way in that maze and finally died of fright.

She took the final turns through the barrels at a trot, breathing a sigh when she reached the stairway. The door above her beckoned, so she gathered her skirts and climbed the wooden steps.

Upon reaching the landing, she tried the door and found it unlocked. She stepped into an empty, shuttered room illuminated by a smoking lantern that hung from the center rafter. Dust lay upon a threadbare blanket across the wooden floor, the fine grit undisturbed except for a narrow path of footprints that led to a second door opposite the first. Isabeau followed that same path. Her fragile slippers left faint imprints alongside the trail of bare-soled smudges. She heard the murmur of voices even before she reached the second door.

It opened onto a room slightly larger than the first, into which crowded two score or more people. The only light came from the stubby candles that burned at the room's far end. She saw people of every hue—Negro, mulatto, quadroon. She also made out a few pale faces interspersed with the dark ones. Apparently, tonight's ceremony had attracted Creoles besides herself.

Isabeau made her way to a corner where she could see everything yet remain inconspicuous. The other spectators paid her no heed. Voices rose and fell, punctuated by an occasional cough or laugh, quickly cut short. The air hung with the pungent odor of unwashed bodies.

Isabeau brushed the tendrils of hair that clung to her forehead. Taking a lesson from her last expedition, she had dressed with care, wearing beneath her grey wool cloak a simple gown of serviceable blue serge modestly buttoned to the base of her throat. In such an outfit, no one could possibly mistake her for a *prostituée,* she assured herself. Still, as the room grew more oppressive, she began to envy the women who wore shapeless cotton shifts.

She found herself struggling against an unexpected drowsiness, when a drum began to throb. Its beat was so soft that Isabeau first thought she was hearing her own heart. The crowd's restless murmur stilled. The drum grew louder, accompanied by a swell of sound from the spectators. Soon the tempo quickened, and a second drum joined the first. Their sounds mingled in a complicated rhythm of beats, building to a crescendo.

Isabeau covered her ears and backed away, stopping only when she felt the splintered wall against her back. *Mon Dieu,* surely the sound must be heard all across the ramparts!

Then, without warning, the drumbeats ceased.

In the silence, the crowd fell quiet and turned at a movement in the far corner. Isabeau saw a dusky-skinned woman emerge from the darkness. She walked toward the table, garbed in a transparent white shift tied up so that it exposed her slim legs. Unlike the other Negresses, mulattresses and quadroons present, all of whom wore their hair covered by the traditional *tignon,* this woman had let her mahogany-colored locks stream down her back. A cascade of gold filigree hung from her earlobes, while a gold collar encircled her slim neck. When the candlelight threw her fine features into sharp relief, Isabeau gasped. It was like witnessing an ancient high priestess come to life.

The worshipers took up their murmur, and Isabeau heard a word repeated throughout the crowd. She finally made out a woman's name.

Ophelia.

Despite the closeness of the air, Isabeau felt a sudden chill. Why, that was the name written in the note to Lili, she realized in surprise. This summons was no hoax, then, despite her uncle's claim. But what connection could a voodoo queen have with her cousin?

As if on cue, the crowd parted, so that Isabeau now stood separated from the rest. The quadroon turned and looked straight at her. In a smoky voice, she demanded, "Why have you come?"

"I wish to learn the whereabouts of my cousin's child," Isabeau replied. Her voice was low but clear as she took a step forward.

Ophelia—for Isabeau had decided that it was surely

she—regarded her for a moment. "What do you offer
the spirits?"

"I . . . I did not bring anything," she answered in
surprise, for the note had mentioned nothing of this.

"What do you offer the spirits?"

Unnerved now, Isabeau glanced about her. The other
worshipers pressed closer, and only with an effort did
she suppress the urge to flee. Then she realized that she
did have something, after all.

"Wait," she cried, fumbling with the strings of her
reticule. She reached past the pistol and searched until
her hand closed on a coin—the gold piece her uncle
had given her. She held it up for everyone to see. As
the coin gleamed in the candlelight, the crowd subsided,
and Isabeau awaited Ophelia's response.

"Set your offering upon the altar."

Isabeau obeyed. She placed the coin between the
cabalistic symbols crudely chalked upon the surface.
The voodoo queen favored her with a regal nod. "Your
offering is acceptable. I shall contact the spirits and
learn the answer to your question."

Isabeau resumed her place, then glanced around to
learn what might happen next. Two of Ophelia's followers produced a basket filled with bottles, which they
passed among the crowd. Each person took a swallow
and then handed on the container to his neighbor. Isabeau was watching the activity with trepidation, when
a hefty, thick-featured woman pressed a sticky bottle
into her hand.

"Drink."

A refusal sprang to her lips, but her protests died
away as she took in the woman's disheveled air. The

Negress wore the usual cotton shift, though hers was
streaked with filth and dampened by half-circles of
sweat beneath her arms. Black hair sprang from her
head in tiny plaits that gave her a Medusan look.

As if sensing Isabeau's dismay, the woman smiled.
Her action was more a savage baring of teeth than a
gesture of friendship. Isabeau heard the insistent note
in her tone as she repeated, "Drink."

What if she refused? Isabeau accepted the bottle, wiping its mouth with her palm before taking a hesitant
sip. The cloudy liquid savaged her throat. With an effort
she managed to swallow it. As she lowered the bottle,
the woman forced the container upright against her
mouth again.

Isabeau's cry of protest was lost in a gasp as the liquor
gushed past her lips. She shoved away the bottle, but not
before she choked down a mouthful of the potion.

"No more," she wheezed out. The woman grinned as
she took her own turn at the half-empty bottle and then
disappeared into the crowd.

Seconds later, the drums resumed their beat. Isabeau
put a hand to her forehead and gazed bleary-eyed at the
altar. Ophelia reached inside a large wooden box someone
had, in the intervening moments, placed atop it. With a
satisfied smile, she lifted out a long, dark shape that rip-
pled thickly in her grasp. She draped it about her shoulders, and Isabeau caught back a cry when she realized
that the object was an enormous mottled python.

The quadroon stepped forward and began a languid,
writhing dance that matched the reptile's undulating
moves. As the drums grew louder, the spectators swayed
as one at the edges of the shadows. Despite herself,

Isabeau found herself edging closer, repelled and yet fascinated by the ritual movements.

Slowly, the woman drew the python between her legs and along the curves of her body in an obscene mimicry of the sexual act. Desire contorted her dark face as she welcomed the intimate caresses of her serpent lover. At the sight, Isabeau moaned and turned away, frightened now by the surge of erotic emotion that gripped her as she watched Ophelia's gyrations.

Sainte Cécile, what was she doing here among these people?

She tried to push her way through the crowd, but they formed a living barrier that pressed her forward. Perspiration trickled down her dress front, yet she felt chilled despite the closeness of the room. Each drumbeat pounded painfully into her skull, until she thought she must surely scream.

A woman's shriek rent the air, and it took an instant for Isabeau to realize that the chilling sound had not come from her own throat. She turned to see Ophelia collapse into waiting arms of her followers. The python slid to the floor, where it curled around the quadroon's ankle and lay still.

A moment later, the voodoo queen struggled upright and reached into the box again, withdrawing a small canvas sack. She untied it and pulled forth a flapping bundle of white feathers that proved to be a rooster. At the sight, the crowd began a new chant, this one a strange jumble of patois punctuated by handclaps as they slowly swayed around their queen. Ophelia grasped the bird by its spurred legs and held it high above her head. Frantic squawks were drowned out by the worshipers' song as it built to a crescendo.

Then, without warning, Ophelia grasped the rooster's head and tore it from its body.

Blood spurted in a dark red fountain from the flapping carcass. The sight drew a shout of approval. Ophelia swung the headless bird around her, raining its blood upon the spectators. With a cry, they surged forward, arms spread wide to receive the unholy baptism.

Isabeau stood stunned, as droplets splattered against her cheek, and trickled across her lips. She retched as she tasted its coppery warmth. Frantically, she scrubbed at her face with her sleeve, trying to hold down the bile in her throat. Her gaze dropped to the floor where Ophelia had tossed the lifeless rooster. As she watched in horror, the python slowly uncurled from its mistress's ankle and unhinged its massive jaws to grasp the limp, feathered bundle.

Isabeau swayed, but even as unconsciousness threatened, she heard the quadroon's voice. "The child, Regine, is not yours to take!" she cried over the sound of the drums. "The spirits have claimed her for their own."

Mon Dieu, what did Ophelia mean by spirits? Isabeau glanced about, jostled by the host of dancers. Helplessness gripped her as she turned back toward the altar, where the voodoo queen now stood alone.

Then Ophelia smiled, and Isabeau's tenuous hold on her emotions snapped. With a despairing cry, she stumbled for the door. No one moved to stop her. She grappled with the doorknob and half fell into the outer room, then ran blindly toward the exit. As she fled down the

stairway into the night, the warehouse door shut behind
her, snuffing out all but an echo of the drums.

Her breath tore from her throat in sobs as she made
her way through the barrels. Her skirts swirled about
her ankles and caught on the wooden casks, threatening
to trip her. Once, she stumbled over a discarded timber,
but fear kept her upright as the rough wood raked her
ankle. When she cleared the final row her steps faltered.

Beyond the sugar shed lay a pile of crates, and she
stumbled toward them. There, she gulped down welcome
breaths of cool, fresh air. Away from the heat and the
beat of drums, she felt her self-control return.

Once her heartbeat slowed, she ventured a look at the
sheds. No one had followed her. In fact, she doubted
that anyone other than Ophelia had noticed her headlong
flight. Still, she didn't care to remain on the dock any
longer than necessary. She started toward the spot where
she'd left her hired carriage.

- Please, let it still be there.

She lacked the strength to track down another coach.
Once she passed the structures that blocked her view
of the main road, she chided herself for doubting the
driver. The coach waited, though likely the poor man
had been mystified by the sounds from the sheds.

She was within a few yards of the vehicle when she
stopped and stared in disbelief. The elegant conveyance
parked along the wharf was no hired carriage. Once
again, she found herself abandoned near the docks.

She pulled her cloak around her and wrapped her
fingers around the pistol. The touch of metal steadied
her, not that she feared a repeat of her encounter with
the rivermen, she told herself. After all, the night was

still young enough by New Orleans standards that another carriage should be easy to—

She froze as the sound of a muffled footstep came from behind her. Easing the pistol from its velvet wrap, she glanced around. Shadows spilled in black patches from the warehouses and cloaked anyone who might be lurking alongside them. She knew that this section of the wharf was not abandoned, for a faint light glowed in the upper window of the building next to her.

"Who's there?" she called softly.

The noise, whatever it was, did not repeat itself. Feeling foolish, she slipped the gun back into her reticule and managed a smile at her imagination. The voodoo ritual had simply set her nerves on edge.

Then a hand clamped over her mouth as she tried to scream.

Twelve

Sweet Jesus, was he going to have to listen to that damn drumming all night long?

Tark set down his whiskey glass and cocked his head, listening past the silence of his office. The sound drifted to him from across the wharf, floating like the dying echoes of a summer storm. Though he had heard their song half-a-dozen times since he had taken up residence on the wharf, he always had to repress a grimace each time the unmistakable rhythm commenced.

He raised his glass and drained it, then reached for his bottle. He splashed out a generous portion of the amber liquid, much of which ended up on the desk. He set the bottle aside, then lifted the tumbler in a defiant gesture to those unknown men of the night.

The first time he heard the drums, he had dismissed them as a product of his imagination, for the docks were alive with the sound of creaking timbers and the stirring of the river. Certainly, no one would spend nights within deserted buildings pounding out this strange rhythm. He soon learned that drums did indeed sing in the night.

His scant knowledge of those African-rooted beliefs came from Elisabeth, who belonged to a voodoo cult headed by the quadroon procuress, Ophelia. Initially, he had tolerated his mistress's interest in that dark religion as the passing fancy of a bored society woman. At her urging, he had participated in a few private rituals of her own devising—rituals that proved to be interesting variations on the act of coitus. He had attributed the erotic results to the aphrodisiacal power of the drugs, rather than to occult spells.

He began to take her preoccupation with voodoo more seriously as time went on. The final straw came when she began to talk of evil spirits, claiming to have seen one of those walking dead known as zombies. Prompted by equal parts of curiosity and concern, he accompanied her to one of Ophelia's ceremonies held on the moss-draped banks of Lake Ponchartrain.

Rather than offering an outlet for genteel debauchery, the so-called voodoo ritual instead proved an exercise in sadomasochism unrivaled by anything he had ever before witnessed. Spurred on by the savage beat of drums, men and women fell upon each other in a frenzy of mindless lust. Cries of orgiastic ecstasy mingled with screams of fear and pain. He realized that nothing would have put a halt to the madness. He doubted Elisabeth even noticed when he quit the place in disgust, since by then she lay across a makeshift altar, while a feather-bedecked Negro painted cabalistic symbols on her naked flesh.

The echo of the voodoo drums lingered in his mind for a long time after, and when the sound again rose from the silent wharf, he had recognized it as the same he had heard on the banks of the Ponchartrain. Recalling the brutal revelry of that night, he never was tempted to track the drums to their source.

Now, the drums beyond the window fell silent. Tark took another swallow of whiskey. The day before, he had depleted his stock of smooth Kentucky bourbon, and Tom Sullivan had magnanimously supplied him with several bottles left over from a sizable cache seized in a raid. What Tark was now drinking, that man had assured him, was "genuine, guaranteed-to-get-ya-roarin'-drunk-if-it-don't-blind-ya-first" rotgut.

Drunk he most definitely was, though still this side of insensibility. Tark held his hand a few inches from his face, managing to count at least five fingers. He took another swig and reviewed the past few days.

With the last of his shipping contracts save for the *Esmeralda* fulfilled, he had spent the week wandering the docks and running up a tab at the Albatross—that was, when he wasn't holed up in his office drinking alone. Tracking down the man responsible for his plight had lost its urgency, since nothing of his company remained to be salvaged. But even while the days blurred into a hopeless cycle of drinking and walking, one memory continued to burn within him.

. . . saved you from quite an unpleasant fate . . . they've lost or gambled away every cent . . . by morning, you'd have found yourself leg-shackled to the little slut . . .

The words had repeated themselves in a silent, taunting litany, delivering each time another blow to his already damaged pride. Hearing them again in his mind now, he choked out a heated curse that did little to ease the anger he'd nurtured since the cotillion.

He had known from the moment he laid eyes on her that she was trouble, he savagely reminded himself. Yet he had gone out of his way to see her again. He had made a public fool of himself over Mademoiselle Isabeau Lavoisier. What made the situation more lamentable was the fact that, knowing she had tried to trap him into marriage, he hadn't been able to forget her.

The click as the office's inner door swung open made Tark sit up. Alma clomped into the room. Her stocky figure was bundled in bright flannel. Her grey hair trailed over her shoulder in a braid.

Tark blinked, his anger momentarily forgotten. Never, in the more than half-dozen years she'd worked for him, had Alma Crenshaw appeared before him in a state resembling dishabille. He suspected this lapse boded ill where he was concerned.

"Care for a nightcap?" he drawled, hoping to forestall the expected lecture.

His gesture to the bottle sent it tottering. Even as he made an ineffectual grab for it, the housekeeper moved with speed and checked the bottle. Her look spoke volumes, though she felt compelled to add a verbal postscript.

"I think you've had enough for the both of us," she began and planted her fists on her hips. "I'll not stand by and encourage this foolishness."

"We've had this particular conversation before," Tark said and met her sour gaze with a quelling look of his own. His tongue seemed more unwieldy than usual. He continued, "How I spend my nights is my concern."

"I quite agree, Mr. Parrish, and that's why I've come to tell you . . . that is, I wanted to say . . ."

Consternation replaced her righteous air as she plucked at the sash of her thick robe. Watching her, Tark set down his glass again and frowned. *Alma Crenshaw, at a loss for words?* He'd not expected to witness such a sight in his lifetime.

"Sit down, Alma, and tell me what's on your mind," he demanded.

The woman complied. The color rose high in her cheeks as the silence between them stretched. Finally, the syllables tumbling over one another, she replied, "I don't know how best to tell you this, Mr. Parrish, so I'll just say it outright. Ned Deaton made me an offer of marriage this afternoon, and I accepted."

"Well, it's about damned time he got around to asking you." The lazy grin that broke across his face broadened when Alma blushed still brighter. His sentiment was sincere as he lifted his glass, and added, "Much happiness, Alma. You deserve it."

"Well, I just don't know." The housekeeper shook her head, resuming her air of stern capability. "I don't feel right about leaving you here, especially with the way things are right now. Maybe I could stop in once a day and—"

"I'll be fine, Alma, never you fear."

Her expression reflected doubt despite his assurances. He went on, "You've actually set my mind at ease. You see, I've decided to leave New Orleans once this last shipment is settled."

In truth, the idea had only now crossed his mind. Why not start over again somewhere else, free of the stigma that would always cling to him here? He could head west—to California, perhaps, or Washington. Hell, he might even go back to St. Louis.

With enthusiasm for the first time in days, he finished, "With you safely married, I can leave town with a clear conscience—so don't even think of refusing him."

"Well, Ned does need my help with the tavern," she conceded. "Lands, you never saw such a pigsty as that storeroom of his. And his books are a disgrace."

"Then it's settled. When do the nuptials take place?"

"Next week. At our age, there's no need to put off things any longer than necessary," she explained. "And we would be pleased if you would stand up as a witness."

"I'd be honored. Just let me know when and where."

Before she could reply, the voodoo drums resumed their beat, though the sound was almost lost in the wind. Alma glanced toward the shuttered window.

"There goes that heathen racket again," she exclaimed. "How a good Christian is supposed to get a moment's rest with that infernal noise going on, I just don't know."

"It'll end soon enough."

Giving in to weariness, Tark dragged himself from his chair. He immediately discovered he was drunker than he'd thought, for he had to catch at the desk for support. "I think I'll call it a night. Why don't you take off the next few days to finish making the wedding arrangements?"

Leaving Alma to turn down the lights, he headed for the hallway, negotiating the stairway with more difficulty than usual. Once in his room, he had to steady himself on the windowsill. He glanced from the unshuttered window out over the wharf.

A frown creased his forehead as he noticed a figure standing at a short distance below. The docks attracted their share of people at night, but a woman alone? His frown deepened. Even the boldest prostitutes preferred the streets to the wharf after dark. He shrugged and started to turn away, when the woman stepped into the moonlight, giving him a clear glimpse of a familiar face.

The sight momentarily took him aback. He watched her for several moments before finally staggering to his bed. Logic dictated that he was the victim of a whiskey-induced illusion.

He lay for a time clutching its edges as he willed the room to stop spinning. Once the sensation of motion subsided, he tried to sit up long enough to strip off his clothes, then gave up the idea. His last thought before unconsciousness took hold was that the comforting embrace of alcohol at last had turned fickle. Why else would he have imagined that, standing beside the woman who looked uncannily like Isabeau, had been the one man he had prayed never to lay eyes on again.

A man named Franchot Calvé.

Her assailant took his hand from Isabeau's mouth, and she faced him. She gazed into familiar golden eyes.

"M'sieur Calvé," she gasped, clutching his arm to steady herself. *"Mon Dieu,* but you frightened me." When he made no reply, her relief faded, and she asked, "Why are you here? Did Oncle Henri send you?"

Calvé regarded her with impassive golden eyes. Suddenly she wasn't sure whom she would rather face—him or Ophelia. "My coach is nearby," he said, as he gestured toward the carriage. "Come with me."

She had little choice but to follow him, for his grip on her arm was unyielding. He helped her into the elegant conveyance and took the seat across from her. A lamp burned within its well-appointed confines, denying her the mantle of darkness. Isabeau tried not to flinch under his silent scrutiny, though she felt rather like a butterfly helplessly pinned to a board.

He must have been the man who was involved with Lili, after all, she decided in dismay. How else could he have known of the voodoo ceremony, unless he was part of all that had happened? Still, that didn't explain what he was doing here now.

"Where are we going?" she demanded as the carriage lurched forward.

Calvé pulled out a cigar and lit it. His eyes glowed for an instant as the match flared. Once more bypassing her question, he merely said, "We must talk."

"As you wish, *m'sieur.*"

She settled against her seat and clung to her air of bravado, though she was aware of the threat that the man represented. Now, smoke wafted through the carriage, and its sweet, acrid scent combined with the effects of the liquor she'd imbibed, and made her head spin.

Everything appeared oddly skewed, as if she now viewed her surroundings from the wrong end of a telescope. Although Calvé still sat across her, when she hazily reached out her hand, it seemed she could not touch him.

Mon Dieu, *what is wrong with me?*

Fright tightened around her, and she swallowed against the unpleasant metallic taste that lingered in her mouth. The liquor she had drunk at the voodoo ceremony must have been drugged.

She struggled to sit upright, but spiraled back into

dizziness. The pressure of a hand around her wrist halted that plunge. Isabeau caught her breath and weakly leaned against the seat, while, from somewhere far away, she heard Calvé speak.

"Do not try to fight it, *ma chère*. The effects will pass. In fact, you may find the sensation pleasurable."

His voice took on a hollow quality, as if he spoke to her from a dream. She managed a nod. The gesture took every bit of her concentration to perform. Still, she could hear and understand every word he spoke to her, although summoning a reply seemed a great effort.

She sighed and let her bleary gaze travel over her companion. Monsieur Calvé was indeed the most handsome gentleman she had ever seen, she decided. Why should she worry about lost babes and voodoo queens, when she could give herself up to this seductive languor?

His voice now seemed to echo in her ears. "I believe, *mademoiselle*, that the time has come for us to discuss a few matters—such as your *cousine*, Lili, and her child."

Then the baby truly did exist.

The realization momentarily pierced the haze that had enfolded her, and she tried to focus her thoughts. Perhaps Monsieur Calvé intended to acknowledge the child, after all. Summoning her voice, she managed, "Are you—"

"—the babe's father?"

Calvé's laugh held a disquieting note as he finished: "I fear not, *ma chère*. Lili merely came to me for help after Henri disowned her."

"Then who . . . is he?"

"A groundskeeper at the Ursuline convent. It seems that, unknown to the good sisters, Lili had formed a *tendre* for the boy. In addition to being unsuitable, he lacked honor, for he pursued the situation to his advantage—and to his eventual . . . downfall."

Calvé's eyes shone with the harsh brilliance of gold coins in the dim light of the carriage. *He killed that young man,* Isabeau guessed, yet she could summon little sorrow over the youth's violent end. If not for him, Lili would be alive. But what had prompted Monsieur Calvé to intervene on her behalf?

"Your *cousine* and I struck a bargain," he anticipated her question with the same accuracy. "I offered a haven away from the convent and to settle a generous sum on her once the child was born. For her part, she agreed to a small . . . favor."

Just as Philippe has done.

The realization flitted through her mind as Calvé continued, "Lili remained awhile at the convent, acting as my liaison with the Ursulines' Mother Superior. You see, I needed the Mother Superior's knowledge of the archbishop and his residence—the daily routine, what buildings on that property were accessible."

When Isabeau stared at him, unable to determine what connection there could be between the Frenchman and the former Ursuline convent, he smiled.

"I had need of a place in which to store certain smuggled . . . goods. Lili convinced the old woman to provide access to one of the service buildings, repeating what I had told her—that the crates contained supplies bound for Caribbean missions. Later, when the nun finally questioned Lili's story, I paid her a visit and suggested that the archbishop would be interested to learn she was a willing participant in the proceedings. As you might guess, the Mother Superior agreed to continue our arrangement. As for your cousin . . ."

Calvé paused to draw on the cigar, then surveyed her through a haze of smoke. "Your *oncle* and the sister told you that Lili died of a brain fever, did they not?" At her nod, he went on, "I fear that they are mistaken in this. You see, *ma chère,* Lili did not fall ill. She was murdered."

Murdered.

Alarm shuddered through her. Painful as the acceptance of her cousin's death had been, the idea that someone had deliberately taken the girl's life was almost unbearable. With an effort, she protested, "But the physician who attended her claimed . . ."

"Then he was a fool." Calvé bit off the words. "No doubt if he had made a thorough examination, he would have found that her sickness was induced by outside forces. Unfortunately, my time has been taken up by numerous important transactions of late, and I have been remiss in my dealings with Ophelia."

At Isabeau's murmured exclamation, he favored her with a humorless smile. "I see you are confused, *ma chère.* Did I neglect to tell you that I entrusted your *cousine* into Ophelia's care while she awaited the child's birth?"

Lili, left in Ophelia's care? Isabeau shivered at the notion. But why had the quadroon summoned her to the voodoo ceremony, and refused to give up the babe? And why—

"Why did she hate Lili enough to . . . murder her?" Calvé shrugged. "With Ophelia, anything is possible.

I believe, however, that she had a practical motive. She needed Lili's baby."

The child, Regine, is not yours to take. The spirits have claimed her for their own.

Ophelia's words came back to her with horrifying clarity, and Isabeau stared up at Calvé as he went on, "Voodoo is a powerful religious and political belief among many of the city's people of color, and they will stake their alliance with the most powerful voodoo queen."

"Ophelia wants to be this queen," she murmured.

The Frenchman nodded. "So do many others. To prove her power surpasses that of the rest, she will use the baby as a ritual sacrifice."

"Mon Dieu, can you not stop her?"

In her mind she found herself choking back a scream. As a child, she had heard stories of voodoo queens and voodoo doctors, and the rituals they performed. She had always dismissed them as tales meant to frighten children into good behavior, nothing more. Yet if Monsieur Calvé were to be believed . . .

Calvé regarded her through the smoke. "I can stop her, *ma chère,* but whether I do so depends upon you."

"A favor," she managed, even as she found herself slipping back into that drug-induced twilight. "You will help me . . . in return for . . . a favor?"

"We understand one another, then," Calvé said with an approving nod. The carriage jerked to a stop, and he reached over to unlatch the door. "I have returned you home. In a few days, I will let you know your part of the bargain. Until then, the child will remain safe."

Isabeau took his arm and climbed from the coach. The night air washed over her. Its coolness lightened

the fog that enveloped her. Vaguely, she was aware that
Calvé held her in his arms.

"What about Ophelia?" she softly asked as she glanced
up at the man. "She must be . . . punished."

His gold eyes gleamed coldly. "I will deal with her
in my own way," he replied, and she shivered. He pulled
her closer and traced the smooth outline of her throat.

His eyes no longer glinted with the harshness of metal but instead burnt like twin suns. She should pull
away, she realized, yet his touch sapped what remained
of her will. But when she thought he was about to kiss
her, he merely put her away from him and murmured,
"Sweet dreams, *ma chère.*"

She stumbled past the wrought-iron gate into the
courtyard, where she collapsed onto a stone bench. A
moment later, she heard the crack of the driver's whip
as Calvé's carriage was pulling away.

Only after the rumble of wheels was no more than
an echo did she make her way into the house. She
climbed the main stairway and then paused a moment
outside Philippe's room. His door was ajar, and she saw
in the moonlight that he was not in his bed. She felt a
measure of relief. At least he was abroad somewhere,
she thought, rather than at home to question her.

Once in her room, Isabeau struggled from her
sweat-stained gown and splashed water into the basin.
By now, the languor had begun to pass, yet she felt
uncomfortably warm, as if she lay in the grips of some
fever.

She dampened a cloth and wiped her face and breasts,
trying to cool the burning sensation that permeated her
flesh. When this brought no relief, she stripped off her

pantalets and camisole, splashing the chill liquid over her nakedness. She shivered as the cool air caressed her bringing relief. But the heat that held her doubled in intensity as she recalled the feel of Calvé's hands against the softness of her throat.

Hesitantly, she touched her hands to the place. She slid her palms down toward her breasts, feeling her nipples tighten as she imagined his long, elegant fingers tracing their rosy contours.

A warm ache blossomed between her thighs, and she moaned aloud, wondering how his lips would feel, pressed against the hollow of her throat, where her pulse pounded an erratic rhythm.

But now another man held her, a man whose calloused palms roughly caressed her. She gasped with pleasure, knowing that he, and not Calvé, was the one for whom she'd waited, wanting him with an urgency she didn't understand. His lips seared her flesh as he kissed her; his fingers burned a path from her pale breasts to the soft curve of her hips. The hot ache between her thighs grew unbearable, and she longed for something—anything—to ease the tension that gripped her.

"No!" Isabeau cried out in a strangled voice. Her eyelids flew open, and she glimpsed herself standing alone before her dressing-table mirror. Shame crimsoned her cheeks as she gazed at the glass, barely recognizing the wanton image it reflected.

"No," she repeated, this time more softly. She didn't want him. Why, she didn't even like him, she told herself, not daring to think his name lest the image return. The drink had set her aflame with desire for a man she barely knew.

She snatched her dressing gown from its hook and flung it around her, so that no hint of flesh showed along its scalloped neckline. The burning feeling slowly subsided, replaced by a weariness that left her trembling.

After she made her way to bed and crawled beneath the coverlet, her thoughts continued to tumble wildly. She had no doubt that Calvé spoke the truth, that Lili had been murdered. Yet who would believe such a tale? She could offer no proof—not even the letters that Oncle Henri had burned. But even if she could not seek justice, she might yet find Lili's child and return the babe to her rightful family. But at what cost to herself?

A favor, the Frenchman had termed it.

Isabeau allowed herself a bitter smile at the thought. Had Mephistopheles approached Faust in the same manner? While Monsieur Calvé might not demand her soul in payment, she suspected that dealing with him might indeed prove akin to bargaining with the devil. Still, the memory of the voodoo ceremony she had witnessed this night steeled her resolve. *Mon Dieu,* how could she leave an innocent baby to such a fate and still live with herself?

No matter the Frenchman's price, she must pay it.

Thirteen

The sign swung in the morning breeze, its black letters proclaiming the name Parrish Co., Ltd. Philippe halted and stared at it. The placard appeared recently painted, unlike the building from which it hung. Years of sun and rain had taken their toll on the warehouse, so that its original color was faded to the anonymous grey worn by every structure on the wharf.

Philippe unfolded the scrap of paper that Calvé had left with him the day before. Another glance confirmed that the Frenchman's elegant scrawl matched the painted words above him. Within this ramshackle building, then, he would find the *américain* who would forge the final, vital link of Calvé's plan. Philippe's task was to ensure the man's cooperation by whatever means necessary.

Philippe frowned. Though he had never met the *américain,* he was well acquainted with Monsieur Tark Parrish's reputation.

Wealthy. Shrewd. Ruthless.

Those were a few of the words he had heard used to describe the man when he put in an appearance. He was accepted into polite society, Philippe knew, because of his money—that, and the rumor that he had been a hero of sorts during the war.

The *américain* had served as a blockade runner in that conflict. This much, Philippe had learned from Calvé. Philippe was also privy to the fact that the claim of wealth no longer held true, though society was still unaware Parrish had suffered a reversal of fortune.

But other tales followed him, so that no family of any repute—Creole or *américain*—deigned to receive him. Common knowledge had it that, years before, Parrish had drunkenly assaulted a young Creole woman and been forced to wed her. A few people dared to suggest that the girl's tragic drowning a few months afterwards was no accident. Parrish had murdered her, they whispered, and then terrorized his servants into testifying that their master had been nowhere near the river that day.

Whether such gossip was true or not, Philippe didn't care to speculate on. He marched into the shipping office.

He paused as the dark-haired man seated behind the desk shut his ledger and stood. A half-empty whiskey bottle and a glass sat within arm's reach of him. Those items, combined with his disheveled appearance, bore mute testament to a night spent in hard drinking.

Not a good sign, Philippe glumly decided. He turned his attention back to the *américain,* glimpsing for a moment what seemed to be a startled spark of recognition in the man's blue eyes. An odd reaction, Philippe thought, since Parrish would hardly have call to know him. But that recognition—if indeed it had ever existed—vanished behind a bland professional mask as the man asked, "What can I do for you?"

"You are Monsieur Tark Parrish?"

"I am." The expression of expectancy faded, replaced by a look of challenge.

"Then we have business to discuss, *m'sieur.*"

Deciding that the *américain* shared with him a distrust of outsiders—which in Parrish's case meant Creoles—Philippe ignored the man's reply and continued, "I wish to arrange the transport of certain goods."

Parrish sat back down, the action triggering a squeal of protest from his chair. "And just where would this shipment be bound, Mr.—"

"—LaSalle," Philippe supplied after a heartbeat's hesitation. "As for the cargo, I wish it shipped to Sevastopol . . . on the coast of the Crimea," he swiftly clarified when Parrish quirked a brow.

At his explanation, the *américain* gave a smile. "I'm well aware of its location, Mr. LaSalle. Still, Sevastopol is hardly a common destination."

"Does this mean you cannot make such arrangements?"

That possibility had not occurred to him, and Philippe felt sweat begin to dampen his palms. *Mon Dieu,* what if Parrish refused the shipment outright, without even giving him the chance to explain his proposal? How could he admit such a failure to Calvé?

He summoned his haughtiest manner. "Might I sit down, *m'sieur?*"

"Suit yourself."

Parrish gestured at the horsehair sofa beside the desk. Philippe sat and presented a sheet of paper. "Here is an inventory of the cargo I wish to be shipped," he began as he unfolded the page and started ticking off items. "Bed linens, crockery, farm implements, and so on—complete with estimated values, of course. The goods must leave New Orleans the night of February thirteen."

He waited for Parrish to note that this date marked the end of the Carnival season, less than a week away. For his own part, he found Calvé's timetable ample reason for suspicion. But perhaps an *américain* would find nothing odd in conducting business during the final hours of Mardi gras.

When the man merely nodded for him to continue, Philippe set the manifest atop the desk. "Now, *m'sieur,* can you perhaps make these arrangements for me?"

"Perhaps."

Parrish's tone indicated otherwise; still, he took up the list and began to survey it. Philippe settled against the sofa to study his new associate.

He'd always considered *américains* uncivilized— brusque, aggressive, and possessed of a tendency to run rough-shod over class distinctions. This man proved no exception. Even in repose, his expression reflected the arrogance and ruthlessness that grated upon the soul of every gently reared Creole. Whether or not the rumors were true, Philippe found himself uncomfortably certain that, in his own way, Monsieur Tark Parrish was as dangerous a man as Franchot Calvé.

That guess proved a certainty when the *américain* tossed the paper onto the desk and fixed him with a cold glance. "We know that you could get anyone to handle this shipment. Why approach me?"

"It is your reputation for efficiency," Philippe replied, for he'd anticipated such a question. "I require a man of experience, and you seemed most suited to—"

"Bullshit."

Philippe blinked. "I beg your pardon, *m'sieur?*"

"I said, bullshit."

Parrish took up the list again and crumpled it, then let it drop back onto the desk. "My guess is that you're trying to move contraband. You don't want a legitimate broker. You're looking for someone stupid enough or desperate enough to risk defrauding the dock authorities in return for a sizable profit."

He smiled, but Philippe detected no hint of humor in those ice blue eyes. "Since I'm no fool, LaSalle—or whatever the hell your name really is—it follows that you think I'd reason to take that risk. Am I right so far?"

"Yes . . . or rather, no . . . that is—"

Philippe fell silent as two realizations struck him. First, Parrish knew he was lying and would make no polite attempt to pretend otherwise; and second, the only way he could win him over was by dealing in a straightforward manner.

Philippe thought back to last night when, following his rendezvous with Bandy and Grubb, he had contemplated the problems inherent in recruiting the *américain*. Striking an equitable agreement bore a similarity to playing poker. With determination and luck, even a novice could set down his cards and walk away from the table a winner.

He kept that thought in mind as he withdrew a bulging envelope which he laid beside the crumpled page. "Very well, M'sieur Parrish, we will play it your way. I have some cargo to be shipped, and you are in need of contracts. I've already secured several bids on goods such as are listed on that bill of lading. This should cover your standard fee."

He nudged the envelope so that the crisp bills within

fanned onto the table. Though the *américain's* expression remained impassive, Philippe glimpsed in the man's eyes a hint of desperation that belied his apparent indifference. Philippe went on, "I've included an additional sum to handle any . . . unforeseen expenses."

"You mean bribes."

"As you wish." Philippe kept his tone even. "Once the ship weighs anchor with my goods safely aboard, you'll receive a second envelope containing an identical amount."

"And suppose I'm not interested in your proposition?"

Philippe let his gaze travel about the shabby office. "As I see it, *m'sieur,* you cannot afford to refuse my generous offer."

"And as I see, *monsieur,* I can refuse whatever offer I damn well please." With those words, the *américain* leaned back in his chair and flipped open his ledger again, implying that the interview was over.

Philippe sank into his seat and considered his next move. Surely Calvé hadn't underestimated the seriousness of the man's financial situation. Chances were that Parrish was himself a gambler, and his apparent refusal was simply a ploy to sweeten the pot. If so, the best resource was to call the man's bluff.

"You have made your position clear, M'sieur Parrish, so I will waste no more of your time," he heard himself calmly reply. Not waiting for an answer, he stood and reached for the envelope.

Almost simultaneously, the *américain's* fingers closed on his wrist. "I didn't say I was refusing your offer, Mr. LaSalle," Parrish softly countered as he, too, rose to his feet. "I was merely pointing out that I had that option—no matter what advantage you think you may have over me."

He gestured Philippe back toward the couch. Philippe resumed his seat. "Then perhaps we might discuss the terms of our agreement," he suggested in a bland tone.

Parrish scowled as he sat down and reached for the envelope. He riffled through the bills, then tossed the packet back onto the table. "There's the matter of my fee," he bluntly stated. "I'm not taking any chances on your vanishing once the cargo is afloat. I want the entire amount up front."

"That might prove difficult, *m'sieur.*"

Philippe frowned and pretended to consider the request, though in fact Calvé already had authorized him to make such a concession. No need to let the *américain* know that, of course.

"Very well, Monsieur Parrish, I will see what can be done. In the meantime, you may begin making arrangements for a ship and the laborers to transport the merchandise. Consider this money as simply a down payment—that is, if we have a deal."

"We have a deal," Parrish agreed.

Philippe noticed that the man didn't bother to offer his hand, but he dismissed this omission as another example of the typical *américain* disregard for manners. He rose and stiffly nodded. "I will contact you on Saturday with the location of the goods and the balance of your fee. Until then, *m'sieur.*"

Only when he was outside the office did Philippe allow a grin to spread across his face. *Mon Dieu,* he had done it! He had maneuvered the *américain* into accepting the shipment, and on his own terms.

With a jaunty spring in his step, Philippe continued along the wharf, heedless of the workers who jostled him or the odors that assailed his refined senses. No more midnight excursions to the river for him. He would limit his forays to salons and sitting rooms, as befitted his station. After all, fresh from this success, he could hardly fail to find himself risen to a valued position among the Frenchman's ranks.

Tark strode to the window and watched the Creole make his way through the throng of dockworkers and tradesmen. Finally, out of habit, he spared a glance at the sky. The morning air held a threat of rain, and the wind-raked clouds matched his mood.

He stalked back to the desk and flung himself into the chair. It responded with a sharp metal shriek that echoed his own frustration even as it set his head pounding again.

Damn that cocky Creole bastard.

He should have thrown the dandy out of his office the moment he saw that faked bill of lading—hell, the instant he recognized him. Hungover as he was, Tark retained enough of his faculties to realize that this man who called himself LaSalle was the same Creole who had escorted Isabeau at Clarisse Dumas's cotillion—the very man he had pegged as the chit's brother.

The thought sent another stab of pain through his temple. He leaned back and took a swallow of whiskey, hoping it might counter the effects of last night's excesses. Instead, his stomach roiled, and it was all he could do to shut his eyes and pray the sickness would swiftly pass.

Once that sensation ceased, he found himself recovered but hardly primed to handle the situation he faced.

"Just what in the hell is their game this time?" he muttered. Obviously, the brother knew of his precarious financial state, so perhaps the Lavoisiers had abandoned the idea of trapping him into marriage, and had adopted some other, more subtle campaign.

Tark smoothed the manifest and glanced over it again. *Bed linens, crockery, farm implements.* To anyone reading the list, it would appear that "LaSalle" was outfitting a missionary expedition.

He put aside the paper and took up the envelope once more. Its weight made his hands tremble. He'd stake his life on the fact that the Creole—LaSalle, Lavoisier, it made little difference—was trying to move contraband. Did the youth have some reason to involve him in illegal activities? Or maybe his offer was straightforward, and the matter of his sister's failed ploy was a coincidence.

Tark's grip on the envelope tightened. Instinct told him that someone of Lavoisier's youth and class did not embark upon a smuggling career on his own, that he was a liaison for someone else. But whom?

He would be a fool to pass up this opportunity, despite the likelihood that the scope of the contract fell outside the law. Given his circumstances, he was beyond worrying about any action the dock authorities might take, should he be caught.

Tark tossed the envelope onto the desk. Its bulging contours held his gaze. He could make the necessary arrangements, as he had overseen countless transactions during the war, and in the months that followed. A few discreet questions would reveal into whose palm he

could count bills, buying temporary blindness and a
measure of deafness.

So why not just do it?

Tark took a swallow of whiskey. He had operated
aboveboard for years now, and look where it had gotten
him. With what Lavoisier was offering, he'd have the
stake he needed to start afresh far from New Orleans.
As for the legalities—hell, it wasn't like he had agreed
to kill someone. Why, then, should he let a little twinge
of conscience stand in the way of self-preservation?

*But you swore to yourself years ago that you'd never
do this again,* an inner voice reminded him. *You decided
to put that all behind you when you lost Belle Terre.*

Tark reasoned that he hadn't yet done anything illegal.
Why not make some inquiries into Lavoisier's dealings
and learn who the Creole was working for? He could
always hand back the cash and tell the little dandy to
find someone else.

Deeming the matter settled, he grabbed the envelope
and unlocked his bottom desk drawer. Tonight would be
a good time to begin his inquiries, he decided as he
stowed the cash in the strongbox he kept hidden there.
He had promised Elisabeth to escort her to the opera,
where a number of his former associates would be in
attendance. A few questions and he just might end the
night possessed of the answers he needed.

Splendor.

No other word could better describe the French Opera
House, Isabeau decided as she and Philippe made their
way up the wide stairs leading to the main entrance.

She had made her debut in Paris, and had never before seen inside the pilasters and colonnades of the building's Greek Revival exterior.

The wait had been worth it. She gazed in admiration around the opulent foyer decorated in shades of red and gold. The brilliant colors were reflected countless times over in the shimmer of ornate mirrors and in the flash of crystal chandeliers. Yet she knew that the opera house was more than an elegant establishment offering its patrons genteel entertainment. It was said by many to be the soul of Creole society.

Indeed, New Orleans and opera were well-nigh inseparable. She could remember Maman humming snatches of one aria or another. The familiar notes would accompany each flash of the needle as she did her fancywork. As for Papa, he would return from an evening out to regale her and Philippe with selections from that night's performance. And the well-to-do were not the sole patrons. She had heard tales of many a poor Creole family that had forgone a meal so they could attend a performance.

Now, however, the pressure of her brother's foot atop her satin slipper pulled Isabeau from her musings. *"Mon Dieu,* Titi," she muttered, "must you crush my toes at every step?"

"It's not my fault, Isette," Philippe protested. "Surely you didn't expect we'd be the only ones here tonight."

Hearing the distress in his voice, she regretted her complaint. Philippe had been looking forward to this evening, and he couldn't be blamed if her anticipation fell short of his own. She had not shaken the horror of last night's expedition to the wharf.

Isabeau suppressed a shiver. Her sole comfort lay in

the fact that, though they were to share Monsieur Calvé's box, he would not be there. As Philippe explained it, the Frenchman habitually purchased a box for the season but rarely attended the opera himself . . . a bit of good fortune, she told herself, for she doubted she could face the man as yet.

She sidestepped a pair of young dandies and frowned. She had not told her brother of her encounter with Calvé, nor did she intend to do so—until she had sorted out the events. *Mon Dieu,* given the effects of the drugged liquor she had been forced to drink, she found herself unable to say with certainty what portions of their conversation had been real, and which she might have imagined.

A matron clad in white gauze jostled her, returning her attention to the matter at hand—making her way through the throng of elegantly attired opera-goers. Still another person trod upon the hem of her sea-green gown, and Isabeau reached for Philippe to keep her balance. When he stumbled against her, she shut her fan to guard its feathers from harm, and landed an elbow in Philippe's midsection.

"Oomph," he wheezed out and clutched his ribs with one hand. With the other, he steered her past a knot of aged gentlemen toward the doors leading to the inner theater.

"Here we are, Isette." He sighed in relief and gestured toward the stage area. "Now, feast your eyes on this uncommon elegance."

She followed his gaze, not surprised to find that the stage and its surroundings were as fabulous as the foyer. Four tiers of boxes and seats, all richly appointed with

crimson damask and gold scrollwork, curved in a graceful semicircle around the stage. They receded upward,
seeming to float one atop the other, with the fourth gallery all but touching the high ceiling. A pair of immense
gold-framed mirrors flanked the proscenium and reflected the theater's splendor.

The people who filled the theater provided a grand
display, Isabeau decided as she and Philippe threaded
their way past the less costly seats to the private boxes
situated at either side of the stage. The gentlemen were
decked in their finest, while the ladies shimmered in
costly fabrics and sumptuous jewels. Interspersed with
the sound of gay chatter was the flutter of ostrich-
feather fans being plied against the heat, by the two
thousand or more opera aficionados who crowded the
theater this night.

Barely had she and Philippe settled upon chairs upholstered in tufted red velvet, when her brother scrambled to his feet again. "Look, Isette, there's Marcel and
Cammi."

Philippe waved until he caught his friend's attention,
then gestured the pair to join them. Isabeau judged that
he was less glad to see the St. Johns than he was anxious to brag of his new-found acquaintance with Monsieur Calvé.

"Do join us," he ushered them in with unctuous civility. "As you can see, we are privileged to be the
guests of Franchot Calvé. I believe you have heard of
that gentleman?"

"You actually know him, Philippe?"

Cammi, clad in a bilious shade of pink, first gaped
in disbelief and then pursed her lips in envy, as she

ignored Isabeau's words of welcome. Marcel appeared
no less impressed by Philippe's words, though he remembered his manners and offered Isabeau a bow. He
wore a subdued version of Philippe's flamboyant coat,
and trousers topped by a bright embroidered waistcoat,
and he cut a handsome figure.

On impulse, she told him as much, and was rewarded
by that gentleman's blush. Noting his friend's discomfiture, Philippe donned a sly smile. "Take care, Isette,"
he warned her in a mock-serious tone. "Any more flat-
tery, and Cammi will be forced to ask what your intentions are toward her brother."

"Don't play the fool, Titi."

Isabeau's reproof held more than a note of sharpness,
for his inadvertent reference to Marcel's proposal tempered her pleasure in the evening's entertainment. Marcel, however, made no reference to their conversation
of the previous week, but only blushed more deeply and
stuttered, "P-perhaps I should pour the ch-champagne
now?"

He busied himself with the bottle chilling in a bucket
behind the seats. Cammi and Philippe shared a pair of
opera glasses and took turns lambasting the other thea-
tergoers. Isabeau accepted the champagne Marcel proffered but, she found her thoughts returning to the
painful truths she had learned from Monsieur Calvé.

*And just how deeply is Philippe involved in all of
this?* she wondered with a glance at her brother. If he
suspected that Lili's death stemmed from unnatural
causes, he would never have kept the knowledge to himself. But were his ties to Calvé stronger than his loyalty
to his own family?

She let her gaze travel about the opera house, until a blaze of color in the uppermost gallery caught her attention. There, in the seats where no Creole would deign to sit, were the *gens de couleur,* the people of color. Isabeau studied them with curiosity, for she knew those dark-skinned people only as servants or laborers.

Tonight, all wore their Sunday best—some dressed in garments faded and patched, but neatly pressed. Others were decked out in such finery that, save for the shade of their skin, they were all but indistinguishable from their Creole counterparts. Two or more dozen Negro men sat attired in elegant dark suits, hats perched upon their knees and exuding dignified reserve. The women of color, however, succumbed to no such similar constraint.

With their vividly hued silks and taffetas festooned with ribbons and plumes, they reminded Isabeau of brilliant tropical birds. Their gowns were cut to display more flesh than any Creole woman dared show, while their bold glances belied the rigid decorum with which they conducted themselves. Several of the younger Creole men stared at the mulattresses and quadroons with open admiration, even as the Creole women pointedly ignored the presence of their darker sisters. Their sexuality pervaded the air like musky perfume.

She glanced away, uncomfortable all at once, and turned her attention to the *loges grillées,* the screened boxes scattered throughout the theater. Traditionally reserved for persons in mourning—or those other patrons who desired privacy—they were outfitted with lattice panels that could be raised and lowered at will. Tonight, the *grilles* of many such boxes were flung up so that their occupants could be seen, as well as see.

The screened box directly across from them held two
elegantly attired women—one pale and blond, the other
dark-haired and dusky-skinned. Odd, Isabeau thought
with a frown, that an unescorted woman would be in
attendance, particularly at night. Perhaps the young
blonde was a recent widow, accompanied by her maid.
Satisfied with that explanation, she started to glance
away, when something of the pale girl's demure pose
reminded her of someone else.

"Quickly, Philippe, your opera glasses," she demanded
as, snatching the tiny binoculars from him, she gazed
back at the box.

Barely had she focused on its occupants, when the
quadroon stood to lower the lattice screen. Isabeau
glanced at the golden-haired girl before she was hidden
behind the panel, but that brief look was enough to set
her heart racing.

"Is something wrong, Isette?" Philippe asked and followed her gaze.

As he spoke, the lights dimmed, while the orchestra
began its opening notes. Isabeau shook her head and
managed a careless smile, as she turned her attention
back to the stage, where the curtain was rising to applause.

"It's nothing, Titi," she murmured as she joined in
the clapping. He eagerly leaned forward. Like countless
other Orleanians, he embraced opera with the enthusiasm and respect of a connoisseur.

Isabeau focused her own attention on the stage, chid-
ing herself for her momentary lapse into fancy. With
last night still fresh in her mind, she was simply letting
her imagination get the best of her. That could be the

only explanation for the fact that, in the latticed box across from them, she thought she had seen her dead cousin, Lili.

Fourteen

" . . . though he denied every word, of course. You are listening to me, *chéri*, aren't you?"

Tark gazed past the lattice screen of their box, letting Elisabeth's words drift over him like so much wood smoke. Even had he been inclined to respond, he doubted she would have let him get a word in. Several weeks had passed since the last time he had accompanied her to the opera, and he had forgotten why he vowed never to suffer through another such evening. Now, with the curtain not yet risen, he found his memory quite refreshed.

"But look." Elisabeth leaned closer to the *grille* and directed her opera glasses at the couple below them. "M'sieur Carpentier has dared to bring his bride out in public. I can see why he kept her hidden these past weeks," she added with spiteful glee.

Tark sighed. God only knew how he had resisted the urge to gag the woman, take his pleasure with her, and be gone before the curtain even rose. Only the possibility of tracking down information about Lavoisier's activities—that, and the suspicion that Elisabeth would relish such treatment—kept him in his seat.

He was spared further commentary when the curtain rang up to thunderous applause. What followed was, in his view, a test of endurance like those midnight hours riding at anchor during his blockade-running days. The audience, however, greeted each aria and chorus with enthusiasm, seemingly unaware that the first act was dragging. Finally the curtain fell, signaling the intermission.

"We need more champagne," he stated before the applause had died away, offering the only excuse he could devise to quit the box without exciting Elisabeth's suspicions. Leaving her occupied with her opera glasses, he brushed past the heavy velvet curtain at the rear of the box.

Once in the dim hall, he paused to savor the comparative silence it offered, then started toward the stairs. He reached the main foyer a moment later and saw that half the audience already filled it.

As he'd hoped, his gaze lit almost immediately on a former client, a florid-faced fellow American by the name of Jack Shelton. The man possessed little refinement, Tark recalled; but he had substantial business acumen. An attractive young brunette clung to his arm. Her painted face and daringly cut gown eliminated any likelihood that she was the man's wife.

"Why, Tark Parrish! Long time, no see," Shelton boomed with a grin as he stopped to wring Tark's hand. Then, with a glance at the woman beside him, he added, "This here's my, er, niece, Suzette."

"Mademoiselle."

Tark acknowledged the woman with a nod. She favored him with an arch smile in return, letting her kohl-darkened gaze travel boldly over him. He ignored the blatant appraisal and turned to Shelton. "I didn't realize you were a connoisseur of the French Opera, Jack."

"I'm not," that man replied, forgetting his supposed relationship with his companion long enough to give her an overly familiar pat. "Suzette insisted we come, so here we are."

"A stroke of good fortune for me," Tark turned the conversation in his direction, "since I've been meaning to talk with you."

"Well, I'm always glad to listen to a sharp fellow like yourself."

The man edged closer and lowered his voice to what was, for him, a confidential undertone. "I sure was sorry to hear about your, er, situation. All the boys down at the Exchange were talking about it. Still, if you ever put together another big deal like that one last year, we might just do us some business again."

"Actually, I have a project in the works. The details are confidential, of course . . ."

"I'm the soul of discretion," Shelton assured him in a pious tone, and then gave a wolfish grin. "Are we talking cotton or sugar?"

"Neither. The project concerns a humanitarian shipment of sorts bound for the Crimea—Sevastopol, to be exact."

He hesitated when the destination drew no reaction, then plunged on, "Are you by chance acquainted with a Mr. LaSalle . . . or a gentleman by the name of Lavoisier?"

Shelton shook his head. "Can't say as I am. Do these fellows belong to the Exchange?"

"It's doubtful," Tark answered, careful to keep the disappointment from his tone. "At any rate, our negotiations are in the preliminary stages, so I've got a few snags to work out before we sign the contracts. Once that happens, maybe you and I can continue our discussion."

"You name the time," the man agreed, then pinched his companion's rouged cheek. "Listening to a bunch of foreign folks singing sure builds up a powerful thirst in a man. C'mon, Suzette, let's get us some refreshments."

Tark continued through the crowd, casting about for other business acquaintances. Chances were slim that anyone would recognize the Creole's name, but he might as well—

Tark halted when a familiar female form exited the main theater a few paces ahead of him. The alabaster smoothness of her skin was set off by a pale green gown of gauzy fabric which did an admirable job of emphasizing her curves. She wore her hair much as she had the night of Clarisse's cotillion. The raven locks were caught up above her nape so that they cascaded down her neck in elaborate disarray.

So, my sweet Isabeau, our paths cross again.

He kept his distance and watched the tantalizing sway of her gown as she moved down the foyer ahead. He doubted she had noticed him, for she appeared absorbed in conversation with her companion, a blond chit he remembered seeing with her at that same ill-fated party.

The pair paused at the door of the ladies' retiring room and vanished inside. Abandoning his plan, Tark took up a position behind a screen of palm trees a few feet away. It seemed that fate had conspired in his favor. What better time for that conversation with Lavoisier's sister that he'd promised himself?

Tark leaned against the wall. If he could separate her from her companion, he might get the answers he needed. And this time, he vowed, he wouldn't be distracted with imagined promises and the honeyed sweetness of her soft flesh. Tonight, he would snare the chit with the same sensuous trap she had set for him.

"I am fine, Cammi," Isabeau insisted. "Philippe merely trod upon my foot before the performance."

"But you said you were in pain, and you do look quite pale. Perhaps I should summon a physician."

This suggestion was made in an inordinately hopeful tone of voice, and Isabeau caught back a sharp retort. Trust Cammi to find a way of drawing attention to herself. She pushed aside that complaint, however, for her sole concern was freeing herself of the girl.

"Do rejoin the others, and I will be along shortly," she urged brightly, her gaze meeting Cammi's in the gilded mirror. "After all, it would not do to let Philippe out of your sight for too long."

"I suppose you're right." The girl's expectant smile dissolved as she added, "Just don't blame me when you're forced to hobble about for the rest of the season while I'm dancing at the Carnival balls."

Isabeau waited until the girl had left, then gave her reflection a critical glance. Cammi was right. She did look pale, though the cause was not so much the pain of her injured foot, as the turmoil in her breast.

That turmoil stemmed not only from Monsieur Calvé's revelations of the night before. She couldn't dismiss the superstitious chill that had gripped her since her glimpse of the blonde who looked so like Lili.

Not that she believed in ghosts, she reminded herself,

nor was she prone to hallucinations. Still, curiosity compelled her to satisfy herself that the wraith was flesh and blood.

She turned from the image in the glass and made her way back to the crowd. Several minutes remained before the intermission would end, time enough for a hasty search of the upper halls before she must return to her own box. She continued through the foyer toward a curtained stairwell she'd recalled seeing just off the main hall.

Two landings above her, the staircase opened onto a dimly lit corridor that was empty, at least for the time being. Here, the chatter of the crowd was muted, so that the rustle of her satin gown against the cool marble floor sounded inordinately loud.

Gilded lamps cast an uneven glow, revealing here and there the same sumptuous colors and textures as adorned the rest of the opera house. She paid little heed to her surroundings, however, for she was intent instead on mentally recreating a reverse image of where the mysterious pair had been seated.

She followed the twisting length of the corridor past several private boxes, glancing at the occupants before halting at a partially curtained alcove halfway down the hall. If she remembered correctly, this was the box. She cautiously peered past the draperies, noticing a furtive movement within its darkened depths. Then a moan of passion assailed her, and she realized that she had stumbled upon a lovers' tryst.

An impulse she couldn't explain held her there, cloaked in shadows as she watched the pair. The bright lights of the theater trickled through the lattice screen

that had been pulled down for privacy. The harsh glow
fell in an uneven pattern, revealing a richly dressed
woman sprawled upon the alcove's tufted bench. Her
skirts were hiked well above her knees as her hefty,
balding companion groped beneath her voluminous
petticoats.

The woman's eyes were closed, her face taut with passion as the man fumbled with his trouser buttons and then
awkwardly positioned himself between her spread thighs.
Isabeau caught her breath, and a flush heated her cheeks
even as she found herself helpless to turn away from the
sight. Now, the woman had locked her silk-sheathed legs
over her lover's hips, and the pair's tentative movements
were giving way to frantic thrusting.

In the next moment, that rhythm ended with the man's
guttural gasp of climax. The woman's answering cry
broke the spell, and Isabeau took a step back. Not bothering with an apology—for she doubted the pair had noticed the intrusion—she turned and fled down the hall.

She stopped at the end of the corridor and leaned
against the wall. Though the coupling she'd witnessed
had lacked both beauty and tenderness, for a brief moment, she had longed to change places with that other
woman, had wanted to know how it felt to have a man
broach that secret citadel of her womanhood.

Mon Dieu, what was she thinking?

Isabeau straightened, and pushed aside the wanton
images. How could she be so distracted, when her efforts should be concentrated on finding the girl? Worse,
she was thoroughly turned around now, so that she
couldn't even guess where her own box was.

With a frustrated exclamation, she peered down the

corridor that angled into the one where she now stood. Halfway along its length sat a plump velvet settee, past which rose yet another stairway. She hesitated, then started toward them. Since her ghost hunt had proved a failure, and the opera would soon recommence, she might as well take time to regain her bearings before returning downstairs.

A moment later, she sank onto the sofa and leaned back with a sigh, with her bruised foot now throbbing in earnest. Cammi's gloomy prediction echoed in her mind, and Isabeau managed a wry smile. *Philippe,* mon frère, *if you* have *crippled me at the height of the Carnival season, I shall be hard-pressed ever to forgive you.*

She tugged off her right slipper, grimacing at the stab of pain as pressure eased on her flesh. She dropped the shoe to one side, then raised the hem of her gown to expose a trim ankle and calf.

She extended her leg and flexed her foot. The sheer fabric revealed a swollen, discolored spot on her instep where Philippe's shoe had connected. Still, the injury was not severe. Once she returned home, she would soak her foot in cool water and then bind it, and by morning she should be fit again. As for the next few hours, she would just have to grit her teeth against the pain.

The sound of footfalls rounding the corner in her direction made her forget her discomfort. Even as she realized the unseemly spectacle she presented with her bared leg and disarrayed gown, a familiar voice assailed her.

"What a charming tableau, *mademoiselle.* I trust I haven't kept you waiting in that pose an unduly long time."

Though she would have recognized Monsieur Parrish's American accent anywhere, she glanced in his direction to confirm the worst. Crimson stained her cheeks at the thought of their meeting in Madame's courtyard, when the red-haired woman had interrupted their reckless kiss. Why did it have to be he?

She tugged down her gown and shut her eyes for an agonized moment, raging against fate and praying that the *américain* would be gone once she looked up again. By the time she reopened her eyes, he had crossed to where she sat.

She struggled for a semblance of dignity as she slowly met his gaze. Despite her unease, she couldn't help noticing the way his elegant clothes emphasized his muscular form. He was dressed much like any Creole, but he never would be taken for one of them. It was the air of controlled aggression he projected, she decided, an attitude unlike the contrived languor typical of those other gentlemen. He appeared quite sober tonight. With any luck, he might not even recall their previous, unfortunate encounter.

She braced herself for a crude jest at her expense, but he merely said, "It seems our paths are destined to cross, Mademoiselle Lavoisier."

"I can assure you, M'sieur Parrish, that it is not by my choice."

She averted her gaze in curt dismissal. Any man who possessed a vestige of decency would take the hint and leave her. For that reason, she was not surprised when the *américain* ignored her snub.

"Since we might be considered old friends by now,"

she heard him say, "surely you won't object if I join you."

Isabeau promptly swung back around to face him. "I have no desire for company, *m'sieur,* especially—"

Before she could protest, Tark had seated himself beside her and propped his arm across the back of the settee, so that his fingers were casually brushing her bare shoulder. She edged away, assuring herself that the shiver she felt was one of revulsion.

She cast about for a retort that would put the man firmly in his place, when she saw his gaze drop to her one shoeless foot. She groped beneath the bench for her discarded slipper. To her horror, Tark, with a single fluid move, bent and retrieved the satin slipper, then favored her with a sardonic smile.

"You seem to have a propensity for losing your footwear, *mademoiselle.* It calls to mind a story I once heard from my grandmother."

His reference was not lost on her—*Mon Dieu,* did he think she had cast him in the role of a fairy-tale prince?—and she blushed again, though this time the high color was born of outrage. "I'll thank you, M'sieur Parrish, to return my shoe at once," she managed to say through gritted teeth as she made an undignified grab.

Tark evaded her attempt and dangled the slipper beyond her reach. "You should be more careful with your belongings, my sweet Isabeau," he answered in mock remonstration. "Who knows what price you might find yourself paying to reclaim them?"

The sight of the rugged *américain* twirling the slipper by one bright ribbon should have amused her, but Isabeau didn't laugh. This was no juvenile prank, she realized. He had some reason for seeking her out tonight. Still, she would not give him the satisfaction of knowing how he had unnerved her. In a cool tone, she replied, "I will not bargain with you for what is already mine."

"As you wish."

Tark headed toward the stairs, her slipper firmly in his grasp. Isabeau, realizing that he intended to abscond with her shoe, leaped up from the settee.

Her bruised foot met unyielding marble with enough force to make her gasp, but fury overrode her pain. Ignoring the cold chill beneath her stocking foot, she hobbled after him, catching up as he reached the staircase. Heedless of the possible consequences, she shoved past him and climbed the first few steps, then turned to block his way.

"Give me back my shoe, *m'sieur,*" she exclaimed, and punctuated that demand by thrusting out her hand.

Tark crossed his arms over his chest, tucking the sea-green slipper in the crook of his elbow. "So you've decided to negotiate, after all." He leaned against the balustrade, as he stared up at her with a speculative expression. "I must warn you that, once refused, I drive a hard bargain."

"Bargain?"

Isabeau regarded him in disbelief. Despite the ludicrous nature of the situation, she sensed a veiled malice in his words. No doubt he hadn't forgotten the public humiliation she had heaped upon him at Madame Dumas's cotillion. Had he chosen tonight to exact some perverse payment for her actions?

Keeping a wary eye on the man, she considered her options. Her attempt to wrestle the shoe from him had ended in failure, and a second try would not prove any more successful. Of course, she could return to her seat minus one slipper, but how would she explain its loss? Even Philippe would not believe that she had misplaced it. Her best recourse lay in playing the *américain's* game.

"Very well, M'sieur Parrish, tell me what you want in exchange for returning my shoe."

"Nothing of significance," he assured her with a cold smile, "merely some information about your brother."

"About Philippe?"

Isabeau frowned. What connection could exist between the two men? Indeed, the *américain's* behavior seemed hardly rational. "If you wish to meet my brother," she curtly replied, "I suggest you search him out, yourself, rather than waylaying me in the corridor as you have."

"That won't be necessary. Your brother and I have already met—though, at the time, he called himself by the name of LaSalle."

He continued to regard her with a chill expression, and Isabeau took a step back. *Mon Dieu,* was she dealing with a madman? Already, she regretted the impulse that sent her chasing after him, rather than fleeing when she had the chance—slipper, or no.

"My brother is Philippe *Lavoisier,*" she stressed in the tone usually reserved for the addle-witted, "and we are unacquainted with anyone named LaSalle. You have made a grievous error, *m'sieur,* but if you'll return my property—"

"There's no mistake." His tone was flat, yet his ice blue eyes glinted. "Your brother paid me a visit this morning and offered me a substantial bribe to ship contraband for him. So leave off with the coy games, Isabeau, and tell me just what the hell you two want from me."

"Philippe . . . *bribed* you?"

Isabeau kept a tone of polite disbelief, though her thoughts flew wildly. She had seen for herself the bank draft signed by Monsieur Calvé. Bribing Tark Parrish had to be the favor the Frenchman had demanded of Philippe. Apparently, the *américain* didn't yet realize that her brother was employing someone else's money— but that didn't explain why the man would suspect her of being involved in the scheme. No matter, she must protect Philippe.

"As I said, *m'sieur,* you have made an error," she continued with frosty politeness, praying her voice would hold steady. "I know nothing of my brother's business activities. Even if he did approach you, as you claim, you most certainly misunderstood his intent. Now return my shoe, and I'll gladly pretend this unfortunate incident never took place."

Tark considered her request before favoring her with a wolfish smile that sent a shiver through her. "I sense that you're not being quite truthful with me, my sweet Isabeau. However, I might be inclined to accept you at your word . . . given the proper persuasion on your part, of course."

His gaze left her no doubt of his meaning. Righteous outrage overcame her apprehension as she tugged off her other slipper and brandished it before him. "If you require persuasion, perhaps this will suffice. Since you seem so enamored of that shoe, you should have its mate," she retorted, and impulsively hurled the slipper.

It bounced harmlessly against his chest and landed at his feet, where it lay like a bright-plumed dove felled by a hunter's shot. Almost simultaneously, the second shoe joined its fellow on the marble step, striking with a muffled plop that sounded inordinately loud. She looked up to meet Tark's gaze. For a brief instant, he appeared as stunned as she by her action. Then his eyes narrowed in a sign more ominous than any outright display of anger.

Prudence overruled indignation, and she instinctively turned to flee. Before she could manage more than a step toward the upper landing, however, he caught her wrists and shoved her back against the wall. The move pinned her between him and the gleaming brass banister, cutting off her means of escape.

A shaft of fear shot through her, and with an effort she bit back a cry. She would not let this barbaric *américain* see how he had frightened her, she vowed. Her resolve proved fleeting, however, when he addressed her again.

"No more games, *mademoiselle*," he clipped out in the dangerously soft tone she had grown to dread. "You and your brother are up to something, and you're not leaving here until I find out what it is."

Fifteen

"I have no idea what you are talking about," Isabeau gasped out, as she struggled against him.

He easily countered her attack, his lips twisting in a smile of disbelief as he replied, "Is that so? Don't think I've forgotten your little performance in Clarisse's courtyard the other night. Was trapping me into marriage your idea, or your brother's?"

Isabeau's laugh held only a trace of hysteria. "Do you actually think that I would lower myself to marry a man like you? Why, you arrogant, overbearing . . . *américain!*"

She spat the last epithet with venom and then subsided in acknowledgement of her captor's strength. From the landing above drifted the orchestra's muted strains, and she realized the next act had begun. No doubt Philippe would search for her if she didn't return soon. Should her brother see her at this man's mercy, *mon Dieu,* he would feel compelled to confront the *américain,* perhaps even challenge him to a duel. And should Philippe not prove the victor—

Her distress must have been apparent, for Tark's grip on her loosened. "You're trembling, my sweet Isabeau," he observed with exaggerated solicitude. "Do I make you nervous?"

Isabeau shook her head, though she found herself unable to meet his gaze. He stood inches from her, so close she could breathe the remembered smell of him— a clean hint of soap mingled with the spicy scent of his flesh. He had held her this close the night he had kissed her, with warmth radiating from his body, and his mouth insistent in its demands. She instinctively sensed that he, too, had not forgotten that moment of intimacy.

"Please, let me go," she pleaded in a tremulous voice she barely recognized as her own.

His blue eyes darkened, their expression unreadable in the dim light. "Not until we finish our little talk." He released her wrists and slid his hands up to her bare shoulders. "You remind me of someone—a Creole girl— whom I knew long ago," he murmured as he stroked her warm flesh. "She was beautiful, too—the kind of woman that can drive a man to distraction. Do you know what that means, my sweet Isabeau?"

She shook her head, confused by this softening of his manner, following as it did upon cold anger. Then he smiled down at her, and she caught back a cry at the implacable expression she saw in those ice blue eyes.

"It means, my little temptress, that he'll do anything to possess her—the consequences be damned."

With a deliberate gesture, Tark reached out and traced the silken swell of one breast above her tightly laced bodice. She moaned and shut her eyes, her lashes a dark velvet fringe against the pale curve of her cheek. The reaction brought a bitter smile to his lips.

Nicely done, mademoiselle. *Have you perhaps considered a career upon the stage?*

With a calculated move, he grasped the banister, so that he held her trapped between his arms. She tried to back away. The satin of her gown rustled enticingly against his thighs, and he felt his loins tighten in response.

Damn the little bitch, she knows just what she's doing to me.

A moment before, his resolve had been defeated by the feel of her warm flesh beneath his hands and the intoxicating scent of her perfume. He had conquered that weakness, at least for a time. But even reminding himself how she and her brother had schemed against him could not cool his desire.

"Please let me go, *m'sieur,*" she repeated in a voice little more than a whisper.

The faint protest rekindled his anger. "But we've only now begun, my sweet Isabeau," he reminded her. "Surely you haven't already tired of the game?"

"I swear I don't know what you are talking about. I only wanted to—"

She broke off with a gasp as he stroked his thumb across her other breast until its peak strained against her gown. This time, she struggled against his touch, while her lips trembled as if on the verge of speech. Whether she would have voiced pleasure or protest, he never learned. He pulled her into his arms.

His mouth captured hers with a ferocity that drew a cry of protest from her. He thrust his tongue between her parted lips, probing her soft depths with abandon. The taste of her kiss was as he remembered, sweet with champagne and desire. After a moment, she countered his aggressive exploration with a tentative flick of her tongue against his. His body stiffened in instant response, while primitive exhilaration sung in his veins. He swept his hands down her back and along the swell of her hips, molding her soft curves to his own hard, hot form. But even as need threatened to consume him, one corner of his mind echoed with the cold voice of sanity.

Sweet Jesus, you're playing right into their hands, just as you did the other night—just like you did with Delphine and her father.

With a shuddering effort, he broke free of the embrace. She blinked and stared up at him, her midnight blue eyes wide with confusion—or was it calculation? Either way, the sight of her flushed cheeks and swollen lips filled him with loathing, though whether the emotion was directed at himself or at her, he didn't know.

"Is this how it's supposed to go?" he demanded in a harsh voice he barely recognized as his own. "Do I take you right here upon the stairs, where anyone might chance upon us? Or do we find an unoccupied box, so I can ravage you in relative privacy—at least until your brother makes his prearranged appearance?"

When she offered no reply, another possibility occurred to him. "Or maybe your brother wants me to have you," he suggested in an insulting tone. "My reward for services rendered, perhaps?"

"Mon Dieu, no."

The choked denial made him pause, even as he marveled again at the chit's acting skill. Had Elisabeth not warned him of the girl's intent, had he not already heard her brother's lies, he might have been swayed by the anguish in her pale face.

As it was, Tark favored her with a cold smile. "I suggest, my sweet Isabeau, that you tell your brother he'd better play straight if he wants to deal with me. No more chance meetings between you and me; no more carefully orchestrated rape attempts. Otherwise, he can find someone else to move his contraband."

"But it was not Philippe's idea to bribe you. M'sieur Calvé—"

Her slim fingers flew to her lips in a vain attempt to stop the words. With one corner of his mind, Tark registered how the blood had drained from her face and wondered if his own features reflected that same stunned expression. Her slip had been inadvertent, he was certain. He mentally reeled as if he'd been dealt a blow.

It couldn't be the same man.

The name had to be a coincidence.

Surely she couldn't mean—

"Franchot Calvé," he clarified her words, and somehow was not surprised at her reluctant nod. Sweet Jesus, his old enemy had come back to New Orleans, and even at this very moment might be . . .

". . . here, at the opera house?"

"No," she countered in a panic-stricken tone. "We are using his box tonight while he is otherwise occupied—that is all I meant to say, *m'sieur.*"

He barely noted her reply. He had long suspected that the Daedalean maze of lost contracts and so-called accidents he'd been stumbling through these past months was of someone's deliberate making. Now, Isabeau had handed him that long-sought length of twine that might mean his escape from that labyrinth—a figurative lead to the one man who possessed both the motive and the means to bring him to the brink of ruin.

So what in the hell are you going to do about it?

Now that the first shock of that revelation had passed, common sense took hold. Until he knew just what Franchot's plans for him were, his best defense lay in letting his old foe think he had the advantage of surprise. And the only way to keep up that pretense was to assure Isabeau that Franchot's name meant nothing to him . . . and then get the hell out of there.

"So your host is Franchot Calvé," he repeated. "I knew a man by that name years ago—though last I heard, he'd long since gone abroad. But we're not here to talk about your friends, *mademoiselle*. We are discussing you and your brother."

"As you say, *m'sieur*," she agreed, her relief apparent. "I will give him your message."

"See that you do."

Tark spared her a final look, but now her pale features reflected only composure. She accepted his dismissal of his past acquaintance with Franchot, and he wondered if she had been aware of his connection to the man—not that it made a difference. Her association with the Frenchman was sufficient to damn her in his eyes.

He turned and started up the stairs. The orchestra's cheerful notes greeted him as he reached the landing. In the past, he'd always dismissed the French opera as little more than a melodramatic exercise—tales of unrequited love, supernatural occurrences, and remarkable coincidence.

After the events of tonight, however, he could almost believe that fate did play a telling role in the lives of men.

As the sound of Tark's footsteps faded, Isabeau sagged against the gleaming banister and pressed her fingers to her bruised lips. *Mon Dieu,* had she gone quite insane? Bad enough that she had let the *américain* kiss her, but to welcome his advances with the abandon of a riverfront strumpet!

She shut her eyes at the memory. Why, it hadn't even mattered that she knew what kind of man he was—not when he touched her. Years of convent rearing and rational thought had proved no match for her traitorous body. Even worse was the way she had betrayed her own brother by mentioning M'sieur Calvé's name to the *américain.*

At the thought of Philippe, she realized how long she had been absent from the rest of her party. She hurried down the few steps to scoop up her discarded slippers and pull them on. Her first priority must be to return to their box before Philippe came for her. Later she would find some way to repair the damage her unthinking words had caused.

She descended the stairs and hurried down the hallway toward the main corridor. A second stairway halfway down its length took her to the next lower level, where Monsieur Calvé's box lay. To her relief, she found that she recognized this section of the theater. A moment later, she dropped breathlessly into her seat and managed a shrug at her brother's questioning look.

"Did Cammi not tell you I was temporarily indisposed?" she murmured to him. "Of course, I am quite well, now."

A burst of applause from the rest of the audience forestalled Philippe's reply. Isabeau joined in with an enthusiasm that left her brother no choice but to take her at her word.

Until the final curtain, she feigned interest in the activity on stage, while her thoughts were embroiled in a more immediate drama. Not only was Philippe's safety at stake now, but also her own, and that of the child, Regine. Tomorrow, she would confess to her brother her own involvement with the Frenchman, and together they would fix upon a course of action. But who, she wondered, posed the greater danger to them—Monsieur Calvé, or the *américain?*

For her own self, she already suspected the answer.

For once, Tark had no quarrel with the opera's prolonged final act. Instead, he accepted it as a reprieve of sorts—he could lean back in the darkened box and let his thoughts spin themselves into some kind of order. Sensing his mood, Elisabeth remained silent, but only after she'd pointed out with considerable asperity the fact that he had returned minus the promised champagne.

As the action drew toward a conclusion, Tark satisfied himself on a few points—the first being, Why hadn't he learned of Calvé's return long before now? The most likely explanation was his own self-imposed exile from Creole society, combined with his former partner's reclusive nature. Franchot had kept a low profile, he recalled, disdaining company. In a city the size of New Orleans, their paths might never have crossed.

But why the subterfuge? Tark remained unmoved by the plight of the star-crossed lovers whose story was drawing to a close below. If Franchot had sought revenge, why go to the trouble of ruining a man over a period of time, when a few dollars flashed in any riverfront alley would buy his prompt murder?

He glanced at Elisabeth, whose attention was now riveted on the stage. She yawned and stretched like a discontented feline, and the exaggerated movement caused her daringly cut gown to slip even lower, exposing a brightly rouged nipple. Seeming oblivious to her growing state of undress, she leaned nearer the *grille,* affording him a better view of her bared breast.

Tark watched her with a dispassionate eye. His affair with Elisabeth had begun at the same time his business woes started, he realized now. While he held a certain affection for her, he had never believed that her feelings stemmed from any emotion other than lust. Now, he couldn't dismiss the possibility that something—or someone—else might have prompted her interest in him.

Then again, subtlety was never Elisabeth's hallmark. Tark spared her another look. She had managed to shrug off the other sleeve of her gown, so both pale, full breasts gleamed whitely in the subdued light of the box. Earlier, he would have found her brazen behavior amusing. Now, he wondered if her bold ways were merely designed to disguise some more devious purpose.

Damn you to hell, Franchot, you'll have me suspecting every person in the city before you're through!

By now, the action on stage had ended with the death

of the opera's young hero and heroine—an outcome of which he approved in his current state of mind. As the lights came up, he made his decision. He would play his role as Calvé's hapless victim at least until he knew the man's intention. And this time, his old partner would find him a more formidable foe.

Once Elisabeth had rearranged her gown into some semblance of modesty, they left the box. Avoiding the main hallways, they made their way to a darkened doorway at the rear of the theater. Outside, the threatened rain had begun, and Tark moved into the cold drizzle which heralded the start of a full-blown storm.

He waited in the open for his hired coach, welcoming the chill mist. He felt no discomfort, but rather the exhilaration that came from abandoning sterile warmth and embracing the elements.

To his surprise, the cold sent a surge of sexual desire through him, so that when their carriage rumbled from the shadows, he wasted no time in pulling Elisabeth beside him. She unfastened the bodice of her gown to let her ample breasts spill free of the confining laces. With a groan, he waited only long enough to unbutton his trousers before surrendering himself to her expert ministrations.

She eagerly knelt between his spread legs and closed her lips over his throbbing shaft. Within moments, her skillful technique combined with the motion of the carriage to bring him to a violent climax. She didn't wait until he'd fully spent himself, however, but pulled away in midthrust so that his seed spilled hotly across her white breasts. As he sank back against the leather seat, she straddled his thighs and guided his hand beneath her lifted skirts. With sure strokes, he helped her find her own release.

Afterwards, as she rearranged her gown and he re-buttoned his trousers, it occurred to him that he'd gained nothing more than a measure of physical relief. He'd never questioned the lack of emotional satisfaction in their lovemaking, but now he found their relationship hollow. *So what would you prefer?* a mocking voice within him asked.

Tark searched his heart, but found no answer.

Sixteen

Tom Sullivan leaned forward with the air of a man about to impart an ageless truth.

"Listen up, boys," he told the dockworkers gathered around him at the bar. "If you ever find yerself losin' at cards one night, an' this fella"—he stabbed a forefinger at Tark—"offers to stake you in return for a favor someday, do what I shoulda done."

A gap-toothed grin spread over his face as he continued, "Tell him thankee kindly, then chuck yer hand, an' don't look back. Otherwise, you'll find yerself sloppin' around the city on a piss-poor day like today 'stead of spendin' the afternoon drinkin' like any sensible man."

The appreciative guffaws that greeted this pronouncement were lost in the clamor from the laborers who crowded the Gilded Albatross this night. Tom acknowledged their plaudits and awaited Tark's reply. Tark settled on the barstool beside his friend, but before he could counter the man's jibes, another voice joined the conversation.

"If you ask me, Tom, you got off right easy on that deal," Ned Deaton exclaimed as he produced an empty glass and an unopened whiskey bottle from behind the bar.

The plump tavern owner poured a shot and set it in front of Tark, then wiped his gleaming forehead with a rag and winked at the other patrons.

"Seems like that was the same night Tom swore his wife would have his hide if he came home busted one more time," he continued. "I don't know about you boys, but I'd sooner crawl around in the mud awhile than face Tom's missus when she's in a lather."

Tom joined in the laughter, though he took a mock swing at the barkeeper. "It's a good thing you pour the best beer in town, Ned, else we'd be drinkin' to yer memory right now. And that'd be a right shame, seein' how you'd be leavin' yer new missus a widow afore she's ever a wife."

"Now, don't you be making sport with my blushing bride-to-be," Ned promptly warned, then tempered those words with a grin as he tossed his rag over his shoulder and started toward the other end of the bar. "Alma's a fine, sweet-tempered woman," he called back to them, "and she'll take her broom to any man who claims otherwise."

With a grin at the truth of that sentiment, Tark grabbed his whiskey and turned to Tom. "Let's get this over with," he said and motioned toward the sole empty table in the establishment.

Chairs scraped loudly as the pair settled in the far corner. Tark scanned the room, his gaze taking in the scarred tables and battered chairs. Behind the rough-carved bar stretched an oversized mirror. The crack across its width had appeared courtesy of a long-ago, mug-hurling customer. The mirror's splotched surface reflected the opposite wall, upon which hung the requisite painting of a recumbent nude. Affectionately dubbed "Sonya" by the tavern's regulars, that blowsy female leered from her bright canvas with genial impartiality—rather like some patron saint of drunks, Tark decided.

The Albatross was a comparatively new addition to the numerous taverns, groggeries and dance halls that crowded Girod Street, a violence-racked avenue near the waterfront in the city's American section. Catering to a motley cross-section of dockworkers, sailors, sneak thieves, and harlots, the area rivaled its French Quarter counterpart, the infamous Gallatin Street, for mayhem and bloodshed.

Ned's place was, however, a step up from the scourge of so-called "barrel houses"—establishments where the unwary could drink their fill for a nickel a glass, with the understanding that they would be robbed and stripped upon leaving the premises. At the Albatross, the portly owner made sure that his customers left possessed of their clothing and cash, if not their wits. That policy, along with Ned's liberal extension of credit and the Albatross's proximity to Tark's warehouse, were the primary reasons Tark frequented the place.

Now, satisfied that the surrounding din would afford them a measure of privacy, he asked Tom without preamble, "What did you find out?"

"He's your boy, all right. I checked out the addresses you gave me. The records confirm that a Frenchman name of Franchot Calvé owns a fancy house out on St. Charles Avenue, and a couple of other places, besides."

Tom took a gulp of beer, paused for a belch, and continued, "Seems he up an' disappeared not long after the war ended—just about the time you had that there . . . trouble of yers. He showed up in town again 'bout three years ago, opened up the St. Charles place to live in, an' turned the one on Gravier Street into a gamblin' hall. The house on Rue de Fleur—that's a little side alley off Basin Street—he set up as a fancy bordello. It's run by a high yella name of Ophelia, calls herself a hoodoo queen."

"I'm familiar with the woman."

Tom quirked an eyebrow. "Times can't be too tough, if you can afford to dip your wick there."

He plucked a battered notebook from his jacket pocket and thumbed its dogeared pages. Tark curbed his impatience with a sip of whiskey, reminding himself he was fortunate to have secured the man's services. Long before they had struck up a friendship, he'd known of Tom Sullivan's reputation for uncovering confidential information. Most of the city's other policemen had their primary interest in taking bribe money from local officials.

Not that Tom was averse to lining his pockets for the right cause. The night patroller staged well-publicized raids on the waterfront brothels, ostensibly to soothe the outraged morality of the town's prominent citizens. Tom had confided to him that, in reality, he limited his forays to exclusive bordellos whose wealthy patrons gladly paid him to overlook their peccadilloes.

"Here we are."

Tom held the book at arm's length and squinted at his notes. "Seems this Calvé feller is involved in all kinda deals—shippin', gamblin', prostitution . . . hell, even bankin'. Anythin' that'll make a buck, he's got his fancy hands in. From what I can tell, it's all strictly legit—but just barely, if you get my meanin'."

He got it, all right. Tark had learned over the course of his past dealings with Franchot that the man had a genius for—among other things—skirting legalities. Now that his suspicions of the previous night were confirmed, he asked, "What about his connection to the girl's brother, Philippe Lavoisier?"

"I went to that other address you gave me and poked around a bit. He and the sister—a nice piece of work, that—live alone there . . . neighbors say the parents died in a fever epidemic a few years back." Tom consulted yet another page. "Seems that a coupla years after her folks died, the girl's relations packed her off to Paris. She just got back a few weeks ago—left 'causa some scandal over a Frenchy nobleman."

"Go on."

The night patroller snapped shut his book and tucked it back into his pocket. "The brother's a gambler, got hisself in a bind with someone name of Rivard—one of them moneylenders who collects his debts one way or another, but just a pussycat next to a fella like Calvé."

Tom took another swallow of beer and continued, "My guess is that the brother went to Calvé, who paid off his note for him. Anyhow, while I was lookin' 'round today, I caught sight of the brother—recognized him right off, too."

"Recognized him from where?" Tark prompted when Tom paused for dramatic effect.

The man flashed his gap-toothed grin. "He's the same young pup I caught the other night wanderin' 'round the old Ursuline convent—you know, the place where the archbishop's livin' like some kinda king. Anyhow, the boy was all dudded up with a fancy waistcoat an' frilly shirt. Kinda spoiled the effect, though, since he looked like he'd been rollin' in the mud with some two-bit doxy."

Tom chuckled at the memory. "He was standin' at the gates with a loaded cart, like he was makin' a delivery. Only reason I let him go was 'cause some old nun came out an' said things was square." The night patroller hesitated in his account, then asked, "Not that it's any of my business, but do you mind tellin' me just where in the hell *you* fit into all this?"

"I can't, Tom—not just yet. But believe me, as soon as I know what's going on, I'll let you know."

"Fair enough," the man said. "Does this mean we're quits?"

"Consider us even," Tark agreed, and signaled the barmaid for another round. "Now that you've given me somewhere to start, I think I'll do a bit of looking around on my own."

"Suit yourself."

The night patroller favored him with the tolerant nod of a professional to a neophyte as he lurched to his feet. Tark watched him make his farewells to the other patrons and then shoulder his way through the tavern's batwing doors into the night.

After the doors had swung shut Tark reached into his pocket. With the same care he would use in handling a newly honed knife, he extracted an oversized envelope and withdrew an invitation then propped it on the table before him.

Seeing it, anyone else might have admired the foiled

and painted card with its rendering of a sultry harem girl and the year, 1872. After what Tom had told him, Tark viewed it in a different light. The elegant invitation seemed like a mocking challenge meant for him, alone.

Tark tipped the card so it sprawled open to reveal the printed words inside. The gleam of the gold-embossed letters was dulled only slightly by the tavern's smoky light. He scanned the brief lines once more, though he already had committed them to memory.

Ophelia's House of Discreet Entertainment for Refined Gentlemen and Ladies. An evening of Seductive Pleasures. Your presence is requested at a Masquerade Ball this Friday Evening, the Ninth Day of February, at Ten O'Clock. By Invitation Only.

Tark rearranged the fragments of information he had gleaned since that night at the opera house. Until a few minutes ago, they had formed no more than a fragile web of conjecture. Now, he had reason for his suspicions.

He gave the card a final glance before tucking it away. If Tom was correct, he had been within arm's length of his former business partner for months now. The question was, had the invitation to Ophelia's masquerade ball been intended as an innocent diversion, or was it yet another strand in the plot Franchot was weaving around him?

"Here's your drink, mister."

The blond barmaid leaned forward, whiskey glass in hand, her move causing the loosely gathered neckline of her blouse to slide still lower. With calculated nonchalance, she set down his drink and straightened, but only after affording him a prolonged view of her pendulous breasts.

When he made no response to her overture, she prompted, "How's about some company?"

"Just the drink."

He tossed the girl a coin in payment, not bothering to conceal his lack of interest. He had a few hours to kill before the masquerade began, and he intended to spend that time with Ned's whiskey. Sober, he would be apt to dwell upon the foolhardiness of blindly walking into his enemy's lair, and then abandon the entire scheme.

He felt the reassuring pressure of the revolver tucked into the rear waistband of his trousers. Not that he foresaw confronting his old foe tonight, but he'd be damned if he would chance going up against Franchot unarmed.

He took another sip of whiskey, thinking back to Tom's comment regarding Philippe Lavoisier and a cartload of goods. Strange as the entire situation was, that fact was particularly puzzling. Having access as he apparently did to Church property, why would Franchot choose to store the contraband at the old convent in the middle of town, when the new Ursuline convent lay directly at the water's edge a scant two miles downriver?

Tark seized upon and then dismissed several possible answers to that question before making a decision. Rather than second-guess his old enemy, he would just take a little midnight tour of the old convent grounds and see for himself what, if any, illegal goods were stored there. Anticipation threaded through his veins in a way he hadn't experienced for years. With a little luck, tonight he just might find the means to exact his revenge from the man who had nearly destroyed his life.

* * *

"Do calm yourself, Titi," Isabeau urged as she pressed a snifter of brandy into her brother's hand. "We need cool heads tonight, if we are to prevail."

"Calm myself?" Philippe repeated. *"Mon Dieu,* first you tell me you've spent your nights cavorting about the docks with superstitious Negroes and dealing with a dangerous man like Calvé. If that weren't enough, then you go on to admit you've been associating with an *américain* whose reputation would give any sensible female pause. Now, you ask me to calm myself?"

He sank onto the chair behind his desk. Isabeau moved to his side. Philippe had been abroad most of the day, so that only now had she found the opportunity to confront him. He had confirmed his own involvement with Monsieur Calvé's schemes with relief, and she realized that her brother was no more comfortable than she with such dealings.

Emboldened by his admissions, she had related the events of the past two weeks—her mysterious summons to the voodoo ceremony, her conversation with Oncle Henri, and her meeting with the Frenchman after the ceremony. Her encounters with the *américain,* however, she had carefully edited. Mindful of Philippe's obsession with convention, she played down their meetings at the cotillion and the opera, and emphasized Tark's suspicions concerning the shipment.

But it was not that she feared her brother's censure, she realized; nor was it the possibility that Philippe might demand satisfaction for the man's bold actions. Rather, it was because she still found herself drawn to

Tark, even though he had proved himself little better than a scoundrel. If she could not understand her feelings, how could Philippe?

Unwilling to deal with that question, she glanced at the library door. She'd had the foresight to shut it before engaging Philippe in conversation, accurately predicting his reaction . . . not that a closed door would forestall Lucie. No doubt the girl had already taken up her position outside, and would report back to her true master—or mistress—every word they spoke.

Still, she had made the eavesdropping servant's task more difficult, Isabeau thought in satisfaction as she caught her brother's hand in hers. "I know you are angry, Titi," she began, "but I explained what little choice I had. Now, we must form a plan to rescue Regine and deliver ourselves from Monsieur Calvé's clutches."

"We must do nothing," Philippe exclaimed. "I will handle this situation alone."

"And what do you propose to do—tell the *américain* that it was all a mistake and take back the money you gave him?"

Isabeau cleared a place amid the stacks of papers on the desk, so she could sit on a level with her brother. "And what of Regine?" she demanded as she settled on the desktop. "Surely you do not think Monsieur Calvé will forget our agreement and return her to us."

"I'll think of something."

"Do not be too harsh on yourself, *mon frère,*" she replied, hearing the frustration in his voice. "Much of what has happened is as much my fault as yours."

She reached beneath her for the stiff envelope whose corner poked against her thigh and idly toyed with the slim packet. "After Oncle Henri refused to help me, I did not know who to trust. And then, when Monsieur Calvé offered his assistance, it seemed so simple—just a favor in return, he said. To be sure, I do not yet know what he wants of me, but it could not be anything so difficult . . ."

She trailed off as Philippe repeated, "Just a favor. Why, he had me scrambling about the riverbanks at midnight, making deliveries like a lackey. I ruined my best pair of shoes that evening, too."

"Alas, Titi . . . you *have* suffered, have you not?"

Isabeau made this last observation with an ironic curve of her lips that drew a smile from her brother. Their moment of understanding ended, when Isabeau noticed the handwriting on the envelope she held.

"Philippe, why did you not tell me that we received another message from Ophelia?"

Her brother grabbed for the envelope. Twisting from his reach, she pulled out the card it contained and stared at the bit of pasteboard in surprise. "Why, it is an invitation to a Carnival ball tonight," she exclaimed as she took in the elaborate illustration and read the summons.

A *masquerade* ball.

The word reverberated in her mind, and her breath caught in anticipation. What simpler means to gain entrance to the quadroon's exclusive brothel than with a printed invitation—and what better way to search the place for clues to the child's whereabouts, than in costume?

"*Mon Dieu,* Philippe, you have had the solution to our problems all along," she exclaimed. "All we need do is slip away from the other guests and search the house for—"

"Don't be absurd."

Philippe made a successful grab for the invitation and held it at arm's length. "What would Maman and Papa have said if I let my own sister set foot in such a place? The people who frequent that establishment are hardly the type—"

"But the card said 'ladies,' " Isabeau pointed out. "And besides, *you* must have been there before, to receive an invitation."

Her brother rolled his eyes heavenward, as if in hope of divine intercession. "That's different. A gentleman is expected to indulge in such . . . diversions. The only females who will be there are women of loose virtue, or married society ladies who don't care if scandal trails in their wake."

He grasped the pasteboard in both hands and tore it in half, then tossed the two pieces onto the desk with a flourish. "You will not, for any reason, set foot in that brothel, do you understand me? I told you I would handle the situation alone, and I will."

"Very well, Philippe," she softly agreed, dropping her gaze. "If you don't want my help, then perhaps you would not mind if I attend a small affair given by one of Cammi's friends tonight?"

"Not at all."

He resumed his usual genial tone, and with exaggerated gallantry helped her down from her desktop perch. "Don't let all this unpleasantness spoil the Carnival season for you. After all, we still must find you a husband, when all is said and done."

A husband.

The thought of marriage had been the last thing on her mind these past days. His assumption that she could put aside recent events, reminded her that, much as she loved him, her brother was no different from any other man. He saw her as nothing more than a giddy, woman-sized child, unable to take upon her shoulders any more responsibility than deciding what gown to wear.

Well, mon frère, *I intend to prove you wrong.*

He started for the doorway, and she followed, pausing when they reached the threshold. "I should send Cammi a note that I will be attending the cotillion, after all," she explained and started back toward the desk.

Mindful of Philippe's presence in the doorway, she pulled several sheets of writing paper and an envelope from one drawer, setting them on the desktop as she searched another for blotting paper. She gathered stationery and blotting paper into a neat stack. With a smile at her brother, she quit the library, with the pages gripped tightly to her chest.

When she reached the privacy of her room she extracted the torn pasteboard she had managed to conceal within the writing supplies. Determinedly, she pieced together both halves and then silently reread the final line of gilded words.

By Invitation Only.

Seventeen

"Don't bother waiting."

With those terse words to the hack driver, Tark climbed from the coach and stepped onto Chartres Street. He kept clear of that yellow light that spilled from the nearby streetlamp, waiting in the shadows until the man whipped up his team and clattered down the road. After the carriage had faded from sight he headed toward Ursulines Avenue.

The hollow ring of his boots on the *banquette* accompanied him as he strode the few short blocks toward the convent—or, rather, the archbishop's residence, he reminded himself. Midnight was near, and a winter wind had risen to greet it, drawing a veil of clouds across a half moon.

The rain had left oily puddles in the streets and a chill in the air. Tark drew his well-worn jacket against the cold, careful to avoid the glances of the opulently garbed people bound for one exclusive Carnival ball or another. Not that he feared being taken for one of them since he was dressed in dark, nondescript clothes. In fact, none spared him more than a cursory look.

A few minutes later, he stood at one corner of the thick, stucco-on-brick wall that embraced three sides of the property's perimeter. He continued down Chartres Street toward the porter's lodge that served as the main entry. There, a formidable wooden door barred his way. Tark gave it a tug and discovered that the entrance was locked. Undaunted, he continued down the *banquette* until he found a second wooden gate, also fastened from the inside.

So what did you expect—that the archbishop would wait up for you?

Tark spared a look around him. Satisfied that he was not being watched, he squinted through the ill-fitting planks of the gate to gain a better look at the grounds.

Facing him was the former convent building . . . now the archiepiscopal residence . . . an imposing, three-storied structure with its arched portico and white-stuccoed facade. To his left, and situated at right angles to the old convent building, was the austere St. Mary's church. To his right was the small bishop's service building, the rear wall of which faced Ursulines Street and formed a section of the estate's perimeter wall.

Those three main structures formed an open, lopsided "U" that occupied much of the property, which was cleaved by a section of wooden cross-fencing. On one side of that fence, a formal garden stretched from the portico to the lodge; on the other, within the shadow of the trees that shielded the service building, sat a pair of ramshackle outbuildings. If his assumptions were correct, one was the object of this night's expedition.

Tark found himself appalled by his former partner's use of the place to store contraband. On the other hand, as a former blockade runner, he had to admit that the set-up was ideal. Who would suspect Church officials

of complicity in such a scheme—not that the archbishop, himself, would be a participant in Franchot's
smuggling activities. No doubt the Frenchman had
found a less powerful victim, such as the nun whom
Tom had mentioned, to carry out his orders.

Reluctant to speculate on what threat Franchot had
used to gain the sister's cooperation, he studied the thick
wall before him. It stretched half again as high as he,
but represented only a nominal barrier for a man determined to scale it.

With a fluid leap, he caught hold of the wall's top
edge. He found that the smooth stucco finish had worn
away in sections to expose the brick beneath. That rough
surface bit into his wind-chapped hands even while it
afforded him ample purchase to scale the wall. He
hoisted himself atop its substantial width and looked
below. The splash of moonlight that illuminated the
courtyard showed it to be deserted. Carnival or not, the
archbishop and his retinue apparently kept regular hours.

So far, so good.

He grimaced at the banal words as he awaited the
rush of anticipation that, during his smuggling days, always had surged through his veins before each mission.
All he could summon tonight, however, was a grim
sense of purpose as chill as the night air.

He eased down the other side of the wall, dropping
to the soft ground below where a welcome blanket of
shadows unfurled. He crouched there, wrapped in darkness, and waited for an alarm to be raised.

When none sounded, he brushed away the grit from
his palms, then patted his jacket pocket. Reassured that
the few crucial supplies he carried had not been lost in

his climb, he made his way through the darkness. A brash wind chased after him, scattering leaves across the grounds.

By the time Tark crossed the short distance to the outbuildings, he had dismissed the nearest of the two as a possible repository for a shipment of any size. He chafed his hands along his upper arms to warm himself and considered the other building. Larger than the first, it faced the Ursulines Street wall and fell within the shadow of the service building, providing a greater measure of concealment. Still, anyone with a key could slip past the gate and, within the span of a few minutes, unload contraband into either shed. Convinced that both buildings bore investigation, he made his way to the first.

Its knob turned readily beneath his hand, though rusty hinges—no oddity in the damp climate of New Orleans—squealed a protest at his intrusion. He belatedly tried to muffle the sound by holding the door. Hell, he might as well have shouted his location, for all the care he had taken not to draw attention to himself. The problem was, he was getting too damn old for this kind of—

He froze as distant voices drifted to him. A blade of unease sliced down his spine, and he debated whether to confront the speakers or vanish. No doubt the door had alerted them to his presence, and even now they were combing the area for intruders.

Summoning an explanation was no problem. His role as shipper gave him authorization to inspect the cargo at will, unconventional as the hour was. But even so, word of his visit would certainly be conveyed to Franchot. He wasn't ready to tip his hand—not until he knew what lay behind the Frenchman's recruitment of him.

The voices drew steadily closer, punctuated now by female laugher and a man's echoing guffaw, and Tark released the breath he'd been holding. The sound came from the avenue beyond the wall. He waited until the voices faded, and he pushed past the shed's open door.

The room contained nothing more damning than garden tools, a pushcart, and a worktable. With a reflexive oath, he shut the door and turned to the second outbuilding.

The door was guarded by an oversized padlock, which Tark studied with a practiced eye. Because he'd had occasion to repossess a number of shipments, he'd become skilled at picking locks. This one would be easy.

He plucked from his pocket a curved length of stout wire and inserted it into the keyhole. With a few deft twists, the lock yielded, and this door swung silently inward at his touch.

Oiled hinges.

Tark managed a smile. Someone had taken pains to ensure access to the building, with a minimum of noise. If Franchot's shipment was indeed stored somewhere on the premises, this had to be the spot.

Moonlight streamed through the door long enough for him to glimpse stacks of wooden boxes. Once inside, he was left with only the trickle of illumination provided by one grime-covered window. One could barely separate dark shape from shadow. At least it was warmer inside than out, he thought, grateful that the closely fitted planks of the walls deflected the rising wind. He took a cautious step forward.

He tripped on a tangle of lumber, but caught himself before he hit the dirt floor, mentally cursing himself for drinking so much. The last thing he needed was to injure himself while prowling on archdiocese property.

A ludicrous vision flashed through his mind of black-robed priests discovering him the next morning, helplessly pinned beneath a jumble of crates. *Sorry, Fathers. Forgive me my trespasses.* He gave a derisive snort at this literal application of the Lord's Prayer, certain the archbishop would fail to appreciate the jest. He decided to risk a light.

He plucked forth a wooden match and candle stub, which he promptly lit. Now, he could make out numerous crates and barrels stacked head-high throughout the shed, leaving only a single aisle, that he could span simply by stretching his arms to either side. At his feet lay the broken packing case he had stumbled over.

Tark was tempted to kick the heap, but he snapped off a section for use as a makeshift candleholder. A glance around him revealed a pry bar within easy reach. Selecting a crate at random, he carefully forced its lid.

Bed linens and crockery.

Tark dug through the box, unable to believe what he saw. Only the farm implements were lacking to complete the bill of lading, which he had dismissed as fraudulent. Knowing Franchot, he concluded that the crate was a decoy. The real shipment, whatever it might be, must be elsewhere.

Working cautiously in the aisle's confines, he pried open half-a-dozen boxes. Each contained items almost laughably mundane—woolen blankets, packets of seed, new pairs of men's boots. By now, the air within the shed had grown oppressive, and his linen shirt clung to his damp torso. He stripped off his jacket and applied his bar to yet another crate, with similar results.

Could he have been wrong in thinking he'd been bribed to take part in smuggling? Or, worse, had he simply deluded himself all the way around, weaving from old grudges and unfounded suspicions this flimsy cloth of conspiracy? Perhaps he had experienced an unprecedented string of coincidences.

Then he shook his head. Everything fitted together too neatly—his failing business, the encounters with Isabeau, his dealings with her brother—each move without doubt choreographed by Franchot Calvé. Contraband was stored here, and he intended to find it.

Taking up his candle and pry bar, Tark moved down the aisle. Almost immediately, he spotted against the far wall a long, narrow crate reminiscent of certain cargo he had smuggled during the war.

Pay dirt, he thought as he forced up the top. The action revealed a row of tools. One by one, he removed them, finally exposing a false bottom a dozen inches below the top edge. He gently pried up the panel, then lifted the candle for a better look.

The flickering yellow light caught the dull gleam of rifle barrels—at least a score of them, Tark judged. He quickly applied his bar to a nearby crate. It too held a small arsenal. A closer survey of the stacks revealed almost two dozen similar boxes. Assuming each held twenty or so carbines, Franchot had accumulated weapons enough to outfit a small army.

But whose?

Tark took a rifle and pulled the bolt to see if the

chamber was empty. He snapped back the bolt and sighted down the barrel, then slowly set the hammer into place. This was no old-fashioned, single-shot piece he held, but a sleek Winchester repeater—fresh from the factory, judging by the sticky film that coated the exposed metal.

He lodged the weapon back in place and absently rubbed his greasy fingers against his trouser legs. In the flickering light, he could make out stenciled markings—sanded down, but not obliterated—that confirmed his suspicions as to the rifles' origin. Their previous destination, he couldn't guess. It had not been a military shipment, since repeating rifles were still rarely the army's weapon of choice.

It was barely conceivable that Franchot had purchased the rifles. Then his only crime would be attempting to smuggle them out of the country. But no matter how the Frenchman had come into possession, the question now was the identity of the buyer for whom the weapons had been diverted.

"Whose war are you supporting, Franchot?"

The candle guttered beside him. He realized that he'd been in the shed for a good quarter hour—ample time for someone to have noticed light in the window.

Tark tamped the wooden lids back into place and restacked the crates, then propped the pry bar where he had found it. He ground the candle into the dirt with his bootheel. He had left a few faint footprints on the hard-packed ground, but those were indistinguishable from the scuffs already there.

He snatched his jacket and made his way to the door, easing it open enough to see that the grounds remained empty. He locked the door, and stealthily made his way back to the wall.

From this angle, it appeared a formidable barrier. Whatever the reason, he scaled the wall less easily this time, losing his footing a time or two before he managed to hoist himself over the top. Eager now to be out of there, he slid down the other side, landing with a thump on the *banquette* below.

"And what the hell do ya think yer doin'?"

The voice boomed out behind him, and at the same instant a beefy hand clamped down on his shoulder. Tark registered the menace he heard in the voice.

In quick succession, he broke free of the man's grasp and spun about; then, noting that the newcomer brandished a cudgel, he reached for his pistol. Prepared to draw the weapon, he assumed an aggressive stance and countered, "It's none of your goddamn business what I—"

He broke off in midsentence as the man moved from the shadows, and Tark realized who he was confronting. With a shake of his head, he relaxed his grip on the pistol, admitting, "Sweet Jesus, Tom, but you scared the hell out of me."

"Serves ya right," Tom Sullivan exclaimed with a flash of his familiar gap-toothed grin. "I thought sure I'd caught me some no-account river rat bent on thievin' from the archbishop."

Tark managed a grin in return and displayed empty palms. "Sorry to disappoint you. You'll have to settle for trespassing, instead."

"Trespassing, is it?" Tom's shrewd gaze never wavered as he tucked the cudgel into his belt and gestured

Tark to follow him. "And here I woulda guessed you was just takin' the night air. I don't suppose this has somethin' to do with our conversation earlier tonight, now does it?"

"It does," Tark acknowledged as he fell in step. Once they were away from the grounds, he continued, "Remember how you said that Franchot Calvé had a hand in several questionable ventures, but nothing that wasn't this side of legitimate?"

The night patroller shook his head in disgust. "He's a slick 'un, all right. I can't think of nothin' I'd like better'n to nail his fancy French hide to the wall."

"Well, Tom, you might just get your chance." Tark halted, turned to the older man, and asked with triumph in his voice, "What do you know about a stolen shipment of carbines?"

Franchot Calvé pulled open the French doors and stepped onto the gallery overlooking the entry of Ophelia's elegant bordello. He stood there, silhouetted against the pale yellow light from the room behind him, and surveyed the street below.

Shouts and laughter drifted up from the steady stream of passers-by trooping along the *banquette,* intent on an evening's revelry. From the ballroom on the floor below, an orchestra's sound was echoed by music from the bordellos that stretched all along Basin Street. Without a doubt, Carnival season was drawing toward its peak.

Calvé allowed himself a cold smile. In general, he had little liking for vulgar, mindless displays, such as *Mardi gras.* While revelers cavorted with no thought beyond the next moment's pleasure, he was ensuring his place in history.

In a gesture long since become habit, he reached into his waistcoat pocket and pulled forth a small object. He studied it in the palm of his hand. Crude, he determined, little more than a few broad strokes carved into a bit of ivory. Its value to him, however, lay not in its material or workmanship, but in what it represented.

A pawn is the least valuable soldier in a chess player's army, virtually powerless against any other piece, and routinely sacrificed in the playing of the game.

Calvé closed his fingers around the piece of ivory, remembering his father's words, spoken almost a quarter of a century earlier—spoken as Michel Calvé had handed him a carved piece little different from the one he now held. *Remember, my son, that most men in this world are content to be pawns. You must be the chess player.*

He had carried that piece as a token for the next three years, until Sevastopol. There, amid the fighting, he lost it along with things he valued most . . . including his father. Still, he clung to Michel's philosophy, even after his capture and imprisonment by the Russians.

A few weeks later, after the fall of Sevastopol, he had replaced that pawn with another removed from the Paris drawing room of one Claude Lavoisier—a recently returned diplomat and the one man who . . . had he so chosen . . . could have put a halt to Michel's execution. Claude had voiced no protest over the theft, strangled as he had been with his dressing-gown sash.

"Franchot, I must attend my guests. Let us be finished with this discussion."

Drifting to him from the private parlor behind him, Ophelia's voice was petulant, not sultry. Calvé glanced at the chess piece in his hand. This was a recent acquisition, and resembled the pawn he had carried from Claude Lavoisier's home almost seventeen years earlier. An appropriate irony, he decided with another cold smile, since he had removed this piece from a set belonging to that same man's grandson.

Tucking away the chess piece and, at the same time, putting aside that particular matter, Calvé turned to the quadroon. "Very well, *ma chère,*" he replied. "Tell me what displeases you about your role in this affair."

Ophelia halted before the pastry-laden table near the red velvet settee and chose a tiny, pink-iced cake from the plate. Her fingernails gleamed like blood against the pale confection as she lifted it to her painted lips and took a slow bite.

"You promised me the brat," she replied, licking the white crumbs from her fingertips and then slanting him a look of feline discontent. "Now, you say I must return her to you. My people demand proof of my power, Franchot. As their queen, I must—"

"There are other babes to be had." He bluntly dismissed her complaint. "A woman of your . . . connections . . . can surely procure another infant without problem."

"But I want this one!"

She gave a toss of her head and stalked about the room. The train of her white silk gown swished behind her like the tail of a frustrated cat. Calvé studied his

mistress with the same detached interest a collector
might take in an exquisite work of art.

Of the many women he had known, Ophelia was the
only one ever to have held any claim on his emotions.
She lacked the passivity cultivated by other quadroon
women whose livelihoods depended on the largess of
their white male benefactors. She exuded a queenly arrogance that veiled her contempt for the way of life that
her beauty and skin color had forced her to accept.

When he had first encountered her, defiantly offering
herself for sale on a crowded street corner, she had been
little more than a girl—though never had she been
young. Indeed, he had glimpsed in her green eyes a
timeless wisdom that spoke of knowledge better left
alone.

With disdain, she had shunned his offer to become
his mistress, swearing she would never be dependent
upon any white man. Her response had intrigued him.
Newly arrived from France as he had been, he still knew
that women of color in New Orleans traditionally sought
such arrangements. Instead, she and he became partners
of a sort—he, as the owner of a small brothel near the
waterfront, and she, charged with its running.

That partnership had proved profitable to them both.
Within a short time, Ophelia parlayed her percentage of
the earnings into this establishment, which catered to
those wealthy men and women in search of discreet sexual diversion. He indulged his own dark passions there,
with anonymous girls plucked from the waterfront
streets . . . and quietly disposed of in some trash-filled
back alley, once he had taken his pleasure with them.

Ophelia's involvement in the world of voodoo indirectly served him, as well. Her clandestine connection to many of the city's more prominent citizens provided him with blackmail victims, along with a source for information not readily available through other channels. Her own growing power among the people of color did not concern him. What did, was her defiance these past months.

Calvé surveyed the woman before him. Ophelia's flashes of rebellion were becoming more frequent. He found himself forced to weigh her usefulness against the liability inherent in her growing lack of respect. Should the scales tip against her, he would find himself with no choice but to decide her fate.

"The babe will be returned to its family," he now told her, curious to see whether or not she would defy him.

She halted, and he could see the rage banked behind her slanted green eyes. "As you wish, Franchot. And now, I must return to my guests."

The unmistakable contempt he heard in her words sparked his own anger. With a swift move, he gripped her wrist, noting with satisfaction her fleeting grimace of pain before she swiftly schooled her features into an expression of unconcern. With the same quick move, he clamped his free hand about her throat so his fingers spanned the silken contours of her slender neck.

"One last thing, *ma chère*. Just remember who you were . . . and who made you what you now are," he softly said, his fingers biting into her flesh. "I am life to you, my beautiful Ophelia . . . and I can as easily be your death."

When she gave a sullen nod, he eased his grip on

her throat and lightly stroked the bruised flesh. "Do not worry, *ma chère*. I will find another way to reward you for your loyalty."

"Yes, Franchot," she murmured, veiling her eyes with her heavy lashes as she pressed her sleek form against his.

At her touch, he found himself consumed by the familiar surge of sexual arousal that always followed his moments of anger. Not bothering with any preliminaries, he took her with the same sort of savagery he reserved for those nameless young women whose terrified screams compounded his enjoyment.

Ophelia, however, welcomed his brutal caresses with sharp cries of pleasure, matching his violence with her own. Afterwards, as they lay spent upon the blood-red settee, Calvé felt his doubts slip away. Clever, Ophelia might be, he told himself, but hardly a match for him.

She was, after all, only a woman.

Eighteen

Almost before Isabeau's hand left the brass knocker, the door of 12 Rue de Fleur opened. This time, not the housekeeper, but a stern-faced Negro whose girth nearly matched his immense height, stepped forward. Dressed in expensive red-and-gold livery that barely contained his bulk, he scrutinized her with the disdainful silence of a professional servant.

Isabeau held her ground and stared back, grateful for the beaded white domino that concealed much of her face. She plucked forth her gilded invitation—carefully restored with a bit of paste—and waited while the surly doorman studied it. Finally, he stepped aside and arranged his dark features into what she presumed was meant to be a hospitable smile, saying, "Welcome to Madame Ophelia's House of Discreet Entertainment, where your every pleasure is satisfied."

This speech was delivered in a bored monotone. Isabeau decided as she stepped into the foyer that the man had been hired for his musculature, rather than for his personality. With the first of the evening's hurdles now passed, she glanced around her in guilty interest.

The brothel's interior proved no less grand than its facade. In the foyer, she counted half-a-dozen gleaming

crystal and gold fixtures mounted on the walls, and cas-
cading from the ceiling. As she made her way into the
main hall, black marble stretched beneath her slippers
like a frozen winter's stream—spanned at intervals with
costly Oriental rugs. Only the scarlet damask and velvet
in the furnishings hinted that this was no ordinary establishment.

While she surveyed her surroundings, another immense liveried Negro stepped forward to take her cape.
Isabeau relinquished it with some misgivings, on account of her costume. But for the anonymity her mask
provided, she would never have dared wear it in public.

The outfit was an impulsive creation, fashioned when
it occurred to her that she risked discovery by appearing
in a costume she had worn to a previous function. Then
she glimpsed her chemise-clad figure in her dressing-
table mirror, and inspiration had seized her. Recalling
the statue of the huntress, Diana, that had graced Madame Dumas's courtyard—*Mon Dieu,* would she ever
forget it!—she plied her needle with a skill the Ursuline
nuns would have praised, even as they would have been
shocked by her purpose.

She created from her shift a Roman tunic and transformed a length of bed linen into a toga. Her hair, she
tied into a cascade of ringlets adorned with ribbons,
topped with a crescent-shaped brooch to represent the
moon. Lacking a bow, she settled for a javelin . . . in
reality, a square-edged, wrought-iron arrow salvaged from
a discarded section of fence behind her home's old slave
quarters.

The overall effect had proved satisfyingly classical
and—in her eyes—more than a little scandalous. It was

not so much the way the gown's sheer fabric clung to
her slim curves. Rather, it was the feeling of freedom
that the costume offered. Now Isabeau glanced in the
foyer's oversized, gilt-framed mirror and smiled. Un-
hampered by yards of petticoats and stays biting into
her flesh, she felt light enough to drift through the hall,
rather than tread the marble.

Conscious of other newcomers behind her, she put
aside such thoughts and started for the music and lights
of the ballroom. At its threshold, she halted and steeled
herself against any depravity she might encounter beyond those double doors. After all, everyone *knew* what
went on in brothels . . .

The sight that greeted her was, upon first glance,
blessedly mundane. A score of costumed couples whirled
about the floor to the strains of a small orchestra. Other
guests clustered about the perimeter of the room. Laughter and champagne flowed freely. In fact, the revelry was
little removed from that of those respectable cotillions
she had attended over the past weeks.

As she scanned the room, however, she noted shocking differences. The majority of the guests were male,
and most were intoxicated. They indulged in licentious
behavior, staggering about the ballroom in various states
of undress and boldly fondling their female companions.

The women were behaving in a wanton manner no
Creole hostess would tolerate. Their bright-hued costumes revealed as much as they concealed. Several
women were sporting skin-tight gowns with side seams
slit almost to their thighs. Alongside such creations, her
own costume appeared nothing short of demure.

On the dance floor many couples were entwined in

embraces so intimate that Isabeau blushed beneath her mask. One man had tugged down the bodice of his partner's gown to suckle her bared breasts, while another couple retreated behind a gilded screen apparently provided for such contingencies. So caught up was she in the spectacle, that she forgot the guests who had followed after her.

"Let's dance, my lovely lady," proposed a slurred voice behind her, reminding her that she was not alone. Startled, Isabeau swung about to face a man of average height who sported a harlequin costume and swayed slightly.

"I think not, *m'sieur*," she retorted and planted the javelin before her. The man eyed that makeshift weapon as if debating whether or not he risked impalement by pressing his suit. Finally, he thought the better of his demand.

"Damn cold bitch. There's plenty others more than willing," he muttered and turned, only to stumble over the plump Spanish grandee behind him. Both men made ineffectual grabs at nonexistent supports before collapsing in a multicolored heap before the appreciative guests who milled about the hallway.

Carrying a javelin has its advantages, Isabeau decided as she turned to the ballroom. By now, optimism had begun to replace her foreboding. Appalled as she was at the goings-on here, she was less uneasy than she had feared. Ophelia's clientele were obviously wealthy and accustomed to genteel surroundings, confining themselves to refined debauchery. Nonetheless, she could not contain the nagging worry that one guest or another might recognize her for an interloper and raise an alarm.

Isabeau bit her lip, still uncertain of the ultimate wisdom of her plan. Perhaps she should leave now, before her charade was found out . . .

But Regine is depending on you, she reminded herself. Besides, no one had cause to question her presence there, nor could anyone recognize her unless she removed her mask. All she needed to do was blend in with the other guests, which meant she must start behaving like one of them. With that in mind, she accepted a glass of champagne from a passing servant.

Although she had not supped that night, she finished off the sparkling wine in one long swallow—not that her intention was to become as inebriated as those around her! Philippe, she recalled, often referred to alcohol as liquid courage. She might need a measure of bravery before the night was over.

Barely had she lowered the glass from her lips than another footman replenished it with more of the bubbling, straw-colored liquid. She downed that with equal haste; it was not as if she were not used to an occasional glass of wine.

The champagne took effect more swiftly than she had expected, leaving her light-headed. That feeling eased into a pleasant numbness that bolstered her confidence, just as she had hoped. What was there to worry about, after all? Why, she would simply search the place, find Regine, and then flee with the child before anyone was the wiser.

Absently setting aside her empty glass, she studied the guests more closely. Her gaze lit on a red-enameled door across the room from her, through which a constant stream of party-goers passed. There, she would begin her search.

She tightened her grip on the javelin—*Mon Dieu,* surely it was not the champagne that suddenly had disrupted her equilibrium!—and made her unsteady way through the crowd. A moment later, she found herself ushered into a lushly carpeted salon. Crimson-globed fixtures mounted along all four walls filled the room with an unearthly pink glow and revealed tables arranged for faro, roulette, and keno. Gamblers flashing staggering sums of cash vied for position along the felt-topped tables, while those with pockets less deep clustered around the broad mahogany bar that stretched the length of the room. The few women did not play, but draped themselves in decorative disarray across chairs upholstered in red velvet.

Hardly a likely hiding place for a child, Isabeau told herself. No, she would have to find a quieter section of the brothel . . . a room far removed from the customers.

She made her way back through the ballroom, ending up in the main hall. The number of guests seemed to have doubled since her arrival, so that the corridor now teemed with masked revelers. Many were headed toward the far end of the hall, where a graceful curving staircase led upward. No doubt the second floor was where the establishment's "discreet entertainment" was conducted.

Javelin firmly in hand, she moved toward the staircase, striving to maintain a casual air. Though the upper story seemed a more logical place to hide the babe, the thought of searching those rooms brought another blush to her cheek. Still, she mounted the first step, when another liveried servant moved to block her way.

"Paying customers only, lady."

Red-haired and doughy-faced, this man lacked the height of his fellow doormen, but rivaled them for girth. Unlike the hapless harlequin, he appeared undaunted by her javelin. Still, with a jerk of his thumb, he added, "There's a room across the hall, where you can watch for free."

"Merci, m'sieur," she faintly replied, unsure just what he meant but anxious to draw no further attention to herself with questions. *Sainte Cécile,* but this was proving far more difficult than she had anticipated. At least she had not encountered the procuress, Ophelia. She doubted she could face the woman with equanimity.

The anteroom to which the man had directed her was opposite the ballroom and had attracted its share of the guests. Like the gambling salon, this room was carpeted and dimly lit, with low-slung couches lining its walls. Its focal point, however, was an immense, gilt-framed mirror that spanned almost the entire far wall.

No, not a mirror.

She bit back a stunned gasp, barely able to credit the sight before her. Rather than reflecting the room and its occupants, the glass instead offered a view of the lit cell behind it. There, a plump, black-haired woman of middling years and a rail-thin, blond man likely half her age knelt naked together atop a silk-draped bed. Seemingly oblivious to their audience, the woman broke free of the embrace and lolled back against the pillows, spreading plump thighs wide to reveal a thatch of dark hair. The man buried his face between her legs, and his

Wish You Were Here?

You can be, every month, with Zebra Historical Romance Novels.

AND TO GET YOU STARTED, ALLOW US TO SEND YOU

4 Historical Romances Free

AN $18.00 VALUE!

With absolutely no obligation to buy anything.

YOU ARE CORDIALLY INVITED TO GE SWEPT AWAY INTO NEW WORLDS OF PASSION AND ADVENTURE.

AND IT WON'T COST YOU A PENNY!

Receive 4 Zebra Historical Romances, Absolutely Free!

(An $18.00 value)

Now you can have your pick of handsome, noble adventurers with romance in their hearts and you on their minds. Zebra publishes Historical Romances That Burn With The Fire Of History by the world's finest romance authors.

This very special FREE offer entitles you to 4 Zebra novels at absolutely no cost, with no obligation to buy anything, ever. It's an offer designed to excite your most vivid dreams and desires...and save you $18!

And that's not all you get...

Your Home Subscription Saves You Money Every Month.

After you've enjoyed your initial FREE package of 4 books, you'll begin receive monthly shipments of new Zebra titles. These novels are delivered direct to your home as soon as they are published...sometimes even before the bookstores get them! Each monthly shipment of 4 books will be yours to examine for 10 days. Then if you decide to keep the books, you'll pay the pre ferred subscriber's price of just $3.75 per title. That's $15 for all 4 books...a savings of $3 off the publisher's price! (A nominal shipping and handling charge of $1.50 per shipment will be added.)

There Is No Minimum Purchase. And Your Continued Satisfaction Is Guaranteed

We're so sure that you'll appreciate the money-saving convenience of home delivery that we guarantee your complete satisfaction. You may return any shipment...for any reason...within 10 days and pay nothing that month. And if you want us to stop sending books, just say the word. There is no mini mum number of books you must buy.

It's a no-lose proposition, so send for your 4 FREE books today!

YOU'RE GOING TO LOVE GETTING

4 FREE BOOKS

These books worth $18, are yours without cost or obligation when you fill out and mail this certificate.
(If the certificate is missing below, write to: Zebra Home Subscription Service, Inc., 120 Brighton Road, P.O. Box 5214, Clifton, New Jersey 07015-5214

Complete and mail this card to receive 4 Free books!

Yes! Please send me 4 Zebra Historical Romances without cost or obligation. I understand that each month thereafter I will be able to preview 4 new Zebra Historical Romances FREE for 10 days. Then, if I should decide to keep them, I will pay the money-saving preferred publisher's price of just $3.75 each...a total of $15. That's $3 less than the publisher's price. (A nominal shipping and handling charge of $1.50 per shipment will be added.) I may return any shipment within 10 days and owe nothing, and I may cancel this subscription at any time. The 4 FREE books will be mine to keep in any case.

Name _____

Address _____ Apt. _____

City _____ State _____ Zip _____

Telephone ( ) _____

Signature _____
(If under 18, parent or guardian must sign.)

LP1294

Terms, offer and prices subject to change without notice. Subscription subject to acceptance by Zebra Books. Zebra Books reserves the right to reject any order or cancel any subscription.

TREAT YOURSELF TO 4 FREE BOOKS.

An $18 value.
FREE!

No obligation
to buy
anything, ever.

ZEBRA HOME SUBSCRIPTION SERVICE, INC.

120 BRIGHTON ROAD

P.O. BOX 5214

CLIFTON, NEW JERSEY 07015-5214

AFFIX
STAMP
HERE

blond head bobbed as he performed some unseen action—apparently a painful one, Isabeau judged, since his partner writhed about the bed with her kohled eyes shut and her painted lips twisted in a grimace of silent agony.

She dragged her mortified gaze from the pair and looked around her. Several of the guests ignored the display, casually drinking champagne and chatting. Others, however, viewed the coupling as fine sport, indulging in ribald jests and coarse laughter as the blond young man finally mounted his partner and began a frenzied thrusting. Isabeau found herself among those who simply beheld in silence this drama of the flesh that had nothing to do with love.

"Do you prefer to watch, my sweet Isabeau," came the soft words behind her, "or shall we take our own turn behind the window?"

Foreboding followed disbelief as Isabeau struggled to maintain her composure. Muffled though it was by his mask, the voice was unmistakably that of Tark Parrish—but whatever was the *américain* doing here? She tightened her fingers around her wrought-iron arrow, wishing all at once that she had not dulled her senses with champagne. Every instinct shouted for her to run, but logic demanded she try to bluff her way through the situation. Indeed, how could he be certain of her identity?

She remained facing the window, lest she confirm his guess with a betraying glimpse of her eyes or lips. "You are mistaken yourself, sir," she replied, assuming a harsh accent unlike her usual silvery tones. "I do not know you—nor do I care to make your acquaintance."

"Then perhaps I can change your mind."

Tark reached around her waist and gripped her makeshift javelin with either hand, pinning her to his chest. One squared edge of the iron pole bit into the tender flesh just below her breasts in a sensation that—so long as she kept her breathing shallow—stopped just short of being painful.

"Don't bother screaming," he warned as she drew gasped in outrage. "No one here gives a damn if you're willing or not, and plenty of them would be glad to join in our fun."

And she would call unwelcome attention to herself. Isabeau struggled for calm, reminding herself that she couldn't afford to attract the others guests' notice lest someone wonder why she was there.

"Let me go, M'sieur Parrish," she demanded in a low tone. "You may believe that no one would come to my aid, but I do not."

"Shall we put it to a test, then? Scream away if you choose, my virgin goddess—but I think you'll find the results little worth the effort."

She didn't need to see his face to know that his ice blue eyes gleamed with challenge. Another look at the guests convinced her that he spoke the truth. Several of the merrymakers, apparently bored by the spectacle, already had filtered from the room. The remaining guests were intent on the action behind the window.

Reluctantly conceding that the *américain* indeed had her at his mercy, she breathed an unladylike oath that drew a harsh sound of amusement from him.

"I see we've come to terms, then," he observed, and lessened the pressure on the bar so that its cold surface just grazed her slim form. "Permit me to compliment you on your choice of costume—though it's a pity I seem to be the only one here who understands your little joke. But then, mythology has always been one of my passions."

He gave that final word a twist, and Isabeau's cheeks flamed at the allusion to that night in Madame's courtyard. "Your passions do not interest me, *m'sieur*," she managed. "As for my costume, I hardly chose it for your amusement."

"Nonetheless, I find myself entertained," he murmured and shifted the bar so its sharp edge pressed more firmly against her. "Now, what is your pleasure, *mademoiselle*—watching, or participating?"

Had her arms not been pinned to her sides, she would have clapped her palms to her ears to block out his tempting words. *Sainte Cécile,* the champagne had muddled her reason and filled her with wanton yearnings.

"You flatter yourself, *m'sieur*," she replied with as much spirit as she could muster, though indeed her protest sounded weak even to her own ears. "You are overbearing, crude, and distinctly unappealing—and I have no interest in you, whatsoever."

"But that's not the impression you gave the other night," he replied, his words a whisper in her ear. "You wanted me just as much as I wanted you."

"T-That is absurd."

Her denial trembled. She was all too aware of the intimate way he held her, every ridge of his muscular form searing her flesh through her costume. Equally unsettling was the weakness in her knees so that any attempt at flight was impossible.

"Leave me alone, *m'sieur*," she added when he made

no response. "You can find any number of willing women here, without forcing yourself on me."

"I don't intend to use force."

His words were a threat—and a promise. She made one final attempt at protest. "But I have never—"

The soft thud of her javelin as it hit the floor cut short her words, even as the sound spurred her to action. She pulled from his grasp and spun about, then caught back a cry. Once, she recalled, she had dubbed the man a demon of sorts. Tonight, he appeared the personification of Lucifer.

A superstitious thrill shot though her as Isabeau studied him. He wore elegant black evening clothes relieved by the white splash of his silk shirtfront. His face, however, was not that of a mortal man, but that of an incubus—unrecognizable . . . and undeniably dangerous.

A second, closer look stilled the frantic beating of her heart. It was a mask, unlike any she had ever seen. It was crafted of fine leather—shiny and black, as if it had been stripped from the devil's own hide—and carefully molded to the planes of his face. With almost invisible slits at its mouth and nostrils, the mask concealed him from forehead to chin. Behind the slanted cutouts lay a shadowed, unwavering gaze.

Abandoning his mocking air now for the softly dangerous tone she knew so well, he told her, "We have business to discuss, you and I . . . and since privacy is essential, I suggest we adjourn upstairs."

"But I cannot go up there with you," she gasped, and took a step back.

Tark caught her wrist. "I'll give you a choice. You can accompany me upstairs to one of the rooms so we can talk, or you can make your ascent slung over my shoulder. The decision is yours."

"You would not dare—"

"I would."

The finality of those two words convinced her that he would carry out such a threat. Indeed, she guessed that the *américain* might prefer the latter alternative— though that was one pleasure she intended to deny him. But by agreeing to this mysterious discussion, she would gain access to the brothel's hitherto forbidden upper floor. Perhaps the risk was worth it.

But is it he that you do not trust . . . or yourself? a voice within her spoke up. She took a deep breath and met Tark's gaze. "Very well, I will accompany you."

In a gesture that could have been either gallant or mocking, he inclined his head and wordlessly gestured her to join him. Isabeau squared her slim shoulders and complied, though the effort it took to set one foot before the other required all her concentration. When she reached the stairs she halted before the same red-haired man who had sent her on her way minutes before. This time, he barely spared her a glance as he turned his attention to Tark and repeated, "Paying customers only."

Tark reached into his jacket pocket and plucked forth a brass token. Seeing it, the man nodded and moved aside. After they were on the landing above, Isabeau stared about her with unbridled curiosity as they began to move down the dimly lit hall.

A series of red doors lined either side of the carpeted corridor, each entry sporting a tiny brass hook and marked with a gilded numeral. Tark halted beside number 10, where a simpering brass Cupid dangled from the hook. Snatching that figure from its mounting—no doubt the Cupid's presence indicated an unoccupied room—he threw open the door.

"Wait here."

With that command, he left her and plunged into the darkness. A moment later, the doubtful comfort of a gaslamp's glow spread through the shadows, and she took a step forward. Even as she stared in amazement, Tark closed the door behind her.

"Welcome to every virgin's nightmare," he said and shot home the bolt.

Nineteen

What she had expected to encounter within that room, Isabeau could not say . . . but the actuality surpassed her wildest imaginings! She removed her mask with trembling fingers, conscious of her blush as she gazed in silence. *Sainte Cécile,* had she mistakenly entered some earthbound antechamber of hell?

The gaslamp provided minimal light, so that shadows clung to the room's sleek black walls, lending it an air of sullen wickedness. Hanging from a convenient rack were what she assumed to be tools of debauchery—riding crops, fetters, and leather harnesses. Black silk bedding draped a narrow four-poster, from each corner of which dangled a heavy gold cord with a loop tied at its end. At the sight, she caught back a gasp. Surely those gleaming ropes were not meant for tying someone spread-eagle across the counterpane!

Her gaze went to the black enamel table beside the bed. Its surface was covered with leather and metal devices neatly laid out like instruments in a surgeon's dispensary. She saw that some were designed to be strapped on, while others were apparently meant to be wielded at the participants' discretion.

A host of possibilities flashed through her mind and

sent her head reeling, much as the champagne had done.
But while she struggled to maintain an outer calm, Tark
made his way to the table. Glancing over its varied of-
ferings, he selected what appeared to be an oddly-
curved, three-tined fork. Brandishing the tool, he turned
to Isabeau and asked, "Would you care for a demon-
stration?"

"Y-you must be quite mad, *m'sieur,*" she choked out
and clutched the mask to her breast in a protective gesture.

A bit squeamish for your role, aren't you, my sweet?
With that thought, Tark set aside the probe and allowed himself a grim smile. No doubt Franchot had neglected to warn her that acting the wanton might require
a stint in the brothel's infamous "Marquis de Sade
Room." To her credit, she had yet to shriek or swoon,
as any other gently reared Creole *mademoiselle* would
have felt obliged to do in her place. Still, the color in
her face proved a barometer of her thoughts. His own
were concealed behind the mask, for which he was
thankful. Otherwise, she might read in his features the
uncertainty that had gripped him.

From the first, he had thought her no innocent, a con-
viction that had been strengthened by her responses to
his every overture. Now he wondered if he could have
been mistaken about her experience—and her motives.

The question nagged at him as he tried to reconcile
the reality of the girl before him with the image of the
brazen temptress. Though she held her head high, he
could see the fright that touched her dark velvet eyes,
reminding him how young she was. In her virginal white
costume that consisted of little more than a shift and a

length of linen, she appeared vulnerable . . . a dove among wolves. It seemed ludicrous to believe she was a distraction sent by Franchot to hold him at bay. Still, how could he explain her presence here tonight?

Tark bit back a curse and plucked off his mask, carelessly tossing it onto the table. One lesson he had managed to cull from his past mistakes was that a deceitful heart often lurked behind the most innocent face. He'd be damned if he would be fooled again.

"Let's dispense with the niceties, *mademoiselle*. I want to know what kind of game your brother and Franchot Calvé are playing with me."

She met his words with a defiant gaze, though he was gratified to see her step back. "I told you the other night that I know nothing of my brother's business affairs. As for M'sieur Calvé—"

"—you merely borrowed his box for a pleasant evening at the opera," he finished with sarcasm. "I'm afraid you'll have to do better than that, my sweet. You see, I paid an unannounced visit to the old Ursuline convent tonight to take a look at that so-called cargo I've been paid to ship—and it's damn sure not just linens and crockery."

She brushed aside that bit of intelligence. "Then you know more about the situation than I, M'sieur Parr—"

"You lying little bitch."

Blinded by a flash of anger, he strode across the room and grasped her chin with one hand. "When I spied you and Franchot together on the docks a few nights ago, I got the impression that the two of you were quite good friends—so don't bother playing innocent with me. I want to know what the hell is going on here."

Tark swept her up in his arms and carried her to the bed, dumping her unceremoniously onto the black satin coverlet. He promptly looped one of the gold cords about her wrist. Then, at the cost of a battered jaw as she flailed wildly against his attack, he pinned her beneath him while he secured her other wrist and both ankles with the remaining ropes.

Her struggles then ceased, though whether from exhaustion or fear, he was not sure. He lay a moment longer across her stiff form, trying to catch his breath while fighting a surge of arousal.

Entangled as they were, like lovers lying spent after a bout of frenzied coupling, he was all too aware of the fact that her soft curves were not encumbered by the usual stiff corsets and yards of petticoats. Her toga lay tangled at the foot of the bed, while her white satin slippers had been lost in the struggle. A moment's work would divest her of that makeshift tunic she wore so that he could—

With a curse, he got to his feet, ignoring the tightening of his loins as he snatched a riding crop and turned again to look down on her. "Now, *mademoiselle,* let's begin again," he harshly demanded from his vantage point beside the bed. "Tell me what you know about Franchot's plot."

At sight of the whip, Isabeau could manage only a frightened croak in reply. *Mon Dieu,* was this what he had meant by "talking?" She gave a futile tug at her ropes and tried to stem the panic that threatened to overwhelm her. Tied with arms and legs scandalously widespread, so that her skirts rode up almost to her thighs and her breasts strained against her sheer gown, she was totally helpless . . . and completely at the mercy of this barbaric *américain.*

Even as she hesitated to answer, he flicked the crop against his palm in a gesture that sent a shiver of trepidation through her. She swallowed against the sudden constriction in her throat. How he knew of Monsieur Calvé's agreement with Philippe, she could only guess. What mattered was that he not learn of her connection with the Frenchman. The safety of Lili's baby depended upon it.

She wet her lips with her tongue and attempted a reply. "I-I know nothing about any plot," she whispered the lie. "I am acquainted with M-monsieur Calvé, it is true, but only because he is my Oncle Henri's friend."

"And did your uncle approve that midnight meeting on the docks with his . . . friend?"

"I-I had disobeyed my *oncle,* and Monsieur Calvé came after me at his request." That was true enough, she told herself as she awaited his response.

Maybe she isn't lying.

At that possibility, Tark was swept by a wave of self-disgust made all the more profound because he found himself aroused by the sight of her lying bound and helpless before him. Sweet Jesus, had he really sunk so low as to abduct and terrify a young woman . . . to satisfy unfounded suspicions? He knew the pleasure that Franchot had taken in manipulating people around him, like pieces on a chessboard. Maybe she was what she appeared to be—a marriage-minded *mademoiselle* intent on luring a seemingly wealthy man to the altar.

You fool, she's only trying to save herself, the cynical voice inside him countered. Once before, he had been ready to accept a woman's honeyed words of explanation, and he had paid dearly for that folly. Never would he make the mistake he had made with Delphine. This time, *he* would call the shots.

"Sorry, my sweet, but I'm not buying your story," he drawled, and was rewarded by the flash of fear in her dark eyes.

His gaze moved deliberately down her body, taking in the slim curves brought into sharp relief by the glow of the lamp mounted above the headboard. Her struggles had hiked up her skirt and loose, lace-trimmed pantalets, affording him an unhindered view of her trim legs and a tantalizing glimpse of what lay beyond. On impulse, he trailed the tasseled tip of the riding crop along the pale inner flesh above her knee.

"I'll give you one more chance," he went on, allowing himself a grim smile as she made a futile attempt to draw back from his reach. "Tell me what you know about Franchot's plan to smuggle rifles to Sevastapol."

"Leave me be, *m'sieur*," she softly cried, then bit her lip as he applied his whip with the same languorous stroke to her other leg.

Tark shook his head in mock reproach. "You try my patience, *mademoiselle*. Don't force me to take more extreme measures to make you talk."

"But I-I know nothing—"

She broke off with a cry as he flicked the crop against the sensitive flesh just hard enough to leave a faint red mark. "Wrong answer, my sweet," he softly remonstrated her. "Now, what shall it be, truth or lie? Pain . . . or pleasure?"

Spurred on, he let the whip skim the silken folds of

her chemise, halting just above her waist. After a heart-beat's pause, he used the crop to circle first one pert breast, and then the other. Each nipple hardened into a tempting bud that strained against the fabric of her bodice.

Tark allowed himself a smile at the sight. Unwitting victim as he had been of her passionate embraces during their encounters, he would enjoy giving her a taste of her own medicine. Let *her* find out what it was like to be driven to the brink of climax, only to be left unsatisfied. By the time he finished with her, she'd be begging for relief . . . and gladly telling him everything she knew about Franchot Calvé.

As the leather tassel continued its fingerlike strokes along her breasts, Isabeau strained against her bonds. She would not give this barbarian the satisfaction of crying out, she vowed. Still, it took all her effort not to plead for mercy when he yanked the hem of her gown over her waist.

She felt a hot rush of blood to her face as embarrassment won out over fear. Save for her pantalets, she was bared from the waist down, with the most intimate secrets of her body exposed to this barbarian's gaze. Had she been able to swoon at will, she would have done so this moment.

"Pain or pleasure, my sweet," she heard him whisper. "You gave me no answer, so I fear it's up to me to make that choice for you. And luckily for you, my choice is . . . pleasure."

He drew out that last word in cold satisfaction. She could not suppress a cry of fright. No one save Tark even knew she was here tonight, she realized in despair. He could do as he pleased with her. If she had listened to Philippe, she would be safe at home now, instead of at the *américain's* mercy.

As wanton images of the couple in the viewing room flashed through her mind, she felt the frayed edge of the riding crop explore her body. She shut her eyes, but that failed to stem the unfamiliar sensations that had nothing to do with fear.

He had promised her pleasure but, *Mon Dieu,* he was inflicting exquisite agony, instead! Her skin was on fire, reacting to every stroke of the crop. She could feel the leather tassel trail with tantalizing slowness along one bare leg, then the other, giving her a shiver of pleasure. Mortified by her body's response and aware of Tark's gaze, she tried desperately to clamp her thighs together. The cords forced her to remain spread upon the black satin coverlet in this wanton pose.

Had he stopped there, she might have retained a measure of control over her traitorous body. Instead, he moved the whip past her knees, halting when he reached the silken tangle of pantalets bunched around her thighs. Her eyes flew open, and she caught a frightened breath, dreading his next move. *Surely he could not intend to—*

He deftly slid the crop across the narrow section of sheer silk stretched taut across the delicate folds of skin that lay at the apex of her thighs. She cried out then—a soft, desperate sound that was lost in Tark's harsh laugh.

"Have you reconsidered your answer, my sweet?" he asked, continuing to move the whip in languid circles along that sensitive ridge of flesh. "Just say the word, and I'll stop."

"But I . . . have nothing . . . to tell you."

By now, she felt close to tears, even as she grew

aware of a spiraling tension centered deep within her.
She arched toward him, feeling a moist warmth between
her legs and a strangely pleasurable ache that had blossomed at the very core of her womanhood. What she
was doing was wrong—*Mon Dieu,* it was sinful!—but
that was lost in this overwhelming need of the flesh.

The whip fell away a moment later, and this time her
moan was in protest. She sagged back against the coverlet and shut her eyes, vaguely aware that she should
be embarrassed. Instead, it was all she could do not to
beg Tark to touch her again with the same pleasuring
strokes.

She bit back that plea. By now, it had occurred to
her that perhaps she had been mistaken about the brunette whom she earlier had watched in the viewing
room. Maybe pleasure, and not pain, had contorted the
woman's painted face and racked her plump form.

The sudden creak of springs accompanied an unexpected weight at the foot of the bed. Startled, Isabeau
opened her eyes only to meet Tark's ice blue gaze.
Stripped now of his jacket and waistcoat, he knelt between her legs and loomed over her. She shrank against
the pillow, trepidation warring with anticipation as she
realized how vulnerable she was. At least he no longer
wielded the riding crop, she saw in relief.

"I think it's time we come to an understanding, my
sweet," he told her, his voice rough with emotion that
she could not identify.

She wet her lips with a flick of her tongue, trying to
summon a reply. For she felt drained of reason, unable
to resist the wanton voice that insisted she give herself
up to Tark.

"Don't fight it, my sweet," he urged in a low voice, seeming to read her every thought. "Just let me satisfy you. That is what you want—isn't it?"

"Yes," she softly breathed, feeling a shameful heat rush through her even as she arched her body toward him once more. "Oh, yes."

His answering groan resounded with equal parts desire and surprise. "Sweet Jesus, but you're hot and ready," he rasped as one hand met the damp silk of her pantalets and slid past their open seam. Embarrassed, she turned from the need she could read in his eyes, even as she instinctively opened her thighs wider still.

His searching fingers brushed the soft curls there and promptly found the tiny bud of pleasure within the delicate folds of her flesh. With practiced strokes, he caressed that sensitive nub, roughly demanding as he did so, "You need me, don't you? Tell me I'm the only one who can satisfy you."

"Only . . . you," she breathlessly agreed, feeling her damp, swollen sex open like a dew-drenched blossom in his hand. He continued to manipulate her with light strokes until she feared she would swoon—or even more likely, die. *Mon Dieu,* never had she known that a touch could bring such pleasure.

Watching the erotic play of emotion that stamped her flushed features, Tark was seized by the same sudden hot need. The cynical voice within reminded him that this was not how it was supposed to go. *He* was supposed to bring *her* to the peak of climax and then leave her unsatisfied. Instead, he had become caught up in the same passionate tide. His fingers were slick with her sweet juices. The faint sharp scent of her drew an answering response from him. Already, he had been half aroused at the sight of her partially nude form. Now, he felt his loins tighten and swell with a sudden, painful heat that drove him to the edge of his self-control.

"Let me put an end to both our suffering," he said in a hoarse voice, as he fumbled with one hand at his trouser buttons while probing with the other at the tight opening to her body. "That is what you want, isn't it?"

"Oh, please," she gasped and writhed with unrestrained pleasure beneath him.

Taking those soft words as assent, he groaned and let his engorged member spring from its confinement. Not bothering to remove the rest of his clothes, he positioned himself between her thighs just as shudder after shudder racked her. He echoed her pleasured cry with a strangled groan and mindlessly thrust into her.

He registered an unexpected instant of resistance to his entry and a sharp cry of pain. The realization was lost, however, in the burning need that wiped out all thought save the compulsion to quench that lustful fire.

With a few quick strokes, he found his own hot release, spilling his seed deep within her in a series of thrusts that seemingly went on for minutes. Spent at last, he collapsed atop her slim form and waited for his heartbeat to slow and his breathing to return to normal.

As he regained a measure of his equilibrium, it slowly dawned on him that something had not gone right. Puzzled, he rose to meet her gaze and was stunned to read pained accusation in her dark eyes. All at once, he recalled that momentary resistance when he had driven into her, and the way she had cried out the instant he had thrust past that barrier.

Sweet Jesus, she really had been a virgin!

He took in her pale face with its traces of tears and was consumed by a surge of self-loathing. Silently damning himself as a brutal despoiler of maidens—sweet Jesus, why the hell hadn't she told him she never had been with a man before?—he rolled off her and scrambled to his feet. With almost panicked haste, he refastened his trouser buttons, all too aware of the traces of blood and semen now staining the dark fabric.

Embarrassment sent a tide of color up the back of his neck as he turned toward the bed. He should make some apology, he realized, but he found himself totally at a loss for words. The best thing he could do was untie the chit and get the hell out of there, before he did any more damage.

She flinched when he reached toward her, though she lay there with stoic calm as he tugged at the knots that bound her. Her flesh was cold beneath his touch now, and he saw with another stab of guilt that the cords had left red welts upon her skin. The most telling proof of his callous actions, however, lay in the rust-colored stains drying on the snowy silk of her pantalets, that sign visible even in this dim light.

Damn it, why hadn't she told him?

The question burned as he worked to free her. If she had screamed, or asked him to stop . . . but, sweet Jesus, she had responded so eagerly to his every touch, he never would have believed that she was still a virgin.

Unraveling the last knot, he caught her hand in his and dragged her to her feet. "The game's over, *mademoiselle*," he wearily rasped out. "Go home to your brother, or to Franchot, if you prefer—hell, go anywhere you want, just so long as I never have to set eyes on you again."

She made no reply but simply stood there, pale and composed. He was reminded of a fragile porcelain statue that had been carelessly broken and then carefully pieced back together again. When he began to fear she might remain in that still pose forever, she reached for her discarded gown. With precise, almost jerky moves, she wrapped it around her and then pulled on her slippers before gazing up at him again.

"I . . . I may leave?" she asked, wariness vying with relief in her expression. "Then, you believe me . . . that I know nothing about Monsieur Calvé?"

He gave a harsh laugh. "If you want the God's honest truth, I don't know what to believe, anymore. Now, get the hell out of here, before I change my mind and tie you back onto that bed."

She fled toward the door like a trapped forest creature unexpectedly freed from its snare. A heartbeat later, she was gone in a flurry of white linen. Tark stared at the door she'd left ajar and then sank onto the bed, doubly damning himself a fool. Which action, he wondered, had been more stupid—setting free the one person who could serve as his link to Franchot, or mindlessly satisfying his need for her . . . a need that had burned in his veins from their first meeting on the docks?

He rubbed his hands across his face, then glanced beside him. On the coverlet lay the white domino Isabeau had worn. He turned it in his hands, letting the cool glass beads absorb the heat from his fingers. Then, in a compulsive gesture, he tossed it onto the table alongside his own sleek leather disguise.

It occurred to him now that they both had shed their masks. What good had it done either of them—and what harm had he caused by his actions tonight?

Don't look back.

The words reverberated in her mind as Isabeau clutched her makeshift tunic about her shoulders and all but flew down the darkened corridor. She bypassed the main stairway and headed for a shadowed juncture beyond. There, the line of red-painted doors led to a second hall that veered off at right angles from the first.

Reaching that sanctuary, she halted and sagged against the gold-flocked walls to catch a sobbing breath. Why Tark had let her go, she could not guess—but neither would she fail to take advantage of his change of heart, abandon though she must her plan to search the brothel's upper floor. For the moment, the plight of Lili's child paled against what had occurred within that black-walled room she had fled.

Mon Dieu, what had she done?

Isabeau drew her tunic more tightly around her as if to ward off the inescapable answer to that question. She had flung away her carefully molded future for a few wanton moments of pleasure . . . and, worse, that she did not regret her actions in the least!

She buried her face in her hands and mentally sorted through the events of the past half hour. Part of her seized upon the most convenient excuse, that it had been the champagne, or perhaps the brothel's intoxicating wanton air that had made her take leave of her senses.

Honesty compelled her to admit that she had made her own choice in the matter. She had gone with him to the room and, with only token protestation, had welcomed his touch upon her body. She instinctively had known that, had she screamed or pleaded, he would have stopped short of that final, irrevocable act.

But she had not . . . and he had taken those acts of intimacy to their logical conclusion.

Isabeau flushed deeper at the memory of Tark's assault upon that last citadel of her womanhood. Those few minutes spent in the viewing room had prepared her. She had known, from frank discussions of the convent school's older girls that she had overheard years before, to anticipate a brief moment of discomfort. Instead, she had been caught unawares by a burning pain that took hold of her lower body as he had thrust into her again and again. The brutal ache had given way, at last, to a satisfying feeling of fullness . . . but it was quickly over, and her girlish innocence only a memory.

Still, there had to be more to this union of male and female than what had happened between her and Tark tonight. Isabeau gingerly straightened, aware of the lingering ache between her thighs, tacky now with mingled traces of her virgin's blood and his passionate juices. Oddly enough, she felt not so much violated as claimed— but what hold did either have upon the other, now that desire was sated? That question was followed by a sense of longing that sharpened into disappointment as she recalled his words to her just before she fled.

. . . go anywhere you want, just so long as I never have to set eyes on you again.

She shut her eyes at the memory. *He* had been unaffected by their lovemaking, it would seem . . . and how could she blame him, when he was accustomed to sharing his bed with experienced women like Madame Tremaine? Perhaps he was shaking his head in disgust over her ignorance—or worse, laughing at how easy she was to seduce.

Unable to face that possibility, Isabeau turned her attention to the matter of leaving the brothel without being discovered. She dared not return to room 10 to retrieve her mask. And though no one might recognize her minus the domino, one of the doormen could describe her features to Ophelia, so she could not afford to depart the brothel the same way as she had entered. But surely every house of ill-repute worth the name had a back exit.

She felt her way down the dark corridor toward a pale yellow glow, giving a silent prayer of thanks when that light revealed a second, smaller stairwell. An echo of the orchestra's music and the brothel patrons' chatter drifted up to her; still, that faint commotion did not drown out a nearer sound that set her heart pounding. Was it simply her imagination, or had she just heard the wail of a fretful child?

Spurred on, Isabeau gathered up her skirts and started down the narrow wooden steps, listening for that wavering cry to repeat itself. For the moment, however, she heard only the echo of her light tread against the smooth boards.

Reaching the last step, she found herself in a square, brick-floored kitchen that was empty of servants. By the glow of the kerosene lantern hanging from an exposed rafter, she viewed the plates and cooking utensils that

spoke of a hearty meal recently consumed. One of the
French doors leading from the kitchen to the courtyard
beyond hung ajar, as if someone had stepped out moments earlier. Still, nothing about the room indicated
that a child was being kept somewhere on the premises.

Mindful that the staff might return at any moment,
she made a hasty search of the entire service wing—a
narrow section of rooms that projected from the rear of
the main house to form part of a lopsided U. The laundry and storage areas provided no clues. By the time
she returned to the kitchen, she was on the verge of
conceding defeat. Then another sharp cry came from
the direction of the courtyard.

Sainte Cécile, had someone abandoned the babe to
the night? Heedless now of her own safety, she hurried
past the French door, halting as a shadowed movement
caught her eye. Not daring to breathe, she took a step
forward . . . and sagged in disappointment.

An overfed grey tabby wended its way from the shadows, pausing to fix bright green eyes on Isabeau and
emit the yowl of a hungry feline. When she made no
move, the cat flashed past her on silent paws, vanishing
around the edge of the open French doors and into the
kitchen. A moment later, a crash of pans and a woman's
scolding voice rang through the courtyard, followed by
the prompt reappearance of the tabby.

Isabeau took refuge in the shadows as a Negress,
whom she guessed was the now-returned cook, appeared
on the threshold. Muttering a final imprecation in the
direction of the departed feline, the woman shook her
kerchiefed head and shut the French doors with a bang.

Isabeau bit back a cry of protest, all too aware that

her way back into the kitchen was barred now. The cat had melted again into the shadows, leaving her to find her own way out of her predicament. A chill gust of wind rustled unseen trees, with a sound like furtive footsteps. She shivered and thought of the warm cloak she had left with the doorman. It, too, was now a casualty of the night.

Reminding herself that she was not yet safely out of Ophelia's reach, she glanced about to gain her bearings. The cloud-draped moon gave light enough for her to see that the courtyard ran the length of the service wing. She felt her way across the uneven paving stones until she reached a heavy wrought-iron gate. She peered past the twist of black bars, glimpsing a convenient walkway that ran parallel to the brothel and led to the lighted avenue beyond. Now, if only the gate was unlocked . . .

It was. Isabeau breathed a prayer of thanks and slipped past, reaching the street a moment later. Half-a-dozen empty hacks sat parked along it, and she hailed the nearest, scrambling in with the haste of a penitent seeking sanctuary. Only when the coach pulled away did she sink back against the seat and allow herself a sigh. She was safe, and her anonymity was intact. Though she had failed to find Regine tonight, at least no one had cause to suspect that she had set foot inside the brothel.

No one, that was, save Tark Parrish.

Twenty

Barely had Tark settled at his desk the following day than the door to Parrish Company, Ltd., flew open, admitting a crisp breeze and an irate Creole gentleman.

"The remainder of your fee, M'sieur Parrish," Philippe Lavoisier stiffly explained as he flung a bulging envelope on the desk and fixed Tark with a stare.

Tark leaned back in his chair and met the youth's gaze with a cool look of his own. "Won't you sit down?"

"I think not, *m'sieur.*"

Philippe remained standing, his fists on his hips and his fair complexion a dangerous shade of red. Though no less fashionably attired than at their last meeting, today he bristled with energy. Watching him, Tark was reminded of a ruffled banty cock prepared to fly against all barnyard comers.

Or, an aggrieved relative ready to challenge the man who had compromised his sister's honor.

That was a distinct possibility, Tark judged with a twist of his lips. He had played into the Lavoisiers' hands by bedding Isabeau, and it seemed he was to pay the price for that folly. He suppressed a moment's guilt over his part. Virgin or no, she must have been aware of what could happen should she pursue him to the brothel. He'd be damned if he would take the blame for what had transpired between them.

He reached for the envelope and made a show of verifying its contents, all the while weighing his current situation. Philippe would follow Claude Blanchard's lead and demand a hasty wedding on behalf of his sister. Failing that, the traditional Creole solution entailed pistols for two upon the field of honor at dawn.

While never one to back down from a fight, Tark wasn't eager to risk his neck over the chit's lost virtue—especially when she had been a willing participant in her own deflowering.

Willing? an inner voice contemptuously questioned that last rationalization. *Hell, what other choice did she have, considering she was tied up the whole damn time?*

Dismissing that self-accusation, Tark acknowledged a third possibility.

Philippe might overlook the brothel incident, since killing his business associate would hardly be a prudent move. Tark casually tossed the envelope onto the desk. "This appears to be in order, Mr. LaSalle, and—"

"That charade is no longer necessary," the younger man interjected. "I am aware that you have discovered my identity, so let us proceed to more pressing matters. Have you made arrangements for my ship?"

"Everything is on schedule, Mr. Lavoisier," Tark began again. "The *Star of the Mediterranean* docked this morning and is scheduled to remain in port until day after tomorrow. I've persuaded her captain to weigh anchor thirty-six hours later than planned—midnight on the thirteenth, to be exact. Your goods will be loaded at the last possible minute, and I foresee no problems with the dock authorities."

The Creole dropped his arms to his side and took a step closer. "I will want to supervise the loading, of course."

"Of course."

"And this *Star of the Mediterranean* will travel all the way to Sevastapol?"

Tark shook his head. "The freighter will make a stop at Lisbon, and then continue on to Constantinople. Once it docks there, your shipment will be transferred to a smaller Turkish vessel for the last leg of the voyage. I also requested accommodations for one—hardly a luxurious cabin, I'm afraid, but quite adequate compared to most freighters."

"And you have no doubt that this captain will follow those instructions, that the goods will arrive safely?"

"Let's just say Captain Considine is the best seaman that money can buy," Tark answered.

Philippe considered that ironic statement for a moment before nodding. "It seems you have everything under control, M'sieur Parrish," he grudgingly conceded. "You will find the shipment stored upon the grounds of the archbishop's residence. I will arrange for a man to meet you at the side gate at nine o'clock Tuesday evening."

"Nine o'clock, it is." Tark pushed back from his desk and stood, anxious to put an end to this interview. "If everything is settled—"

"One moment, *m'sieur*. There is one thing more we must discuss."

Sweet Jesus, here it comes, Tark thought, not that he blamed the younger man. The question was, did the Creole intend to end the matter here and now, or would he insist upon an early morning jaunt to the Dueling Oaks?

Praying the youth's choice would be the former, Tark kept an expression of polite expectancy and raised a brow. Philippe hesitated, then burst out, "Let me warn you, *m'sieur,* that your reputation precedes you. I insist that you cease your crude attempts to court my sister. She will marry a Creole gentleman, and no other."

"Court? Marry?" Tark shot him a look of appalled disbelief. Surely the chit hadn't interpreted what had happened between them last night as some kind of offer! "What in the hell are you talking about?"

"Isabeau has told me that you two have spoken together on numerous occasions—without her family's knowledge or approval, I might add—so I can only assume . . ."

Philippe paused. "If I learn that your intentions were less than honorable, M'sieur Parrish, I will have no compunction about killing you for the insult you offered my family."

With those words, the Creole turned on his heel and marched out the door. Tark stared after him for a stunned moment before settling back behind his desk.

So you didn't tell your brother about last night.

The realization that the Lavoisiers apparently had abandoned the idea of blackmailing him into marriage brought him a momentary sense of relief. Now, he could keep a safe distance from the chit, and continue as if nothing had happened. That glimmer of relief dissolved into a bitter wave of regret . . . though what was there to regret, except that he had waited this long to avail himself of her?

Not daring to examine the emptiness that weighed upon him, he shoved aside the question and turned to the cash-filled envelope that lay on the desk. It demanded another kind of action. He snatched the money and stowed it in his strongbox.

Tuesday night was little more than seventy-two hours away, he reminded himself, yet he had learned nothing more about the carbines' origins or their final destination. More importantly, he still hadn't figured out the motive behind Franchot's recruitment of him. The first thought was that the situation was a set-up, and the dock authorities would be waiting to arrest him once the shipment was safely aboard. Carrying the scenario to its conclusion, however, meant that they would also confiscate the rifles—which could hardly be Franchot's intent.

And which puts me back to square one, Tark thought. What he had to do was step back and examine the overall picture. At first glance, it appeared deceptively uncomplicated, just a straightforward smuggling scheme that was—

—meant to do nothing more than throw me off track, he finished in sudden comprehension. Sweet Jesus, that had to be the answer. Why else had he managed to uncover the tie between the Lavoisiers and his old foe? Franchot must have planned it from the first, employing mystery and misdirection with the skill of a vaudeville magician.

Tark shoved back his chair and got to his feet, needing action to help him order his thoughts. Likely, the rifles played some role in the Frenchman's plot, he told himself as he paced the small office. On the other hand, the ruse to smuggle them from the country was probably just that . . . a gambit. But considering the lengths to which Franchot had gone in keeping up the pretense, the payoff of this particular scheme—whatever it might be—must be enormous.

Tark halted beside his desk and opened a drawer to reveal the revolver that lay gleaming against the pale wood. His fingers closed on the cold steel, then hesitated. As often as he had imagined seeing his old foe lying dead at his feet, he could hardly kill him in cold blood. The legalities aside, there was something distinctly unsatisfying in ending a long-held grudge with a single bullet.

"I'm not letting you off that easily, Franchot," he softly vowed as he slid the drawer shut and stood. Three days remained before Tuesday, time enough for him to gather his resources and confront the Frenchman. First, however, he had personal responsibilities to resolve.

He could rest easy concerning Alma. She was packing for a visit to her sister's home near Baton Rouge, where she would remain out of harm's way until the wedding. The doughty housekeeper would have made a formidable ally, Tark thought with a smile. He suspected Alma would regret having missed giving Franchot Calvé a piece of her mind.

The question of Elisabeth might prove stickier. Tark paced the room, debating how best to handle the situation. That night at the opera house, he had made his decision to end their affair. To his mind, that relationship was a thing of the past. Still, he owed his former mistress the courtesy of telling her so to her face. He did not relish the prospect.

Past experience told Tark that she would not accept his decision with good grace. He'd be lucky to get out of there in one piece, he thought, as he grabbed his jacket and headed for the door. Once he had settled matters with Elisabeth, his next move would be to meet with Tom Sullivan. And soon—

"And soon, Franchot, you and I will meet for one last time to put an end to this war between us."

The midafternoon sun brought welcome warmth as Isabeau passed through the wrought-iron gates of St. Louis No. 1, one of the city's oldest Creole cemeteries. In the distance, the Angelus bells began to ring, and Isabeau paused to repeat the familiar prayer. When their final echoes had died away she carefully passed along the graveled walk through rows of above-ground crypts.

Embellished with everything from simple white-washed finishes to gleaming marble statuary and intricate black ironwork, the tombs crowded together in jagged rows to form one of New Orleans's so-called "cities of the dead." Here, along with countless other Orleanians, the Lavoisier family dead had found their final resting place. It never occurred to her to be fearful there. The cemetery was simply a gathering place for friends and family—a peaceful spot where the specter of death had no business setting foot.

A few moments later, Isabeau halted before an imposing structure fenced in black wrought iron. *No tiny oven vault for the Lavoisiers,* she thought with pride.

Many families could afford only the miniature crypts—"fours," as the Creoles called them—that stacked one atop another to form the cemetery's outer wall. *Her* relatives had once been wealthy enough to commission a free-standing, multivault tomb complete with a trio of marble angels pointing heavenward.

She read the names carved above each vault, pausing at two of them: Jean-Paul and Thérèse, her parents. She stood caught up in her memories; then she sought out the most recent of the Lavoisier dead.

Her first visit here upon her return home had been hasty, the briefest paying of her respects to Lili's memory. Now, her guilt over her cousin's death had faded, replaced by a need for comfort that only this earthly reminder of her could provide.

"Tell me what to do, Lili," she whispered, reaching with unsteady fingers to trace one stark character of her cousin's freshly cut name. Its marble edge nicked her flesh, and a drop of blood slid tearlike along the chiseled letter. That pain was lost, however, in the dull ache of her heart.

She had donned for this pilgrimage a sober grey gown and black-veiled hat . . . though it was as much for her own lost innocence as for her departed cousin that she lamented. She sank to the nearby wrought-iron bench and unthinkingly swabbed at her finger with a lace handkerchief to staunch the thread of blood. With the clarifying light of day upon her, she could see now the enormity of what had transpired last night.

Sainte Cécile, had she been quite insane?

That moment during which she had surrendered her virtue surely had been insanity. In a single night, she had forgotten every lesson in duty and honor she had ever learned, and had surrendered herself to a man without the benefit of marriage. Such an action was unthinkable . . . sinful. And worse, no respectable Creole gentleman would ever have her now.

Isabeau swallowed back a sob of disappointment at the thought of her future. As an unmarried woman, she would be consigned to the thankless role of "Tante Isette," playing aunt to Philippe's future children and living off the largess of his family. She would grow old without a husband or children of her own, living vicariously through others. Indeed, it must have been madness. Nothing else could explain her actions, save for—

Love.

The word drifted swanlike through her thoughts, the syllable fraught with uncertainty and exhilaration. She straightened, feeling the ebb and flow of blood in her face as she confronted this unexpected possibility. Her girlish fancies paled beside the emotions Tark drew from her—yet how could she love the man, when she barely knew him! After what happened last night, she could never face him again, let alone speak to him of such turbulent emotions.

Not that he was likely to return that sentiment. Chances were that he already had consigned the memory of their lovemaking to the farthest corner of his mind. But even if his attentions had not been entirely unhonorable . . .

Should she inform her brother that an *américain* dared to court her, he would rage and insist she marry a Creole . . . a gentleman. Someone like—

"—Marcel."

The word fell from her lips in a rush of relief tempered by only a twinge of guilt. The solution before her all along. Marriage to Marcel would guarantee her security and respect. Also, she had not allowed herself to consider the most dire possible consequence of last night's encounter, the fact that she might well be with child. If so, a hasty marriage was her sole recourse. As for the fact that she was no longer a virgin . . .

Isabeau had always heard that a man could tell the difference between a maid and an experienced woman. Still, there were ways one might mimic that virgin state. What harm could such a deception bring? After all, it was not as if she had betrayed their marriage vows. Indeed, she would tell Philippe this very day that she had decided to accept Marcel's suit.

But what about love . . . and desire?

Ruthlessly, she ignored the fervent voice. She would make Marcel a dutiful wife, she vowed. She would be satisfied with the warmth of friendship that always had existed between them. What did it matter that, married to him, she would never experience the reckless rush of passion that she had known with Tark—the kind of passion that threatened to consume her very soul?

The sound of footsteps on the walk broke through her thoughts, and she glanced around her. She could not see the intruder—not that this person's presence need alarm her, she reassured herself. Most likely it was a caretaker, or someone come to pay his respects to a departed loved one. When the footfalls moved closer, however, her nerve failed her. Gathering up her skirts, she hurried past the nearest bend in the path, only to collide with a familiar, well-tailored figure.

"M'sieur Calvé," she gasped out, unable to conceal her dismay.

The Frenchman reached out to steady her, as he acknowledged her words with a humorless smile. "Do not look so surprised, *ma chère*. Surely you have not forgotten that we were to talk again."

When she shook her head, he gestured her back toward the bench. "The time has come for you to learn what favor I require of you," he began without preamble. "I presume you are aware that His Imperial Highness, Alexis Romanoff Alexandrovitch, intends to visit New Orleans during Mardi Gras?"

"You mean, the Russian grand duke?"

She settled again upon the seat and stared at him. Who in the city had *not* heard the news? The town's businessmen had formed a new Carnival organization whose king, Rex, had issued mock edicts in the daily paper in preparation for the event. She continued, "I know that he is to be received by the governor and mayor, and that he will be honored at the Comus parade."

"Quite so."

Calvé smiled down at her again. His tall, lean form was outlined by the white marble crypt behind him. With his graceful stance and mane of bronze hair, he reminded her of those bas-relief sculptures of medieval knights lying in peaceful repose upon their tombs. But surely no knight had looked upon the world with eyes so full of diabolical purpose.

Oblivious to her uneasy regard, he went on, "I have arranged for you to join the delegation upon the grandstand outside City Hall, where His Imperial Highness will view the Comus parades on Tuesday. I have also obtained for you an invitation to the Comus ball, which he will attend that same evening. Upon one of those occasions, I wish you to make the grand duke's acquaintance."

"But how? Why?" she exclaimed, puzzled by their conversation.

Calvé gave a shrug. "I shall leave the 'how' to you—but since Alexis has a reputation for being, shall we say, attentive to the ladies, I foresee no problem. As for the 'why,' your part in this affair is to lure the grand duke from the ballroom. Two of my associates—your brother and *oncle,* to be precise—will join you outside the theater and take His Imperial Highness on an unscheduled tour of the docks."

"Philippe and Oncle Henri . . . the docks?" she echoed with a frown, then caught back a horrified gasp as realization dawned. *"Mon Dieu,* you mean to kidnap him. But I cannot—"

"You can, *ma chère,* and you will, just as Henri and Philippe have committed themselves to my cause. Or have you forgotten that the safety of your cousin's child depends upon your cooperation?"

She grasped the arm of the bench to steady herself as she strove to make sense of it all. "But why kidnap the grand duke?" she finally managed in a shaken voice. "Indeed, *m'sieur,* all of New Orleans knows that you are a wealthy man. Surely you need not hold him for ransom."

"My reasons are of no concern to you," he replied, and a flash of emotion in his golden eyes made her regret asking the question. "The necessary invitations will arrive at your home Monday morning. Since time is short, I have taken the liberty of providing you with an appropriate gown for the festivities. I am certain you will be pleased with my selection."

"But do you mean to . . . to harm the duke?" she pressed on, knowing the futility of that query yet desperate for reassurance. *Mon Dieu,* would she be forced to add a crime worse than kidnaping to her list of transgressions?

Calvé's chill silence answered her more eloquently than any hollow denial. Isabeau shut her eyes, unable to meet the glimmer of madness she now read behind the sun-like brightness of his gaze. *Lili was right,* she told herself in despair. He was no man, but a demon bent on wreaking earthly havoc.

"One last thing, *ma chère,*" she heard him say, and she reluctantly opened her eyes again. "I understand that you and an old friend of mine have furthered your . . . acquaintance, so to speak. May I suggest that you not forget how his late wife, the *charmante* Delphine, met her sad end."

With those words, he sketched a bow and headed back the way he had come, the soft crunch of gravel echoing after him. Isabeau released the strained breath she had been holding. The cemetery's tranquil air lay shattered around her. Shivering, she rose from her seat, anxious now to flee this silent place of death.

If only she had someone whose judgment was unclouded by fear or greed. Marcel seemed a logical choice, honorable and steadfast as he was—yet he would likely insist upon confronting Calvé. She could never live with herself should Marcel, too, fall victim to the Frenchman's schemes. Who, then, could she call upon?

"Madame Dumas," she softly exclaimed, her uncertainty easing. *Mon Dieu,* why had she not thought of this before? The dowager had heard and seen much in her lifetime. Surely her elderly friend could be entrusted with this secret and perhaps offer some word of wisdom.

She hurried past the cemetery's main gate and started down the avenue in the direction of Madame's elegant home. She could not help noticing the streets around her, ablaze now with banners of purple, green, and gold. For days, talk in every parlor and ballroom had been centered on the coming festivities and the honor the Russian grand duke had bestowed upon the city by his anticipated arrival.

What would those same people say, she wondered, if they knew what tragic fate awaited that royal guest of honor—should she be unable to stop Franchot Calvé?

Twenty-one

"Ma chère, you look quite pale."

Madame Dumas bustled toward Isabeau in a flurry of black bombazine. "Bring us the sherry, Robert, and quickly," she addressed her manservant, who had stepped aside in the foyer to let his mistress pass. Then, taking Isabeau's arm, the dowager steered her to the parlor.

"Come, sit down, *chérie,*" she went on, "and tell me what brings you to my door in such a state."

"I-I am quite well, Madame," Isabeau hastily explained, anxious to set her elderly friend's mind at ease. "It's just that I needed to talk to someone."

Still, she made no protest when Madame, with much tsking and clucking, settled her upon the parlor love seat with her feet propped on a hassock and a pillow tucked behind her. A moment later, Robert reappeared at the doorway with a tray bearing a heavy, cut-glass decanter and two small glasses.

"Are you certain you are all right, Miss Isabeau?" the dark-skinned man asked as he set down the tray and poured out a measure of sherry. "Perhaps I should send for Mr. Philippe."

"That won't be necessary, Robert," she assured him with a tremulous smile and accepted a glass.

He gravely awaited Madame's nod of dismissal before leaving them. Isabeau sipped tentatively at the sweet wine, feeling the blood warm her cheeks once more as the alcohol took effect.

Madame, meanwhile, had taken the wooden chair beside her and helped herself to an ample portion of the sherry. Now, she grasped Isabeau's hand in her fragile fingers and demanded in a kindly tone, "Something *is* wrong, *chérie,* is it not? Has some trouble befallen you . . . or perhaps your brother or your *oncle?"*

It was all Isabeau could do not to confess every detail of the past weeks. She stopped short, however, unwilling to endanger the frail old woman before her by revealing anything of Monsieur Calvé's schemes. Who knew what measures the man might take to ensure Madame's silence in that matter?

"I-I'm afraid that I have troubled you for no good reason. I just came to ask you . . . that is, I wanted to know—"

She hesitated, grasping wildly for a logical means to satisfy the old woman. Then, taking herself by complete surprise, she blurted out, "What do you know of Monsieur Tark Parrish?"

Though Isabeau flushed scarlet as she realized what she had asked, Madame clapped her hands as she exclaimed, "I told you I had found the very man for you, *non?* Now, what is it you wish to know, *chérie*—about his family, perhaps?"

Not giving Isabeau a chance to reply, she poured them both another measure of sherry and went on, "As I told you before, our handsome Tark is from a respected St.

Louis family—but his grandmère, she was Creole, and once a dear friend of mine."

The dowager paused for a dramatic sigh. "Ah, but it was so romantic. My friend, Celeste, she fell in love with a handsome *américain*—but her *maman* and *papa,* they did not approve. *Mon Dieu,* but there was a scandal when she ran away to marry her *américain.* They never forgave her, not even when Celeste had a child of her own."

Isabeau found herself eager to glean every scrap of information she could about him. What did it matter that each word was like a grain of salt rubbed into her wounded heart?

"And what of Celeste's child?"

Madame shook her head. "But that is the sad part of my tale. The daughter, she grew up to marry an *américain,* as well—but she chose a man who had no understanding that life, it is to be lived. Even when they had a child, they were not happy."

With another sigh, the dowager went on, "Our Tark and his father, they had always disagreed about everything—but then came the war, and this was, as they say, the final straw. M'sieur Parrish—his *papa*—was a rich merchant, and he believed in the Northern cause. Ah, but Tark, he told his *papa* that the government should not interfere in its people's lives—but rather than fight against his own friends and family, he came to New Orleans and became a great hero . . . a blockade runner," she finished with almost maternal pride. "Of course, I did not learn all of these things until later."

The dowager paused and fixed Isabeau with a knowing look. "And so, *ma chère,* has he asked permission of your brother and *oncle* to court you, yet?"

"I-I think not, Madame," Isabeau faintly replied, her blush deepening. He had hardly treated her as a potential bride. Moreover, she could not picture Monsieur Parrish asking permission for the taking of anything, including a wife!

She straightened in her chair, a frown creasing her forehead. Madame's account of the *américain's* past had given her new insight into the man's character. Knowing what she now did, it seemed unlikely that he would be an accomplice of someone like Monsieur Calvé. Perhaps she might find in him the ally she needed to defeat the Frenchman. Which was the more important, she asked herself, her pride or the rescue of Lili's baby and the undermining of the Frenchman's kidnap plot?

The answer was evident. Setting down her glass, she took a deep breath and slowly asked, "Tell me, Madame, would you trust Monsieur Parrish . . . with your life?"

"So the rifles aren't stolen?"

Tark took a swallow of whiskey, ignoring the raucous banter of those few laborers and dockworkers around him who made up the late-afternoon crowd at the Gilded Albatross. Tom Sullivan evenly met his gaze and spread his hands in a deprecating gesture.

"I didn't say the carbines wasn't stolen," he clarified. "I said no one's reportin' a shipment like that missin'. Mebbe they just ain't noticed it's gone, yet."

"Maybe," Tark absently agreed, though the fact that

the rifles might have been a legitimate purchase seemed to fit this confusing scheme.

While Tom signaled the barmaid for another ale, Tark reviewed what he knew about Franchot's plot thus far. He had decided that smuggling was not the Frenchman's primary objective. It stood to reason that something connected with the weapons was. But an arsenal of that size was usually employed in only one of two ways—to defend a territory from attack . . . or to wrest that piece of land from its rightful owners.

"So what did ya do 'bout makin' the little dandy's arrangements?" Tom's voice broke in on his thoughts.

Tark put aside the question of weapons and managed a smile. "I called in a favor. Remember Petros Considine, captain of the *Star of the Mediterranean?*"

"Ya mean the Greek fella you dragged outa here that day them Kaintuck boys was givin' him and his crew a poundin'?"

"The same. Once I got back to his ship and patched him up, he began celebrating our new-found friendship with a bottle of ouzo. He already was three sheets to the wind—hell, I was pretty damned drunk, too—and by the time we'd gotten halfway through the bottle, he had decided I was his long-lost brother, Stephanos. He spent the rest of the night regaling me with stories about our supposed boyhood together."

Tark grinned at the memory. "Come morning, he had sobered up enough to realize I wasn't a Greek, but he told me he owed me one, anyway."

"So Petros is gonna let you use the *Star* as bait?" Tom asked with a quirk of his shaggy brow.

Tark nodded. "Since she was due for some minor

repairs before she weighed anchor again, I used a portion of my so-called fee to get her out of dry dock early. And Petros has instructed his crew to go along with whatever I say."

"So what's the plan?"

"The hell if I know." Tark drained his glass, then continued, "I've got a crew set to move the shipment from the archbishop's place to the wharf and I booked the passage, just in case Franchot checks up on me. At this point, all I can tell you is to be at the Gravier Street wharf at midnight Tuesday—and be prepared for anything."

"That's one party I ain't gonna miss."

The night patroller grabbed the ale the barmaid had placed before him and downed half of it in a single swallow, then plucked his notebook from his pocket. "I almost fergot. Here's that Frenchy fella's address you wanted," he added and tore a page from the book with a flourish.

Tark reached for the ragged sheet of paper, noticing as he did so that his friend was now eying him with undue interest. "What's the matter, Tom—have I suddenly grown two heads?"

"Nope, but the one ya got looks a mite battered," the man replied with a knowing grin. "I'd guess ya'd been in a bit of a tussle—an' I'd say the lady got the best of ya."

"You're not far wrong, Tom," he admitted, wincing as he touched the scrapes on his right cheek.

His discussion with Elisabeth earlier that afternoon had ended in a full-blown battle. He had expected her to be angered. What he hadn't anticipated was a wave of unbridled fury that manifested itself in a physical assault, complete with teeth, nails, and whatever she could lay her hands upon.

Tark gave thanks for a well-developed set of reflexes. When reason hadn't worked, he'd been forced to restrain her, using the curtain ties to truss her up like a goose bound for market. He'd deposited her on the parlor sofa and made good his escape, but her vitriolic shrieks had echoed out onto the streets.

"Women," he muttered the age-old plaint, and was rewarded with a grunt of assent from his friend.

"They're a curse an' a blessin'," Tom sagely intoned, then spoiled the effect with a gap-toothed grin. "Speakin' of which, I'd best be headed home, afore the missus decides to track me down. I'll keep my ears open, though, an' let ya know if I hear anythin' more about yer, er, friend."

Tark watched the night patroller amble out into the dying afternoon light, then turned his attention to his empty glass. While he debated the wisdom of ordering another shot, the blond barmaid from the previous evening sauntered over to his table.

"There's a gent out back that wants to see you," she informed him, her tone cooler than it had been last night. "Says he has some unfinished business with you."

Tark glanced toward the rear exit. "Don't tell me," he wearily said, "he's medium height, slim build, dark hair . . ."

. . . and goes by the name of Philippe Lavoisier, and is starting to become one hell of a pain in the ass.

"I suppose that's him." Her shrug caused her dingy

chemise to slip off one narrow shoulder. "You want me to tell him you're busy?"

"I might as well get this over with," Tark muttered. He tossed a few coins onto the table, then spared the barmaid a considering look. The chit was attractive, he determined. No doubt she was also healthy, since Ned didn't allow diseased girls in his place. And since he had time to kill . . .

Sensing a potential customer, she abandoned her sulky air to sidle closer. "I'll be around when you get back," she purred, "just in case you need a bit of comfort, after all. Just ask for Emma."

She scooped up the coins, then brushed against him as she headed back toward the bar, hips rolling. Tark let his gaze linger on her a moment longer. He should have been tempted to take her up on her offer. Instead, the prospect was off-putting—rather like sitting down to a meal of bread and beer after already having sated himself at a champagne and oyster feast.

He started toward the back. Ned was busy pouring drinks for the rowdy group of rivermen who'd just staggered in. He could only spare Tark a quick nod as he walked past. Returning that casual greeting, he turned down the narrow hall that led to the back door. It, in turn, opened onto an alley heaped high with broken crates and refuse.

Trying to curb his irritation, which was in danger of flaring into downright annoyance, Tark strode out the battered door. "All right, Philippe, let's get this over wi—"

He stopped short as he came face to face with a dark-haired riverman whose greasy features looked vaguely familiar. Beside him slouched a second, shorter man, who gave a nasal laugh.

He remembered there had been three drunken dock-workers that morning he'd rescued Isabeau from their clutches. The last of the trio made his presence known. "Well, if it ain't the fancy man," came a rough voice behind him, seconds before a splintered plank connected with Tark's back.

"Mister Parrish left late this morning. I don't know when to expect him back."

Though the stocky housekeeper's tone brooked no argument, Isabeau stood her ground. That announcement was not the only unsettling news she had received in the past minute. The first was the fact that the *américain,* who was by all accounts wealthy, actually lived in this ramshackle warehouse! She spared another glance at the office of the Parrish Company, Ltd., tightening her grip on the scrap of paper bearing its address—a note written in Monsieur Calvé's unmistakable hand and found in Philippe's desk. Now that she had gotten this far, she would not turn back.

"Please, *madame,* it is important that I find M'sieur Parrish immediately. Do you know where he might have gone?"

"I don't hold with that *Madame* nonsense," the woman shortly replied, though Isabeau sensed a hint of approval in her tone. "You can call me Alma, just like everyone else. And why is it so important that you see him, Miss—"

"—Isabeau," she supplied, "Isabeau Lavoisier. Please,

Alma, I must find him. I can't tell you why, it is just that . . ."

She hesitated, unsure just how much she might reveal and still convince the housekeeper of her mission's importance. Any explanation could sound melodramatic or, worse, foolish. She took a deep breath and simply said, "I need his help."

"The Gilded Albatross," Alma replied. When Isabeau stared at her in confusion, she gestured toward the main avenue and added, "It's a tavern on Girod Street, just off the wharf."

"Merci, madame—Alma," she breathed with relief and turned to leave.

The housekeeper put out a restraining hand. "You can't go there by yourself, child. The Albatross is no place for a lady, even though my Ned runs an honest house. Why, it attracts every kind of lowdown, mean, ornery—"

"If M'sieur Parrish is there, then I shall feel quite safe. Besides, I am not completely helpless, as you see," she added, and reached into her reticule to withdraw the pepperbox pistol.

Alma eyed both her and the gun with misgivings. "I just don't know," she said with a shake of her head. "Why don't you wait here for him? I'll have to leave in a few minutes to catch the Baton Rouge steamer, but you're welcome to stay awhile."

Isabeau spared a glance at the sun, which already was stretching charcoal shadows across the wharf, then turned in the direction Alma had indicated. It should take only a few minutes to walk there, she told herself, and determine if he was still there. On the other hand, should she choose to await him here at the warehouse, she might find herself in for a long night—in spite of Alma's assurances.

"Don't worry," she reassured the older woman as she tucked away the pepperbox. "I will be quite fine alone."

"I guess I can't stop you, then, short of tying you to a chair," the housekeeper conceded. "If you don't find Mr. Parrish, just go up to the bar and ask for my Ned. Tell him that I sent you—and that he'd best see you home safely, if Mr. Parrish can't."

"I promise I will," Isabeau agreed, giving the woman a hug before starting toward the tavern.

Her walk was brief, though it gave her time to think over her earlier conversation with Philippe. She had returned home from her visit with Madame at almost the same instant he had rounded the corner, a thoughtful frown marring his features. His distracted air . . . a mood unusual for her normally carefree brother . . . had worked in her favor.

With a heartfelt if hasty "thank *le bon Dieu,*" he had agreed to inform Marcel of her acceptance of that gentleman's proposal. Her explanation of her plans for that evening—"another Carnival ball, *mon frère,*" she had offered, silently asking forgiveness for that lie—had been met in the same casual manner. He had not mentioned that her simple gown was hardly the appropriate attire for such a festive event.

Still puzzling, she halted before a dubious-looking establishment huddled between two other unkempt structures. Above this building's front door hung a sign with the crude rendition of a gold-tipped seabird reassuring her that she had found the Gilded Albatross. She took a tentative step past its threshold, peering through the smoke at a haphazard arrangement of tables. Two dozen or so rivermen in various stages of intoxication had gathered—their freely hurled threats and curses were punctuated by bursts of coarse laughter. Tark, however, did not appear to be among them.

Drawing her cloak about her, she made her way toward the bar. The bedraggled women appeared permanently propped there. All were clad in dingy chemises, over which they wore black or brown skirts cropped to expose their thin ankles. They met her gaze with hostility, and Isabeau hid her disdain. She addressed herself to the florid-faced man busily washing glasses behind the bar.

"Are you Ned?"

The man glanced up at her, his round face reflecting surprise, and then, concern. "What's a pretty young girl like you doing here? Can't you see, this is no place for a lady."

"Hey, I'll make a place for you, sweet thing," called a man from the far side of the tavern. "Send her over here, Ned."

"That's right, *lady*. We'll show you a good time," a second riverman boasted.

Ned gestured at the nearest barmaids. "Flora, Katie, get over there and keep those fellows happy." He turned back to Isabeau. "I'm afraid I'll have to ask you to leave, miss. The fellows here . . . well, they aren't used to ladies. Now run along and—"

"Alma said you would help me, *m'sieur*. I'm looking for a gentleman . . ."

"Alma sent you?" His distraught expression began to

clear. "You're looking for someone in particular? Not your husband, I hope? I don't want any trouble."

"Please, Ned, I must speak with M'sieur Tark Parrish. Alma said he was here, but I don't seem to find him. I assure you, it's very important."

"You're looking for Tark? He was here a minute ago. Seems he walked past and nodded . . ."

When the bartender hesitated, the remaining barmaid spoke. "He went out the back way to talk to some gent—said he'd be gone just a minute." The doxy fixed Isabeau with a knowing look. "He asked me to wait for him until he got back . . . said he wanted a bit of comfort, if you know what I mean."

"He did head outside," Ned remembered, though his smile faded when Isabeau started for the rear door. "Wait, you can't go back there."

The door in question opened onto a short hall. A stairway lay at one end, while at the other a splintered door hung ajar. She made her way to it and peered cautiously around its edge.

The alley beyond lay awash in shadows; still, she readily made out the brawling forms of the three rivermen who previously had accosted her at Ophelia's brothel. This time, the object of their attention was Tark.

The trio had pinned him against the far wall, and were pummeling him with more vigor than finesse. The thud of bare knuckles against flesh was muffled in their shouts as the three attacked him from all sides.

She saw that even as Tark met each onslaught with a returning jab, his defenses were weakening. Unless someone helped him, it would be a matter of moments before he was at the rivermen's mercy.

Isabeau jerked the pepperbox from her reticule and pointed it at them. "Let him go."

Barely had the echo of her words died than the men halted, letting Tark sag to the ground. At the sight, she choked back a cry and stepped closer, gesturing with the pistol. "Leave us be."

The fat man squinted in disbelief, then burst into laughter. "Why, it's the same Frenchy gal what wouldn't play friendly," he said between guffaws, swiping at his bloodied nose. "Guess she's changed her mind—haven't ya, girlie?"

Isabeau bit her lip. *Mon Dieu,* she couldn't just shoot them. Yet, brutal men like these could hardly be reasoned with. "I swear, *m'sieur,* if you don't leave right now, I'll . . ."

"You'll what? Ya gonna plug all three of us, girlie?" The fat man leered and wet his lips. "Tell ya what, you come on over here an' apologize, an' I might even let your fancy man live."

"You tell 'er, Bill," the short man mumbled through rapidly swelling lips. "You're more'n a match for the little slut—gun or no."

"I'd think twice about calling the lady's bluff, if I were you," came an ironic drawl from behind them.

Tark dragged himself upright against the scabbed wall, his air casual despite the steady trickle of blood from a gash above his left eye.

If he was surprised to see her there, he gave no sign but went on, "I've seen our sweet Isabeau put a bullet in a man just as pretty as you please. She never blinked, not even the time some poor fellow's blood splashed all over her new muslin gown. Of course, if you gentlemen are determined to test her mettle . . ."

He trailed off with a shrug, and Isabeau willed her hands not to waver. She knew Tark was bluffing—the question was, would their assailants believe him?

The short man spat blood and shook his head in disgust. "Hell, I don't aim to get kilt by some fancy piece," he exclaimed and started toward the street.

The others muttered their assent and trotted after their companion. Isabeau lowered her pistol and sagged against the brick wall behind her.

"And just what in the hell kind of stunt was that?"

Before Isabeau could respond, Tark had crossed the alley in half-a-dozen quick strides and planted himself before her. "I didn't ask for your help, and I damn sure didn't need it."

"Didn't need it?" Isabeau was mortified to hear her voice quavering on the edge of tears. "How can you say that, when there were three men fighting you? *Mon Dieu,* you're bruised and bleeding, and they might have . . ."

She stopped short when his forbidding expression warned against further debate, though the sentence finished itself in her mind. *They might have killed you.*

"I could have handled them." His clipped tone put a halt to that line of discussion, while his gaze dropped to her gun. He gave a snort of disgust. "Sweet Jesus, where in the hell did you get that relic?"

He yanked the pepperbox from her grasp and broke it open, then unloaded it. "This thing hasn't been cleaned in a good ten years, and the ammunition's got to be older than that. Do you have any idea what would have happened if you'd been fool enough to pull the trigger?"

When she shook her head, he went on, "Probably not a damned thing . . . which would have been inconvenient as hell. So do us both a favor and toss it into the river on your way home. Or, better yet, I'll get rid of it for you."

He flung the gun and its bullets toward the alley's far end, where they landed in a pile of broken whiskey bottles. Then, without a look back, he strode out onto the street.

Though her first impulse was to rush after him, she headed to the rear of the alley, intent on retrieving her discarded weapon. After all, even so useless a gun as the ill-maintained pepperbox would be better than nothing, should she encounter any other riverfront thugs.

She hastily sifted through the glinting brown shards until she recovered both pistol and bullets. By the time she stepped from the alley, Tark had already put a good block's worth of distance between them.

She fleetingly contemplated hurling the weapon in the direction of his well-muscled back. She had risked her life to save his, yet all he did was belittle her effort and leave without thanks! More than her pride was at stake.

Dusk had wrapped the city in a grey blanket, so that she just made out Tark's figure before he rounded a corner. She couldn't afford to lose sight of him, lest he was bound for some destination other than his warehouse.

Or in case he succumbed to his injuries and collapsed in some dark alley. That last possibility spurred her to action. Tucking the pepperbox in her reticule, Isabeau hurried down the *banquette* after him.

Twenty-two

Tark rounded the corner and halted alongside a boarded-over tavern. There, he abandoned his pretense of vigor and sagged against the listing doorway.

Sweet Jesus, but he felt like he'd been trampled by runaway horses! Still, he was lucky that his attackers had settled their score with fists, rather than knives or guns. Otherwise, he would not have walked away from that encounter.

He stifled a groan. By now, the gash over his eye had bled enough so that he felt distinctly light-headed, while his battered ribs screamed in protest with every breath, this not to mention the fact that his right hand was swollen to twice its normal size and was throbbing like a voodoo drum.

He put his uninjured hand to his forehead. Though his fingertips came away tacky, the cut seemed to have stopped bleeding. A few moment's more rest, and he could make his way to the warehouse to continue his suffering in relative comfort.

Tark shut his eyes, content for the moment to remain upright and conscious. As his dizziness subsided, the one nagging question regained his attention.

Just what in the hell had Isabeau been doing in the alley behind the Albatross?

In those agonizing minutes while he desperately had prayed for someone to provide assistance, he'd had in mind Tom or Ned. *She* had been the last person he expected.

Now, it occurred to him that his shabby treatment of her had been poor thanks for the chit's timely intervention. Embarrassing though it was to have been saved by a girl brandishing an ineffective weapon, it was a damn sight better than subjecting himself to the rivermen's pummeling. But what had prompted her to be there in the first place? Surely she hadn't come to the waterfront looking for him.

Or had she?

Despite his blinding headache, Tark gamely struggled with the question. Clearly, her actions were prompted by something other than fancy, since she had ventured alone to a part of town where many men would never set foot. Courage, she had in spades. What he didn't understand was why she wanted to see him again . . . or why she had risked her neck to save his. Hell, in her place, he'd have let the rivermen do their worst.

The sound of footsteps on the splintered *banquette* roused him from his half-stupor. He opened his eyes and met her stricken gaze, then asked in resignation, "Can't I go anywhere in this city without you or your brother trailing after me?"

"*Mon Dieu,* Tark, you truly are hurt," she exclaimed, seeming not to have heard his jibe. "You need a physician, and bandages, and—"

"What I need is a bed . . . preferably, my own," he cut short her diagnosis and pushed away from the wall.

She reached out to steady him, and he acknowledged that he was glad to see her. It wasn't that he could use some assistance in making his way home. The real concern in her face made him realize how long it had been since anyone had shown interest in his well-being.

Seven years too long.

Memories of that ill-fated night in Claude Blanchard's garden flashed through his mind, and he pulled free of Isabeau's grasp. He'd let a woman take advantage of him once before, and he had paid dearly for the luxury. He'd be damned if he would make the same mistake twice.

"Don't you remember what I told you last night? In case you've forgotten, this time I'll make myself perfectly clear—I don't ever want to set eyes on you again."

Coolly, he registered the hurt that flashed through those midnight eyes. Then anger stamped hard lines across her aristocratic features, and he saw her wall of Creole civility crumble to let a torrent of words spill past.

"From the moment we met, you have plagued me with your unwanted presence—yet each time you dare pretend that *I* am to blame for our paths constantly crossing. And then, last night you . . . you—"

She broke off and flushed. "You are nothing but a barbaric *américain,* and the only reason I sought you out today is because I need your help to stop Monsieur Calvé."

She paused for breath, her chest heaving with the effort, and Tark let a smile twist his lips. "You need my help," he slowly repeated. "I don't see why—unless whoring for Franchot has perhaps lost its appeal for you?"

That final calculated taunt had its intended effect. Her palm met his jaw with a solid crack that echoed through the silent street. When she drew back in preparation for another onslaught, however, he caught her wrist in a punishing grip.

"I wouldn't try that a second time," he warned, releasing her so that she stumbled. "The mood I'm in right now, I might hit you back. Do us both a favor and get the hell out of my life."

But would he have a life without her?

The realization hit with sudden, unprecedented clarity. Bloody and battered as he was, he felt the familiar hot stirring of his loins at the thought of possessing her. But it was more than just physical attraction that held him enthralled.

From that moment on the dock, he'd been drawn to her like a thirsting man to water. He needed the cool, sweet relief of her pride . . . her honesty . . . and her passion. With her he could regain those qualities of his own that he'd thought lost forever—stupidly flung away on that sultry night so many years ago.

Before he could voice that flash of insight, she turned and fled down the *banquette*. Reflexive pride held him a moment where he stood, watching her charcoal gown blend with the light of dusk. Then, he started after her.

Isabeau heard footsteps behind her and quickened her pace, hiking her skirts with one hand and angrily swiping at tear-filled eyes with the other. It didn't matter where she went. All she cared about was putting as much distance as possible between herself and that barbarian.

Barely had she gone a block when her breath began to tear from her and her side started to ache. Her pulse pounded with a vengeance, so that only when she felt his hand on her shoulder did she realize that Tark had caught up with her. The unexpected pressure threw her off balance, taking him with her as they careened against a whitewashed brick wall. Her cry echoed Tark's choked curse as they tumbled headlong onto the rough-hewn *banquette*.

She lay stunned for a moment, bright pinpoints of light dancing before her eyes. She finally caught her breath, only to find she was sprawled across Tark's lap, while he lay half-propped against the offending wall.

With more speed than grace, Isabeau struggled upright, then glanced back at Tark. His eyes were closed, and his lashes a sooty smudge against a complexion now as chalky as the brick wall against which he lay. Surely, he was not—

"*Mon Dieu,* h-he is dead."

"Not hardly," came the ironic drawl from the supposed corpse, "but I'd probably feel a damned sight better if I were."

Tark opened his eyes and dragged himself up beside her. The cruel hand of grief that unexpectedly had gripped her heart released its hold, and she let out her breath in a tremulous sigh. Then, she recalled the reason for her flight, and her relieved smile faded.

"Not so fast, my sweet."

Tark grasped her arm before she could scramble to her feet. He reached his other hand to brush her cheek, his ice blue eyes regarding her now with warm emotion. "I believe I owe you thanks for what you did back there at the Albatross, and an apology . . . that is, if you can find it in your heart to forgive me for last night."

Forgive him?

Isabeau stared at him in stunned silence. In ruthlessly taking her maidenhead, he had robbed her of more than her innocence, yet in asking her pardon, he was admitting culpability for his actions—and perhaps conceding that he was not unaffected by their lovemaking.

Thoughts of Marcel and her impulsive engagement fled, and she gave a nod. Tark's expression lightened, but his tone remained serious as he went on, "I know I have much to answer for, but I think we should find a more private place to talk."

Realizing what an unseemly a spectacle the pair of them made, sprawled like vagrants on the wooden walkway, Isabeau scrambled to her feet. "We can talk at your office."

Tark waved aside the hand she offered and stood unassisted, though she could tell from his pain-taut features that the effort was costly. It wasn't until after they had traveled half a block that he deigned to lean against her for support.

"How in the hell did you find me?" he abruptly demanded, hand on her shoulder as they navigated the walkway. "If that dandified brother of yours sent you wandering the waterfront alone, I'll—"

"It was your housekeeper, Alma, who told me where to find you. As for my brother, he does not know where I am . . . or that I was looking for you."

She hesitated, groping for the explanation that she

mentally had been rehearsing since she had left Madame's home earlier that afternoon. "I know Philippe has involved you in some illegal scheme, but he had no choice in the matter, just as I had none. Then Madame Dumas told me how, during the war, you were . . ."

When she hesitated, Tark obligingly prompted, "I was what?"

"A h-hero."

Mon Dieu, he must think her as foolish as some starry-eyed debutante. Yet so she had been, following her conversation with Madame that afternoon. She had listened in amazement while the dowager related a few of Tark's more dangerous exploits from years before. According to Madame, the *américain* was a man to be reckoned with.

She glanced over at him, glad the dim light hid her blushes. "You are the only one I can turn to. You must stop him, before it is too late."

"Stop him? You mean, your brother?"

Isabeau shook her head. "The one you must stop is Monsieur Calvé. You see, he plans to kidnap the Russian grand duke the evening of Mardi gras."

"So what happens once your brother and uncle escort the grand duke from the theater?" Tark prompted as he sprawled atop his bed and listened to Isabeau's tale.

She didn't reply, busy as she was adjusting the pillows behind him. While she reached for the basin and towel, Tark suppressed a smile.

She had balked at setting foot in his bedroom, until he explained with unarguable logic that he would eventually have to make his way up the stairs. He had refrained from pointing out that, considering the intimacies they already had shared, it was late for her to be worrying about such niceties. She had conceded that she couldn't have him risk further injury by attempting the ascent on his own.

"I do not know," she answered, sponging away the dried blood that streaked his face from temple to jaw. "All M'sieur Calvé told me was that they would take the duke on a tour of the docks. Could they perhaps mean to hold him there until the ransom is paid?"

"Perha—"

His word ended in an involuntary grunt as fire seared his brow. "Sweet Jesus, what in the hell are you putting on me?"

"The label said 'Kentucky's finest bourbon.' I found almost a whole case of it downstairs." A smile touched her lips as she pressed him back against the pillows. "Now, lie quietly. You've a bad cut, and I must clean it."

"That rotgut is liable to do more harm than good," he darkly predicted. When she took a swipe at his cut, he gritted his teeth and concentrated on the sight before him, finding it a distraction from the pain of his forehead.

Isabeau leaned over him, one slim white hand brushing back his hair and the other wielding the whiskey-soaked towel. Her position afforded him an enviable view of her small, firm breasts, for the neckline of her demure grey gown revealed a shadowed hint of the enticing valley between them. With an effort, he resisted the urge to press his face against that soft flesh, instead letting his gaze roam her smooth white skin. With equal enjoyment, he breathed in the hint of her perfume, a floral scent whose sweetness was intensified by her body's warmth.

"There," she pronounced and pulled back to survey her handiwork. "How do you feel?"

"Like I've been in a fight."

Actually, aside from his lacerated forehead and battered ribs, he felt pretty good. Maybe the impromptu brawl had allowed him to vent his frustrations—or maybe it was the fact that he had gained an ally.

Debating just how rapid a recovery he could make and not arouse her suspicions, he favored her with a smile. "Shall we consider the score between us equal, then—a rescue for a rescue?"

"I think we may." Her answering smile was tremulous as she lowered her gaze to the bloody cloth she held. *"Mon Dieu,* but I was afraid. What made those rivermen come after you, when you had only frightened them off that morning?"

"Pride," he promptly guessed, feeling a sudden kinship with his assailants. Hell, his own self-esteem had absorbed a similar blow. "Remember, Isabeau, that few men will tolerate being made a fool of before another man . . . let alone being shown up in front of a woman."

"So that was why you were so angry at me for interfering," she exclaimed. "Why, you actually would have preferred for me to let them beat you senseless."

"Let's just say that I would rather fight my own battles—even when it's three against one."

And even when the big guy takes me by surprise and hits me from behind. Deciding this line of discussion had taken too personal a tack, he seized upon their original topic. "Tell me what else you have learned about Franchot's plans. Did he say why he wants to kidnap Alexis?"

Isabeau shook her head. "I have told you everything I know. Now, what must we do to stop Monsieur Calvé?"

"First of all, you can forget the 'we.' "

Ignoring her cry of protest, he swung his legs over the side of the bed and stood. "You'll do your part that night by luring the grand duke outside, just as Franchot has instructed you. Afterwards, I'll want you the hell out of there."

"But what of my cousin's child? I told you, Monsieur Calvé will not release Regine unless I cooperate." She tossed aside the towel and glared at him. "Don't think to put me off. I will do what I must to save her."

"Don't be a damned fool."

Turning his back on her, Tark glanced at his washstand mirror. He put a hand to his brow, then ran his fingers down his bruised cheekbone. Still, save for the blood on his shirt, he appeared little worse for his experience. With a grimace he swung around to face her again.

"This isn't some parlor game," he went on as he tugged his shirt free and unfastened its buttons. "In case you haven't guessed, our friend Franchot is a dangerous man. Once you're no longer useful to him, he's liable to send his thugs to slit your throat and leave you in some back alley. If you want to get out of this mess alive, you'll do what I tell you."

"But I cannot let you take all the risks . . ."

Isabeau's voice trailed as she watched him shrug out of the bloodied shirt. It was one thing, to be unchaperoned as she attended the needs of an injured man. It was another to be alone with the man, now that he was half-dressed and apparently recovered. But as she reminded herself of this, her gaze fixed in unwilling fascination upon his bared torso.

Outside, the winter sun had extinguished itself in the waters of the Mississippi. A pair of flickering gaslamps provided the room's sole illumination. Their sooty shadows emphasizing his muscular shoulders and arms. Crisp black hair covered his chest and veed downward along his flat stomach, continuing to tantalizing depths beneath the waistband of his trousers. She recalled their first meeting on the dock, when the sight of him so casually dressed had first stirred in her the same dangerous desires.

With an effort, she dragged her gaze upward to meet his. Though his eyes held a cynical gleam, they also reflected a spark of sensual awareness that sent warmth threading through her. She thought of last night and the satisfying sensation of oneness during those few brief moments that had changed her life.

Tark let the shirt fall and started toward her. "Don't tell me you're having second thoughts about our partnership, my sweet. I thought we were suited, you and I. And if we *are* to be partners, we must trust one another . . . don't you agree?"

"But I do trust you," she softly protested. It no longer mattered that she was a Creole, and he was an *américain*. Neither did she care that the common ground between them was doomed to trickle away like so much river mud. For now, she would give herself up to Carnival madness and follow her heart.

She searched Tark's gaze, his expression calling to mind a man she had seen wager a sum on a roll of the dice. The gentleman in question had lost the gamble— and with it, his entire fortune. She could have a hand in the outcome. She could determine whether or not the *américain* won his wager.

He has as much at stake as I do, perhaps more. She realized with a woman's instinctive wisdom that he had lost his faith in life and in love . . . and that he needed her help to win it back. All at once, it seemed somehow right to seal their unspoken bargain with a joining of their flesh.

"I trust you," she whispered again. "Let me show you how much I do."

Twenty-three

Her challenge stopped Tark cold.

"Show me?" he repeated, not daring to believe her offer. Anxious as he was to bed her again, it occurred to him that her capitulation might stem from something other than desire. Pity for his battered state, perhaps? Or, even worse, maybe she viewed their lovemaking as a necessary exchange, the use of her body in return for his help against Calvé.

At the thought, cold despair wrapped around his heart. Once he would have welcomed such an encounter with its freedom from any emotional bonds. Now, however, he realized he needed more than the physically satisfying but emotionally barren release that came with a simple joining of their bodies. He needed . . .

Love, he slowly finished the thought, elated by the possibility. For years, that emotion had been absent from his life. Unexpectedly, it had returned, finding a niche while leaving him unprepared for the consequences. How could he expect Isabeau to reciprocate his feelings, given the role that desire had demanded?

She reached a hand to his face, and desire overrode thought. Heedless of the consequences, he pulled her into his arms and captured her lips with his.

She made no protest but encircled his waist with her slim arms. Encouraged, he slid his hands down her back and eased his palms along the gentle swell of her hips, pressing her to him so she could feel his arousal.

When she moaned at this intimate contact, he penetrated her parted lips with his tongue to probe her mouth in unhurried strokes. Slowly at first, and then with increasing boldness she parried his thrusts, pressing closer so that her silken gown caressed his bare chest. Desire gave way to something stronger, hotter . . . an unfamiliar hunger that stemmed from his very soul.

Abruptly, he broke free of their embrace, shaken by the intensity of his reaction. When she looked up at him, he saw her dark eyes reflect the same uncertainty as she whispered, "Do I not please you, Tark?"

"You'll do."

His harsh breathing lent an edge to his casual reply. When hurt flashed across her features, he gathered her back into his arms. This, too, was unexpected, the urge to reassure her overwhelming his need to shelter himself from his own emotional storm.

"You please me very well, my sweet," he murmured, capturing her slim white fingers and pressing her palm to his chest. "Feel my heart, the way it beats faster at your touch. I need you . . . more than you could ever know."

Barely were those words spoken than he regretted them. Sweet Jesus, the blow to his head must have sent him raving. To his own ears, he sounded like nothing so much as a youth suffering an acute bout of calf love.

But Isabeau barely heard his words, for anticipation now warred with uncertainty. With her hand across his bare flesh, she could feel the texture of his chest hair and the warmth of his skin taut across muscle. Beneath her fingers, his heart throbbed a beat that matched her own racing pulse.

Remember what happened to Lili, a censuring voice warned, to no avail. Stronger than the bonds of propriety, than of any fear of being seduced and abandoned, was the growing sense that her fate and Tark's were somehow intertwined. Even if she fled him now, she would one day find herself in his arms again.

"What would you have me do next?" she softly asked, knowing that the question sealed her fate.

He gave a smile and fingered the neckline of her gown. "I think things will progress more smoothly if we rid you of this."

With a few deft moves, he unfastened the small buttons that ran halfway down the back of her gown. She scarcely breathed as his fingers paused on the last pearly disk. He undid it with deliberate casualness and then eased the gown off her shoulders.

Her impulse was to cover herself, but something in his gaze held her motionless as he slid the heavy gown down her hips. Finally, he let the dress puddle around her feet alongside his discarded shirt.

With practiced moves, he divested her of corset cover and corset, leaving her clad only in a chemise, drawers, and petticoat. "We're making progress, my sweet. Shall I continue?"

Her whispered assent ended on a sigh as he slowly plucked the tortoise-shell pins from her hair. When the last skittered from his fingers to the floor, allowing her black tresses to spill free, he slid his hands down her neck and along her back.

He paused at the curve of her waist and then moved upward again until he gently cupped her breasts. She gasped as he caressed their rosy peaks through the thin fabric of her chemise, his touch sparking a warm glow between her thighs.

"You like that, don't you?" he murmured, gently nipping her earlobe. "I want to hear the words. Tell me that you like the way I touch you."

"I . . . I like the way you touch me," she breathed. The admission ending in a moan as his lips moved down her throat, pausing to explore the hollow where her pulse beat a frantic rhythm.

Then he tugged at tapes binding her petticoat, so that it slid in a silken whisper down her hips and to the floor. Just as quickly, he unfastened the narrow ribbons of her camisole. Cool air caressed her breasts as he pushed aside the confining silk. Now, only her drawers and stockings remained as a flimsy barrier against his sensual assault.

"Sweet Jesus, you're so beautiful."

Tark reached out a hand and stroked first one breast and then the other. Her nipples tightened as she strained against his hand, the heat of his fingers all but searing her flesh. Then he dropped to his knees and took one hardened peak in his mouth. His hands encircled her waist as he alternately nipped and suckled each sensitive bud.

She moaned with pleasure and reached out to revel again in the sensuous feel of his flesh beneath her hands. Mirroring his earlier touch, she lightly stroked his chest, marveling at the similar way his flesh responded to her touch.

All at once, he straightened in her embrace with a sharp intake of breath. *"Mon Dieu,* your ribs," she gasped in dismay as she saw in the dim light the bruises from his earlier altercation. Gently she ran her fingers along the discolored flesh. "Is it very painful?"

"That's not what hurts," he rasped out with a grin.

"Then what does?"

"This." He grasped her hand and stroked it across the hot, bold outline of his erection. "I'm afraid you're the only one who can relieve this agony, my sweet."

He released her fingers and tugged at his boots and trousers, until he stood naked before her. She let her gaze travel down his muscled chest past his flat stomach. His engorged manhood jutted proudly from the dark thicket at the apex of his long, muscular legs.

"I trust you're satisfied with what you see," he said, his grin holding a touch of savage pride.

With an effort, she tore her gaze free. Her religion stressed the shame inherent in the naked human form, yet she found it difficult to embrace that tenet. The muscled limbs and boldly chiseled arousal of this man embodied primitive male beauty . . . a virility that made her ache to feel his touch again. The Mother Superior might brand her a sinner for harboring such thoughts, but eternal damnation seemed a small price to pay for such bliss.

He moved closer until his manhood brushed her silken pantalets. "Touch me," he urged as he tangled his fingers in her hair and pulled her closer. "Wrap your hands around me and feel how much I want you."

Hesitantly, she stroked her fingers along the thick length of his staff. When it quivered like a silk-sheathed sword beneath her hand, she slowly repeated the gesture. She heard his groan and saw in his half-closed eyes pain mingled with pleasure. Emboldened, she cupped her free hand around the twin pouches at the base of his distended rod, marveling at how soft and yet how heavy they were. She gently continued her rhythmic stroking, feeling a frisson of excitement heat her blood and bring a damp warmth between her thighs.

He pressed himself more urgently against her hands, a few warm drops of liquid now spilling across her palms. She realized all at once she wielded a power over him that he was helpless to resist. But before she could further test her new-found mastery, he eased himself free from her grasp.

"If you keep that up much longer, my sweet," he said with a ragged grin, "I'm afraid our lovemaking will be over almost before it's begun."

He slid his fingers beneath the narrow waistband of her pantalets. With a quick move, he freed the tie, so that the last wisp of fabric shielding her from his hungry gaze slid to the ground.

"Sweet Jesus."

His words fell somewhere between a curse and a groan as he swept her up and carried her to the narrow bed. "I'm sorry there's not a more comfortable place for us," he said as he straddled her. "Next time, we'll find a big bed with satin sheets . . . but right now, I want you so damn bad this will just have to do."

"I-I do not mind," she truthfully murmured and lifted her mouth to his.

He thrust his tongue savagely between her lips and kissed her with an exhilarating ferocity. She arched against him, feeling the blunt tip of his manhood against her as he stroked his swollen shaft along her stomach, at first slowly, and then with increasing urgency.

The damp warmth between her legs spread as she moved along with him, brushing her nipples against his chest until pain and pleasure became one. Then he thrust one knee between her legs, his hand moving down her body to the apex of her thighs.

"Let me touch you," he urged, his breath hot against her lips as he broke free of their kiss. "Let me give you the same kind of pleasure you give me."

His fingers found the sensitive nub between the twin folds of delicate skin, his touch sparking the same hot tingling she remembered. She moaned and instinctively spread her thighs so that he could freely caress that soft bud of flesh.

"Sweet Jesus, you're so hot and wet," he rasped out, positioning himself above her. "Do you want me inside you now?"

"*Mon Dieu,* yes," she pleaded and arched against him.

With an answering groan, he eased between her legs so that the blunt tip of his shaft throbbed at the entrance to her body. She tensed, remembering all too clearly the sharp pain that had assailed her the first time he had penetrated her. He sensed her uneasiness and rose up so that his ice blue gaze met hers.

"I promise you, it won't hurt like that again. Just . . . trust me."

His words ended on a groan as he slid deep within

her tight sheath. She caught her breath, overwhelmed by the sensation of fullness but relieved that the expected pain was only an instant's discomfort.

"It's all right, now," she whispered and trailed her fingers along his back, feeling the quick play of muscles beneath her hands as he reacted to her touch. He began to move slowly within her, and the faint burning between her thighs blossomed into an ache of pleasure.

"Wrap your legs around me," he urged her. "That's good, my sweet. Just relax and move with me."

His mouth captured hers again, and she eagerly parted her lips, allowing his tongue to probe her mouth with the same sure strokes that mirrored his movements between her thighs. And with that final surrender fell the last vestiges of her trepidation.

This lovemaking was different from last night's. Gone was the sense of threat that had accompanied their first hasty coupling. Instead, it was a mutual passion that this time sprang, not from anger, but from desire.

Now, she was conscious of nothing more than Tark's harsh breathing and the frantic clashing of their hot, sweat-slicked flesh as he penetrated her again and again. The pulsating throb between her thighs grew to an unbearable crescendo. Just as she knew she couldn't take any more of that glorious agony, it peaked in a burst of pleasure that made her cry out.

He echoed her cry with a harsh sound of triumph and drove into her with a final fierce stroke. She felt the thrusts as he found his own release, spilling his hot seed until, with a shudder, he relaxed atop her.

Sated, she wrapped her arms around him while his rapid heartbeat slowed. Then he rose up and smiled with the same affection she had glimpsed in him earlier that night. "Was I right, my sweet? Was it better this time?"

Feeling shy beneath his warm scrutiny, she blushed. "It was wonderful, but now I feel so strange, like I could laugh and cry at the same time."

"That's just how you're supposed to feel."

His smile broadened into a lazy grin as he rolled off her and lay back against the rumpled sheets, cradling her so her cheek was pillowed on his shoulder. She nestled there contentedly, savoring the warmth of his flesh and breathing the heady scent of sweat and whiskey that clung to him. He dozed off, and she let herself consider the most telling consequence of her actions.

She had betrayed Marcel.

Little matter that their betrothal had only just been settled, or that the banns had not even been read. What mattered was that she had set aside that obligation to indulge her new-found desires. The question was, could she marry Marcel now?

She harbored no illusions that Tark loved her, though she realized now that she had lost her heart to him long ago. But what truly mattered was the security of her family. Did she not owe them the satisfaction of her brilliant match, so that she spare them lives of financial hardship? Surely her own happiness must play only a secondary role.

The thought sent a shiver through her, so that she drew one of the discarded blankets across her for comfort. At her movement, Tark stirred beside her. "Are you cold?" he whispered against her hair.

When she nodded, he turned and scissored one long leg over hers, locking her body against his. Propping himself on one elbow, he idly traced his fingers along the soft curve of her cheek. "Is that better?"

"Much better," she agreed, drawing comfort from the warmth of his gaze. She realized that he had lost the hard, cynical expression that usually masked his features. Minus that guarded reserve, he appeared little older than Philippe, she thought with pleased surprise.

He caught her look and quirked a brow in inquiry, twining his fingers through hers. "Tell me what you're thinking."

"I was merely deciding that you are not so old as I had first thought," she admitted, then blushed when she realized the confession might offend him.

To her relief, his smile broadened. "I may have a few years on you, my sweet Isabeau," he said, moving his thumb in circles against her palm, "but I can withstand any activities you have a mind to try."

"I will remember that." She tried for a light tone, uncomfortably aware of her naked state. Shy now, she disengaged her fingers from his and sat up, pulling the coverlet nearly to her chin. What *did* one talk of afterwards? she wondered in embarrassment. The weather, perhaps?

Tark paid no heed to her sudden modesty, but merely sat up against the bedstead. Unlike her, he contented himself with only a sheet draped across his lap to conceal his nakedness. She clutched her blanket more closely and studied him from beneath lowered lashes.

He had lapsed into abstracted silence, his ice blue gaze fixed on the flickering gaslight. Then he glanced over at her, and she saw in him that familiar attitude of detachment she had come to dread. Was he concerned about the grand duke's kidnaping, or could it be that he regretted their lovemaking?

Isabeau shifted uncomfortably beneath the wrinkled quilt, all too aware that the man with whom she had shared the most intimate secrets of her body was the same man who now held her fate in his hands. She trusted him—*Sainte Cécile,* perhaps she even loved him!—yet he was little more than a stranger to her, despite their moment of shared passion.

She struggled to sort her thoughts, but the question she finally blurted was, "Is Madame Tremaine truly your mistress?"

Even as she spoke the words she wished them back, appalled at her brazenness. No woman of refinement would dare mention so indelicate a subject to any man.

When he did answer, the reply was the one she dreaded. "Elisabeth and I are intimately acquainted. I'm sure if you ask, she'll be glad to elaborate on some of the more interesting facets of our relationship."

"And do you still . . . love her?"

Love?

Tark bit back a crude retort as he considered the question. Just what *were* his feelings for his former mistress? Once, she had amused him with her unrepentant self-absorption and her astute manipulation of those around her. She also had satisfied his physical needs with a skill that no other woman he'd ever encountered could surpass—yet he had never experienced with her the soul-searing gratification he had found tonight. In fact, the sole emotion he could summon in connection with her was fervent relief that their relationship was ended.

Isabeau awaited his reply, so he answered truthfully, "No, I don't love her."

"But how can that be? If you took her for your mistress, surely you must care for her."

"With women like Elisabeth, love and sex tend to be mutually exclusive endeavors. Hell, love is rarely a prerequisite for bedding any woman."

Too late, Tark realized just what those heedless words implied. "What I meant to say was, a man and woman need not feel guilty should they choose to share physical love outside of marriage," he explained, but not swiftly enough to forestall the bewilderment that flashed across her face. Trying to banish her stricken expression, he added, "As for Elisabeth . . . don't worry, my sweet. She's out of my life for good."

Her fleeting smile at those words faded when she continued, "When I talked to Monsieur Calvé today, he called you his old friend and said I should keep in mind how your wife died. What did he mean?"

The question was one he had been dreading. In the aftermath of their lovemaking, however, Tark found himself oddly eager to reveal to her the truth about Delphine and Belle Terre. But by laying bare those secrets, he ran the risk of losing her. Still, what other choice did he have, if he wished to rebuild his life with her as its foundation?

Carefully choosing his words, he began, "If you're to understand why I became embroiled in Franchot Calvé's schemes, you'll first have to know how I came to own Belle Terre . . . and how I woke up one morning to find myself married to a scheming little baggage by the name of Delphine."

Twenty-four

"Belle Terre was my plantation a few miles outside the city . . . canefields, good pasture, a home overlooking the river," Tark went on. "Once, the property belonged to Clarisse Dumas. After her husband's death she left it in the care of her staff and took up residence in town."

"I remember the place," Isabeau said, a frown marring her brow. "Once, when Philippe and I were children, we stayed there until the fever season was over. But how did you come to own it?"

"Clarisse suffered her share of financial reverses during the war. She couldn't afford the exorbitant taxes slapped on the estate by the Reconstruction government, but I could. And since I was like a grandson to her . . ."

Tark smiled at the memory. Actually, the dowager's reasons had been couched in slightly more biblical terms—something to the effect that she would sooner burn the place and sow the land with salt than let Northern scum defile her home.

"At any rate, Clarisse sold me the place for a song. The following week, Alma Crenshaw showed up on my doorstep and informed me that I should hire her as housekeeper.

"With Alma's help, I refurbished the house and moved in, only to learn that my Creole neighbors considered me no better than any Yankee interloper." His smile turned bitter. "It came as quite a blow to my vanity when the people I'd considered my social equals looked down their collective noses at me."

His tone self-deprecating now, he went on, "You see, my late father was a wealthy St. Louis businessman. I spent the first twenty-four years of my life playing the role of heir before a crowd of anxious mothers and marriage-minded daughters. I accepted every privilege as my due . . . only to find myself in for a rude awakening once I'd settled here."

"But your wife," Isabeau interjected. "I thought she *was* a Creole."

"She was. Her father had lost his fortune during the war and when he learned I had a substantial inheritance to draw upon, he graciously overlooked the fact I was an American."

"Then you loved her?"

"The only love involved was that of Claude Blanchard for my bank account. He invited me to a cotillion and arranged for half the parish to discover me and his daughter in a compromising position. I was drunk at the time and in no condition to protest my innocence."

Not that he could have offered any defense for what he'd done. The truth remained that he had brought much of his misery on himself.

"In one fell swoop, Claude managed to saddle me with his slut of a daughter and every cent of his debt, while looking a sympathetic hero to all his neighbors."

He fell silent, tempted to ease the pain of his aching

body with a few sips from the whiskey bottle beside the bed. Memory forestalled his hand.

"The rest of the story is not too pretty. Are you sure you want to hear it?"

He was gratified by a moment's reluctance in her face before she nodded. Still, he hesitated. Physical intimacy was one thing, emotional sharing was quite another. Was he ready to let her see into his heart?

Taking a deep breath, Tark plunged on, "I decided to make the best of the situation, to try to make the marriage work . . . not that I had any example to go by. My own parents' marriage had been cold and joyless. Hell, they couldn't even move beyond indifference to hatred—too much emotion involved, you see.

"My good intentions lasted long enough for me to learn that Delphine had her own ideas about wedded bliss. She made no secret of the fact that she despised me for who I was and what I represented. By the end of our second week together, she had moved out of my bedroom. By the end of the third, she had taken her first lover."

That admission, at least, held no pain for him. From the first, he had his suspicions concerning his wife's actions. Had he been so inclined, he might have demanded an explanation. The fact had been that he hadn't given a damn what she did, so long as she was discreet.

"I knew about Delphine's infidelities," he went on, "but all I cared about was saving Belle Terre. Clarisse had entrusted me with a legacy. I didn't think I could face her again if I lost the estate . . . which I was in danger of doing."

But there had been another reason he had let Delphine

go her own way. Soon after their hasty marriage, he found something to ease his own needs—that smooth, dark bitch known as bourbon. She brought him comfort and oblivion by the bottleful, never demanding anything for her services . . . until one summer afternoon months later, when the liquor had exacted one hell of a payment.

Omitting for the moment this portion of his tale, Tark continued, "Between Blanchard's debts and my own—not to mention the way Delphine spent her way through every month—my capital was almost depleted. The only thing that saved me was striking up a partnership with a man who needed me to help launch a full-scale smuggling operation."

"A man," Isabeau echoed, her tone grim as his. "You mean, Monsieur Calvé."

Tark nodded. "The money was damned good and what I did was little different from what I'd done as a blockade runner. As for the legalities, I had no qualms since the Reconstruction government was bleeding the city dry. Then I learned that while I was risking my neck for silks and whiskey, my wife was entertaining my business partner."

Tark had left Baton Rouge a day early, his trip cut short by a narrow escape from that city's port officials—the second such unpleasant encounter in a month. Angry, drunk, and guessing that this turn of bad luck was no accident, he had returned home to find Delphine gone and the servants given the afternoon off.

Tark reflexively clenched his fingers at the memory. Some impulse had compelled him to search the place for any clue as to her whereabouts, starting with the lower floors and ending up in her bedroom. *Her bed-*

room. Sweet Jesus, how he'd hated that room with its pink silks and satins. Draped in softness, it should have been a dainty, feminine retreat. Instead, it reminded him of some great, ravening mouth that could swallow an unsuspecting male whole.

After a cursory search, something on her dressing table caught his eye. Amid the clutter of cut-glass perfume bottles and silver-backed brushes sat a tiny alabaster figure. It was a pawn . . . the very pawn that Franchot Calvé carried about as a talisman.

"I must have been half mad that day," he said, his tone taut with long-suppressed anger. "I know that by the time I headed for the riverbank an hour later, I was thoroughly drunk. And when I found her there, waiting . . ."

He swallowed the bitterness that rose in his throat and fell silent. This part of the story, he could not bring himself to tell her, yet the image remained deeply etched in memory.

It had been hot—a suffocating heat that clung to the earth like some desperate, sweating whore unaware that her attentions were unwelcome. Instinctively, he had left the well-tended grounds and followed the curve of the river where it bordered the property. Lush vegetation provided welcome coolness . . . and privacy.

She stood in a sunlit clearing, her back to him. The sharp crack of a branch beneath his boot sent her spinning to face him, not knowing it was he and not her lover who lurked in the shadows.

She wore only lace-trimmed pantalets, torn so that he could see the damp, golden vee of curls between her white thighs. Pale breasts jounced lightly at her movement, their white flesh marred by livid bruises. In a calculated gesture, she lightly cupped those globes, so that their swollen pink nipples pouted from between her splayed fingers.

The body of a woman; the face of a child. He had been lured once before by that tantalizing combination, and he again found himself unwillingly aroused, even knowing that another man had used that lush flesh minutes before. Bourbon-soaked desire fueled his anger and sent hot lust singing through his veins. She was his wife, by God, and he would take her if he damn well pleased!

He advanced on her, intent only on slaking that need. Delphine shook back her hair, littered with bits of leaves and took a step forward. "Franchot," she purred in childish satisfaction, "I knew you would—"

She broke off with a gasp, realizing her mistake. He halted, stunned by the knowledge of just how big a fool she had played him for this time. Sweet Jesus, she had cuckolded him with his business partner—a man he considered a friend! But even as he grappled with that double-edged betrayal, Delphine favored him with a sly smile.

"What is the matter, cher, do you not still want me?" She moved closer, so that he could smell the sharp scent of spent lust that clung to her, and her tone took on a contemptuous edge. "You wanted me badly enough that night in my father's gardens. You were drunk then, too, just like you are now. Tell me, cher, is that the only way you can take a woman?"

Tark shook his head as rage and helplessness alternately swept him. Sweet Jesus, if he could only recall what had happened next, after he seized her by the shoulders, his fingers biting into that soft white flesh.

She had made no cry of pain or protest, but merely laughed up at him—and then he had looked into those deceitful blue eyes and told her he would kill her for what she had done.

"I don't remember anything else about that afternoon," he continued in a flat tone. "I woke up the next morning at the Albatross with one hell of a hangover and no idea how I'd gotten there. It wasn't until after I made my way home that I found out Delphine was dead."

He heard Isabeau's soft intake of breath and winced. How was he to convince her of his innocence, when he wasn't even certain of it himself? Yet when he ventured a look at her, concern was reflected in those midnight eyes, so that the uncertainty that clenched his gut eased.

"Tell me what happened to her," she softly urged.

Tark took a deep breath, wanting now to tell her everything he had pieced together about those lost hours. "Her groom had spent his afternoon fishing not far from where I'd found her. Just before dusk, he saw her floating face-down in the river, snagged on a submerged tree limb. She was naked, so everyone first assumed that she had gone for a swim and drowned. Then the physician noticed the pattern of bruises across her throat, and talk turned to murder."

"But why suspect you?"

"One of my neighbors recalled seeing me ride by that same day, around noon," he replied with a careless shrug. "When no one could find me that night, the local officials concluded that I had cut short my trip with the intention of returning home unobserved and quietly murdering my wife . . . planning, of course, to make my public appearance the next day in time to play the bereaved spouse."

"Mon Dieu," Isabeau softly breathed. "But what proof did they have?"

"It was all circumstantial—and all pretty damn convincing. Hell, it made sense . . . a faltering marriage, a faithless wife, a husband unable to remember anything that might have proved his innocence."

He shook his head. "What saved me was Alma's testimony. It seems she had returned to the estate just as I rode out. She told the judge the reason she was certain it was me was because my gelding and I had practically trampled her. She also testified that she'd noticed Delphine standing near the riverbank, and that she had been very much alive at the time. So I was set free."

"And everything went back to normal, afterwards?"

"Not quite, my sweet," he answered with a humorless smile. "I returned home to Belle Terre again only to find the place empty. My creditors had taken advantage of my enforced absence to repossess everything."

"But what of M'sieur Calvé? Could he not have intervened in your behalf?"

"He left New Orleans the same day I was arrested . . . and departed one hell of a lot richer than he'd come, thanks to me. So, you see the kind of hero you found yourself," he ended with a shrug. "Do you still want my help now?"

"You are the only one I can trust," she said and reached a hand toward him.

He caught her fingers and drew her to him with a fierce possessiveness more powerful than desire. This time, when their lovemaking reached its peak, his release came in a sharp series of shudders that left him feeling joyously spent and yet renewed. As he lay there afterwards, entangled in her embrace, well-worn yet timeless phrases of love rose to his lips, so that he was tempted as never before to bare his heart.

Sleep claimed him, however, before he could murmur the words.

A distant thud thrust Isabeau into wakefulness. She sat up with a start, momentarily disoriented. Only when she glimpsed Tark's tall, naked form silhouetted against the moon-streaked window did she recall where she was.

Sainte Cécile, she had slumbered away a good portion of the night! She drew the bedcovers to her chin, wondering what had awakened her, when the pounding she had heard in her dreams repeated itself. Someone demanded entrance to the warehouse. But what could be so important that it could not wait until after dawn, unless the caller was—

"Philippe," she breathed in horror, picturing her brother at the door below, prepared to defend her honor. But how could he have guessed—

At her strangled cry, Tark turned from the casement and started toward the bed. "It's only Tom—my night patroller friend," he reassured her as he pulled on his discarded trousers. "He's probably got some more information about Franchot's shipment. I'll find out what he wants and get rid of him."

He paused and lightly brushed her lips with his. "Go

on back to sleep, my sweet," he murmured. "I'll be back in a few minutes."

She waited until he had padded from the room before wrapping a quilt over her nakedness and climbing from the bed. Though dawn was still a good hour away, she was fully awake, thanks to her disquieted conscience. She turned up the gaslight and gathered her strewn clothes, then splashed water from a chipped white china pitcher and made a hasty toilette. Her stiff limbs bore testament to unaccustomed delightful exertions as she drew on her chemise and pantalets.

She ventured a glance in the washstand's mottled mirror and saw that the evening's labors had left other marks on her, as well. Her lips still bore traces of swelling, and a small red bruise stood out on her throat. Her dark eyes looked larger than usual, touched with purple shadows. With her hair tumbling about her shoulders in an ebony cascade, she looked just like a woman who had been thoroughly and completely satisfied by her man.

She promptly gathered up her scattered hairpins and bundled her hair into a hasty knot. The style tempered her wanton air, she decided after another glance in the glass. Nothing, however, could banish the contented smile on her lips.

She turned from the glass and headed toward the woodstove in the room's far corner. The weather had been mild these past days, so the stove had seen little use. A chill hung in the air this morning, however, so she pulled open its door and stirred the grey ash. Unfortunately, no convenient ember lay buried within the cinders.

She had resigned herself to a chilly wait, when she heard the hollow echo of men's voices emanating from the open stove. Someone must have left the door on the furnace in Tark's office ajar, she reasoned, so that the connecting pipe served as an amplifier of sorts.

Isabeau hesitated, recalling Tark's reminder about the fate that awaited eavesdroppers. It had been a true enough consequence that night of Madame's cotillion, but this situation was different. With all that lay at stake, she was obligated to learn whatever she could by any means. Her conscience eased, she crouched beside the Franklin.

"—ain't 'bout him," asserted a rough, unfamiliar voice that presumably belonged to Tom. "It's 'bout yer lady friend, Elisabeth Tremaine."

Elisabeth Tremaine? Isabeau's heart lurched at the thought of her red-haired rival. But had he not implied that he had broken off his affair with the woman?

"What about Elisabeth?" came Tark's answer, and relief swept her at the unmistakable note of irritation in his tone.

Tom didn't immediately answer, and she heard the creak of floorboards that accompanied booted footsteps as the man moved about. Not daring to breathe, Isabeau leaned closer to the stove.

Finally, she heard his rough voice again. "There ain't no easy way to say it, so I'll tell ya flat out. Coupla fellas fished Missus Tremaine outa the river not more'n two hours ago. The doc says she drowned, but to my mind it weren't no accident. She had bruises on her throat, an' on her shoulders. Looks like she was murdered."

Twenty-five

Murdered.

The word drifted through the stovepipe in a hollow echo, and Isabeau swallowed back a horrified cry. Much as she disliked the woman, she could never wish such a fate upon her. But why had Tom felt compelled to bring such news now?

She heard Tark softly swear, though his next words held only cold rationality.

"Do you have any idea who did it? What about that so-called voodoo cult she belonged to? Have you talked to—"

"We do have one suspect," Tom interjected. "You."

No, Isabeau silently cried, even as a small serpent of suspicion uncoiled in her breast. Surely it was coincidence . . .

Tark gave a harsh, wordless sound of disbelief. "I hope to hell this isn't your idea of a joke, because I'm damn sure not laughing."

"It ain't no joke."

Tom's words were heavy with regret, yet Isabeau sensed the determination in his voice. "I talked to that fancy butler of hers, an' he says the two of ya had a real knockdown fight yesterday afternoon. Said ya had her trussed up tighter'n a nun's knees."

When Tark made no denial, the night patroller continued, "The fella also said that soon as he untied her, she took off after ya, an' that's the last time they seen her alive. Looks a mite suspicious, don't it?"

"I know how it looks," Tark clipped out, "but she didn't give me much choice. Hell, you saw what she did to my face. That was the only way I could get out of there in one piece, short of laying her out cold."

The floorboards creaked again as the men moved about, but Isabeau barely heard the sound above the pounding of blood in her ears. *He could not have killed her.* Still, suspicion sank cold fangs into her heart as she recalled Tark's bitter words concerning his faithless wife. She had confessed her infidelity, only to be found drowned in the merciless waters of the Mississippi. Now, Elisabeth Tremaine had met a similar end.

Though Tom's next words proved unintelligible, Tark's reply sliced rapierlike through the room. "The last time I saw her was at the house. She might have come looking for me, but she sure as hell never found me."

"Now, don't get all riled up," the other man urged in a reasonable tone. "I ain't said that I think ya kilt her. I'm tryin' to show ya how some folks might see it that way."

"Damn it, Tom, it couldn't have been more than thirty minutes from the time I left her place until I talked to you at the Albatross—not to mention the fact that I was on foot, and that it was broad daylight. So unless you're suggesting I carried her body through the streets . . ."

"Like I said, I ain't pointin' no fingers," the night

patroller went on. "Lemme do some more checkin' but in the meantime, ya'd best lay low fer awhile."

Their voices faded as Isabeau heard the office door open and shut, followed by the sound of a single set of footsteps. A moment later, she heard the wooden screech of a drawer being pulled open, and the faint but unmistakable clink of glass against glass.

With trembling fingers, Isabeau refastened the stove door and stood. She pulled on the rest of her clothes, vaguely aware she was shivering with a chill that had nothing to do with the unheated room.

Murdered. She drew an uncertain breath, her gaze held by the pattern of shadows from the flickering gaslight.

She curled her fingers so that her nails bit into the tender flesh of her palms, welcoming the pain that served to anchor her to the present. *It is only coincidence,* she assured herself. *Tark had nothing to do with Madame Tremaine's death, and Tom will prove it.*

She was struggling to fasten her corset, when she heard Tark's footsteps on the stairs. He halted in the doorway, his expression unreadable. "You're leaving."

"I-I must be home before daylight, or else Philippe will worry."

The gaslamp's glow didn't quite reach his face. Still, she sensed a watchfulness about him as he moved from the shadows and caught her corset strings, lacing her with an efficiency that did not surprise her.

With the same casual skill, he fastened the buttons of her gown, his fingers pausing to rest upon her bare shoulders. At her reflexive shiver, he turned her and gathered her against his bare chest, his embrace forging a bond of hard, muscled flesh that brought unexpected comfort.

"Are you cold, my sweet?" he murmured against her hair. "I can warm you, if you want."

Then he kissed her, not with the demanding passion of last night, but with an unspoken need that drew from her an instinctive response. She gave herself up to his caress, tasting on his lips the smoky tang of whiskey. If only she had never overheard that conversation, she could be lying in his arms again.

With a reluctant sigh, she broke free and gazed up at him, knowing what she must ask. "Your friend, did he want anything . . . important?"

She sensed his withdrawal even before he released her. "It was just business," he explained, his ice blue gaze hinting at neither guilt nor innocence. "It seems I have a few details left to work out before Tuesday night."

But what about Madame Tremaine? Tell me that you had no hand in her murder.

No explanation was forthcoming, however. Instead, Tark reached into his wardrobe for a fresh shirt, then pulled on his boots. When he faced her again, she saw that the remote, cynical *américain* had returned, his dangerous air enhanced by the angry gash across his forehead and the cool regard in his eyes.

"I'll see about finding you a carriage."

Isabeau gathered her reticule and followed him into his office. He indicated the horsehair sofa where she might sit, then made his way onto the wharf.

Isabeau glanced about the dimly lit office, taking in its shabby air and the mismatched collection of furnishings. Her gaze lit on the stove that had played a vital role in the past moments' drama.

No accident. Bruises on her throat. Murdered.

Surely Tark must have a reason for keeping silent. Still, she couldn't readily dismiss the uncanny similarity between the deaths of two women who had played such intimate roles in Tark's life. In the flickering half-light of the gaslamp, she noted an opened bottle of whiskey and an emptied glass on the desk. Had Tark turned to liquor to dull his grief? Or, more frightening, had he perhaps spent those few moments after Tom's departure indulging in some private celebration?

"*Mon Dieu,* no!" she cried and leaped to her feet. She was letting her imagination run wild. No proof of Tark's guilt had been offered; no witness had stepped forth to claim Elisabeth Tremaine had died at his hand. Why, even Tom had said he didn't believe Tark was guilty.

But did the night patroller know about Delphine and the way she had died?

The outer door reopened with a soft click. Isabeau spun about, praying that nothing of her uneasy thoughts was reflected on her face as she met Tark's ice blue gaze.

"You'd best hurry," he said without preamble. "The hack driver is anxious to call it a night."

Something in his expression, however, suggested that Tark's patience was strained. Isabeau was ready to protest this unceremonious dismissal, when a sharp sense of loss welled within her.

For all her fears and suspicions, she could not free herself of the tender emotion that bound her to him.

She was willing to lay aside her doubts, and yet he would not confide in her.

"Wait," Tark abruptly said and caught her arm. "We agreed last night to fight our way out of this damnable coil together—as partners."

His fingers were warm against the silken barrier of her sleeve, his touch a reminder of the intimate pleasure she'd experienced at his hands just a few hours ago. She steeled herself against the wanton desire that heated her flesh and ignored the husky note of promise she heard in his voice.

"You need not worry that I will hold you to any vows you made. Both of us said and did many things that we might now . . . regret."

"And do you regret what happened, my sweet Isabeau?" he softly demanded, with an unfathomable expression in his blue eyes.

She met his gaze and took a deep breath, prepared to deny her heart . . . and then shook her head. "I regret nothing," she whispered, longing to fling herself into his embrace and forget everything but the comforting warmth of his touch.

As if reading her thoughts, he drew her into his arms. "I don't regret anything, either," he murmured. "Not the silken feel of your soft flesh or the way you trembled so sweetly at my touch. And I don't regret how it felt to be one with you . . . to hear your cries of passion."

She glimpsed the fiercely possessive light in his eyes and the uncertainty that had gripped her heart loosed its hold.

"So now that we are well and truly partners," she said with a smile, "what do we do next?"

He gave a rakish grin. "I have one or two suggestions we could pursue, though I doubt the driver would be gracious enough to wait around while we explored them."

Before she could propose that they forget about the hired carriage, Tark gently disengaged himself from their embrace.

"We have almost three days before the Comus ball to come up with a plan. For now, I want you to go home and act as if nothing untoward has happened. Anything your brother or Franchot asks, you agree to. Can you do that?"

"Of course."

The words fell reluctantly from her lips, for her heart ached with the need to tell someone of her new-found love. For now, however, she would be content with keeping that emotion to herself.

Tark gave her a nod of approval and grasped her arm. "We'll need to talk again—tomorrow, perhaps," he said and purposefully steered her toward the coach waiting beyond the warehouse.

He paused at the vehicle's open door. "Can you arrange to be at the Albatross on Monday at noon?"

"If that is what you want, but why can't we meet here—"

She abruptly recalled the conversation between Tark and the night patroller. Lay low for awhile, Tom had suggested. It seemed Tark was taking that warning to heart.

"The Albatross, tomorrow at noon," she repeated, her contentment darkened by the shadow of her earlier suspicion.

Trust him, a voice within her urged. Just because he had assumed a posture of guilt didn't mean he had committed the crime. But the rough kiss Tark gave her before helping her into the coach seemed spurred by a sense of finality—as if he feared he might never see her again.

With a snap of reins, the carriage jerked forward. Isabeau glanced back to where Tark stood in the open doorway, unmoving within the slash of lamplight. His silhouette reflected the mystery of some earthbound spirit—but whether that of angel or demon, it remained to be seen.

She settled against her seat with a sigh and gazed out the window to the river beyond, where a pearly edge of dawn lay along the horizon. By the time the sun burst into the full glory of day, she would be safely home and in her own bed.

She shut her eyes and let the coach's bumpy course lull her. All too soon, the hired carriage pulled up short outside her courtyard gate.

Light blazed from the house's lower level, and foreboding swept her as she climbed from the vehicle. Her unease grew when she noted her uncle's carriage waiting along the *banquette,* its matched bays snorting and blowing in the crisp air. Nothing could have brought her relative calling before dawn, save that he and Philippe had learned of where—and with whom—she had spent last night.

She crossed the threshold and halted in the entry. Last night's impromptu prevarication lay heavily on her conscience, but she had seen no other way to allay her brother's suspicions. Unless someone had seen her leave the Gilded Albatross in Tark's company, she had only to remain firm in her denials.

"Isabeau! Blast it, niece, where have you been?"

Henri's voice rang through the hallway as he strode toward her, his face flushed with anger. "Philippe . . . is he with you, then?"

"Philippe, with me?" she repeated in unfeigned confusion. "I have been out all evening, and—"

"Then you don't know."

Henri ran a distracted hand over his face, looking years older than his age. "It's not yet dawn. We might still be in time to stop him, before it's too late."

"Stop who?" She caught her breath in horror as she recalled her brother's distracted air last evening. *"Mon Dieu,* has Philippe challenged someone?"

"Franchot Calvé," her uncle flatly replied. "Your fool of a brother has demanded satisfaction from the city's deadliest marksman."

Henri Lavoisier's well-sprung carriage thundered along the deserted streets, the rhythmic crack of his driver's whip splintering the early morning silence. Within the enclosed coach, Isabeau watched in dread while the night sky inexorably faded into dawn.

What had possessed Philippe to risk his life in such a manner? Proficient as he was with both pistol and blade, he surely must have known that Calvé possessed an even greater skill. And if the Frenchman wounded him, or worse . . .

A childhood memory resurfaced, flashing through her mind with cruel clarity though she had been barely six years old that summer night. The heat had lingered well after midnight and the air, thick with the promise of rain, had swathed her in a suffocating blanket that no amount of restless movement could dislodge. Frustrated mosquitoes whined beyond the frothy net enveloping her narrow bed, their high-pitched song unceasing.

Just after dawn, her restless slumber was disturbed by doors slamming and a woman's keening. Creeping from her bed, Isabeau had knelt with Philippe in the shadow of the upper landing. Hands tightly clasped, they peered through the intricate wrought-iron stair rail and watched the drama below.

Tante Aurore lay half swooning in their mother's arms. As the front door crashed open once more, tears flowed down Aurore's painted cheeks.

Isabeau and Philippe watched in dismay while their father stumbled through the doorway, supporting the half-conscious Henri. Blood stained his silk shirt and seeped through the crude linen bandage wrapped around his shoulder. She had not needed Philippe's whisper to understand that her beloved relative had suffered a grievous wound.

"A duel," he explained with boyish importance. A gentleman had pressed his unwelcome attentions upon their aunt, and Henri had reacted as any Creole would have . . . he had challenged the man upon the field of honor.

The confrontation had proved deadly. From the frantic conversation below, she learned that Henri had dispatched his young opponent—though luck, rather than skill, had won the day. Even so, the hapless victim had gotten off a shot before dying beneath the infamous Dueling Oaks.

Isabeau shook her head at the memory. Young as she'd been, she had sensed that all was not well between her aunt and uncle. Years later, it had occurred to her that Henri might have fought the duel out of duty rather than to preserve his wife's honor. She had wondered, as well, if perhaps Tante Aurore's tears had been for the slain young gentleman.

That memory fresh in her mind, she glanced over at her uncle, his face drawn in anger. Did he also recall that long-ago morning, or were his thoughts focused on more immediate concerns?

A moment later, the carriage halted on the outskirts of the old Allard Plantation, time-honored site of Creole dueling where as many as ten *affaires d'honneur* had been fought in a single day. Isabeau choked back hysterical laughter. Trust the tradition-loving Philippe to have chosen this place to conduct his own fight.

By now, the sky blushed a rosy pink, illuminating the expanse of green lawn dotted with ancient live oaks, their gnarled branches dripping with grey Spanish moss. Isabeau stared up at them in awe, for many of those trees had stood sentinel for nigh on a century.

Was it only her imagination, or did those oaks seem alive with some mystical power, nourished as they had been by the blood of countless Creole gallants?

The morbid thought lingered even as she spied a flurry of movement beneath one distant trio of oaks. Through the tattered veil of mist that clung to the damp ground, she glimpsed two carriages and the soberly clad gentlemen who waited with solemn purpose. A short distance from them and partially obscured by the fragile drift of white, two men stood ten paces apart. Both were stripped of their jackets, pistols at the ready.

"Mon Dieu, no," Isabeau gasped out, recognizing her brother's slim form. She wrenched the door handle, not caring that the duello prohibited blood relatives from advancing within two hundred yards of any such meeting.

Henri had already alighted from the coach and swung her to the ground. The damp grass soaked her fragile slippers, but she barely noticed that discomfort.

"Perhaps there is still time to halt this madness," he said and started at a dead run toward the mist-cloaked clearing.

Isabeau hurried across the spongy ground after him, snatches of prayers whirling through her mind. Then a man's low voice floated to her, the distant words unintelligible yet weighted with finality. She was halfway to the clearing, when the combatants raised their weapons.

"Philippe," she cried, stumbling to a halt.

Her plea was lost in the belch of smoke and roar of gunfire as the pistols fired. As the reverberation died away, she waited with fatalistic calm for one man or the other to collapse in a pool of blood. Then a veil of mist rose up to conceal the pair, but not before Isabeau saw that both men remained standing.

Relief swept her in a wave so powerful that she sank to her knees in the damp grass. Perhaps honor was satisfied now. But even as she breathed a prayer of thanks that Philippe had been spared, a shout broke the silence.

"Bring the carriage," came a hoarse voice she barely recognized as belonging to Marcel St. John. "He's been wounded."

Wounded. Isabeau stood and frantically scanned the mist that concealed the combatants. Which man had fallen? It could not have been Philippe, she assured herself, for she surely would have heard Henri's voice above the rest.

She rushed to the sheltering trio of oaks and with a wordless cry shoved past the men gathered like mourners around the still figure at their feet. Blood darkened the crisp white linen of his shirt, while the spreading mist dampened his pale face. The scene blurred before her disbelieving eyes, but not before she heard a familiar voice beside her.

"I suggest you transport your brother to a physician, *ma chère,*" Calvé murmured in silken tones. "I fear he may be dying."

Twenty-six

A crystal snifter cradled in one hand, Tark propped booted feet upon the massive cherrywood desk and leaned back against the butter-soft leather of the over-sized chair. He took a considering sip of his unwitting host's cognac, then glanced around the richly appointed library.

No expense had been spared in decorating the magnificent Garden District mansion that Franchot Calvé called home. Ornate plasterwork adorned the high ceiling and its dividing arches in an elaborate counterpoint to the simple lines of the Baccarat chandelier and carved white marble mantel. Intricately furled draperies of blue and white velvet cascaded from gilded cornices above ceiling-high windows while brocaded upholstery padded the pierced bentwood frames of the furnishings.

Tark managed a grim smile. His former partner had done well, he conceded, likely at little cost. His wealth was born of others' blood and toil—Tark's own, included.

Then he noticed the chessboard atop the table beside him, its surface inlaid with alternating squares of glossy black and white marble. *The royal game,* he thought with no little irony. Apparently, Franchot had kept his passion for that pastime over the years.

He took a closer look, noting that only a handful of the heavy, cylindrical pieces—some silver, some gold—remained on the sleek marble field. An end-game study, he realized, a carefully prescribed exercise in which White appeared destined to win. The symbolic meaning behind that planned outcome was not lost on him.

Tark shook his head. During the numerous games the two of them once had played, Franchot always took the white to his black. They had been well-matched opponents, their wins evenly distributed and their games often ending in draws.

The contrast came in their playing styles. Franchot's strength had lain in his brilliant if methodical manner of attack—a strategy that utilized pawns to a high degree. His own play ran the gamut from uncomplicatedly straightforward to carelessly erratic. Still, his unorthodox moves often disrupted the Frenchman's expectations.

Impatient now to confront his old foe, Tark shifted in his chair. He'd been awaiting Franchot's return since shortly after dawn, and in that hour had formed some conclusions regarding Elisabeth Tremaine's murder.

The news of her death had stunned him more than he cared to admit, though his feelings for his former mistress fell far short of love. Foremost among his emotions, he realized, was guilt. Though lacking proof to substantiate his theory, he had no doubt that her death was linked to his involvement with Franchot Calvé. What else could explain the similarity between her murder and the death of Delphine almost seven years earlier?

. . . no accident . . . bruises on her throat and on her shoulders . . .

Tom's description had chillingly echoed his own earlier account of Delphine's death. The implications had raised a more disturbing problem, and he had wrestled with that dilemma after the night patroller's departure. How could he expect Isabeau to believe his claim of innocence concerning that years-old tragedy, following as it did on a second murder accusation?

Tark's grip on the fragile crystal snifter tightened. Given the circumstances of the preceding weeks, Isabeau had trusted him far more than he deserved. Still, he deliberately had withheld from her the reason behind Tom's visit, wanting first to find the answers to a few important questions.

And he had made the right choice, despite the fact his decision had put at risk the bridge of trust they so recently had built between them. He only prayed that once this entire unsavory business was resolved, he could make Isabeau understand why he had taken that step.

The uneasy silence that held sway over the mansion abruptly lifted. Now, the echo of hurried footsteps and flustered voices drifted from the main entry. No doubt Franchot had returned and was being apprised of the situation awaiting him. Tark allowed himself a smile. He would have enjoyed watching the same burly footmen who had tried—and failed—to bar him from the residence explain to their master just why they had allowed a certain American entry.

He took another sip of cognac, savoring its smooth amber warmth . . . a comforting warmth, such as heated the gleaming steel of the revolver he gripped in his other hand. By now, the murmur of voices had halted outside the library. He set aside the half-empty glass and raised the weapon that had been casually propped across his thigh.

"Glad to see you could spare me a few moments," Tark drawled, noting that no fewer than six of the liveried footmen loomed in the hall behind the Frenchman.

With a casual flick of the pistol, Tark gestured him into the room, adding, "Tell your men to go, and then close the door behind you. If anyone tries to disturb us before I'm ready to leave, I'll kill you where you stand."

"Do as he says," Calvé instructed his men. "M'sieur Parrish and I are old . . . friends. It would seem we have much to discuss."

Tark waited until the door shut firmly behind them, then set the pistol within fingertips' reach on the desk before him. "I'm here for some answers, Franchot," he flatly stated, "and I damn well expect to get them."

"As you wish, *mon ami*." The Frenchman's words held a familiar note of ironic amusement. "I must confess that your visit is not . . . unexpected."

The oblique admission of guilt hung between them for a few chilling seconds. With a dispassionate eye, Tark noted that the passage of time seemed to have left no mark on the man's coldly handsome features. He exuded the same aristocratic languor that Tark remembered—languor that masked a well-honed streak of ruthlessness.

Tark summoned an equal measure of callousness. "I take it that you wouldn't be surprised to learn Elisabeth Tremaine's body was found in the river before dawn. Rumor has it she was murdered."

"Indeed."

Calvé gave a casual shrug, as if dismissing an unexpected change in the weather. "Had she been content simply to keep me informed of your activities, this unpleasantness would have been avoided. Alas, she was not satisfied with her small role."

"So you killed her and set me up for the murder."

"A stroke of genius, do you not agree? Once your name is mentioned as Elisabeth Tremaine's last visitor, even our incompetent local authorities should be able to make the connection to that unfortunate . . . incident at Belle Terre."

And just what in the hell do you know about that "unfortunate incident." A cold blade of suspicion sliced through him, and he again recalled that long-ago afternoon on the riverbank. Sweet Jesus, what if the Frenchman was the one responsible for Delphine's death?

While one corner of his mind toyed with that question, he addressed Franchot's insinuation. "I presume you have a reason for wanting to see me swing for a murder I didn't commit."

"But you do not understand, *mon ami*," the man replied and started toward the desk. "It is not my intention that you die—"

Tark reached for the pistol and Calvé halted, then spread his hands in a deprecating manner. "Surely you will not begrudge me a sip of my own cognac."

Warily, Tark put aside the weapon, though he didn't relax his guard until after Calvé had splashed a generous portion into a second glass and settled in a chair.

"I must admit, *mon ami*," he said with a slight smile, "that I have missed these little chats of ours."

"I wish to hell you'd quit calling me your friend," Tark coldly interjected, "because I'm damn sure not."

"Ah, but you are wrong—or have you already forgotten that you still are a wanted man? Soon, you will find that I am the only true friend you have left."

The threat in the man's words was unmistakable. Tark clenched his fingers against the urge to pick up his pistol again and put an end to the situation, the consequences be damned.

Play it like a chess game. Franchot's got you checked, and now it's your move.

He met Calvé's golden gaze with a level look. "Let me get this straight. You're offering to help me out of this mess, and in return, I'm supposed to pretend that you weren't the one who got me into the situation in the first place."

The man acknowledged the ironic words with a slight smile. "I am sure that even you must realize that my goal lies far beyond any harmless manipulation of your interests. I have need of your connections and certain . . . talents.

"You may recall that although my father was French, he married a Russian noblewoman. It was for this reason that during the campaign at Sevastopol, he—and later, I—fought alongside the Tsar's men."

Tark nodded, for he'd been privy to that much of Calvé's personal history. "But the war in the Crimea ended almost twenty years ago."

Calvé shrugged aside his observation. "At first, it seemed we would repulse the combined French and English troops—in part, because of my father's knowledge of their weapons and tactics. The old Tsar, Nicholas, acknowledged his efforts with the promise of lands along the Black Sea once the war was over. But the Tsar's generals did not trust a foreigner in a position of command, and so my father was ignominiously expelled from their ranks."

Calvé's urbane mask momentarily slipped, revealing the shadowy predator behind those golden eyes. Almost immediately, however, the civilized facade was back in place.

"Along with his command, my father lost all his wealth and holdings. He swore revenge and offered our services first to the French and then to the Turks. By then, Nicholas had died. Soon after, Sevastopol was captured, and the new Tsar, Alexander, signed the peace treaty.

"But it was too late for my father. Despite the help he had provided Louis Napoleon's forces, he was betrayed by . . . a minor French diplomat. He was executed as a spy—a fate for which I, too, was destined. I will not bore you with the details of my escape and subsequent journey to Paris. Suffice it to say that I remained in that glorious city just long enough to avenge my father's death."

Tark quirked a brow. "What does that have to do with your shipment to Sevastopol?"

"Everything, *mon ami*, everything." The expression in his golden eyes was unfathomable. "You see, I am a man with two motherlands—France and Russia—yet I can never set foot upon either soil again. With no country to call my own, I must carve my own kingdom from those lands for which I have a grant signed by Nicholas, himself."

"Lands that are now under the control of the Turks," Tark bluntly clarified. "Your claim is worthless, so unless you plan to seize the territory by force . . ."

He trailed off, picturing the rifles stored on the grounds of the old Ursuline convent. *Weapons enough to outfit a small army.* And the other supplies, all integral to a missionary effort . . . or a military campaign.

"Sweet Jesus, that *is* what you plan to do," he said with a disbelieving shake of his head. "You're going to march in there with your own personal army and stake your claim."

"Ah, but it is not quite that simple. To accomplish my goal, I have need of someone I can trust, someone who can handle certain delicate diplomatic . . . transactions."

"Transactions such as kidnaping the Russian grand duke?"

Calvé smiled. "I see Mademoiselle Lavoisier has at last confided in you. *Bon.* I had begun to fear I had misjudged her righteous zeal, just as I underestimated her brother's sense of honor."

When Tark raised a querying eyebrow, the Frenchman gave a careless shrug. "I was forced to face young Lavoisier barely an hour ago beneath the Oaks. It was only by happenstance that I did not kill him outright— though I expect he will expire by day's end."

So the cocky little dandy had dared to face Calvé. Though Philippe's common sense might be brought to question, his bravery would certainly not. Aloud, however, Tark replied, "Another outdated display of chivalry.

I thought that kind of thing had gone out with the war's end."

Then he frowned. Sweet Jesus, Isabeau must have arrived home to find her brother near death. If he hadn't been so concerned with his own problems, maybe he would have been there with her—

"—will take his place the night of the Comus ball," Calvé's voice broke through his thoughts. "Near midnight, you and Henri Lavoisier will remove the grand duke from the Varieties Theatre and transport him to the waterfront. While the world's attention is focused on this drama, you will depart for Sevastopol and remain there as my agent, helping to establish an economic stronghold. Once I have come to terms with the Russian government regarding the grand duke, I will join you there."

Tark stared at the Frenchman in ill-concealed dismay. The plan sounded reasonable—yet he knew that the scheme was doomed to failure. He knew with equal certainty that, sometime in the past seven years, Franchot Calvé had crossed the line that separated rational thought from insanity. But the Frenchman had not fallen victim to mere frantic lunacy. Instead, he had succumbed to the single-minded madness of a brilliant man caught in the thrall of obsession.

He met the Frenchman's gaze and shoved back from the desk. "Tempting as your offer is, I'll take my chances with the authorities. Once I tell them about Elisabeth and your plot to kidnap the Russian grand duke, they'll—"

"They will . . . what?"

Calvé casually refilled his snifter, then fixed his golden

gaze on Tark. "Whom do you think they will believe—an influential citizen, or a man thought to have committed a similar crime years before? I rather suspect they will dismiss your claims as the ravings of a desperate man."

"You may have half the city's politicians in your pocket, but I'm still willing to take the risk."

"But what of the risk to Mademoiselle Lavoisier?" the Frenchman murmured, swirling his glass so that the splash of cognac spun like liquid amber. "It would be unfortunate if she suffered an accident such as befell the *charmante* Tremaine. And what of your house-keeper—Alma Crenshaw, is it not? How sad if the would-be bride perished before she was made a wife."

A chill tide of rage swept Tark. Taking a step closer, he raised his pistol. "I should kill you now."

"And what will my death gain you? My servants wit-nessed the way you broke into my home and threatened me with a gun, so you stand no chance of being ac-quitted of the crime. Kill me, and you follow me to the grave. Join me, and—"

"—and partake of riches beyond my wildest dreams." Tark managed a grim smile, ignoring the hatred that twisted in his gut. "Isn't that what you promised me seven years ago, when I was desperate to save Belle Terre? I seem to recall I ended up with less than nothing for my troubles."

"Ah, but that was different." The Frenchman waved aside his protest with a graceful gesture. "Then, you were but another pawn in the game. This time, you shall be my partner."

Partner.

The word rang with irony and promise. Tark realized

that he had been weighing the idea's possibilities, not that he trusted Franchot Calvé after the man's betrayal of him. Instead, his confidence stemmed from the fact that he'd gained and lost two fortunes over the past decade. He was ready to partake again of Lady Luck's bounty. The question was, did the source of his profits matter to him this time?

It did.

Tark shoved aside the tantalizing visions of wealth that Franchot's offer had raised in his mind. To be sure, he had every intention of regaining his fortune—but this time he wasn't going to bargain away his integrity in the process.

The decision made, he turned his attention to his original dilemma, knowing that the Frenchman would drag into his private inferno as many people as possible. He already had been lured halfway down that brimstone path.

He took the first step toward mentally retracing that road by resuming his chair. "Say I agree to this scheme, why in the hell should I trust you—and what makes you think you can trust me?"

Calvé's smile was cold . . . predatory. "Trust has little to do with it, *mon ami*. We are both gamblers, you and I. Just as I gambled that the grand duke would find his way to New Orleans, so I will wager that your desire for vengeance can be supplanted by the lure of wealth and power. You will be gambling that the profits I derive from your abilities would be worth more to me than your life."

"And in the meantime, all I have to do is help kidnap the grand duke and then head for Sevastopol."

"A minor feat for someone of your abilities. Besides, *mon ami,* your only other option is to spend the remainder of your days trying to prove you are innocent of murder."

Tark leaned back in his chair, matching the Frenchman's chill smile. "Franchot, old friend, I do believe you've convinced me to take you up on your proposition. But tell me something—"

"—what is to become of the Lavoisiers? I am afraid that once the ransom is paid, Henri will be left to his own devices. As for the girl, you may abandon her to her uncle's mercies—or take her with you to Sevastopol."

"I'll consider it."

Tark shrugged and again rose, this time tucking the pistol into the rear waistband of his trousers. Franchot had accepted his change of heart without comment, but he attributed that lapse to overconfidence on the part of his old foe. Likely the Frenchman had determined that the threat to Isabeau and Alma would keep him in line for the next two days.

"I'd better take care of some last-minute details on that shipment," he went on. "If I'm supposed to be with Henri on Tuesday night, I'll need someone else to oversee the loading."

He spared a final glance at the chessboard, then positioned the remaining gold knight between the attacking queen and the imperiled king. "If you need to get in touch with me before then," he casually added, "you can find me at the Gilded Albatross."

Calvé nodded, then raised his glass. "To our partnership, *mon ami,*" he said, his golden eyes reflecting a cold brilliance.

Tark reached for his own snifter. "Our partnership," he flatly echoed and drained the remaining cognac in a single swallow.

Twenty-seven

Isabeau stirred at the murmur of familiar voices. As she drifted closer to wakefulness, a few phrases echoed clearly in her mind.

. . . stayed with him all night . . . hard to tell . . . the physician said that if he survived the first hours . . .

She opened her eyes to find that she lay fully dressed upon the chaise in her brother's room, a shawl draped across her. She stretched her cramped limbs and focused blearily on Philippe's bed. To her surprise, Oncle Henri and Madame Dumas stood beside it, their attention fixed on the still form beneath the blankets. Was someone ill, or—

"Mon Dieu, Philippe." She scrambled to her feet as the memory of yesterday's duel returned with horrifying clarity. Her uncle and Madame had turned at her exclamation, but she barely noted their presence. Instead, she started toward the four-poster, every detail of the morning before playing again through her mind.

Philippe's white linen shirt had been awash in blood as he lay beneath the oaks. Marcel's mild features were distorted with fright as he tried to staunch the flow. Franchot Calvé, his golden gaze impassive, had casually

tossed aside his still-smoking pistol and made his way
back to his own carriage.

More chilling was the memory of the Frenchman's
final words to her before he quit the field. *Our arrangement still stands,* mademoiselle—*whether your fool of a
brother lives or dies.* She had understood then the rage
that had driven Philippe to this act of madness. Had she
possessed a working pistol, she would have put a bullet
through the man without a second's remorse.

With Marcel's help, she and Oncle Henri had transported the unconscious Philippe home and located a surgeon of sorts, dearly purchased for his discretion.
Though ill-tempered and stinking of brandy, the man
had determined that the ball had caused no major damage. In the next breath he warned them that blood loss
and the possibility of infection could easily finish the
job. When Isabeau frantically pressed him for a more
exact prognosis, the old man reeled off a battery of instructions, admitting that, if the gentleman survived the
next twenty-four hours, he might pull through.

And he *had* survived the night, Isabeau saw with a
surge of relief. She halted before the bed and grasped
Philippe's limp hand. Now, his skin was warm to the
touch, unlike those frightening hours when his chill
flesh seemed drained of blood. Still, the waxy pallor of
his face and shallow rise of his chest beneath a heavy
wrapping of bandages did little to reassure her.

"He is improved," she heard Henri murmur, though
his doubtful tone belied the hopeful words.

She gently laid her brother's hand atop the coverlet.
"Has he regained his senses yet?"

Henri shook his head, his aristocratic features drawn

into lines of weary sorrow. "He does appear to be simply sleeping now. Perhaps that is a promising sign."

"Perhaps," she agreed, then managed a smile for the old woman. "It was good of you to come, Madame."

"Ah, but I only wish there was something I could do, *ma chère,*" the dowager softly exclaimed and clasped her black-gloved hands. "First, your dear *maman,* then your *papa . . .*"

Her aged features crumpled in sorrow before she managed a valiant smile. "But Philippe, he will be fine—of that, I am sure. Now, *ma chère,* go with your *oncle,* and I shall stay with your brother for a time."

"I *would* like to bathe and change my gown," Isabeau ruefully agreed, running a hand through her tangled curls. Yesterday's hastily donned grey gown was in a sadder state, its creases likely permanent. Before she could accept the dowager's offer, however, the bedroom door flew open.

Camille St. John rushed forward in a flurry of ostrich plumes and green-and-yellow gabardine. "Marcel refused to summon me a carriage," she peevishly explained, "so I had to walk."

She stopped short at the sight of Philippe and shrieked, then dropped to her knees beside the bed. "But h-he didn't tell me how badly Philippe was h-hurt," she wailed, then glared at her brother now standing in the doorway, panting for breath.

The red-faced Marcel swiped at the perspiration beading his forehead and managed an apologetic look. "I'm sorry," he gasped out. "She slipped out of the house when I wasn't watching."

"You can't make me leave," Cammi retorted, and promptly burst into tears. "Philippe n-needs me—"

"Come along, *ma fille*," Henri interjected and pulled the girl to her feet, steering her toward the door. "There, now, you'll do him no good with your caterwauling."

"Perhaps she might stay, Oncle," Isabeau impulsively suggested, hearing in Cammi's plaint genuine anguish. "I can show her what must be done."

Marcel's uncertain gaze wavered between her and his weeping sister. "If your *oncle* thinks it is wise—"

"It is a wonderful idea," Madame opined. "After all, Isabeau cannot spend every waking hour—"

"Can't a man . . . get a moment's peace . . . in his own home?" came a faint voice behind them.

The halting complaint cut short any discussion as effectively as a shout. The group turned toward the four-poster, where a pale but conscious Philippe struggled to sit upright.

"Is everyone . . . just going to . . . stand there," he gasped out, "or will someone . . . help me?"

Isabeau was the first to react. With a heartfelt "thank *le bon Dieu*," she rushed to her brother's side. "The physician said you are to keep still, Titi," she happily scolded and began tucking the blankets back around him.

A babble of questions and well-wishes poured from the rest of his friends and family. Before she could propose that they leave the invalid to recuperate, however, a high-pitched voice rose above the rest.

"Quiet, everyone," Cammi demanded, gloved fists on her hips as she surveyed the room's occupants. "Can't you see that you're disturbing my patient?"

Her patient! Isabeau looked up, only to find the girl's gaze upon her.

"You may stay, Isabeau, and show me what must be done," she regally proclaimed. "Everyone else is in the way."

Seemingly oblivious to the stunned reaction that her pronouncement caused, Cammi continued, "M'sieur Lavoisier, you may escort Madame Dumas downstairs for a cup of *café au lait*. Marcel, you return home and tell Maman I'll be staying here until Philippe is well again."

Isabeau waited for the expected indignant protests over Cammi's high-handed dismissal. To her surprise, however, the others cleared the room without demur, leaving Isabeau with a self-satisfied Cammi and a thoroughly miserable-looking Philippe. Though obviously weakened by his brief exertion, he gripped her hand in an unmistakable attempt to forestall any such plan.

Sympathetic as she was to her brother's plight, she ignored his woeful expression and repeated for Cammi the doctor's instructions. After all, she reasoned, she could not continue to care for Philippe by herself—especially when Lucie mysteriously had disappeared sometime within the past day.

Isabeau concluded her explanation by describing how to clean the wound and rebandage it. By then, Cammi's ruddy complexion had paled. Still, her gaze never wavered, and Isabeau wondered if she had misjudged the girl's feelings for Philippe.

Summoning a smile of unfeigned relief, she said, "It was good of you to come, Cammi. I know you will be of great help—and I am sure that Philippe is equally grateful."

Cammi settled herself in the hard-backed chair beside the bed. "I always nurse Maman when she has the headache," the girl confided, "and she says she could not do without me. I even missed seeing the Grand Duke Alexis disembark this morning for Philippe's sake."

"The grand duke," Isabeau faintly echoed. *Mon Dieu,* she almost had forgotten the Russian nobleman . . . that, and the fact she was to meet Tark today at the Gilded Albatross.

"I thought that Alexis's steamer was to have arrived yesterday."

"It did, but His Highness stayed aboard last night, instead of attending the opera as everyone planned." Cammi leaned forward, eyes agleam with satisfaction as she lowered her voice. "I heard that Miss Lydia Thompson—the actress, you know—was there with him . . . and for the entire night, too."

"Lucky dog," came the faint observation from the sickbed.

Cammi shot her patient a peevish look, but Isabeau barely attended the girl's retort. The past two days, she had clung to the hope that she might somehow encounter the grand duke and warn him of his impending danger. If Alexis could only be dissuaded from attending the ball tomorrow night, Monsieur Calvé would be forced to abandon his scheme. But now, it seemed she had no choice but to uphold her end of her agreement with the Frenchman.

"—hardly as interesting as the rumors about Elisabeth Tremaine."

Cammi's careless words brought Isabeau to the present with a start. "What did happen to Madame Tremaine?" she said in feigned ignorance. "Surely not a scandal . . ."

"Why, haven't you heard? It was *murder.*" The girl gave an exaggerated shiver. "She was strangled and thrown into the river—but that's not the exciting part."

Cammi lowered her voice to a dramatic whisper. "The newspapers say the killer is that *américain,* Tark Parrish—the very man we saw at Madame Dumas's cotillion. And just think, Isabeau, you actually danced with him!"

"It was only one waltz," she protested, avoiding her brother's gaze lest he read guilt in her eyes. He had been shocked enough by her admission that she had spoken with the man unchaperoned. *Mon Dieu,* if he ever learned what had happened these past nights . . .

She turned instead to Cammi, asking, "But how do they know that M'sieur Parrish is guilty? Did someone see him kill her?"

"Of course not, but everyone knows that he murdered his wife in the same way. Besides, she was his *petit amour*—though I can't believe any woman of refinement would let her name be linked with him. And if that were not enough," she concluded, "the man hasn't been seen since the afternoon of the murder."

"But that does not signify a thing," Isabeau retorted, then fought down a blush when Cammi gaped at her.

Let her wonder what she will, she defiantly thought, her charitable feeling toward the girl fast fading. Still, Cammi's last words seemed to indicate that Tark had eluded any pursuers—though whether she would find him at the tavern remained to be seen.

Philippe, who was silent through this exchange, spoke up. "I'm hungry," he plaintively began. "Cammi, could you bring me . . . a little something—"

He trailed off and sagged against the pillows with a dramatic groan. Cammi sprang to her feet, the issue of Tark's presumed guilt apparently forgotten. "But of course, Philippe. Let me ring for the maid."

"I am afraid that is impossible," Isabeau put in. "Lucie has vanished without a word—unless you gave her notice, Titi?"

Philippe weakly shook his head, and she gathered from his expression that he, too, suspected the mulattress's disappearance was no coincidence. But surely the girl could cause them no further mischief.

"Don't worry, Isabeau," Cammi said and started toward the door. "I *can* cook. Maman says a lady should be familiar with all household tasks, so that she can properly supervise her staff, assuming she has one."

Isabeau waited until the girl left, then faced Philippe. With a crooked smile, he said in a stronger voice, "I couldn't think of any other way to get rid of her."

"You should have kept her here to protect you, Titi, because I'm tempted to shake you until your teeth rattle."

Isabeau paced the small room, ready to vent her fearful anger now that her brother's injuries no longer appeared life-threatening. *"Mon Dieu,* whatever possessed you to challenge Monsieur Calvé? Surely you must have guessed that he intended to kill you."

"It was a matter of honor, Isette, and I—"

"Honor! All you men are alike, with your notions of honor—and then you expect us women to patch you up, so you can fight again."

"But you didn't tell Henri why I issued the challenge?"

Isabeau shook her head. "He did ask, but I mentioned nothing about Monsieur Calvé and his plans. I told him that your grievance was personal—but you cannot blame him for being upset, *mon frère*. How do you think he must feel, knowing you almost were killed by a man he considers a friend?"

Philippe's expression reflected equal parts resignation and trepidation. "You'll have to tell him the truth. We have no other choice."

"But I cannot. If Regine is to be saved, I must do as Monsieur Calvé asks, unless I . . ."

She hesitated, mindful of her brother's weakened state, then determinedly went on, "I can ask Monsieur Parrish for his help. After all, he is already involved in the scheme, and—"

"The *américain!*" Philippe struggled upright, color flooding his cheeks. "Why, the man's nothing but a common murderer and may even be in league with Calvé. I forbid it, do you hear me—"

His outburst ended on a gasp and he sagged back against the pillows. From his pallor, Isabeau knew that this time he wasn't feigning his distress. She rushed to his side and tucked the blankets around him again, relieved that his exertions hadn't started his wound bleeding afresh. Once he was comfortably settled again, Isabeau again perched on the bed's edge.

"Listen to me, Titi," she began. "I know you do not trust Monsieur Parrish, but I must enlist someone's help. Besides, I-I already have spoken to him about the matter."

"You what?" Philippe choked out. "How could you . . . an *américain*—"

"I know I should have asked you first, but Madame Dumas vouched for his bravery. And he has no love for Monsieur Calvé, of that I am certain. He has agreed to help me, so let that be an end to it."

Philippe's reply was lost in a clatter of crockery as Cammi trotted back in, proudly bearing a dish-laden tray. With a flourish, she set it on the bedside table and beamed at Philippe. "I fixed just the thing to tempt your appetite. A soft-boiled egg, pineapple with port wine, *beignets,* and of course, *café au lait."*

"It does smell good," Isabeau agreed and rose before Philippe could stop her. "Titi, I will leave you in Cammi's care."

To her relief, he swallowed any protests along with the bite of egg Cammi offered him. Isabeau secured a pastry for herself and hurried from the room. Downstairs, the parlor clock struck eleven times, reminding her that morning her appointment with Tark was but an hour away.

A short while later, Isabeau made her *adieux* to Cammi and a surprisingly cheerful-looking Philippe and set out, ostensibly to run the departed Lucie's errands. As her hired coach neared the waterfront, however, she saw that the streets were almost impassable.

"It's 'cause of that there Russian fella," explained her driver when she leaned from her window to question the delay. "Ya shoulda seen all them ladies crowdin' 'round to get a look at him. Didn't no one pay mind to the mayor when he started speechifyin'. They was all just asmilin' and awavin' . . ."

Isabeau resumed her seat and impatiently toyed with her reticule. What if Tark had left by the time she arrived at the Gilded Albatross? How could she get word to him before tomorrow night?

Her concern grew when the carriage stopped, its way blocked by other coaches trying to negotiate the same intersection. By the time her own conveyance finally reached the waterfront, it was well after noon.

She paid the driver and made her way past the tavern's swinging doors. This time, the dimly lit establishment was almost deserted. Two lanky dockworkers sat at a far table contemplating their empty mugs. The only other customer was a stocky, middle-aged *américain*. With no regard for propriety, he boldly fondled the breasts of the sallow-faced barmaid who straddled him.

Isabeau averted her gaze, but not before the grey-mustachioed man favored her with a knowing leer. Suppressing a shudder of distaste, she made her way to the bar. Ned Deaton stood behind its polished length, drying mismatched glasses.

The man's cherubic features played host to a range of emotions before finally settling on polite expectancy. "Good day, miss," he exclaimed, then whispered, "Mister Par—that is, your gentleman friend told me to expect you. You'll find him upstairs"—he jerked his head, indicating the familiar back hallway—"second door on the right."

"*Merci,* M'sieur Deaton."

So Tark *was* here. She managed a smile, grateful that the man's tone held no hint of censure. What story Tark might have told him, she couldn't guess, but surely Ned must have wondered why a young woman like herself frequented a waterfront tavern. With an involuntary glance at the hefty *américain* seated behind her—*Mon Dieu,* he stared as if she were some street-corner doxy!—Isabeau started toward the stairs.

Josiah Grubb unceremoniously shoved aside the barmaid he'd been pawing and lurched to his feet. He ignored the slut's indignant protests and tossed a coin onto the table, then spared another look after the Creole girl. Damn, but he'd give a gold eagle to see that highfalutin' Philip Lavoisier's face when he learned what his pretty little sister was doing—and who she was doing it with!

Not that he could blame that Parrish fella. Grubb rubbed one beefy hand down the thick bulge in his trousers. He'd never had much use for proper women—hell, they were always so gussied up, that by the time a man finally unwrapped the package, he'd about lost interest in sampling what was inside—but he wouldn't say no to a tumble with this gal. Come tomorrow, she'd be needing someone new to scratch her itch, seeing how Tark Parrish wasn't going to be around to do it for her.

Grubb gave a satisfied grunt and headed for the exit. He could do with a bit of relief, himself, but he knew better than to sidestep Mister Calvé's orders. A quick poke sure as hell wasn't worth his life.

He shouldered his way through the batwing doors and stepped out onto the *banquette,* squinting against the early afternoon sun. He waved down a hack, then spared a glance at the paper he plucked from his waistcoat pocket. This next errand was one he was going to enjoy.

Suppressing a chuckle, he gave the driver his destination, a house in the French Quarter belonging to one Monsieur Henri Lavoisier.

Twenty-eight

Isabeau glanced in dismay along the empty hallway whose series of identical doors reminded her of Ophelia's brothel. It proved the only similarity, however, between that elegant establishment and this waterfront counterpart.

Rather than the gaudy luxury that the Basin Street house boasted, this place offered indifferent neglect. Greasy, unfinished wood floors creaked beneath her feet, while the stained plaster walls appeared in danger of collapse. The stench of urine, stale beer and unwashed bodies assailed her but couldn't mask the pervading odor of spent lust.

She shut her eyes and took a steadying breath. *Sainte Cécile,* she was alone in a waterfront tavern, on her way to meet a man who might be guilty of murder! More compelling, however, was the anticipation that swept her at the thought of seeing Tark again. With it, thoughts of Marcel and her engagement faded like shadows banished by the coming of dawn.

She rapped on the door. When no voice answered, she bit her lip in consternation. Surely Tark would not have left the tavern without telling Ned. She hesitated another moment and then gave the handle an experimental twist.

The door squealed open a few inches, allowing her a glimpse into the curtained dimness. The disheveled bed indicated that he had indeed stayed the past night. Now, however, the room was empty.

Or was it?

She checked her first impulse to call out Tark's name. What if someone had been here before her? *Sainte Cécile,* perhaps Monsieur Calvé's men had tracked Tark to this place and overpowered him, leaving him for dead. Maybe those same men still waited inside for her to blindly walk in.

She gave herself a mental shake. If there *had* been a struggle, the commotion would have been audible to anyone in the barroom below. Likely he had just stepped out for a minute. With that thought in mind, she pushed past the door and entered the tiny room.

The door slammed shut behind her, while a hand clamped around her throat and cut short her cry of fright. In the next instant, the cold barrel of a revolver seared her cheek as her unseen assailant dragged her back against him in an unyielding embrace.

Isabeau froze, any thought of resistance driven from her mind by the gun at her head. She had steeled herself for the brutal impact of a bullet when a disbelieving voice behind her choked out, "Sweet Jesus, it's you."

The pistol fell away from her face, and the cruel pressure around her throat immediately eased. Gasping for breath, Isabeau swung about to lock gazes with a familiar pair of ice blue eyes.

With an oath, Tark set the pistol on a nearby table

and stalked to the window, jerking aside the faded quilt that served as a curtain. Dull light filtered through the grimy window to dispel much of the gloom. She could see now that he appeared much as he had that first morning on the docks, unshaven and attired in a shirt and trousers that were in sore need of a flatiron. Though weariness stamped his features, his watchful gaze held no hint of fatigue.

He crossed to her and caught her by the shoulders. "What in the hell were you doing, skulking outside my door like that?"

"I was not skulking. I was coming to see you—just as we agreed."

She pulled from his grasp, her earlier fear forgotten with this unfair accusation. "I know I'm late, but I had to explain things to Philippe . . . and then streets were so crowded. And besides," she finished in a righteous tone, "*I* should be the one who is upset, since *you* were the one who had a gun pointed at m-me . . ."

To her mortification, that last word trembled on a sob. She took a deep breath and willed herself to remain dry-eyed. She had not once given in to tears these past two days, so why should she cry now?

In the next moment, the anger in his eyes faded. "You're right, and I'm sorry," he stiffly admitted. "It's just that I've been cooped up in this damned place with nothing to do but stare at the walls and worry about whether or not you're safe. I'd heard about what happened to your brother."

He ended on a questioning note, and Isabeau managed a smile. "Philippe is much better. I left him in the care of a marriage-minded young woman, so he shall have to get well if he wishes to escape her clutches."

"Then I predict a full recovery," Tark replied with an answering grin.

His words banished the constraint between them. Ruthlessly, she ignored the voice in her head that reminded her of her duty. All that mattered was the need she could see reflected in Tark's eyes—a need that matched her own.

Seeking the comfort of his touch, she moved closer. He reached out as if to brush his fingers along her cheek. Then, abruptly, he turned away, the aborted gesture serving more cruelly than a slap. What had she done to warrant his disdain? she bleakly wondered.

"There's another reason why I'm on edge," he began, and she heard uncertainty in his voice. She realized that his recriminations were directed, not at her, but at himself.

"I wanted to tell you before you left yesterday morning, but the timing didn't seem quite right. I suppose you've heard about Elisabeth Tremaine's murder?"

Though the question was casual, she sensed a wariness in him that sent her heart racing. Now her suspicions would be put to rest—or else, confirmed. Not trusting herself to speak, she simply nodded.

"That was what Tom's early morning visit was all about. As luck would have it, she and I parted on rather . . . unfriendly terms, so I appear to be the logical suspect in her death."

He turned and paced the small room. "After you and Tom left, I paid Franchot a visit—something I should have done a hell of a lot sooner. He was busy shooting it out with your brother at the time, so I had the chance to think a few things through."

He swung about to face her again, his expression grim. "It already had occurred to me that my relationship with Elisabeth was a bit too convenient. Once I learned that Franchot was behind my run of bad luck, I decided he was also responsible for putting Elisabeth in my path—rather like distracting a dog with a bone. Now, with her killer taking pains to duplicate Delphine's death, the only common link besides myself I can find between the two women is my old friend."

"You mean Monsieur Calvé killed her?"

When Tark nodded his reply, relief swept her. *Mon Dieu,* how could she ever have doubted his innocence? "But if that is the case," she asked aloud, "why must you remain in hiding?"

"Franchot made no secret of his guilt when I confronted him. Unfortunately, it's my word against his, which doesn't do me much good right now."

"But why not?"

"Because, my sweet Isabeau, our friend is an influential man, while my reputation is questionable. Tom promised he'd do what he could to clear my name, but without proof, there's not much he can accomplish."

He favored her with a wry smile and started toward her. "When I heard you in the hallway just now, I was certain I was about to be arrested—and I damn sure wasn't going to go quietly."

"But surely Monsieur Sullivan would not come after you, when he was the one who told you to lay low. And he did say that he did not think you were responsible for—"

She stopped short, realizing that she had betrayed her ill-gotten knowledge. A glance at Tark confirmed that her slip had not gone unnoticed.

He halted, his ice-blue gaze revealing no hint of his thoughts. "You knew all along I was suspected of her death. I suppose you eavesdropped on my conversation with Tom?"

"Y-your voices carried through the stovepipe. All I meant to do was stir the coals, but then I heard the two of you talking . . ."

She lowered her gaze to her clasped hands. He surely would despise her for her lack of trust or, worse, dismiss her as simply a meddling child.

"You knew," he softly repeated, "yet you said nothing at all—no questions, no accusations."

He lightly caught her chin, tilting her face to meet his gaze once more. "Do you know, my sweet Isabeau, that I agonized over whether or not to tell you about what had happened. I already had admitted that my wife drowned under mysterious circumstances—and that even though I was cleared of any involvement, I can't remember to this day if I was responsible for her death."

He let his fingers slide away, but she could still feel a tingling heat where he had touched her. His eye held a chill watchfulness, however, when he demanded, "What would you have done if I'd tried to explain how another woman I'd been involved with had been found murdered in a similar fashion—and that I was innocent of that crime, as well?"

"I would have said that I believed you."

Her words were little more than a whisper, but they were enough. With a groan, Tark pulled her to him in a crushing embrace, his lips capturing hers.

She gave a soft moan of surrender, opening her mouth to him so that he could freely probe its soft secrets. As he did, a heat within her flared into a burning need that spread through her body in a swift spiral of desire.

She gripped the linen of his shirtfront and boldly molded her body to his, welcoming the exquisite ache of her breasts as they pressed against his chest. He responded by sliding his hands down the swell of her hips, kneading her buttocks with a gentle yet insistent pressure.

Instinctively, she let her own fingers travel lower to find the hot evidence of his arousal. With trembling hands, she fumbled at his trouser buttons until she had freed him. As her fingers closed around that throbbing shaft, he groaned again and moved rhythmically against her palms, each stroke matching the urgent plundering of his tongue.

A moment later, he broke free of their kiss and eased his stiff rod from her grasp. His ice blue eyes dark with desire, he harshly whispered, "Let me love you."

"Oh, yes, *mon cher.*"

Tark's insistent fingers promptly plucked at the tiny buttons of her jacket and skirt. Barely had those garments settled in a bottle-green pool at her feet, than he made equally short work of her petticoats. Now, she stood before him clad only in her stockings, drawers, and chemise, that last item cinched by a light corset.

When he reached out to unfasten that silk-covered bit of canvas and bone, however, she protested, "But it is still daylight."

He shot her a ragged grin. "So it is, my sweet. What difference does that make?"

"But I cannot . . ."

She blushed and trailed off in dismay. *Mon Dieu,* it was one thing to make love at night in a darkened room. It was quite another to cavort about stark naked on a sunny afternoon.

Her appalled look drew a short laugh from Tark. "I'll make a bargain with you," he offered in a voice taut with amusement and desire. "This time, we'll manage with a minimum of undressing."

He led her to the narrow bed—a battered piece of furniture that looked far more uncomfortable than the one they had shared two nights before—and gave her a rueful glance.

"At least the sheets are clean. That's the one amenity Ned offers in this place." He sat on the edge of the bed and tugged off his boots, then sprawled back against the pillows and eyed her in some amusement. "I'm afraid, my sweet, that those drawers will have to go."

Her blush deepened as she eased off her fragile slippers and hiked up her chemise. She untied the waistband of her pantalets, letting the silky white undergarment slide to her ankles, then dragged her mortified gaze back to Tark.

He had rearranged his trousers so that his erect shaft jutted from the black hair curling above his well-muscled thighs. He lazily ran one hand along that swollen member, then caught her wrist with the other.

"I think, my sweet Isabeau, that you should ride astride," he said in a husky voice and gently guided her onto the bed. "If I can't see your lovely body, let me watch the passion as it plays across your face."

She lifted her chemise and straddled him, bracing her hands against his broad chest. The blunt tip of his manhood quivered against the delicate folds between her spread thighs, and she slowly rubbed herself against him, the soft petals of skin growing slick and swollen with every stroke.

With a choked exclamation, Tark fumbled beneath her chemise until his hands cupped her hips. He slowly guided her onto his rigid member, and she caught her breath, savoring the wanton and now-familiar fullness of him as she settled onto his thighs.

"Now ride me, my sweet," he harshly urged, rocking her back and forth atop him.

Tark matched her rhythm with urgent thrusting of his own, the rough fabric of his trousers raking her bare buttocks in a way that was both painful and erotic. By now, her hair had escaped its pins to brush her cheeks and throat. She shook back the errant locks, glimpsing her own image in the mottled mirror beside the bed. The wanton creature reflected there was yet something of a stranger to her. This time, however, she found no shame in embracing that other self as a symbol of her new-found womanhood.

Tark promptly recaptured her attention as he tugged down her chemise to expose her breasts above the tight confines of her corset. His fingers found her nipples, lightly pinching them until they hardened into twin buds of sensual pleasure. She moaned and offered her breasts for him to suckle. His lips closed over first one, and then the other pale globe with an urgency that drew a shudder from her very depths.

She closed her eyes, unable to contain a cry of satisfaction as his hot mouth feasted on her. Just when pain and pleasure threatened to become one, he sank back against the sheets again.

"Open your eyes," he demanded.

She obeyed with a sigh. "Watch me," he urged in the same husky tone. "I want to see my passion reflected in your eyes . . . and I want you to see just what it is your sweet body does to me."

She sat upright once more, her arms braced behind her on his muscled thighs. Her gaze never left his as she moved her hips in that ages-old rhythm. His face was taut and sheened with perspiration now, and she knew that he was on the verge of climax. She felt the first dizzying stirrings of her own release and bit back a moan, wanting to prolong this ecstasy for as long as possible. Then he slid one hand back under her chemise, finding that sensitive button of flesh that was now ripe with desire.

At his touch, the coiled heat within her exploded as shudder after shudder racked her. Her cry of joy was echoed by Tark's own harsh shout as he thrust upward in one final savage move. She felt his seed pump into her in a series of hot bursts, his expression reflecting primitive triumph.

Slowly, she settled against him, a satisfied lethargy stealing through her. She reached with trembling fingers to touch his face, lightly skirting the cut that marred his brow. His bruises had begun to fade and were barely visible beneath the dark stubble of whiskers along his jaw.

She traced one corner of his mouth, and he caught her hand in his. He brushed a kiss along her palm and then pulled her to him so that she lay contentedly against his heart.

"Now what do you think of making love in broad daylight?" he asked several minutes later once both their heartbeats had slowed.

She met his grin with a shy smile. "I think I like it quite well," she admitted even as she realized her scandalous state of dishabille. She promptly eased herself off his now-flaccid rod, then got to her feet. Now that the embers of desire were safely banked, she recalled the purpose for her visit.

"We must discuss our plans for tomorrow, and then I must return home," she said, guilt weighing her words as she gathered up her discarded clothes.

Tark got to his feet, casually rebuttoning his trousers and tugging on his boots. Without comment, he offered her the clean scrap of cloth that had been draped over the headboard. She accepted it with a blush and using the tepid water in the washstand pitcher, sponged away the sticky fluid on her thighs.

By the time she finished dressing, she had regained a portion of her self-possession. Tark, however, now appeared ill at ease. "Before we make our plans," he hesitantly began, "there's something else we must discuss."

His words hinted at that earlier uncertainty she had

sensed in him. Puzzled, she waited for him to continue.

"I've had a lot of empty hours to fill since Sunday," he went on, fixing his gaze on the nonexistent view. "I've spent most of them thinking about the conversation your brother and I had the other morning. He somehow had formed the impression I was courting you. It wasn't until after that impromptu brawl you interrupted that I realized he had hit upon the truth."

Isabeau stared in dismay at his rough-hewn profile, silhouetted against the window's hazy light. Surely Philippe had emphasized that duty meant a match between her and any *américain* was impossible. Now, she had no choice but to confess her own sins of omission . . . and in doing so, to make him understand that the passion they had shared these past days had been but a temporary madness.

"P-please do not say any more," she choked out, lifting her hand to ward off further words. "It can never be, so let us not torment ourselves."

"What in the hell do you mean, it can never be?"

He turned and closed the short distance between them. "I can't offer you much right now, but in another year or so, I'll be back where I was before Franchot returned. In the meantime, I'll do everything in my power to make you happy."

"But if you mean m-marriage," she whispered, the words falling like rough-edged stones from her lips, "I cannot—"

"Cannot . . . or will not?"

Despite his aggressive stance, she recognized a pain in his eyes that mirrored her own. "If you're turning me down, you're damn sure not walking out of here without first giving me some kind of explanation."

He gripped her shoulders and pulled her closer, so that she could see her own image reflected in the gemlike glitter of his eyes. When he spoke again, it was in that dangerously soft tone she knew so well.

"When we made love, you wanted me just as much as I wanted you. I could taste the desire on your lips, I could hear it in your sweet moans when you gave yourself to me—so it can't be that you find me repulsive."

She mutely shook her head, unable to deny his words. Satisfaction gleamed in his eyes, and his lips twisted in a smile.

"Then maybe it's the fact that I'm an American," he went on. "Just like the rest of them, you don't mind sharing my bed, but your delicate Creole sensibilities quail at the thought of making it a legal arrangement. Or maybe"—and he traced his fingers down her cheek in a gesture that should have been affectionate but was instead oddly threatening—"maybe it's just the goddamn money."

"Non," she cried, pressing her clasped hands to her breast as if to shield her heart. "None of that matters, not anymore. If only I had known how you felt . . . I knew you perhaps desired me, but I could not believe—"

"Couldn't believe that I might love you?" He shook his head in despair. "I guess I can't blame you. Sweet Jesus, I think I knew the truth that first moment I saw you on the docks, but I was too damned proud to admit it, even to myself."

He hesitated, and it was all she could do not to fling herself weeping into his arms. As it was, her answer bordered on a sob when she repeated, "I-I cannot. You see, *mon cher,* I am already betrothed."

Twenty-nine

"You're already . . . betrothed?"

Tark repeated her words in an oddly hushed voice. She nodded, steeling herself against an angered response. Instead, he gave a harsh laugh that sent a shiver through her.

"Let me get this straight. The whole time that you've been taking your pleasure in my bed, you were engaged to marry someone else?" When she managed a miserable nod, he persisted, "Who is the lucky gentleman?"

"His name is M-Marcel St. John. He is from a very respectable Creole family—"

"I'll bet he is," Tark cut her short, his words edged now with sarcasm. "So tell me, do you intend to inform your fiancé that he's getting used goods, or do you plan to surprise him on your wedding night?"

She blanched at those cruel words, even as the sound of hurried footsteps echoed from the hall beyond. With a muttered oath, Tark grabbed his pistol from the table, just as the door burst open.

"Oncle Henri!"

The disbelieving words escaped her at the same instant that Tark raised the revolver level with her relative's chest. Heedless of her own safety, she shoved past

Tark and flung herself between the two men. *"Sainte Cécile,* do not shoot him."

Isabeau saw the cold purpose in Tark's blue eyes dissolve into something akin to fear. An instant later, he had lowered the revolver and swiftly released its hammer. That steel click was echoed by a similar metallic sound behind her, and she belatedly realized that her uncle, too, was armed.

"Sweet Jesus, are you trying to get yourself killed?"

His voice raw with fury, Tark dragged her to him. She bit back a cry, unable to understand his manic reaction. Then she saw the naked relief that stamped his features and realized that his anger had been born of fear for her safety.

"Unhand my niece," her uncle's heated voice behind her demanded. Isabeau turned to see him tuck his pocket pistol into his waistband, his handsome face mottled with outrage. Prudently, she disengaged herself from Tark's grasp.

She saw that he had resumed his emotionless mask, his earlier anger now banked beneath the chill blue ice of his eyes. Henri made no such similar attempt to conceal his emotions.

"A man came to my door less than an hour ago. He told me I would find my niece in this particular waterfront tavern—and in the bed of an *américain."*

He spat that last word like an epithet. "I threatened to have this . . . person horsewhipped for his insults, and now I see to my everlasting shame that he spoke truth."

"But you do not understand," she protested. "I merely—"

"You merely let this rutting *américain* take his pleasure with you!" Henri gave a contemptuous gesture at the mirror. "Look at yourself. I can see it in your face, how you let him use you . . . ruin you . . . and yet you dare deny what you have done."

He spared a contemptuous glance at Tark. "Be grateful, M'sieur Parrish, that our mutual acquaintance has seen fit to charge you with an important role tomorrow night. Otherwise, I would not hesitate to kill you for the dishonor you have brought to my family."

Isabeau flinched beneath his brutal verbal onslaught. The contempt in her uncle's face was a more telling mirror of her appearance than the mottled glass beside the bed. How could he believe any protests of innocence when her swollen lips and disheveled air spoke all too clearly of the past hour's events?

"I am sorry, *oncle*," she helplessly began, though her apology was cut short by Tark.

"I'm not surprised to find you know quite a bit about whoring," he interjected, his tone edged with contempt as he set aside his own pistol. "You see, I've done a little checking into your private affairs. You've been prostituting yourself for Franchot Calvé on a regular basis for quite some time."

At Isabeau's gasp, Tark glanced down and favored her with a humorless smile. "What's the matter, my sweet? Didn't you know your uncle is as deeply involved as the rest of us in Franchot's schemes?"

When she mutely shook her head, his smile became predatory. "Perhaps you'd also care to know that he will be helping us kidnap the Russian grand duke tomorrow night."

Sainte Cécile, it couldn't be true—yet how else to explain her uncle's cryptic statement about mutual friends? Here, she and Philippe had struggled to spare Henri the anguish of knowing what his friendship with the Frenchman had cost the family—and all the while he had been but another pawn in the game.

"Is it so, *oncle?*" she demanded in sudden bitterness. "Did you know that Monsieur Calvé had involved Philippe and me in his plot against the Grand Duke Alexis?"

"I do not deny my guilt," Henri stiffly replied, "but what I have done has been for the good of our family."

"For the good of our family? What purpose would my brother's death have served?"

"You cannot possibly understand, *ma fille.* It is a matter of honor."

Honor.

The word rang with hollow selfishness. Isabeau met her uncle's righteous gaze as a cold hand of dismay closed over her heart. Henri, for reasons known only to him, had become so obsessed with preserving the Lavoisier name that he saw no shame in perverting his cherished notions of honor to accomplish that goal. More importantly, she also knew that he would never agree to help them prevent tomorrow night's kidnapping.

"You are right, *oncle,*" she sadly replied. "I do not understand."

She glanced at Tark, who met her uncertain look with cool detachment that hinted at nothing of his thoughts. No time remained for them to discuss their plans or for her to explain the reasons behind her betrothal to Marcel. She could only carry on with her role tomorrow night and trust Tark to do the rest—assuming that he did not abandon her to Calvé's mercies outright.

"Come, niece," Henri said. "I find I do not care to remain in this room a moment longer with this . . . américain."

"Since I don't recall inviting you in," Tark drawled, "I'd just as soon you got the hell out of here, myself."

Though his words were addressed to her uncle, Isabeau realized with a sinking heart that his arrogant dismissal included her, as well. She spared him a final beseeching look and started for the doorway. She shook off the arm Henri offered, guilty resentment diminishing her already weakened affection for him. Whatever her weaknesses, they paled against Henri's deliberate treachery—but what manner of secrets could have spurred him to place her and Philippe in mortal danger?

Her own resolve renewed itself. Surely in the final magical hours of Mardi gras, she would find a chance to make Tark understand why she had chosen duty over love . . . and that her decision had scarred her heart forever.

Tark waited until their footsteps faded before he shut the door. Then, with the fatalistic calm of a man who didn't realize he had just been dealt a mortal wound, he sagged against the splintered wood.

Sweet Jesus, what in the hell had just happened?

The answer was painfully apparent. In the space of a few minutes, he had lost the woman he loved and gained a dangerous enemy in her uncle—and made a damned fool of himself in the process.

He winced as he recalled the stunned look on Isabeau's face while he fumbled with the speech he had been rehearsing since last night. No wonder she'd been taken by surprise, since the notion of marriage had come as a shock to himself.

The memory brought a grim smile to his lips. Lying awake just before dawn, trying to ignore the creaking of bedframes and lusty groans that penetrated the room's thin walls, he fond himself taking a long, hard look at his future. What he had seen was not the possibility of bankruptcy, or imprisonment, or even execution. Instead, all he saw was loneliness—and it scared the hell out of him.

The realization had staggered him, for he had accustomed himself to living out his life alone. Since Delphine's death, he deliberately had avoided emotional ties to any women, telling himself that love could only result in heartache and betrayal. But now, he had found a woman for whom he was willing to take that risk . . . and then the chit knocked his pins out from under him with the announcement she planned to marry someone else.

A respectable Creole family.

Tark clenched his fingers, swept by the urge to find this Marcel St. John and tear him limb from limb. He was bound to be an effete dandy with nothing to recommend him but wealth and an impeccable lineage, for why else would he wed a woman who might be carrying another man's child?

His child.

The idea that Isabeau might be pregnant as a result of their affair had not occurred to him until this minute. From her own actions, it seemed she also had not given any thought to the matter. Still, the possibility filled him with a fierce possessiveness that renewed his determination to make her his own—betrothal or no. Only one obstacle stood in his way.

He strode to the window and pried it open. It yielded with a rusty shriek, revealing the wharf where he and Franchot Calvé would soon settle their score. How events might unfold, he couldn't say. One thing, however, was certain.

By midnight tomorrow, either he or the Frenchman would be dead.

Shrove Tuesday had dawned brilliant.

Now, dusk fell with equal grandeur, but Isabeau paid little heed to its breathtaking colors. Instead, she stood poised on the gallery and bleakly surveyed the costumed merrymakers who filled the streets below. With the coming of darkness, the boisterous crowd had shed their masks. Beneath the harsh yellow glow of the gaslamps, they continued the celebration that had begun well before noon.

Isabeau stretched her cramped muscles and lifted her flushed face to the welcome whisper of breeze that had risen. She had spent much of the day mingling with that crowd, a change from past years when she had joined other well-born Creoles in watching the boisterous Mardi gras activity from the comfort of her own gallery. Costumed and masked, she had attended every official ceremony in an attempt to gain the Grand Duke Alexis's royal notice.

"*Mon Dieu,* Isabeau, I still cannot believe you actually stood on the same platform as His Imperial Highness!" Camille St. John's awed exclamation broke through her musings as the younger girl joined her. "I would have swooned with excitement. Tell me again about the Grand Duke Alexis."

"He was quite . . . royal."

Indeed, her first glimpse of Alexis Romanoff had surprised her. Tall and blond, with keen blue eyes and bushy sidewhiskers, he proved as handsome as the ladies had predicted. He also was much younger than she expected—barely a few years older than herself. She also had noticed the envious glances turned her way when she took her place with various dignitaries and social luminaries upon a semicircular platform temporarily erected before City Hall.

Garlanded with evergreens and draped with flags, the grandstand boasted an immense archway of gaslights in anticipation of the Comus parade scheduled for later that night. In the meantime, the elevated structure provided its occupants with an unhindered view of the afternoon's Rex parade.

Isabeau again regaled Cammi with the highlights of that particular event. An enthusiastic crowd watched the proceedings from the bunting-draped galleries that overhung the streets. Lining the *banquettes* were thousands of maskers whose costumes reflected a myriad of characters, including numerous men attired to represent the royal guest of honor in his guise as a Russian naval lieutenant. One masker, in particular, had caught her eye . . . a comical rooster whose bright red feathers and oversized, yellow beak she glimpsed with unsettling frequency.

The merrymakers strolled, strutted, and simpered their way along the streets, forming a brilliant kaleidoscope of color and a raucous symphony of sound. The parade itself reminded her of something from a fairy tale. Rex, white-bearded and resplendent in purple velvet, led the way on a magnificent bay stallion. Behind him followed courtiers mounted on proud-stepping white steeds whose tails and manes were dyed purple.

Among the floats had been a cloudlike creation bearing a grove of silver and gold trees. On still another, a gold-armored knight battled a green dragon who belched purple smoke. Interspersed with these colorful wagons were countless brass bands.

"And every one that came along played that silly song that Lydia Thompson sang in *Bluebeard*. You remember, Cammi, the same tune that Philippe was whistling the other evening." Isabeau hummed for the girl's benefit a few bars of what had become the unofficial song of the day, "If Ever I Cease to Love."

"But they made up new verses as they went along," she continued, "some of them quite ridiculous. Everyone thought it would please the grand duke since he enjoyed Lydia's musical so much—but I think he was offended, instead."

Alexis's reaction to that whimsical song was less remarked upon, however, than an earlier incident. Despite her bleak mood, Isabeau smiled as she related the story.

Heedless of the pleas of the city fathers, His Imperial Highness had refused to sit upon the makeshift throne provided him. Not that she had blamed Alexis. It sat atop a dais over which had been erected a red silk canopy festooned with gold trim, the effect reminding her of something out of Ophelia's brothel. The grand duke, however, had invoked democracy rather than good taste in declining to view the parade from that place of honor.

"He told them that titles were simply nicknames, as Thomas Paine had said, and that he would not insult the people of New Orleans by accepting such undeserved reverence," she finished with amusement.

Cammi, however, gave a disdainful sniff. "What is the point of being a grand duke, if one does not act like royalty?" Then she glanced at the watch pinned to her gown. *"Mon Dieu,* the Comus parade will soon start, and you're not dressed yet."

She all but dragged Isabeau back into the bedroom, where her costume for this night hung from her wardrobe. It had arrived the afternoon before, delivered by a young Negress whose calloused fingers and quiet pride dubbed her its seamstress. Isabeau hadn't been able to suppress an awed gasp when the woman carefully withdrew the dress from its wrappings.

Now, while Cammi helped her out of this afternoon's shepherdess costume and added several petticoats to those she already wore, Isabeau feasted her eyes on the fairy-tale creation before her. Its snowy satin was overlaid with a scalloped skirt of glittered white tulle edged with tiny, iridescent white beads. More beads edged the scooped neckline and cap sleeves, and traced intricate flowered patterns along the gown's bodice. Tonight, beneath the brilliant glow of countless crystal chandeliers, the bits of cut glass would resemble handfuls of diamonds sparkling upon virgin snow.

To accompany the gown was a white garland of beaded silk flowers, lace, and plumes braided into a cascade of snowy ribbons. Completing the outfit was a half-mask of stiff white satin, also beaded and beribboned. She set these aside while Cammi lifted the heavy gown over her head.

Even before the younger girl fastened the hooks that ran down the back seam, Isabeau knew the gown would be a perfect fit. Doubtless some days before, Lucie had secured her measurements from another of her dresses and supplied Monsieur Calvé with that information. Never had she owned such an elegant and sinfully expensive gown, yet how ironic that so beautiful a creation should be put to such evil purpose this night.

"Mon Dieu, Isabeau, you are truly a vision."

Cammi secured the matching headpiece and took a step back to admire her handiwork. Unable to suppress a twinge of feminine curiosity, Isabeau faced her reflection in the cheval mirror, taking in her glittering image with a dispassionate eye. Crystalline white from head to foot, with only her unbound raven curls and midnight eyes to provide contrast, she resembled an ice princess born of some snowbound foreign land. The grand duke could hardly fail to notice her, even among a crowd.

She met Cammi's gaze and summoned a smile as false as the beaded mask she now tied so that it dangled against her skirt. "I feel guilty leaving you here while I attend the Comus ball. Are you certain you do not mind looking after Philippe?"

"Do not worry," the girl replied, her habitual pout nowhere in sight. "Philippe and I will watch the parades from the gallery, just as we did this afternoon."

Humming a few bars of "If Ever I Cease to Love," the girl put the final touches to her ensemble. Isabeau realized that Cammi and Philippe had at last come to an understanding. The knowledge brought a small pang of envy. Though she could never begrudge the pair the joy they had found, she wished her own situation might be as happily resolved. Instead, her troubles weighed upon her shoulders like a leaden cloak she could not shrug off.

Don't worry, Isette, everything will work out.

Her brother's confident words of this morning brought her scant reassurance, for she knew that his bold facade hid frustration over the fact that he could offer her no other support, wounded as he was.

She had given him an account of her confrontation with their uncle the day before—a recitation painstakingly abridged to avoid any mention of Tark. His reaction mirrored her own anger and dismay.

Isabeau suppressed a sigh. Her uncle had not spoken a word to her since they had left the Gilded Albatross yesterday afternoon. As for Marcel, he had been conspicuous by his absence today, though she was grateful for the temporary reprieve.

Her thoughts were still in turmoil a quarter of an hour later, when she tucked the pepperbox in her reticule and bade Cammi and Philippe *adieu*. By now, the streets overflowed with merrymakers so that no carriage could make its way through, leaving her no choice but to walk to the grandstand.

Taking a deep breath, Isabeau let herself be swept away by the growing human current, intent now on her destination—City Hall, where the Grand Duke Alexis waited.

Thirty

"It is tragic, I tell you."

The heavy-set matron in the box beside Isabeau heaved a great sigh, ostrich feather plumes quivering against her too-black hair. "My husband and I approached the royal box, but he refused to shake hands. Why, he barely even acknowledged our presence, *chérie*—but that is not the worst of it."

The older woman leaned toward her, her voice choking on a sob. "The entertainment committee pleaded with him, but to no avail. The grand duke simply refuses to dance with anyone tonight."

Refuses? Isabeau stared in dismay across the makeshift dance floor that transformed the Varieties Theatre into a ballroom. His Imperial Highness, Alexis Romanoff Alexandrovitch, stood in his elegantly appointed box, hand tucked in his jacket as a series of tableaux played before him. Alexis's lack of interest was apparent, and Isabeau felt her heart sink. *Mon Dieu,* how could she hope to lure him from the theater?

Her dismay was all the greater as she recalled her small victory earlier this evening during the Comus parade. She had mounted the grandstand with the trepidation of a condemned prisoner facing the gallows. Above her, the archway of gas jets blazed so brightly that she feared everyone might read the guilt she knew must be written upon her face. At any moment, she expected someone to bar her path . . . and yet no one did.

By the time she took her seat, she even had managed to catch Alexis's roving eye. Meeting that warm blue gaze, she boldly favored him with flirtatious smiles. She might have pursued a more daring approach, had the grandstand not been crowded with others vying for the grand ducal attention. She reassured herself that she would have opportunity enough to speak with him at the Comus ball.

Now, with a hurried excuse to her companion, Isabeau left the box and started in the direction of the grand duke. The temporary wooden floor that had been fashioned atop the theater's rows of seats now played host to countless couples dipping and swirling in time to the orchestra's bright strains. Maskers who earlier had manned various floats milled about in costume, their outlandish clothing a garish contrast to the elegant attire of the other guests. She saw no sign, however, of the mysterious man disguised as a rooster. Doubtless his earlier appearances were nothing more than coincidence.

Silk and satin rustled around her, while jewels flashed beneath the lights of the chandeliers. Talk and laughter offered a festive accompaniment to the gay music. A person could easily lose oneself in the crush, and indeed, the situation was ideal from a kidnapper's point of view. She had only to persuade Alexis to leave his box—but how, when an entire committee already had met with failure?

She halted a short distance from the royal entourage

and studied Alexis's stern figure, wondering at his change in attitude. His apparent reserve was at odds with the rakish joviality he earlier had displayed. Perhaps he *had* taken offense at the Orleanians' boisterous behavior, not to mention the irreverent ditty with which they had regaled him all day long.

What was she to do? Eleven o'clock was almost upon her, and Tark and her uncle would be waiting behind the theater for her and the grand duke.

"Mademoiselle," came a man's unfamiliar voice behind her, "I have searched the ballroom for you, fearing you were but a creation of my own wistful thoughts. Now that I know you are indeed real, would you do me the honor of accepting the next dance?"

At this florid declaration, she swung about to find herself facing a tall, bewhiskered gentleman attired to represent Alexis in a splendid military uniform, complete with gold braid and numerous rows of medals. She started to refuse him, then gave him a second look.

"Y-your Highness," she choked out. For it was indeed Alexis, though his fair hair and sidewhiskers were darkened now with pomade in an attempt at disguise. She started to make her curtsy, when the grand duke put out a restraining hand.

"That is not necessary," he smilingly remonstrated in accented but excellent English. "Tonight, I am simply Alexis, and I wish to enjoy Mardi gras as one of the people. And I do hope you will deign to be my most gracious hostess, *mademoiselle—*"

"L-LaSalle, Your Highness," she impulsively supplied, recalling the false surname Philippe had assumed. Then she glanced uncertainly to the man standing in the royal box. "But who—"

"My half-brother, Stanislaus," he explained, his blue eyes glinting with humor. "The resemblance is striking, is it not? His mother was once a servant in our household . . ."

He trailed off with a shrug and added, "He takes my place on occasion when I wish to move about incognito."

"But isn't it dangerous for you to travel without your retinue?"

Alexis drew himself up proudly, his mustaches bristling. "You forget, *mademoiselle,* that I am a lieutenant of the Imperial Russian Navy. I can take care of myself."

Before Isabeau could form a suitably placating reply, the orchestra struck up a lively air. The music seemed to restore his good humor, for the duke gallantly offered his arm. "From the moment I first beheld you this afternoon, I vowed I would not leave the city until we had a chance to meet. And now, Mademoiselle LaSalle, if you will honor me . . ."

"I-I am flattered, Your Highness," she murmured, praying he would attribute her nervousness to discomfiture at having attracted his distinguished regard.

As they took the first turn about the floor, she took the measure of her intended victim. Up close, Alexis was rather less handsome than she had first thought, his blunted features genial rather than striking. A young bear of a man, she silently dubbed him. Doubtless before he was much older, his girth would match his impressive height. Still, his boisterous charm was undeniable.

Encouraged by her regard, he pulled her scandalously closer. "Would you care to join me tonight for supper . . . and perhaps entertain me with tales of your charming city?"

"I would be honored, Your High—, Alexis," she promptly agreed, certain from the gleam in his eyes that he sought more than casual conversation from her. Encouraged, she went on, "And what do you think of our Mardi gras celebration?"

"It is quite . . . interesting."

"I do not believe you thought so earlier this evening during the Comus parade."

Alexis shrugged. "Ah, but that was because I did not have a lovely young woman such as you to enjoy it with."

"But what about that actress, Lydia Thompson?" she asked, then blushed when she realized how forward her question was.

To her relief, the grand duke appeared to have taken no offense. "Alas, the charming Lydia no longer seems quite so charming, now that I have met you."

Her own smile faltered. *It is not too late. You can still warn him.* Since the real Alexis was supposedly safely out of reach, she could simply tell Monsieur Calvé that her task had been impossible. But then what would happen to Regine and the others?

The music ended with a flourish, and Isabeau took a steadying breath. "It is so warm in here," she said with a flirtatious smile. "Perhaps we might step out for a bit of air."

"An excellent notion," the duke agreed, his manner too eager for mere gallantry as he promptly turned toward one of the nearby alcoves.

"No, not that way," she exclaimed, then quickly softened her involuntary protest. "That is, I fear too many other guests will have the same idea. Let me show you a spot that is a bit more . . . private."

Grasping the royal hand, she led Alexis through the throng toward the back hallway. They reached the darkened, deserted corridor and started down it. "We are almost there," she reassured Alexis.

He halted in midstep and unceremoniously pulled her to him, capturing her lips in an enthusiastic kiss. She gave a muffled gasp and tried to struggle free of his bearlike embrace. The sharp-edged medals that decorated his broad chest pressed painfully against her bodice, so that the expensive fabric of her gown was quite brutally crushed.

To her dismay, Alexis interpreted her frantic reaction as cooperation, and he grew more ardent in his overtures. When he finally allowed her to break, it was all she could do to restrain her urge to give him a resounding slap. Remembering her role just in time, she instead exclaimed in an appalled tone, "Y-your Highness!"

"Alas, my beauty, you must forgive me," he replied in a contrite if breathless voice. "I was so overcome by your charms that I forgot myself."

Isabeau suppressed an inelegant snort. Royalty or not, Alexis was no different from any other man. She composed herself with an effort and gave him an encouraging smile.

"I am not displeased," she said, touching her tongue to her upper lip in a calculated gesture. "It is just that anyone might happen upon us here—but as I said, I know a place . . ."

She trailed off suggestively, and the duke promptly

straightened his jacket. "Tonight, Mademoiselle LaSalle, you are my superior officer. I will follow wherever you command."

"Then let us go now, Your Highness," she replied and led him out into the night.

The throng of maskers that earlier had filled Canal Street appeared to have doubled. Now, as she and Alexis fought their way down the crowded *banquette,* they were all but swept away by a tide of exuberant humanity.

"This way," she cried and grasped Alexis's hand even tighter, fearful lest they be separated in the crush. By dint of much shoving, they reached the gaily painted placard outside the theater's front entrance.

"Let us catch our breath," she suggested, frantically scanning the crowd for her uncle and Tark. No doubt the pair simply was delayed—for who could squeeze a carriage onto the street this night?

She spared another look at Alexis, wondering how best to stall him. She could hardly engage him in conversation, since the blaring of countless brass bands and the ceaseless shouts and laughter made dialogue impossible. Then she realized that any such efforts were unnecessary, since the duke appeared enthralled by the surrounding mosaic of color and sound. Indeed, he looked like a youth about to embark on a grand adventure.

And so he was, she thought with a stab of misgiving, though it was too late now to reconsider her part in the kidnapping. Barely had she reminded herself of that fact, when a man's hand closed over her wrist.

"Might I suggest, *mademoiselle,* that you pretend to be distraught," came Tark's ironic whisper behind her.

She managed a nod and with the tip of her tongue

wet her suddenly dry lips. If Tark's plan entailed her portraying the innocent, then she would gladly assume that role. But her gasp when she looked back at him owed nothing to playacting.

More than once, she had dubbed him a buccaneer. Tonight, he had dressed the part, with tight black breeches tucked into shiny black boots and topped by a loose-cut white shirt unbuttoned almost to his navel. A pistol was casually thrust into the fringed crimson sash that served as his belt, while a square of fabric in the same flamboyant shade was tied rakishly around his head. Though unmasked, he appeared almost a stranger to her beneath the gaslamps' harsh light. The half-healed gash across his temple only enhanced his piratical air.

His eyes glittered with impatience as Tark gave her arm a quick shake, recalling her to her role. She took a deep breath and dutifully exclaimed, "How dare you! Unhand me, *monsieur,* or I will scream!"

"What is the meaning of this!" Alexis's fair skin flushed in anger. "I warn you, sir, to let this young woman go, or I will be forced to—"

He broke off. Surprise supplanted his outraged expression. Directly behind him stood her Oncle Henri, the grim cast to his features at odds with the jaunty gaiety of his Bacchanalian costume. Glancing down, she saw he had shoved a pistol into the grand duke's ribs.

"Come quietly, Your Highness, and no one will be hurt."

Alexis frowned in apparent disbelief. Then his broad features relaxed into a grin, and he nodded. "Ah, I understand. This is a joke—a Mardi gras prank, yes?"

"It's no joke," Tark tersely replied. He pulled Isabeau

to him, his fingers lingering on her throat in a threatening gesture. "Now listen carefully. We have a . . . friend who wants to meet you. Try any heroics, and the *mademoiselle* will suffer for it. Do you understand me?"

The duke surveyed him with disdain. "But you would not dare to try anything in front of all these good people."

"Don't be too sure of that, Your Highness. We could shoot you and vanish into the crowd before your body hit the ground."

Alexis's ruddy complexion paled; still, he drew himself up with royal hauteur and made a final attempt at appeal. "Allow this fair beauty to go, sir, and I will do as you ask."

"She comes with us."

Tark's clipped reply held a note of finality, and Alexis subsided with a shrug. Isabeau gave a silent prayer of thanks that the duke had not called Tark's bluff—if he had indeed been bluffing. Had she not been privy to Monsieur Calvé's scheme, she might have been fearful for her own safety.

Flanked by her uncle and Tark, she and the duke started toward the side street beyond, where the crush of maskers had begun to thin. Isabeau concentrated on keeping her expression one of unconcern lest someone read in her eyes the fact that she was helping abduct the city's royal guest of honor.

The yellow glow from a succession of gaslights spread a sickly illumination over the masses, while the multihued bunting and costumes no longer struck her as magical, but simply as tawdry. Worse, the laughter that filled the streets seemed to have taken on a taunting edge, as if all the crowd were privy to her fall from grace.

A few blocks later, they halted alongside Monsieur Calvé's elegant carriage. Its gold curtains were drawn, while its team of blooded greys stamped in impatience. Here, the festive sounds were a muted echo, while few maskers made their tipsy way down this debris-strewn *banquette*. None paid any notice when Alexis defiantly spun about to face his captors.

"Enough," he declared, folding burly arms across his broad, medal-strewn chest. "I demand to know what is going on here."

"You are not in the position to make demands, Your Highness." The chill tone of Henri's voice echoed the cold expression in his pale eyes as he unfastened the carriage door. "Now, step inside."

"Do not think to frighten me with your barbaric American ways," the duke sputtered. "I am a Romanoff. I can have you flogged for your insolence. I can—"

"You can shut the hell up and do as you're told," Tark interjected.

Alexis sputtered a moment longer and then complied, climbing into the coach with surprising grace for so large a man. Isabeau followed suit, sparing a final look at the street behind her. In the bright halo of gaslights, she spotted her rooster nemesis taking refuge in a shadowed doorway.

Watching his beaked headpiece bobbing from around its edge, she choked back nervous laughter. What must this unknown admirer think to see her setting off with not one, but three gentlemen?

Isabeau obediently settled on the leather seat across from Alexis and smoothed her sadly crushed gown. Tark sprawled beside her, while her uncle took his own place beside the disgruntled duke. At a signal from Henri, the driver whipped up his team, and the coach rumbled off into the night.

She shifted uneasily in the close quarters. The curtains had been tied shut, allowing no glimpse of the passing streets, while the lantern beside her had been turned down. Still, the lamp provided illumination enough for her to study, in turn, each of the three men seated around her.

The grand duke's broad features were stamped with royal anger, and she admired his refusal to display any sign of fear. Doubtless he was cursing his own folly for putting himself at risk. With his half-brother fulfilling his official role, it might be hours before his retinue realized he was missing.

Henri's face reflected more subtle emotions. Not the least among them was an almost palpable hatred directed not at their royal prisoner, but at Tark. Recalling their confrontation the previous day, she fought back a shiver. If the opportunity ever again presented itself, she sensed her uncle would not hesitate to kill Tark.

And what of Tark's intentions?

From the corner of her eye, Isabeau studied the man for whom she had been forced to deny her love. A day ago, she would have taken comfort in his presence. Tonight, an unspannable distance separated them, though they sat so close that the glittering skirt of her gown brushed his calf. Despite his air of apparent unconcern, she could sense a tightly coiled watchfulness about him. She felt that he was aware of her scrutiny—and that he had not forgiven her seeming betrayal the day before.

She gradually grew aware that the carriage had

picked up speed. A few minutes later, its uneven jouncing gave way to a familiar hollow rumble. The wharf.

She tensed, aware that their destination must be close at hand. The remainder of Monsieur Calvé's scheme held as great uncertainty for her as it did for their prisoner. Were they to hide away the duke in Tark's warehouse, or would they instead hold him aboard one of the steamboats that crowded the docks?

The carriage jerked to a halt, and she bit her lip in consternation. Now would be the time for Tark to put into effect any plan. Still, she couldn't suppress her foreboding as she studied her uncle's set features.

"Let's go," Tark clipped out, unfastening the door while her uncle caught up the lantern from its hook. Henri filed out first, flanking the doorway while Alexis clambered out after them. Isabeau prepared to follow, when Tark put out a restraining hand.

"You wait here."

"But I must—"

"You wait here, *mademoiselle*," he repeated in a tone that brooked no argument. Then, in a low voice meant only for her ears, he added, "Don't worry, my sweet. I'll take care of everything."

It was that brief endearment, rather than his promise, that reassured her. She settled back in her seat and watched him climb out, glad she would not have to confront her uncle again. That momentary relief faded, however, when Henri poked his head back inside the door.

"Listen to me, niece," he harshly whispered, "and for once do exactly as you are told. Do not leave this carriage for any reason—no matter what you might hear."

Not waiting for a response, he shut the door and left her sitting in darkness.

No matter what you might hear.

Henri's cryptic words repeated themselves in her mind, renewing her earlier foreboding. Cautiously, she unfastened the curtain ties and peered past the heavy gold velvet, only to distinguish the retreating dark shapes of the three men. Once her eyes adjusted to the low light, she realized with a gasp just where on the docks they were.

"The sugar sheds," she softly exclaimed, taking in the immense structure and familiar rows of barrels. If Calvé's instructions had been for them to take the duke aboard one of the nearby vessels, it made more sense for them to wait in the carriage until the ship was ready to disembark. Why bring Alexis here and risk the chance he might attempt an escape, unless—

"Mon Dieu, no," she whispered in horror as another possibility presented itself. If her guess proved correct, then she dared not sit idly by.

With shaking fingers, she unlatched her door and slowly let it swing open. Though she had not heard her uncle instruct the driver, she could not take the risk that the man might attempt to prevent her from leaving the carriage.

Gathering her skirts in one hand, she eased herself out the open doorway, carefully feeling for the step. She shifted her weight in stages until she had lowered herself onto the wharf. Then, silently, she closed the door and glanced at the driver.

He sat hunched upon his perch staring across the river, moonlight glinting on glass when he raised a bottle to his lips. *He's celebrating Mardi gras, just like everyone else,* she thought in relief, even as off-key snatches of some melody drifted to her.

"If ever I cease to love," he plaintively warbled, "may the grand duke ride a buffalo in a Texas rodeo, if ever I cease to love."

Biting back nervous laughter at this now-familiar refrain, Isabeau fled the shadow of the carriage for the structure looming before her.

Thirty-one

Urgency lent swiftness to her step as Isabeau traversed the molasses barrel maze. By the time she neared the first stairway, the echo of men's voices drifted to her. She slowed and strained to listen, catching only fragments of sentences.

". . . can't possibly succeed . . . playing you for a goddamn fool, Henri . . ."

". . . you who are the fool, Parrish . . . never meant for either of you to leave here alive . . ."

Isabeau choked back a cry, dread seizing her as she recognized the deadly intent behind her uncle's threats. Not only did Henri plan to execute the grand duke here tonight, he also meant to kill Tark.

Sainte Cécile, she had to stop this madness—but how? The whispered rustle of her skirts accompanied her as she hurried toward the open area beyond. Both men were armed, she knew, so that Tark might just as easily kill Henri. She could reason with them, perhaps . . . plead with them, if need be—but even if she prevented the grand duke's murder, how could she hope to resolve this feud between her uncle and the man she loved?

She halted at the end of the barrel maze. In the yellow glow of the lantern, Tark and Henri faced each other, standing twenty or more paces apart with pistols at the ready. Though Tark still wore his pirate's garb, her uncle had shed his laurel-draped white robes and was now attired in elegant black evening clothes. Neither paid any heed to the duke, who waited a short distance away, his hand tucked in his jacket and his expression watchful.

She could not see her uncle's expression. Still, she guessed that his face mirrored the grim purpose she read in Tark's set features. None of the men had noticed her arrival, intent as they were on Tark's words.

". . . only way to save yourself. Franchot has probably already notified the authorities that you are responsible for the duke's kidnapping."

"I will not be swayed by your crude tactics," her uncle replied in a taut voice. "Calvé has arranged for me to leave the city as soon as my business with you two gentlemen is concluded. A ship bound for Sevastopol will disembark from this very dock—"

"The *Star of the Mediterranean*," Tark interjected with a grim smile. "Don't look so surprised, Henri. I'm the one who made those arrangements. And contrary to what Franchot told you, I'm the one who's supposed to be aboard that freighter come midnight."

"That cannot be. I have done all that he has asked of me. I have been loyal—"

"Franchot doesn't give a damn about your loyalty," Tark brutally cut him short, "so don't waste your breath trying to convince me of his honorable intentions toward you."

"Honor! You *américains* know nothing of honor!"

Henri's righteous words rang throughout the shed with equal parts outrage and madness. He raised his arm, so that his pistol was leveled squarely at Tark's chest.

"If you thought to save yourself with lies, you have made a fatal mistake," he went on, cocking back the hammer. "For years, your kind has defiled what we Creoles hold dear. Now you have ruined my niece and brought dishonor to my family—and you *will* pay the price for your actions."

"Oncle, no!"

Isabeau flung herself from the shadows against her relative's outstretched arm. She glimpsed Tark's stunned expression as he caught sight of her and lowered his own weapon. A heartbeat later, the deafening roar of a shot filled her ears.

The moment that followed seemed to pass with incredible slowness, though indeed events unfolded within the blink of an eye. Her head ringing with the echo of the gunshot, Isabeau struggled to catch her balance, then saw that the bullet's impact had sent Tark sprawling against the stairway behind him. A bright flower of blood blossomed against his white shirt before he sagged to the ground.

"Non!" she screamed and started toward him, when her uncle caught her arm in a brutal grip.

"He is dead, *ma fille,*" Henri told her, and despite her anguish she recognized the harsh glee in his tone. "Now let us deal with this other, and then be gone."

"Murderer," she shrieked and struggled against Henri's cruel hold. "Let me go!"

He might still be alive, she wildly reassured herself;

after all, Philippe had survived a similar wound. If she could somehow transport him to a physician . . .

"You will drop your weapon, Monsieur Lavoisier," came an accented voice of command.

Isabeau ceased her struggles and stared in amazement at Alexis, who stood holding a pocket pistol. The duke allowed himself a satisfied smile. "I told you, my beauty, that I could take care of myself, did I not?"

His triumphant expression vanished, however, as he spared a look at Tark. "I am sorry that your lover is killed. He explained how it was you were coerced into helping with this folly. His wish was that no blame be attached to you."

The duke edged toward the barrels and gestured vigorously with his revolver. "I am telling you to drop your gun," he demanded of Henri. "I do not care for you to shoot me in the back when I take my leave."

"You will not get far," Henri threatened, though he let his pistol drop. "My men will search until you are found."

"As you will."

Alexis shrugged and motioned them backward, then caught up the discarded gun. "I only wish, my beauty, that we were meeting under more pleasant circumstances," he added with a gallant nod in Isabeau's direction. "Now, I am off to enjoy your wonderful city."

The grand duke vanished into the barrel maze, his heavy footfalls swiftly fading into the night. Henri rounded on Isabeau, his handsome features distorted with fury as his grip on her tightened.

"See what you have done, niece! How will I explain

this failure to Calvé?" With his free hand, he dealt her a painful slap that dropped her to her knees.

Stunned by his blow, Isabeau could only watch while he stalked over to Tark's prone form and cursorily checked his wrist for a pulse, then plucked the oversized Colt from his slack fingers. Henri stared down at his vanquished foe a moment longer, then spun about in the same direction the duke had fled.

Once the echo of her uncle's footsteps faded, Isabeau struggled to her feet. She ignored her ringing ears and blearily focused on Tark. He had not stirred, and the realization dimmed any hope she nurtured that he yet lived. Choking back a sob, she started toward him. She could not leave without touching him one last time, without brushing his lips with one last kiss—

"Make haste," came Henri's strident voice from behind her. "We must hunt down that arrogant fool of a duke."

"I will not, Oncle," she rashly replied, heedless now of her own well-being. "I care nothing for Monsieur Calvé's schemes."

She broke off with a gasp as Henri raised his pistol even with her face. "If you do not wish to join your lover in death," he softly threatened, "you will come with me now. Do you understand me, *ma fille?*"

She understood him quite clearly—but what could it matter now, when she had no reason left to live? Even as that despairing thought whirled through her mind, however, her uncle persisted, "Have you forgotten this bastard child of my daughter's? If you do not carry out your part in this night's events, the babe will be given

to Ophelia to do with as she will. Can you live with
another death upon your conscience, Isabeau?"

Another death. If she did not carry through with
Calvé's orders, Regine would also fall victim to the
Frenchman's madness. At that thought, she managed, "I
will do what I must, Oncle."

"Then let us be off."

As he led her away, she spared one final glance back
at Tark. He lay bathed in the yellow glow of the abandoned lantern, one arm flung toward her in a supplicat-
ing gesture. For an instant, she thought she glimpsed
the shallow rise and fall of his chest, and her heart leapt
for joy. In the next moment, however, she realized that
it was no more than a trick of the light . . . that the
lantern slowly was flickering out.

The tears began then—not the noisy sobs of disappointment, but the silent anguish of heartbreak. Only
the thought of the innocent still held captive by Ophelia
gave her the strength to turn her back on him.

"Adieu, mon cher," she brokenly whispered as she followed her uncle out into the night.

"You disappoint me, Henri."

Franchot Calvé leaned back against the red velvet
love seat and narrowly studied the older man through a
cloud of blue smoke. He paid little heed to Isabeau,
who stood silent beside her uncle.

They had gathered at Ophelia's brothel in a second-
floor parlor well removed from the establishment's paying customers. Two pairs of French doors stood open
against the mild night, allowing in the boisterous sound

of celebration. From the ballroom below drifted an orchestra's bright strains accompanied by raucous laughter from the brothel's guests. The festive clamor served as an incongruous contrast to the grim drama unfolding within.

She had managed to retain a stoic indifference, though she deemed both men equally responsible for Tark's murder. Still, her earlier hot grief had abated, replaced by cold purpose as she reminded herself that Regine depended upon her. Later, she would mourn for what was lost. Until then, she would hold that emotion tightly to her while she listened and bided her time.

"I entrusted you with a matter of vital importance, and you have failed me," Calvé went on, his golden eyes reflecting the harsh brilliance of coin. "In one brief instant, you robbed me of the vengeance I have sought for almost twenty years—and for what purpose? A few moments of satisfaction of your own."

"But you bade me to kill the *américain,*" Henri protested. "And how was I to know that the grand duke carried a pistol?"

"You are an *imbécile,* Henri . . . a pitiful excuse for a man."

Calvé rose from his seat. Anger distorted his cultured tone as he stabbed out his cigar and continued, "Did I not tell you that Alexis Romanoff is a lieutenant in the Imperial Russian Navy? You should have expected him to be armed . . . just as you should have anticipated Tark Parrish's treachery."

"But—"

The Frenchman cut him short with a vicious gesture and strode toward him. "You will do well to remember that you are but a pawn to be moved about at my whim. I am the one who determines this game's outcome—and I shall reap an eye for an eye."

His words cracked whiplike through the room, taking Isabeau aback. Privy now to the man's dark side, she could well believe that he had murdered both Elisabeth Tremaine and Delphine Parrish.

He halted before her stupefied relative. "Do you truly believe that Alexis Romanoff is wandering the streets of New Orleans, waiting for my men to finish the job you so miserably began? Or do you think it more likely that he has given the authorities a full report of this night's events?"

When Henri managed only a wordless stammer, the Frenchman gave a contemptuous shake of his head. "I should kill you right now," he softly said, "if only to spare the world another fool. Fortunately for you, you may yet prove of use to me. Though Alexis Alexandrovitch lives, I still intend to reclaim what is rightfully mine."

"Tell me what I must do," Henri gasped out. "Whatever you wish . . . but please do not kill me."

Watching him plead for his life, Isabeau felt a detached sort of pity for the frightened man. She swiftly squelched that emotion, concentrating instead on the fact that he had murdered Tark and threatened her life. What did it matter that they shared common blood . . . or that she knew how easily one might bargain with the devil—and in the process barter away one's soul?

Calvé's merciless words broke through her thoughts. "You will remain here until dawn," he told Henri, "when one of my associates shall hand you your final instructions. In the meantime, Ophelia will see to your . . . comfort."

"But I dare not stay in the city. It will be only a matter of time until the authorities find me."

Calvé harshly cut short his disjointed plea. "There has been a change of plans. I shall be the one leaving for Sevastopol at midnight . . . accompanied by your niece."

"Mon Dieu, no."

Isabeau shot Henri a look of anguished appeal. "You cannot allow him to do this, Oncle. If Philippe was not wounded . . ."

Seeing that her uncle would make no protest, she defiantly met the Frenchman's gaze. *She* would not be another of this demon's pawns, meekly following him down his private road back to hell.

Before she could tell him so, Calvé caught her chin in a cruel grip, forcing her to hold his gaze. She shrank from the inhuman light that seemed to burn from those golden eyes. Was it simply madness that drove him, or was it something far more dangerous?

"You should be thankful that your brother is unable to interfere," Calvé told her, "for he would not survive my wrath a second time. I am equally confident that you will find a sea voyage preferable to the fate awaiting you here."

Anger gave her the strength to pull free of his grasp. "You are wrong, *m'sieur.* The grand duke knows I was coerced into helping you. He will tell the authorities I am innocent."

"Do not be so certain of that, *ma chère.* While Alexis Romanoff has the reputation for being easily swayed by a pretty face, he is equally known for his capricious nature."

"Perhaps I am willing to take that risk," she replied with a proud lift of her chin.

She steeled herself against another wave of his anger, but Calvé merely shrugged. "I had hoped you would come willingly. I see I must remind you that I still control this game."

He strode gracefully across the room and tugged at the bell pull. The parlor door clicked open, revealing the same dark-skinned housekeeper with whom she had spoken that first morning as she searched for Lili. Isabeau paid her little heed, however, for her attention was fixed on the blanket-wrapped bundle the woman held.

"Regine," she exclaimed and rushed forward to take the child.

She looked much as Lili would have at that tender age, Isabeau thought with a pang, gazing at the tiny plump face surrounded by a fine halo of golden hair. She ran a reverent finger along the babe's delicate white skin, marveling at its softness. When the child did not stir at her touch, Isabeau gave the housekeeper a worried glance.

"She sleeps so soundly. Has she been ill?"

The Negress shook her head, slanting a dark look at Calvé. "There's nothin' wrong with that chile, 'cept that Madame Ophelia done give her one of them voodoo potions to keep her quiet. Now, don't you worry none," she added at Isabeau's cry of horror, "she'll be fine come mornin'."

Reassured, Isabeau gave her a grateful nod and hugged

the babe to her. She waited for the older woman to quit the room, however, before she again addressed Calvé.

"I kept my part of our bargain, so why not let me leave here with Regine, as you promised. Surely the child and I would be of no use to you aboard ship."

"But you are wrong, *ma chère*. Together, you shall ensure my safe passage back to the Crimea—for no breath of suspicion could fall upon a man traveling abroad with his . . . family."

At his words, it was all Isabeau could do not to clutch the child to her breast and bolt for the door. But how could she make an escape, when a contingent of doormen guarded the brothel? Better she should wait until they were on the streets again.

She took a resolute breath. "If the babe and I accompany you, will you guarantee that no harm shall come to us?"

His silken tone did little to reassure her. "You are quite safe with me—so long as you do as you are told. Now, come."

He gestured her toward the door, though she stopped at the threshold and turned to her uncle. "Please, tell Philippe—"

"He will inform your brother that you willingly accompanied me," Calvé interjected. "I am sure that once he learns of your unfortunate relationship with the deceased Monsieur Parrish, he will concur with your decision. Do you not agree, Henri?"

Henri gave a jerky nod, his autocratic features set in strained lines as he avoided Isabeau's gaze. She realized then that with this last unquestioning act of fealty, her uncle had forged the final link in the chain fettering her family to Calvé. She knew with equal certainty that she had to break those shackles and redeem what remained of her family. But only one solution presented itself—a solution that might cost her very soul.

A glance down at the child she held decided her. She would do it, she silently vowed, if only for Regine's sake. Sometime before the last stroke of midnight, she would murder Franchot Calvé in cold blood.

Thirty-two

From a great distance, he heard the sound.

Its echo was reminiscent of icicles melting beneath a chill winter sun, and by painful degrees it penetrated the buzzing in his head. If he could only manage to open his eyes, he might track down its source and end his torment.

With effort, he raised his eyelids. He promptly discovered he was lying flat on his back beneath a series of rough wood planks. The flickering yellow glow of a lantern did little to dispel the surrounding gloom—or give him a clue as to where the hell he was. Compounding his confusion was the overwhelming reek of molasses that assaulted his nostrils. The buzzing in his head had subsided, replaced by a persistent, agonizing throb, like he had spent the night drowning his sorrows with Tom's rotgut whiskey.

Or like he had suffered a blow to the head.

Memory returned then with sudden, brutal clarity, and he was aware of a searing pain along his side which rivaled that of his skull. Sweet Jesus, the crazy Creole bastard actually had shot him. His head injury had been secondary, happening when the bullet's impact sent him sprawling back against the wooden stairway. As for the sound, it was the echo of dripping molasses from a keg beside him, where doubtless the bullet that had grazed him must finally have lodged.

How long had he been lying here? Minutes . . . maybe even hours? No doubt he had been left for dead, though he knew his wound was minor. But what had happened to the others . . . to Isabeau?

He struggled into a sitting position, fighting at the same time the wave of dizziness that assailed him. Sweet Jesus, his attempt to defuse the kidnap scheme had almost literally blown up in his face. So what the hell had gone wrong—and why?

He had settled on that old standby, reason. Had he succeeded in convincing Henri to abandon his part in the plot, he would have charged the older man with the grand duke and Isabeau's safety. That, in turn, would have freed himself to deal with Calvé.

What he hadn't counted on was the Creole's unreasoning hatred of all Americans—him, in particular—and his desperate loyalty to Franchot. His failure meant that the stakes in this game had been raised drastically. Despite Franchot's glib agreement to free Isabeau and her uncle once they'd played out their roles, he knew the Frenchman had no intention of keeping that promise. He had to find her before—

"So you are alive, after all. Good."

The sound of a man's satisfied words drifted to him, and Tark blearily squinted in the direction of booted footsteps moving toward him. "You . . . got away," he managed in surprise. "But how—"

"As I told the *mademoiselle,* I can take care of myself." The Grand Duke Alexis halted before him, and with a casualness that belied his royal upbringing, sat back on his thick haunches. "You have been insensible for half of an hour, perhaps a bit less. Do not fear, the young woman and her uncle are gone for but a short while."

So Isabeau was safe, at least for the time being. Still, with midnight fast approaching, he didn't have time to spare, he told himself as he unfastened his shirt buttons. The question now was, would he be of much use to anyone in his current condition?

"Ah, but your injury is just, as they say, a scratch," the other man proclaimed. "I have had much worse."

Tark squinted at the spot just below his ribs where the bullet had plowed cleanly through his flesh, leaving a bloody furrow but doing no real harm. Of his two injuries, the blow to his skull was likely the more serious.

He tugged off the scarf still wrapped around his head and gingerly probed the lump that had risen above his nape. The external damage seemed minor, so he groped for the knot that held the sash tied across his waist.

Grasping his intent, Alexis reached over and whipped off the length of cloth with a flourish. "Never fear, my friend, I will make you good as new."

He withdrew from his uniform jacket a gleaming silver flask and poured its contents over the wound. The resulting agony made Tark yelp in pain, even as the vodka fumes cleared the remaining fuzziness from his head. With the same boisterous efficiency, the duke transformed the scarf and sash into a makeshift bandage, then sat back on his heels to survey his handiwork with a satisfied grin.

"See, I tell you I make you well again."

Tark managed a grin in return. "Not bad for royalty," he conceded. "Now, tell me what went on here while I was out. How did you get away?"

Alexis dramatically flashed open his jacket to reveal a pair of mismatched revolvers tucked in his belt. "I am a military man," the duke proudly reminded him. "While your companions' attention is on you, I take them by surprise with my pistol and make my escape."

He grinned and shrugged his broad shoulders. "I think at first only to save myself . . . and then, I change my mind and come back to check on you."

"I'm much obliged."

The sentiment was genuine, for he wouldn't have blamed His Highness if he'd hightailed it out of there without a second look back. Tark glanced around him and saw that his own oversized Colt was missing. No doubt Henri had relieved him of the weapon to replace the one Alexis had commandeered—not that it mattered, since he intended to recover both his revolver and his woman before the night was out.

Anger hastened the return of his strength, so that he struggled to his feet. Even with Alexis's help, however, remaining upright proved a greater feat than he anticipated. Finally satisfied he had regained his equilibrium, if not all his strength, Tark turned to the duke. "You said Isabeau and her uncle left in the carriage. Do you know where they were headed?"

"Alas, no." Alexis frowned into the distance, then brightened. "But wait. The gentleman said he would bring more men that they might track me down. Perhaps you know where he will find them?"

As a matter of fact, he did. Tark allowed himself a grim smile as he and the duke traced their way out onto the wharf again. A contingent of burly footmen had attempted to bar him from Franchot's residence. What better source for Henri to avail himself of convenient brute force?

His smile abruptly faded when he remembered that Ophelia's brothel was equally well staffed. Either place might prove their destination, and time was growing too short for guesswork.

The echo of clumsy footsteps abruptly cut short his calculations. Someone apparently more concerned with speed than stealth was headed in their direction. Tark glanced at Alexis, who plucked Henri's revolver from his belt and tossed it to him. Tark and the duke concealed themselves behind a nearby pile of discarded lumber just before a figure burst from the shadows.

"I-I hear voices. Wh-who's there—"

The newcomer broke off with a squeak as he noticed the pair of pistols leveled at him, while Tark stared disbelievingly at the mild-featured gentleman before them. From the neck down, he was enveloped in a scarlet-feathered suit, the arms of which resembled wings. Beneath one avian appendage was tucked an oversized papier mâché headpiece molded into a rooster's head.

Tark exchanged mystified glances with Alexis at the unexpected appearance of this comically garbed intruder. The young man in question flushed but drew himself up with a dignified air.

"Y-your Highness," he addressed Alexis, juggling his unwieldy headdress to manage a shy bow. "I am p-

pleased to see you are unharmed. I-I followed you and
Isabeau here from the Varieties, but when you did not
leave again with the others, I was concerned. Perhaps
you might tell me what is going on?"

When Alexis made no reply, he turned toward Tark.
"Y-you are Monsieur Parrish, are you not? I saw you
at the cotillion. You forced Mademoiselle Lavoisier to
dance."

He blanched as he noted Tark's bloodied shirtfront.
"Mon Dieu, you've been wounded. I h-heard the shot,
but I had no idea—"

He broke off again, his eyes widened in distress when
Tark cocked his borrowed pistol and stepped toward
him.

"Just who in the hell are you?" Tark grimly demanded, "and what in the hell are you doing here?"

"D-don't shoot."

The young man brandished his rooster mask like a
shield. "I am M-Marcel St. John. Philippe—Mademoiselle Lavoisier's brother—insisted I keep an eye on her
tonight. He said she was in t-trouble, and that it had to
do with His Highness, but he never mentioned—"

"You're Marcel St. John?"

Tark lowered his revolver and stared. Sweet Jesus,
this was his rival for Isabeau's affections? He shook his
head and gave a bitter laugh. He could see now why
she had chosen to take a lover.

Marcel met his contemptuous gaze and shifted uneasily. "I-I fail to see what is so amusing, *m'sieur.* As I
said, I spent several hours watching out for Mademoiselle Lavoisier. When she and her uncle got into a carriage with you two, I had no choice but to follow."

"Then what in the hell took you so damn long?" Tark demanded. "We could have used a little help."

"I-I had a bit of trouble," he explained and anxiously toyed with the rooster head. "I kept up with the coach on foot for a time, but once the streets cleared, I had to hang onto the rear of the carriage. I-I fell off before you reached the dock and walked the rest of the way."

At that last admission, Alexis burst out with a guffaw that he disguised as a cough when the youth indignantly rounded on him. "I could only cling with one hand," Marcel defended himself, "since I had to hang on to my mask with the other. You see, the costume is borrowed, and I couldn't let any harm come to it."

This time, Alexis made no attempt to hold back his laughter, though Tark saw precious little humor in the situation. Time was rapidly ticking past him—and he still had no idea where Isabeau had gone. With a quelling look at the duke, he shoved his pistol into his waistband and rounded on Marcel.

"If you were so damned concerned with keeping track of her, what the hell are you still doing here?" he demanded. "Your Mademoiselle Lavoisier is liable to wind up murdered, unless I find her within the hour. Did you see what direction their carriage took?"

Marcel let the rooster head slip to the dock. Then, recovering himself, he squeaked, "Their d-driver spotted me and I had to conceal myself behind some pilings. I-I rather got stuck"—he waggled one leg, indicating the large rent in his feathered trousers—"and by the time I f-freed myself, the coach was moving too fast for me to catch. But I did hear Monsieur Lavoisier tell the driver something about R-Rue de Fleur—"

"Ophelia's brothel," Tark cut him short, making a quick decision.

Franchot might not wait around to see his orders carried out, so that in the time he needed to rescue Isabeau and return to the wharf, the Frenchman likely would have made his escape. To assure that his old foe didn't slip through his fingers, he had to be waiting at the freighter come midnight. And that meant someone else must stake out the bordello.

"Listen carefully," he tersely informed Marcel, "because I don't have time for stupid questions, and I damn sure don't intend to repeat myself."

Tossing his weapon to the younger man, who caught it with the ease of one accustomed to pistols, he went on, "You'll find them at Twelve Rue de Fleur, just off Basin Street. Go there and do whatever it takes to keep Isabeau safe—and that means shooting anyone who gets in your way. I'll take care of things here. Agreed?"

Marcel vigorously nodded, his mild features taking on a determined cast. "I-I will protect her with my life," he declared, "but it would be helpful for me to know just who I am p-protecting her from."

"Her uncle, for one."

Ignoring his exclamation of disbelief, Tark added, "Henri Lavoisier is just one of your worries. Watch out for Ophelia, the quadroon who runs the place, and a cold-blooded French bastard named Franchot Calvé, who's the one behind this whole scheme. Any of them would gladly make chicken fricassee out of you."

His threat didn't daunt the youth. Instead, Marcel

straightened his shoulders and squared a pugnacious jaw, reminding Tark of a half-grown pup confronting its first stranger. But while Alexis favored the youth with an approving nod, Tark found his patience at the breaking point. "Why in the hell are you still standing here?"

"B-but how will I get there?"

The innocent question had much the same effect on Tark as a pointed stick upon a wounded bear. "Run . . . find a carriage . . . hell, fly if you want," he retorted with a sneering gesture at the youth's absurd costume, "but just get there—or don't you care that your fiancée might end up with a cord wrapped around her pretty neck?"

"M-my fiancée?"

Marcel blinked, and Tark prayed for strength. "Your betrothed," he clarified through gritted teeth. When Marcel simply gaped at him, Tark felt his last vestiges of control give way. "Your intended, your beloved. Goddamn it," his voice swelled into a roar. "Isabeau Lavoisier, the woman you're going to marry."

"M-marry? Isabeau?"

The young man's tone held unfeigned perplexity. "You must have been m-misinformed, *m'sieur.* I offered for her once, it is t-true, but her brother informed me that she t-turned me down. We are good f-friends, and nothing more."

Tark barely heard that last, however, fighting as he was the sudden sick feeling that had settled in his gut. *She had lied about the betrothal.*

Hell, he had even deluded himself into thinking he'd heard genuine anguish in her voice when she turned down his suit. Worse, he had no one to blame for that state of affairs but himself, since his past experience should have been lesson enough. He kept his tone carefully neutral, however, as he replied, "As you say, I must have been mistaken. Now, get the hell over to Rue de Fleur, before it's too late."

"Y-You can depend on me." Marcel snatched up the rooster head, then plunged into the shadows. Tark stared unseeingly after the youth, his earlier sense of urgency dulled by pain at this new betrayal.

"So that is how it is, my friend," came the duke's voice behind him. "You are in love with the beauteous young woman, and you are fearing she does not return your passion?"

Tark met the other man's knowing gaze with a cold look. "I suggest you find your way back to the Varieties, Your Highness," he replied, pointedly ignoring Alexis's question. "Calvé might still decide to send his men in search of you."

"Bah."

Alexis waved away the warning and enthusiastically returned to the subject of Tark's love life. "But how it is you are thinking the young woman is to marry this other one—this one who dresses as a bird? She is perhaps trying to make you jealous?"

"I could stand to borrow your pistol," Tark gritted out, resolutely ignoring the duke's words. "Chances are the freighter's crew has been celebrating tonight and won't be of much use when I confront Franchot."

Caught up in the drama of what he perceived as a lovers' quarrel, Alexis absently handed over his revolver. "When Mademoiselle Isabeau is seeing you bleeding, she is weeping and calling her cruel uncle a murderer. Does this not mean that she is loving you still?"

"What it means is she's one damn fine actress," Tark found himself goaded into retorting. "No doubt that little performance was strictly for your benefit, so you wouldn't accuse her of being in league with Henri."

Or, just as likely, she was mourning the fact she no longer had herself a convenient hero to rescue what was turning out to be every goddamn member of her family.

"But is this also a performance," Alexis mused, "the way she is watching you so sadly in the carriage before—when she is thinking that you do not see her doing so?"

Ruthlessly tamping down the perverse flicker of hope that stirred in his heart at those words, Tark faced the Russian one last time. "Let's get one thing straight here, Your Highness. Whatever might once have existed between me and Isabeau is finished. All I care about now is stopping Franchot from killing anyone else."

"As you please."

Alexis shrugged and gave a good-natured sigh. "I fear that we Russians are the sentimentalists. We would see all love stories have the happy ending."

He straightened and gave a snappy salute. "Farewell, my friend, and much luck. Now, I go back to the celebration." He vanished into the shadows.

Even after the sound of the duke's heavy tread faded, Tark could hear his voice raised in jovial song. The refrain was one he had heard time and again this night, so that by now he had a violent aversion to the ditty.

Still, he could not stop the nonsensical words from running through his mind.

If ever I cease to love,
if ever I cease to love,
may fish get legs and the cows lay eggs,
if ever I cease to love . . .

Thirty-three

The carriage picked up speed as it drew nearer to their waterfront destination. Isabeau hugged the sleeping Regine to her breast, taking comfort from the babe's sweet-smelling warmth. The child, at least, was unaware of the horrors lurking in this night. Isabeau gave a silent prayer of thanks.

A sudden exhaustion swept her, so that it was all she could do not to give herself up to the false refuge of sleep. How easy it would be, lulled by the rhythmic motion of the carriage and the hypnotic glow of the interior lantern as it swung to the same pace.

She blearily focused on Franchot Calvé seated across from her, as he surveyed the passing streets with what she considered remarkable unconcern for a man fleeing the country. A lazy curl of smoke rose from the cigar he idly held, reinforcing his careless air. Briefly, she wondered if she had only imagined that moment in the brothel, when his civilized facade had slipped to reveal the brutal predator lurking beneath.

He glanced her way, and she shivered at the implacable purpose in his golden eyes. How could she have forgotten this was the same man who earlier had threatened her life—and who had killed at least two other

women in cold blood? This brief carriage ride was
merely the first leg of a hellish journey that every instinct warned her must end in tragedy.

She sank her fingernails into her palm, welcoming the
pain that revived her. She had to be ready to seize any
opportunity for escape. Otherwise, she and Regine would
find themselves unwilling passengers on a freighter
bound for a foreign port.

Sevastopol.

Over these past days, she had pieced together enough
snatches of conversation to have forged a logical link
between that destination and the Grand Duke's kidnaping. But what was *her* part in this affair?

No answer came to mind, though she sensed that the
Frenchman's choice of her as hostage had been deliberate. Could it have had something to do with her uncle's unflagging loyalty to Calvé? Barely had she begun
to examine that possibility, than the Frenchman's silken
voice broke the silence.

"Perhaps you would care to know, *ma chère,* just why
I chose you for this particular . . . mission."

He had voiced with his usual uncanny accuracy the
final question that remained in her mind. From his chill
expression, she gathered that she might not care to hear
his explanation after all.

He briefly related his family's history and the later
circumstances surrounding his own role in the Crimean
War. His account paralleled in most respects the local
gossip she recalled hearing. In the next moment, however, she learned that his story involved much more than
wartime struggles.

"Within days of the war's end, while Sevastopol was

suffering under the brutal bombardment of the Allied troops, my father and I were taken prisoner by the Russian forces. Our plight did not lessen once France and England declared victory, and the Tsar sued for peace. You see, our Russian captors declared us criminals—deserters—and we were sentenced to death."

As Isabeau listened in unwilling fascination, he went on, "Our one hope lay with a minor French diplomat involved in the peace negotiations—a man whom my father had known during his youth in Paris. It was not until later I learned that he and my father had experienced a falling out over a *demi-mondaine*. The woman showed a preference for my father."

He paused to draw on his cigar, while Isabeau struggled against foreboding. Calvé had nurtured a grievance for almost two decades. How could she hope to dissuade him from his purpose with mere words?

"I will not shock your sensibilities with accounts of how we languished in that Turkish prison, forced to watch our fellow captives die beneath the lash and the sword. What you will know is that this diplomat—this man who once had been as a brother to my father—had it within his power to halt the proceedings. Instead, he chose to indulge his own bitter envy . . . and so my father fell to the executioner's blade."

Calvé's golden eyes gleamed with an unholy light as he softly added, "I, however, managed to escape that fate—and I saw to it that his death did not go unavenged."

He fell silent, so that the only sound was the clash of shod hooves against uneven cobble. Despite her hatred for her kidnapper, Isabeau admitted an unwilling sympathy for the long-ago horrors he must have suffered. Had it been those brutal experiences that had stolen his humanity and left behind a man devoid of compassion?

But even so, she saw no connection between those distant events and the present. Frantically, Isabeau racked her brains, sensing that her freedom might hinge on that bit of knowledge. Her family had long since emigrated from France, save for her widowed grandmother. Still . . .

Isabeau caught her breath, the thought of her aged relative triggering a long-forgotten memory. Grandmère's husband had been a government official, and his untimely death almost two decades before was whispered to have been murder.

"Perhaps, *ma chère,*" Calvé's voice broke through her thoughts, "you have guessed by now that this diplomat was none other than your own *grandpère,* Claude Lavoisier."

Panicked denial rose to her lips, then faltered as she mentally examined the fearful possibilities the Frenchman's words raised. *An eye for an eye,* he told her uncle. Calvé must have been the one responsible for her grandfather's murder. *Sainte Cécile,* could he mean to kill her, as well?

While she struggled against the craven impulse to plead for mercy, the coach rolled to a halt. Her heart lurched when she saw that their carriage had come to a stop only a short distance from the sugar sheds. With an effort, she tore her gaze from that cursed structure and swallowed the sobs that welled in her throat.

She concentrated instead on the freighter that loomed over the dock, spilling its ominous shadow across the coach. A quarter moon threaded silver light along the wharf, revealing the crates and boxes stacked alongside the coach. She had just time enough to wonder what they contained before the Frenchman again broke the silence.

"You and the child will wait here."

With that terse command, he stepped out onto the wharf. She watched through the open door while he and the driver moved a short distance from the carriage. Farther down the dock, a handful of stevedores toiled with silent efficiency as they transferred more cargo onto the waiting vessel.

Isabeau strained to hear the men's exchange above the lapping of the river and the creaking of sodden wood. She caught snatches enough of the conversation to guess that the coachman was being dismissed. That could only mean that Calvé intended them to board the freighter at once—and that these next few minutes offered her final chance for escape.

But fleeing the carriage unseen would not prove simple. Whether by design or accident, the coachman had maneuvered their vehicle so that it flanked one row of crates, blocking the far door. The other door hung invitingly ajar, but Calvé could not fail to witness her flight should she attempt to slip past them. Too, she could never hope to outrun him, burdened with the unconscious child cradled in her arms. Only one other choice remained, then.

She fumbled with one hand at the strings of her reticule. Carefully, she seized the pepperbox pistol that had become a familiar source of comfort. She drew it forth and, still gripping it tightly, concealed the pistol beneath the tangle of blankets wrapping Regine.

The feel of cold steel strengthened her resolve. Never mind that having witnessed one brutal murder this night, she doubted she could kill the Frenchman despite her earlier vow. She had managed once before to frighten off three men without pulling the trigger. Surely she could do the same again.

She had settled back against the seat when Calvé appeared in the doorway. "It is time," he said, his tone as chill as the metallic gleam of his eyes. "Now, our journey begins."

She bit her lip and nodded. She allowed him to assist her from the coach, careful to keep her gun-wielding hand hidden within Regine's blanket. Her arms had begun to ache from the unaccustomed weight of the babe, and she prayed that her strength would hold out a few minutes longer.

Barely had she set foot on the dock than the driver whipped up his team. A cold breeze spun its way off the river, billowing her white gown and touching the night air with the water's dank, fishy smell. She could hear an echo of the evening's festivities, while along the muddy riverbank, a lone night bird gave its mournful call. Small things, these, yet they spurred her into action.

She hoisted Regine's limp form so that the baby was propped high on her shoulder, then spun about to face the Frenchman.

"I think, *m'sieur,* that our journey is at an end," she boldly declared as she withdrew the pepperbox pistol and pointed it at Calvé. "Go wherever you will—I shall do nothing to stop you—but the babe and I remain here."

"So, the offspring of Claude Lavoisier's whelp dares

show her claws." The Frenchman surveyed her with a cold smile. "Of all your family, you are the only one with the courage of your convictions. Alas, *ma chère,* such bravery, though admirable, will not serve you this time."

"I swear, I will shoot you if you make a move toward us."

"Look around you," he said, ignoring her threat as he gestured at the cargo stacked on either side of them. "Within these crates lie the seeds of a new dynasty—my dynasty—that shall spring from the bloated corpse of the once-great Ottoman Empire. And you, as my consort, shall share in this destiny."

So he did not plan to kill her, after all.

Her momentary relief was supplanted by horror as she grasped his intentions. She was not his hostage, she realized. Rather, she was to be his concubine—doomed to live out her days with a madman.

"No," she gasped out. "It has ended. Your hold over my family is no more. Now leave us, or I—"

"Do not think to stop me," he interjected. "Understand this, *ma chère*—you and the child *shall* accompany me on this sojourn."

"Never!"

She tightened her hold on Regine and stood pistol at the ready. Even so, she was unprepared when the Frenchman, with a savage snarl, abandoned his urbane pose and started for her.

Reflexively, she pulled the trigger.

Rather than the expected hot burst of gunfire, however, the sole response was that of metal striking metal as the hammer fell with an impotent click. Calvé halted in his tracks, shock and fury momentarily distorting his features. Then, with a feral sneer, he moved toward her again.

Isabeau fired a second time, and third, and with each desperate squeeze of the trigger the barrel futilely spun in its moorings. Before she could attempt the final shot, however, a man's ironic words drifted to her.

"I warned you that might happen, my sweet. You should have rid yourself of that relic when you had the chance."

She recognized the voice at the same moment that Calvé's hand closed over hers in a punishing grip. She let the pistol clatter unheeded onto the dock, glancing about her. She must only have imagined those words, she wildly told herself. *Mon Dieu,* it couldn't be—

"So, you are alive, after all." Calvé's silken tone was rent now by savage anger. "I should have known that Henri could not be trusted with even so simple a task as the murder of one *américain."*

"You know what they say, Franchot. If you want a job done right, you have to do it yourself."

Tark stepped out from behind a nearby stack of crates, revolver in hand and ice blue gaze fixed unwaveringly on the Frenchman. Isabeau swayed as if she had been dealt a blow, so that only Calvé's painful grip on her arm kept her upright. In the next instant, however, joy welled in her heart as a single word reverberated in her mind.

Alive. Alive.

Like a parched flower welcoming an unexpected summer's rain, she greedily drank in the sight of him. She suppressed a fearful cry, however, when she saw his blood-drenched shirt and the makeshift bandage around his chest. Alive, he indeed was, but wounded . . . though how serious his injury might prove, she could not judge.

Her first impulse was to rush to his side, but Calvé's pistol in her ribs forestalled that move. Not daring to breathe, she hugged the babe more tightly to her breast and fixed her frightened gaze on Tark.

"The game is over, *mon ami,*" Calvé called out. "Concede defeat, and I may let you live."

He raised his pistol level with her temple, so that its cold barrel lightly brushed her flesh. Nothing—not even that fleeting panic she had experienced at the Gilded Albatross, when Tark had mistaken her for an intruder—had prepared her for the outright terror that now gripped her. Yet it was not her own life for which she feared. *She,* at least, was of some value to Calvé—but what of Regine and Tark?

"Franchot, *old friend,* I think you've got the situation backwards." Tark's impassive blue gaze swept Isabeau but briefly as he raised his own weapon.

"Look around you." He gestured at the nearby crates and barrels, his contemptuous words echoing the Frenchman's earlier command. "You're the one who's lost the game. In case you haven't guessed yet, this freighter is captained by a friend of mine. All the arrangements I made—booking your passage, having these goods transported here—was just for show. I'm not letting you walk away from this one, Franchot . . . not this time."

Sainte Cécile, what was he doing? Surely he must know that they were dealing with a madman.

The Frenchman's fingers bit into her shoulder. "You

seem to forget, *mon ami,* that the safety of this woman and child rests with me. Attempt to stop me, and I will not hesitate to kill them both."

"Just like you murdered Elisabeth Tremaine?"

The blunt question hung between them as Tark moved closer, his gaze never leaving the Frenchman's. "Tell me something, Franchot, did you strangle Elisabeth because she got too greedy, or did you kill her just for the hell of it?"

Rather than protest, the question drew a careless shrug from Calvé. "You should be grateful that I rid you of that particular . . . hindrance. Had I let her live, the *charmante* Tremaine would merely have hastened your downfall."

"Your concern for my welfare is touching." Tark gave a cold smile and glanced at the crates nearest him. "How about it, Tom? Is that confession enough for you?"

"It shore is."

The speaker squeezed his way through the narrow rows out into the open. Isabeau stared in surprise at the heavy-set *américain* who now stood alongside Tark. He drew one pistol of the oversized pair strapped around his sagging belly, then flashed a gap-toothed grin.

"Let me introduce a friend of mine," Tark addressed the Frenchman with mock formality. "Tom Sullivan is a member of the metropolitan police . . . and when it comes to murder, he's immune to threats and bribes. And as he tells it, he has been itching to get his hands on you for some time."

"Indeed? Then I am afraid M'sieur Sullivan must again be disappointed."

Isabeau heard the cold self-assurance in Calvé's reply and shivered. His madness was almost palpable now as, with a none-too-gentle shove, he steered her closer toward the men. "May I suggest, *messieurs,* that you drop your weapons if you do not wish to see this young woman harmed."

"She's none of my concern."

Tark's clipped reply sliced through her heart—but how could she blame him for hating her, after all that had passed between them? She had lied to him . . . betrayed him . . . *mon Dieu,* she might yet be responsible for his death this night!

Something of her anguish must have shown, for Tark spared his first real look at her. Isabeau read no reassurance in those ice blue eyes, but rather a hint of the same madness that gripped her captor.

"Neither of us will be content with a stalemate." He glanced over at the night patroller and harshly added, "This is a private quarrel, Tom. Throw down your pistol, and let us settle things our own way."

Tom kept his weapon level and stubbornly shook his head. "Now, Tark," he began in a reasonable tone, "them's serious charges we got against the man. I cain't jest—"

"Do it."

The night patroller gave a disgusted snort and tossed aside the revolver, then fumbled with thick fingers at the buckle of his gunbelt. He dangled it in his beefy hand a moment, then reluctantly dropped the leather strap onto the wharf and took several steps to one side, arms spread to show he was unarmed.

"Now it's your turn, Franchot." Tark turned back to

the Frenchman and gestured with his pistol. "Let the woman and child go. They're of no use to you—unless, you're afraid to face me in a fair fight?"

The contempt in his voice was unmistakable, and Isabeau felt Calvé momentarily stiffen behind her. Just as swiftly, she heard unexpected cold amusement in his tone as he replied, "Are you proposing, *mon ami,* that we duel here . . . on the docks? I thought that you had no use for—how did you once term it?—outdated displays of chivalry."

"I'm not talking chivalry." Tark's grim smile didn't reach his eyes as he lowered his own weapon. "This is just you and me—no seconds, and no second chances. One man walks away, the other doesn't."

Isabeau's heart thudded as she awaited her captor's reply. She saw her own fearful anticipation reflected in the night patroller's uneasy expression. So taut were her nerves that she started when the Frenchman at last broke the silence.

"Then let us say ten paces, *mon ami,* shall we?"

Thirty-four

Calvé gracefully lowered his pistol and dropped his restraining hand from Isabeau's shoulder. Like a doe freed from a snare, she swiftly edged away, the sleeping Regine clutched to her breast. She halted when her slippered foot connected with something small and hard-edged lying on the dock.

The pepperbox pistol.

Instinctively, she positioned herself so that her billowing skirts concealed the weapon. She saw that the Frenchman's attention was on his own revolver, the sleek silver barrel gleaming in the moonlight as he spun the cylinder. The casual gesture sent a shiver through her, crowding her mind with images of her brother's own near-fatal duel with the man. *Mon Dieu,* how could she bear to witness another such confrontation?

She swayed and would have stumbled had not the night patroller appeared at her side to steady her. "Here, let me help ya, now," he insisted and reached for the unconscious child. "An' don't worry none. Our boy Tark's a crack shot."

As was Calvé.

She gratefully surrendered the babe. Even with Tom's comforting presence, however, it was all she could do

to watch as the combatants took up position several
yards away.

Lacking a second whose duty it was to signal the
duel's start, they instead stood back-to-back. She heard
Tark's muttered, "let's's get on with it," just before the
pair separated, pistols raised as each silently stepped off
the distance.

One, two, she found herself mentally counting each
pace. *Three, four.* She clasped her hands, snatches of
prayers whirling through her mind as she tried to reassure herself that Tark would defeat the Frenchman.

Five, six. But Tark was wounded, and she had witnessed the ease with which Calvé had bested her
brother, a fine marksman in his own right.

Seven . . . Isabeau caught a disbelieving breath as the
Frenchman, in defiance of the duello, halted and pivoted
in Tark's direction . . . *eight.*

She snatched up the discarded pepperbox, forgetting
that it had misfired three times before, intent only on
stopping the Frenchman as she squeezed the trigger one
last time.

Nine.

The pepperbox spat fire and smoke, the sound echoing Tom's warning shout and stopping Calvé in mid-
stride. Her panicked shot had gone wild; still, the
distraction served its purpose. Alerted by some inner
instinct, Tark already had half-turned to face his opponent. The Frenchman's instant of hesitation gave him
just time enough to fire his revolver at the moment
Calvé's pistol discharged.

The simultaneous shots echoed like an artillery blast
across the dock, the brutal sound reverberating for an

inordinate space of time. A moment later, a haze of white smoke drifted downward on the breeze, carrying with it the acrid smell that meant death. Yet, both men remained standing.

Tark remained unmoving, his revolver at the ready and his gaze fixed on his old foe. Isabeau tried to choke out a warning—*mon Dieu,* it had to be another of Calvé's tricks—but the words remained frozen on her lips. Then, almost imperceptibly, the Frenchman swayed and collapsed onto the sodden wharf.

With a relieved cry, she let the pepperbox tumble to the dock and started toward Tark. Joy turned to dismay, however, when he never glanced her way but instead headed toward his vanquished foe. Swallowing back her disappointment, she joined him there. A moment later, Tom stood alongside them, gunbelt slung over one shoulder and the sleeping Regine awkwardly propped against the other.

Like pagan worshipers awaiting some grim ceremony, they surrounded the fallen Frenchman. Sprawled face up on the dock, the man resembled some errant dark angel struck down by a vengeful god. The shallow rise and fall of his chest indicated he still lived . . . but surely not for much longer, Isabeau numbly thought, taking in the rapidly spreading stain of blood across his white silk shirtfront.

Tark tucked away his own pistol and, wincing from the pain of his earlier wound, knelt on the dock beside Calvé. The Frenchman stirred, and his golden eyes flickered open.

"The game . . . is yours . . . *mon ami,*" he choked out, fumbling with one pale hand at his waistcoat pocket. With a travesty of a smile, he made one last gasping attempt at speech. Isabeau could make out only a single syllable—*pawn*. Then the Frenchman gave a final convulsive shudder and lay still, the glow of his golden eyes snuffed out like a candle flame.

The night patroller was the first to break the silence. Thrusting the blanketed child back into Isabeau's arms, he steered her a discreet distance from Calve's body. "Hell, seems to me like he got off right easy."

"He did, at that," Tark grimly agreed, seizing something from Calvé's slack fingers before stiffly rising to his feet again.

Apparently assured that Isabeau and her young charge were safely out of harm's way, Tom rejoined him, demanding, "What's that he was holdin'?"

"It's a chess piece—a pawn." Tark held the tiny ivory figure to the light. "Franchot always carried one about . . . for luck, as I recall."

Her curiosity aroused, Isabeau took a step closer. Though shaped with but a few crude strokes, the figure had a certain grace to its rough lines. Isabeau frowned, for the piece struck her as oddly familiar.

"Why, it is identical to . . . it must be the missing piece from Philippe's chess set," she exclaimed, drawing both men's attention. "But how—"

She broke off in dismay, recalling her first ill-fated meeting with Calvé in their study. She had noticed a single pawn missing from the chessboard, but had attributed its loss to Lucie's careless housekeeping. The Frenchman must have confiscated the tiny figure as some fiendish token of the power he wielded over her family.

"Take it, then. I'd say you've earned it back," came Tark's dispassionate reply as he pressed the chessman into her trembling hand.

Isabeau spared another look at the ivory pawn, then glanced at the grim-visaged man before her. The fact he had broken his self-imposed silence brought scant comfort. She saw no warmth in those ice blue eyes, and nothing in his tone hinted at forgiveness or understanding.

Mon Dieu, even anger would be preferable to such icy indifference. Before she could coax some warmer response, however, the rough mutter of unfamiliar voices drifted to her. Behind her, a dozen or more lank figures were edging like river rats from the shadows. The freighter's crew, she swiftly determined, no doubt drawn by the sound of gunfire.

Tom eyed the curiosity-seekers with a professional eye. "Ya'd best take the lady an' tyke outa here, an' let me handle things from here on. There's a coach waitin' over there"—he jerked a thumb toward the nearby warehouses—"so you can be gone before the real excitement starts. An' don't worry none, I'll see to it that all charges against ya in the Tremaine woman's murder are dropped."

"I'm much obliged, Tom. If there's ever anything I can do . . ."

Tark's taut features momentarily relaxed as he offered his hand to the older man. The night patroller flashed a gap-toothed grin. "Jest remember that the next time I'm holdin' a winnin' poker hand an' ain't got a cent left to wager."

Then he turned to Isabeau. "Ya handled yerself right fine, miss," he went on, the blunt compliment bringing a flush of pleasure to her cheeks. "Our boy Tark owes ya his life."

With a final nod, Tom advanced on the onlookers. Tark waited until the night patroller was out of earshot before he abruptly said, "We're not far from my warehouse, so I'll leave you there for the time being. Alma will look after the two of you until I get back."

"Leave us?" Her earlier numbness thawed into indignation. "Why, you are wounded, and Oncle Henri—"

"—is at Ophelia's brothel, which is where I'm headed. In case you've forgotten, he and I have a score left to settle."

He caught her free arm, steering her and the babe toward the waiting coach. Though chafing at this cavalier treatment, Isabeau held her peace. Her first priority was to see Regine left safely in Alma's care. That accomplished, she would insist on accompanying Tark. She, too, had scores to settle.

They made the short ride to Tark's warehouse in silence, save for his quick appraising look at Regine, followed by a curt, "So there *was* a baby, after all. I would have bet a year's commission that was just another ploy of Franchot's."

A few minutes later, Tark gave his housekeeper a terse account of the night's events, while Isabeau spared a moment's admiration for Alma's reaction. A lesser woman would have indulged in histrionics at the sight of her employer returning home liberally splattered in his own blood. Alma, however, forbore any such displays. To her surprise, neither did the older woman attempt to dissuade him from leaving again.

"Don't worry yourself, Mr. Parrish, I'll see they come

to no harm in the meantime," the housekeeper instead assured him.

Tark gave her the barest of smiles. "I knew I could depend on you."

Isabeau heard the slight emphasis on that last pronoun and frowned. *Mon Dieu,* was he implying that *she* was not trustworthy? The notion was an unsettling one. She might not be able to win back his love, she thought, but she could at least wrest from him a measure of respect.

Her resolution was put to the test when Tark headed for the open door, where the hired coach waited. Reluctant though she was to leave behind the precious burden of her new-found charge, she brushed a fond kiss against Regine's plump cheek. Then, with a few quick words to Alma, she hurried in the same direction.

Tark had almost reached the carriage door by the time she caught up with him. She planted herself between him and the vehicle. "Wait, I'm going with you."

The hell you are.

The unspoken response was reflexive, as was the surge of anger that swept Tark. He should have known she wouldn't be shunted aside so easily, he sourly told himself. Still, the last thing he was going to need tonight when dealing with Henri Lavoisier would be her presence. Distasteful as he found the idea of shooting down the man in cold blood, he would find that task made doubly difficult with her as witness.

So make damn certain she's not there.

His resolve wavered when the chit remained stubbornly blocking his way. Had he simply pushed past her, as was his first impulse, he could easily have abandoned her without a backward glance. His mistake lay in sparing her more than a dispassionate glance.

Earlier tonight, she had played the fashionable Creole miss. The past few hours had taken their toll on her shimmering elegance, however. With her dress crumpled and her raven hair tumbled in artless disarray, she resembled a Girod Street waif masquerading as a grand lady.

With this observation came his realization that she had displayed an admirable presence of mind this night—and was prepared to face more unpleasantness. Though strain was evident in her face, she appeared remarkably composed for a woman who had been kidnapped and then forced to witness her captor's brutal death. Odder still was the fact that she seemed totally unconcerned about her disheveled appearance.

Her behavior ill-suited a scheming female bent on furthering her own aims . . . not that he was prepared as yet to forgive and forget. Still, he somehow found himself agreeing to her request with an abrupt, "Get in, then."

She clambered into the coach in a billow of white satin. With a final word to the driver, Tark settled across from her and attempted to justify this lapse in judgment to himself. No doubt the blow to his head had addled his wits. Still, he was free now to press Isabeau for answers to such questions as, what in the hell did she see in this St. John fellow, anyhow?

The query went unasked, however, as he slumped back and shut his eyes. Not that he intended to sleep, he reassured himself, not with a battered head and a gash that burned like a white-hot iron against his flesh.

Nevertheless, the vehicle's rhythmic motion proved so effective a soporific that he dozed off.

He awakened with a start when the coach halted just off Basin Street. Bleary-eyed, he scrubbed a hand over his face and glanced at Isabeau. Her pale face was etched with worry—or was it only pity?—and he promptly straightened and shot her a baleful look. Under other circumstances, he might have appreciated her feminine concern for his well-being. In his current state, however, he resented it like hell.

"Let's get on with it," he clipped out and wrenched the door handle.

Tark climbed from the hack and started toward the brightly lit brothels that lined Rue de Fleur. The boisterous Mardi gras celebration had continued unabated, the only difference being that most of its participants were decidedly drunker now.

Tark allowed himself a smile as he strode past the wrought-iron gate leading to Ophelia's establishment. The music and laughter that poured from its open doors rivaled the commotion on the street. Given the tide of people surging in and out of the place, he could gain entry unnoticed. All that remained then was to track down Henri Lavoisier.

He was halfway up the flagstone walk before Isabeau plucked at his sleeve and demanded in a breathless tone, "Please, you must tell me what you plan to do."

Tark met her gaze with a level look. "I thought I'd made myself quite clear. I plan to walk in there, find your uncle and kill him."

"Kill him?" she echoed in whispered disbelief. *"Mon Dieu,* you cannot . . ."

She glanced helplessly about her, as if debating whether or not to risk trying to stop him. It was apparent she dreaded witnessing a rematch of their earlier confrontation, a reaction that should have brought him some measure of satisfaction. Why, then, did he feel a vague sense of guilt at forcing her to this pass?

Even as he struggled for an answer, it dawned on him that his urgent need for revenge had waned. He had faced down death not once, but twice in the past couple of hours, and he'd be a fool to go on pressing the odds. More to the point, he would gain nothing gunning down the man. Still, he'd be damned if he would let Henri Lavoisier think he could go around shooting unwary Americans with impunity.

"I'll make a deal with you, my sweet," he proposed. "Convince your uncle to make a clean breast of things to the authorities, and I'll be content to let them handle matters."

"But what if he will not?"

"Then we'll just have to do it my way . . . so I suggest you be persuasive."

Tark started again toward the brothel's ornate door, Isabeau close on his heels. The familiar dour contingent of doormen guarded the entry but even they were not immune to the pervading festive mood, waving in patrons after only cursory scrutiny. Grasping Isabeau's arm, he boldly insinuated them into the ragged line snaking its way inside.

A moment later, they crowded into the marble-tiled foyer with a score or more other newcomers. Tonight, flaming braziers took the place of gaslamps and added a bacchanalian note to the brothel's raucous atmosphere.

Tark used the confusion to his advantage, taking stock of the situation.

Ophelia had anticipated the glut of customers Mardi gras was providing her, for additional maids and footmen appropriately robed in a Romanesque manner had been added to the brothel staff. Security, however, appeared no tighter than usual.

"Let's check the upstairs sitting room first," he suggested and started in that direction. "It's private, with one of the few doors that locks. If our . . . mutual friend . . . has any sense, that's where he'll be holding your uncle."

Mutual friend. Isabeau puzzled over the words as she accompanied Tark up the main stairs. Who could he mean? The ironic note in his voice warned her this was one mystery she might do better not to solve.

They reached the upper level without incident, save that several guests spared a second look at Tark's bloodied costume. Taking her cue from him, she feigned ignorance of this unwelcome scrutiny, though her heart drummed uncomfortably. *Mon Dieu,* what if some guest, less drunk than his fellows, summoned the doormen—or worse, Ophelia?

Those fears were forgotten, however, as she followed Tark down the dimly lit hall. Strains of the orchestra below were no match for the sounds of drunken coupling that issued from behind the familiar red doors. Those lusty moans prompted memories of that fateful night when she first had learned of those pleasures.

Glancing over at Tark, she was grateful for the shadows that concealed her mortified blush. He gave no sign of remembering their first time together but strode grimly down the corridor. No doubt he considered their lovemaking to be little different from the anonymous rutting of Ophelia's customers—and could she, in truth, blame him for his change of heart?

She was spared her conscience's reply when Tark halted before a pair of double doors at the hall's far end. He signaled her to remain silent, then drew his borrowed pistol and reached for one curved brass handle.

The door readily swung open at his touch, revealing an ornate parlor resplendent in Ophelia's trademark colors of red and gold. A pair of curtained French doors facing the street beyond hung ajar, allowing music and laughter to pour in with the cool night breeze.

In grotesque counterpoint to this festivity, the room was adrift with crimson feathers while her uncle and the familiar if unknown masker in the rooster costume, engaged in a silent wrestling match atop the polished parquet floor. Their struggle ended with a crash against a gilted serving cart, the resulting impact all but overturning the water-filled decanter atop it.

"Oncle Henri," she choked out just before he was subdued by his feathered opponent. Intent on rescue, she started toward the pair but was promptly pulled up short by Tark.

"Not so fast, my sweet," he drawled, plucking a stray red feather from her hair. "Let's allow the gentlemen to work out things for themselves."

By now, her uncle's opponent had planted a plumaged knee in Henri's back, effectively pinning him. He whipped a handful of linen napkins from the cart, using one to bind Henri's wrists and another to gag him. That accomplished, the feathered victor scrambled to his feet and gallantly lifted his captive onto the red brocade sofa beside them.

Isabeau dragged her astonished gaze from her relative to the young man who stood panting over him. Swathed as he was in the tattered remains of his costume, it took a moment for her to recognize him. When she finally did, she found herself perilously close to laughter as the evening's last bit of irony fell into place.

The comically menacing masker who had trailed her, this so-called mutual friend of whom Tark had spoken . . . was indeed none other than—

"Marcel!"

Thirty-five

"H-hello, Isabeau."

Marcel St. John smiled and wiped a feathered forearm across his perspiring brow. Then, as if suddenly remembering something, he dove behind the divan, reappearing an instant later with a pistol.

"I-I am glad to see that M-m'sieur Parrish found you well," he went on, pausing for a polite if guarded nod in Tark's direction. "When your *oncle* told me you had left here with M'sieur Calvé, I thought . . ."

"How dare you follow me about the city all day?" Isabeau cut short his explanation. *"Non,* do not try to deny it. I saw you at the Rex parade this afternoon, and then again tonight, outside the Varieties. *Mon Dieu,* whatever possessed you to do such a thing?"

Barely had the accusation spilled from her lips than she regretted her harsh tone, for Marcel was arguably the most innocent of the evening's players. A twinge of guilt assailed her at that realization; still, she awaited his reply.

"I-it isn't what you th-think . . . that is, not really."

Marcel smoothed his threadbare chest plumage in a quick nervous gesture. "Y-you see, Philippe told me what was to happen tonight—that the grand duke was to be abducted, and you were being forced to take part in the scheme. Since he could not watch after you himself, he asked me to do so."

He gestured helplessly toward her uncle. "I-I must apologize to M'sieur Lavoisier but he tried to wrestle away my pistol. Still, M'sieur Parrish did warn me your *oncle* was a d-dangerous . . . a d-dangerous . . ."

He broke off with a hearty sneeze that set awaft another flurry of crimson feathers. That cloud prompted, in turn, a full-fledged sneezing fit that rendered the young gentleman speechless for a few seconds. Isabeau used the brief interlude to study her uncle.

Above the gag of snowy linen, Henri's eyes glinted with the same heated madness she had glimpsed earlier that night, so that she was grateful for the restraining cloth strips about his wrists. What frightened her more, however, was the way his inner madness somehow had skewered his outer form, distorting it into a cruel caricature of her relative.

She fought back a shiver and turned to Marcel, who had gained control of himself. "Do not worry, *mon ami*," she reassured him at his mournful look. "You treated my *oncle* with more consideration than he deserves. I dare say that neither Philippe nor M'sieur Parrish could have done better."

He brightened, and Isabeau forced herself to return his smile. Marcel, too, had faced his share of danger this night—and all for her sake. Surely she could overlook the fact that his presence had put her in an awkward situation.

A blush rose on her cheeks as she spared a glance at Tark. He had shut the door behind him but not yet deigned to join them, his pistol casually clutched in one tanned hand. Judging from his chill smile, he was aware of who Marcel was—which fact went far in explaining his current behavior toward her.

Isabeau lifted her chin and struggled to gather the tattered remains of her dignity. She had not dreamed that these rivals for her affection would cross paths, let alone forge this unlikely partnership. She could only pray that Marcel remained unaware of just how intimately acquainted she was with the *américain*.

"So, Marcel," she brightly began again, "how is it that you and M'sieur Parrish came to know one another?"

"We met on the wharf," Tark answered for him, not moving from the casual pose he had assumed against the door. "He'd been a step behind us starting at the Varieties Theatre. He tracked us to the sugar sheds just in time to see you and your uncle fleeing the scene— and just in time to witness my inconvenient return from the dead. Since he'd overheard your destination, I suggested—"

"You!"

Henri's anguished cry ripped through the narrow room as he worked free of his makeshift restraints and flung them aside. He paid no heed to either her or Marcel, but advanced with determination on Tark.

"I killed you," he choked out, his features darkened with despair. "I made sure you died the honorless death that you so richly deserved, yet you stand here before me alive . . . mocking me."

"Sorry to disappoint you, Henri," Tark drawled, raising his pistol so that its barrel was pointed squarely at the older man's chest. "Unless you care to learn whether or not I'm a better shot than you, I suggest you stop right there."

"Do as he tells you, Oncle."

Isabeau rushed forward and laid a restraining hand on her uncle's sleeve. With a snarl, he shook free; still, her demand had the desired effect, for he stopped short like a dog brought to heel.

"Please, do not make things any worse," she insisted, any sympathy for his plight tempered by her memory of how he had abandoned her to the Frenchman's mercies. "You must go to the police and confess everything. That is the only choice remaining for you, now that Monsieur Calvé is dead."

"*Oui*, Oncle," she added when Henri made a strangled sound of protest. "M'sieur Parrish was forced to kill him in a duel on the docks."

"Dead?" he softly repeated, the unhealthy color fading from his face. "Franchot Calvé is . . . dead? Can it be that I am free, at last?"

He blinked like a sleepwalker come awake. Watching him, Isabeau glimpsed the affable relative from her childhood, and she allowed herself a guarded moment of hope. Perhaps this had been simply a temporary bout of madness. If he indeed had come to his senses the nightmare of the past weeks might at last be over. Though nothing between them could ever be the same, they might yet put the past behind them and start anew.

Then he laughed, a high, thin sound more frightening than his earlier ravings, and Isabeau realized that the madness had won out. There would be only the pain of knowing that her uncle was lost to her . . . as much so as if death had claimed him, along with the Frenchman.

Suddenly, she wanted nothing more than to fling herself into Tark's arms. Safe in his embrace, she could face the madness that assailed them. But now even that haven was lost to her.

Oblivious to her distress, Henri stumbled toward the divan and sagged onto its rich brocaded cushions. "So, you wish me to confess and beg for absolution. Tell me, of what crimes am I guilty?"

"Try kidnapping, conspiracy, and attempted murder," Tark clipped out. "I'm sure the list is longer, but that'll do for a start."

"Kidnaping? Conspiracy?" Henri bared his teeth in a mock smile. "The only other witness to these so-called crimes is the grand duke, himself, and I doubt that so proud a man as he would care to confirm such a tale. And even if he did, need I remind you that you also were involved in that affair? I simply would tell the authorities that I was an innocent man forced by you at gunpoint to become a criminal. It will be my word against yours?"

"Like I told Franchot once before, I'm willing to take that risk."

Tark glanced over at Isabeau, the expression in his ice blue eyes oddly neutral as he tucked away his pistol. She drew a deep breath and held his gaze, gripped by sudden surprise. He was leaving the matter of her uncle's fate up to her. Moreover, he would abide by whatever decision she made.

"I will take the same risk," she declared, praying that

she had made the right choice. "I will testify that you tried to murder Tark."

Henri gravely shook his head. "Alas, *ma petite,* I only did what any man of honor would do. After all, this barbaric *américain* had compromised you—which is what I shall tell the authorities."

His threat, delivered though it was in a gentle tone, made her blanch. *Mon Dieu,* her already tarnished reputation could never withstand such a scandal.

As for Marcel, if her disgrace became public knowledge, he would find himself the butt of ridicule, while Philippe's budding romance with Cammi would likely be cut short in the aftermath of that scandal. How could she justify ruining their lives just to prove her uncle guilty of what some might claim was no crime at all?

Henri smiled and rose to his feet. "So, my accusers do not care to face me. If that is the case, then I will be on my way."

"Do not think you will escape judgment, Henri Lavoisier," came a woman's harsh voice from the direction of the French doors. "You and the others have much yet to answer for."

Ophelia.

Isabeau recognized the familiar husky tone even before she saw the speaker. The quadroon moved with wraithlike grace along the gallery, and she was not alone. From her vantage point, Isabeau could glimpse a second, smaller figure hovering in the shadows behind Ophelia . . . though whether that person was male or female, she could not judge.

The quadroon halted at the threshold and turned toward Tark, her green eyes momentarily dulled by grief. "My footmen told me you were here," she said in an emotionless tone. "I came to warn Henri—I knew the fool was no match for you—but you found him first. I overheard your conversation."

She stepped forward into the light, and Isabeau caught back a gasp. Tonight, Ophelia again resembled some barbaric Eastern princess, dressed in the same simple white sheath she had worn the night of the voodoo ceremony. The chandelier's yellow glow lent a subtle gleam to her amber skin, even as it reflected with a metallic glint off the slim dagger she held at her side.

Sainte Cécile, only a madwoman would dare challenge two pistol-wielding men with no weapon save a blade! Then it occurred to her that the quadroon's unseen companion might be more formidably armed. Before she could form a warning, however, Ophelia lifted her other hand in a commanding gesture to the dark figure behind her. "See what fate awaits those who dare cross me!"

"L-Lili? I-Is that y-you?"

"Cousine? Mon Dieu, how can this be?"

Marcel's incredulous gasp echoed Isabeau's disbelieving cry as a delicate young blonde haltingly joined the voodoo queen. Dressed in a frothy blue gown and with her golden curls floating about her shoulders, the fragile beauty did bear an uncanny resemblance to Isabeau's dead cousin. The only difference she could discern was the curious emptiness of the girl's wide blue gaze.

But how could this possibly be Lili, when numerous people had watched as the girl was put to her final rest?

And, more importantly, if she actually *was* Lili, why did she give no sign of recognizing her own family?

Drawing a shaky breath, Isabeau turned to the men. Henri's face reflected the same denial that she knew must be stamped upon her own countenance, while Marcel appeared in danger of fainting.

The only one seemingly unaffected was Tark, who eyed the girl with chill unconcern. "Does someone mind telling me just what the hell is going on here?"

"Can you not see, M'sieur Parrish, that they are all in shock?" Ophelia silkenly replied. "How would you feel if someone who had long since left this life appeared before you again, no longer one of the dead . . . but not quite one of the living?"

"Not quite one of the living," Tark softly repeated. The words recalled to him Elisabeth's long-ago claim that she herself had witnessed the dead brought back to life. He abandoned his post and moved purposefully toward the quadroon. "You're saying this girl is some kind of zombie that you've brought back from the grave with a voodoo spell?"

"I see you have more than a passing knowledge of our dark religion." Ophelia gave him a mock nod of approval and stroked the blonde's pale tresses, her hand lingering on the girl's bare shoulder. "You are quite correct, M'sieur Parrish. With the help of my spirits, I did bring her back to life."

"Mon Dieu, then she really *is* Lili," Isabeau gasped, feeling perilously close to swooning herself. As a child, she often had overhead the servants' tales of such soulless creatures, but never had she doubted that those

beings were the product of anything other than superstition . . . until now.

"Sweet Jesus, you don't believe this nonsense, do you?" Tark clipped out. "If that girl really is your dead cousin, then there's a logical explanation for what happened." Rounding on the quadroon, he went on, "I don't know what your game is, lady, but I damn sure don't intend to wait around and find out."

"You will wait . . . and you shall listen to me!"

Light sparked from the narrow blade as Ophelia swiftly raised her weapon to Lili's white throat. "Franchot would have come back. My spirits had promised me . . . but instead, you killed him and now you must be punished."

She flashed a hate-filled look in Isabeau's direction. "I was forced to give up the child whose blood would have appeased the spirits. But any blood will do . . . and what more fitting victim than one who has already visited their realm?"

"Don't hurt her," Isabeau pleaded. Marcel now stood at her other side, joining Tark so that they formed a barricade between Ophelia and the door. Henri had roused himself enough to pour a cognac, offering neither help nor hindrance now. "It is over," she went on in a stronger voice. "Why should anyone else be made to suffer?"

"Put so much as a scratch on the girl," Tark bluntly interjected, "and you won't get out of here alive."

"Fool! I have no fear of you," she spat and raised the gleaming blade.

"No!" With that anguished cry, Marcel charged the quadroon, steel flashing as he thrust himself between the weapon and Lili. In the next instant, he slumped to the floor, the knife buried to its hilt in his chest.

With a shouted, "See to him!" flung over his shoulder in Isabeau's direction, Tark raced past the fallen youth and seized Ophelia just before she reached the open French doors.

Isabeau heard the woman's shrieks as Tark struggled to subdue her . . . noted, too, that Lili remained staring vacantly ahead, like some great wax doll abandoned for some newer toy. Then, slowly, she focused on the still form sprawled at Lili's feet, the knife hilt incongruously poking up from the tattered mass of red feathers.

"Oh, Marcel," she whispered and knelt before him, one hand brushing his cheek.

The youth's eyes flickered, then opened. "Wh-what happened?" he demanded. Then, glimpsing the knife still quivering in his chest, he scrambled up and tugged the weapon free, dramatically brandishing it before him.

Isabeau stared in amazement from the unbloodied blade to the hale specimen before her. "Your costume . . . it saved you," she exclaimed, for his suit's feathered outer layer was slashed away to reveal the wire framework beneath. "But if you were not hurt—"

"I-I must have f-fainted." A blush darkened his pale cheeks before he spun about and grasped Lili's hand. "S-She's not hurt, is she?"

"Everyone's fine," Tark replied, clutching the quadroon so that her arms were pinned to her sides. He deposited her on the red velvet settee beside Henri, then pulled his pistol from his sash. "I'll wait here with these two, while the rest of you get the hell out of here. Mar-

:el, send word to Tom Sullivan that I've got the last of
his suspects rounded up."

"Of course." Marcel straightened his feathered shoulders and, gripping Lili's hand, gestured Isabeau to pre-
cede him. "How else might I be of service, *m'sieur?*"

"You've already done your part," Tark replied with
an approving nod. "And I suggest you take the back
way out," he added as Marcel pulled open the hall door.
"There's no telling . . . what in the hell?"

A muted chorus of shouts and screams now emanated
from the floor below, the commotion sharply different
from the earlier tipsy merriment that had filled the
brothel. The orchestra ceased playing just as Marcel offered in a hesitant voice, "I-I hate to alarm anyone, but
I think I smell s-smoke."

As if to confirm his contention, a cloud of grey haze
drifted from the shadowed hallway. The accompanying
odor of burning wood was faint but unmistakable.

"Sweet Jesus, someone must have turned over one of
those damned braziers," Tark exclaimed and strode to
the door, taking a quick look before slamming it shut
again.

Marcel thrust Lili in Isabeau's direction and hurried to
the open French doors, leaning out at a precarious angle
over the railing. "I-I don't see any sign of f-flames below
us."

"If we're lucky, the fire's confined to the ballroom,"
Tark replied as Marcel rejoined him. "All I saw in the
hallway was smoke, so the main staircase is probably
still passable—"

"Stop her! Ophelia is escaping!" Taking advantage of
the men's preoccupation, the quadroon had begun edg-

ing toward the gallery. At Isabeau's cry, however, the
woman abandoned any attempt at stealth and fled in a
swirl of white linen past the open glass doors.

"Forget her," Tark clipped out when Isabeau started
after the dark-skinned woman. "She's just trying to save
herself . . . which is the same damn thing the rest of
you should be doing."

Pausing to grab the linen napkins that lately had been
used to restrain Henri, Tark swiftly dampened them with
water from the crystal decanter, then shoved them at
Marcel.

"Have the women breathe through these. Now, take
them and try the front way. If that's blocked, you can
use the back stairwell at the far end of the hall."

Marcel promptly grasped Lili's limp hand and steered
her toward the door. Isabeau started after them, then
realized that Tark was not behind her. She promptly
halted and spun about to face him. "But surely you
cannot mean to stay behind."

"There's got to be a couple of dozen more people
besides us on this floor," he told her, ice blue eyes alight
with grim purpose. "Probably half of them are in no
shape to walk out of here alone. Don't worry," he added
at her sound of protest, "I'll meet you on the street."

His tone did nothing to dispel her sudden trepidation,
aware as she was that the commotion downstairs was
growing. "But why—"

"Damn it, I don't have time to argue with you. In a
few more minutes, the entire building is liable to go up
in flames."

He dragged her into the hallway and shoved her in
Marcel's direction. "I'm counting on you to get them

out safely," he told that young gentleman. "Now, move it . . . and keep low. The smoke won't be as bad closer to the floor."

Isabeau opened her mouth to protest and promptly choked on a lungful of acrid smoke. By the time she caught her breath, Tark already had disappeared down the hazy corridor, while Marcel and Lili were halfway to the staircase. She hesitated, then glanced behind her once more. Where was—

"Oncle Henri!" she called. Her cry was drowned out by the commotion as the hallway's red doors began to bang open. The occupants spilled forth in various stages of undress and intoxication, all but trampling her in search of the staircase. A few frantic moments later, the flow of panicked humanity abated, and she found herself alone in the corridor.

She clung to the wall and tried to gain her bearings. Dark smoke roiled from the direction that Tark had taken, while the sharp, sweet smell of burning wood permeated the air. Heat had built in the corridor's narrow confines, so that perspiration dampened the bodice of her satin gown. She should flee, she told herself—but how could she leave Tark and her uncle behind?

She fought back panic and started back down the hall. How many doors down from the stairway had the parlor been? Five? Six? By now, smoke filled the corridor in earnest, so that its usual twilight glow was snuffed out. Worse, the acrid fumes that seared her lungs also were making her light-headed.

Belatedly, she recalled Tark's advice and dropped to her knees, her satin skirts pooling around her. The air at that level was markedly fresher, and she gulped in greedy mouthfuls. Then she glimpsed at either end of the hall a bright orange glow that could mean only one thing.

The fire now had spread to the upper floor, blocking off the stairways that were her sole means of escape.

Thirty-six

Taking a deep breath, Isabeau staggered to her feet. The fire was spreading rapidly, so that all she could do now was pray that Tark and Henri had already found their own way out. She turned back in the direction she had come—and collided with a dark shape that materialized without warning from the smoke.

"Sweet Jesus . . . Isabeau?"

Tark's disbelieving voice, rough with smoke and emotion, rang above the growing roar of the fire. "What in the hell are you still doing up here? You were supposed to be with Marcel."

He did not wait for her reply but shoved her, half-stumbling, through the nearest of the red doors and into the very parlor they had left just minutes before. By the time she caught her breath, Tark had slammed the door behind them and whipped off the damp cloth tied over his mouth.

Given the fact she had disregarded his orders, she expected harsh words of censure. Instead, with a groan that was equal parts anger and relief, he pulled her into his embrace.

"I don't know whether to kiss you or turn you over my knee," he rasped out, his arms tightening about her.

"Sweet Jesus, if you hadn't been wearing that white dress, I never would have seen you through the smoke."

"But I could not leave you here," she managed, the words raking her smoke-ravaged throat. "Do you not see, I love—"

"Might I suggest," interrupted Henri's caustic voice behind them, "that you postpone this touching reunion until we are all safely gone from here."

Her uncle clutched his brandy snifter and lounged against the red brocade divan—this despite the haze of smoke that was rapidly filling the room. With a delicate cough, he added, "The gallery would seem to be your best means of escape."

"Then what the hell are we waiting for?" Tark grasped Isabeau's arm and dragged her onto the narrow walkway. Henri joined them, unconcerned, as if they merely had stepped out to enjoy the view.

By now, the fire's roar behind them sounded like that of some angered beast, while acrid smoke poured from beneath the hall door in earnest. Clutching the rail grown warm with the fire's heat, Isabeau sucked in greedy gasps of fresh air and anxiously scanned the crowd gathered a safe distance away on the avenue below.

Amid the rescued brothel patrons and curiosity-seekers, she glimpsed Marcel's crimson-feathered form. He frantically waved, then indicated Lili standing beside him with doll-like placidity. Stemming with an effort the panic that gripped her, she turned to Tark and anxiously asked, "What do we do now?"

"I'll have to find some way to lower you and Henri

to the ground and then climb down myself. One thing is certain, we damn sure can't jump."

Grimly, he pointed. Isabeau followed the gesture to the narrow strip of lawn below, where the brothel's elaborate wrought-iron fence ran almost directly beneath the gallery. Closely spaced rails thrust skyward, their spear-like points gleaming in the fire's orange light. Anyone who plummeted from this particular spot would almost certainly land upon those cruel points.

"The draperies," she promptly suggested, indicating the yards of now-sooty lace that trailed down either French door and puddled with ostentatious abandon along the marble floor.

Tark gave her a quick nod of approval and caught hold of the nearest curtain, yanking it from its moorings, then tore the second curtain loose. A moment later, he had tied both sections together to form a serviceable if bulky rope.

"You first, my sweet," he said with a half-smile and hastily looped one end about her waist. In the same fashion, he tied the remaining free end about him, so they were joined by a lacy umbilicus. Then, before she had time to mull over the risks, he lifted her over the railing.

"Catch hold of the top edge," he urged, steadying her while she kicked aside her trailing skirts to gain a foothold. "All you need to do is ease down until you're holding onto the bottom rail. Once you've done that, let go and I'll lower you the rest of the way. Can you do that?"

"Oui," she murmured and met Tark's ice blue gaze, dark now with grim purpose. Jumbled phrases of love

and encouragement vied with each other as she searched
for some suitable parting words. What finally sprang to
her lips, however, was the undignified squeak of a plea.

"*Saint Cécile,* Tark, do not drop me!"

"Don't worry, my sweet," he replied with a grin. "I
have every intention of seeing you safely down. Just try
to keep perfectly still once I start lowering you."

She managed a fleeting smile in return, then began
the perilous task of half-climbing, half-slipping down
the railing until she clung by her fingertips to the gallery's lower edge. She hung there a few seconds longer,
choking against the hot smoke that blasted up at her
from below. So far, the fire had not reached the street-
front windows; still, she could not suppress the image
of greedy flames licking at her while she helplessly dangled high above the ground. Shoving aside that thought,
she let go and grasped the makeshift rope.

Vaguely, she was aware of the crowd's encouraging
clamor as she began her descent. The lacy loop that
supported her cut into the flesh just below her ribs,
making each acrid breath she drew even more difficult.
She blinked against smoke-induced tears to gaze up at
Tark, who gave no sign that his wound pained him as
he slowly fed out the line. Despite his care, however,
every jerk of the rope sent her swaying.

The fire's roar was punctuated now by the crackle of
burning timbers and the high-pitched shatter of glass as
windows began to give way beneath the onslaught of
heat. Unnerved, she ventured a look down. No more
than a dozen feet separated her from the ground now,
so that her slippers brushed the looming row of dag-

ger-sharp fence rails. All she need do was keep perfectly still.

A rush of smoky heat sent her skirts billowing, and she realized she was in danger of becoming entangled upon the fence's uppermost rails. Quickly, she weighed her options. If she tried to swing free of that danger, the added strain might cause the makeshift rope to give way so that she would wind up impaled upon those pikes! But even if her gown simply caught upon that ornamental iron, she could never free herself in time for Tark and Oncle Henri to manage their own escapes.

"I-I've got you," called a familiar voice below her just as a pair of hands clamped around her ankles to steady her. She glanced down to see Marcel poised upon a short ladder, that piece of rescue equipment no doubt unearthed from some nearby garden shed.

Batting aside layers of satin and tulle, Marcel eased her over the fence and guided her downward. A moment later, her slippers touched solid ground, and she sagged against that young gentleman's feathered chest in relief.

"Merci, Marcel," she croaked out as she unknotted the loop tied around her waist. She let the line slip from her fingers for Tark to reel back in, then glanced up at the gallery.

The sight that greeted her made her cry out in horror. Thick smoke all but obliterated the silhouetted figures of Tark and her uncle, while the house was lit with a hellish red glow. In the next instant, a blast of searing heat drove her and Marcel to join the other onlookers a prudent distance from the flames.

She clutched at Marcel's arm and frantically scanned the upper gallery. The local fire brigade had arrived, but even their modern steam pumpers would prove no match for this inferno. Within minutes, the entire brothel must certainly be consumed—meaning that, at best, only one of the pair had time now to make good his escape.

"He's coming down," rose the cry around her as a shadowy form clambered over the rail. Which man it was, she could not distinguish for the roiling smoke. She *could* tell, however, that his descent was proving even more harrowing that hers.

The drapery rope still stretched from the gallery to the ground, whipping about like some impatient serpent in the night air. The unknown climber caught hold of it and began making his way hand-by-hand down the narrow lace column, much in the same way sailors descended their rigging. The technique had the advantage of speed, but compared with simply letting oneself be lowered to the ground, it also required a greater measure of skill—skill that was being put to the test by the combined forces of smoke and heat.

A gasp tore from the crowd as the climber swung over the wrought-iron fence. He cleared that obstacle with seeming ease . . . and then the makeshift rope gave way with an audible snap.

The man twisted in midfall so that he just skimmed the waiting row of pikes. An instant later, he landed in a motionless heap upon the narrow strip of lawn that edged the fence.

Sainte Cécile, let him be alive, she fervently prayed as she raced toward the prone figure. Heat from the fire scorched her, and glowing embers pelted her as she fell to her knees beside him. With strength born of fear, she rolled him onto his back and searched his soot-streaked face for some sign of life. His eyes flickered, then opened.

"Just got . . . the wind knocked . . . out of me."

With that wheezing explanation, Tark dragged himself into a sitting position just as Marcel joined them. "H-hurry," he exclaimed with a frantic gesture at the flame-engulfed brothel. "I-It's about to g-go."

As if to prove his words, a section of roof caved in, and an anguished groan of timbers rose amid the fire's roar. "But what about Oncle Henri!" she cried, even as Tark shook his head.

"It's too late now, even if he had changed his mind about staying behind. Now let's get the hell out of here!"

With Tark leaning heavily upon her and Marcel, the three started at a dead run toward the waiting crowd. Barely had they reached it when, with a reverberation that held a note of almost-human agony, the flaming brothel slowly collapsed upon itself.

"Oncle Henri," Isabeau repeated in a pained whisper as she watched the brilliant glow of what had become her relative's funeral pyre. If only he had not stayed behind—

"He wanted it to end like this, my sweet," came Tark's voice, taut with sympathy and exhaustion. "I tried to get him out of there, but he refused to listen to reason. I think he felt that by dying, he could atone for his crimes. He found a way to redeem what proved, in the end, to be most important to him . . . his honor."

"Honor." Her voice caught on the word. "And what about the rest of us . . . you, me, Philippe? Now that this night is over, what are we left with?"

Tark's ice blue gaze warmed to the brilliant shade of a summer sky as he drew her into his embrace. "That, my sweet, is something I think we should discuss," he murmured as, ignoring the spontaneous cheers of the Carnival crowd around them, he lowered his lips to hers.

The doleful chiming of Angelus bells heralded the dawn of Ash Wednesday and pierced Isabeau's slumber. She stretched her cramped muscles and blinked against the pale morning sun . . . and then came fully awake with a start.

She was wrapped in an unfamiliar cloak and perched upon a large marble carriage block that spanned the narrow ditch between *banquette* and street. A chill breeze sent stray bits of green, purple, and gold streamers dancing along the flagstones, a tattered reminder of the past night's festivities. The crowd of costumed onlookers had long since dispersed, though a few disheveled maskers were still staggering down the avenue in their various directions home.

Her own appearance must be equally disreputable, she reminded herself with a glance down at her soot-streaked gown, missing a good portion of its glittering glass beads and liberally peppered with tiny burns. Doubtless her face was equally grimy, so that a casual observer might dismiss her as a street urchin who had played at Mardi gras for too long.

She turned her gaze toward the brothel across the street. All that remained of the once-elegant establishment was a smoldering framework of charred lumber and blistered ironwork. From what she had gleaned from overheard bits of the firefighters' conversation, the fire *had* started accidentally—the cause an overturned brazier, just as Tark had speculated. Now, the acrid stench of smoke mingled with the area's usual odors of stale urine and rotting garbage. As she watched, one of the few remaining timbers collapsed upon itself and sent a flurry of white ashes heavenward.

Ashes. Ash Wednesday.

She stiffened at the sound of a familiar footfall. Not taking her eyes from the blackened ruin, she asked in an emotionless voice, "Did they find . . . anyone?"

"Your uncle's body was recovered a short while ago," Tark gently answered as he settled on the slab beside her. "They also found a second body they suspect is Ophelia's. It seems she came back into the building, probably hoping to retrieve some of her voodoo artifacts. The back room where they found her was set up with a kind of altar . . ."

He trailed off, and Isabeau glanced at him, wondering if he shared her thought that the quadroon's spirits had proved no match for more elemental forces. Finally, he went on, "The rest of the guests made it out safely, with nothing more than a few burns and bruises among them. The brothels on either side of Ophelia's place suffered some damage, but not so much that they won't be open for business as usual tonight."

He punctuated that observation with a grin that emphasized his worse-for-wear appearance this morning.

Unshaven and streaked with soot, his face bore a few burns and bruises of its own. His gunshot wound had been freshly bandaged, the snowy wrappings a stark contrast to his singed and smoke-stained pirate's costume.

Mon Dieu, had ever a man—Creole or *américain*—looked more handsome?

The silent question brought with it a pang of longing. Even the memory of his kiss last night, a kiss as hotly passionate as the fire that had burned before them, could bring her no comfort. With the matter of the grand duke's attempted kidnapping settled, and Lili and Regine restored to their rightful family, the ties that had bound them for a time were no more. Tark would go his way, while she would fulfill her own obligations . . . knowing as she did that she would never forget him.

"Why so pensive, my sweet?" his voice broke in on her thoughts. "If you're worried about Regine, I already sent word to Alma. She said she'd be happy to take care of the babe until things settle down. Lili is in good hands, too. Marcel took her home to his mother, since she's obviously in no shape right now to take care of herself."

"But will she ever recover?" Isabeau asked, momentarily forgetting her own troubles. "I know that she is not truly the walking dead, as Ophelia claimed, but something about her seems so . . . so wrong."

"That's another bit of good news I have for you," Tark replied with a grin. "I had a little chat with Tom Sullivan a few minutes ago. He told me that while we were busy with kidnappings and fires, a former servant

of yours named Lucie was paying you an unannounced
visit. Unfortunately for her, your brother's fiancée happened upon her just as she was trying to make off with
a shawlful of silverware and jewelry. Cammi hit her over
the head with a frying pan, tied her to a chair, and held
her there until Tom showed up."

"Cammi stopped her?" Isabeau exclaimed in mingled
delight and awe, then returned to the subject of her
cousin. "Tell me, did Lucie say anything about what
happened to Lili?"

Tark nodded. "She wasn't too anxious to admit anything, until she learned that Ophelia was presumed
dead. Then, she decided to make a clean breast of
things."

His tone turned grim. "From what I understand,
Ophelia slipped your cousin a poison whose symptoms
mimic death—complete with slowed pulse and respira-
tion, so that even a physician could be fooled. Lili's
crypt had barely been sealed and the mourners gone
when some of Ophelia's people showed up and stole
what they believed to be her dead body. When Ophelia
poured another potion into her, it counteracted the poison and revived her enough so that she could hear and
see and move—but not enough so that she could fight
what was happening to her."

"And Ophelia told her followers that she had created
a zombie," Isabeau said with a shiver. "But will Lili
ever be the same again?"

"If Lucie can be believed, the effect of that particular
drug wears off fairly swiftly, but no one can say what
effect the whole ordeal will have had on her. Now she
needs the security of her family around her . . . and if

my guess is right, Marcel will see to it that she doesn't go through her recovery alone."

He paused, his gaze unfathomable, and Isabeau was beset by the suspicion that his words held a much deeper meaning. "Last night on the docks, your friend Marcel and I had a little chat. It seems he was quite unaware of the singular honor you'd done him."

"What do you mean?"

"What I mean, my sweet Isabeau," he softly replied, "is that your so-called fiancé claims you never agreed to be his wife."

"But that is not true!"

Isabeau shot him a frantic look. "Surely you must recall the night of Madame Dumas's cotillion. He asked me to marry him that same evening, and I agreed to give him my answer by Ash Wednesday. And I did . . . or, rather, I told Philippe to tell him that I had decided to accept his suit. You see, after the first time that you and I . . . that is, I did not know what to do afterwards . . ."

She trailed off miserably. *He thinks that I deliberately lied, that I rejected him out of hand.* What other conclusion could he have drawn . . . and what good would it do her to protest her innocence now? But she *would* protest. She would beg, cajole, even scream, if necessary, but somehow she would make him listen, make him believe the truth . . . that she loved him, and not Marcel.

"I think, my sweet, that we should start again from the very beginning," Tark suggested with a grin when she stared at him in disbelief.

Not waiting for her reply, though indeed she suddenly

felt incapable of forming one, he went on, "When a man finds himself unexpectedly staring at death, he gains a little perspective on life. The entire time I was standing on that burning gallery, all I could think was that I might never get the chance to tell you I understood why you had done what you did . . . and that I was sorry I hadn't told you sooner. So now, I think I should get formal permission from your brother to court you. And after that, I—"

"Mister Parrish! Mister Parrish!"

Tark stopped short at the sound of a reedy voice drifting to them from halfway down the block. "Well, I'll be damned," he muttered with a shake of his head as he draped his arm around her shoulder.

Isabeau followed his gaze to see the speaker alight from a shiny black coach and start toward them at a dignified lope. At closer range, the figure proved to be a balding, soberly dressed gentleman of middling years. He halted before them, clutching an expensive bowler in one hand while using the other to mop his high forehead with a snowy handkerchief.

"I stopped by your office," he began his explanation, "but your housekeeper informed me that I might find you here, instead." The man took pains not to stare at Isabeau, though he allowed himself a glance at the brothel's charred remains behind them before returning his gaze to Tark.

"This, my sweet, is Aloysius Burnett," Tark drawled, not bothering to take his arm from around her shoulder or rise from his unconventional perch. "He happens to be one of the city's most respected financiers—and a former client of mine. Mr. Burnett, may I present Made-

moiselle Isabeau Lavoisier, my fiancée . . . that is, if
she will agree to have me."

"*Oui*, I will have you," Isabeau fervently replied and
flung herself into Tark's arms. To his credit, Burnett had
the delicacy to avert his gaze as she proceeded to dem-
onstrate her sincerity with a kiss that any proper Creole
mademoiselle would term shocking.

By the time she and Tark separated, Burnett's pale
cheeks were suspiciously red. "A pleasure to make your
acquaintance, miss," he said with a prim nod in her
direction before turning back to Tark. "May I offer my
felicitations on your upcoming nuptials . . . and perhaps
pass on a bit of news that will make the occasion even
more memorable."

"News?"

Tark spoke lightly, but Isabeau sensed a sudden tension in him that belied his casual tone. He rose from
the granite block and reached out a hand, drawing her
to her feet in a single fluid move. "As I recall, your
last announcement left something to be desired. I trust
this one will prove more edifying."

"Indeed, it shall." The banker gave a smile and
paused for what Isabeau assumed was dramatic effect.
"I had word just after dawn that a freighter by the name
of *Esmeralda* was steaming toward New Orleans. By
my calculations, she should be making port within a
quarter of an hour."

When Tark made no reply, Burnett's hopeful expression turned crestfallen. "I don't understand, Mister Parrish. Your gamble seems to have paid off. I thought you
would be delighted by the news."

He clamped on his bowler and tucked away his handkerchief. "Ahem. Well, perhaps you might care to stop by my office at your earliest convenience, so we can discuss my clients' future contracts with your firm." With a final nod at Isabeau, he started back toward his coach.

"Your Mr. Burnett is indeed an unusual gentleman," she diplomatically observed once the banker was safely out of earshot. "What did he mean by this talk of freighters and investments?"

Tark turned to face her. "What he meant, my sweet Isabeau," he replied with a slow grin, "is that in about fifteen minutes from now, I'll be rich again."

"Rich?" she echoed. "But whatever is the *Esmeralda* carrying that is so valuable?"

"Bananas," he replied, and then gave a mock frown when she simply stared at him. "Don't look so incredulous, my sweet. The Oteris brothers have been importing bananas since the end of the war—and doing quite well for themselves, I might add. I figured they could use a bit of competition."

"Mon Dieu, bananas," she mused with a shake of her head . . . and then laughed. Her sudden carefree air, however, had nothing to do with visions of wealth or power.

Tark's answering chuckle held the same contented note as he offered her his arm. "What would you say, Mademoiselle Lavoisier, if I asked you to join me at the wharf to inspect my cargo?"

She glanced from his disheveled clothes and soot-streaked face down to her own sadly crumpled gown. "I would say, Monsieur Parrish, that I would be proud to join you anywhere."

Her smile was more brilliant than all the *flambeaux* of Comus, as Isabeau delicately placed her fingertips upon Tark's torn sleeve and started down the *banquette* with him.

Author's Note

Woven into 19th century New Orleans' dusty tapestry of Old World European cultures were two slightly more exotic threads . . . those of the African and Caribbean peoples. Their colorful traditions had a marked effect on New Orleans' cuisine, language, and music that has lasted to this day. But with these benign influences came certain darker elements, including the spirit-based worship known as Voodoo.

Marie Laveau (and later, her daughter of the same name) was the acknowledged queen of that obscure religion for much of the 1800s. She was a tall, striking woman of mixed blood who updated the old Voodoo traditions by adding a dash of Roman Catholicism into her rituals and allowing outsiders to witness those ceremonies for the price of admission. Countless Orleanians, black and white, sought her help in such matters as love, money, and health. Her power was such that she even was rumored to have an inordinate amount of influence with various public figures.

But Marie also had her share of enemies. Numerous lesser, self-proclaimed queens periodically tried to wrest control of her followers from her. My character, Ophelia, is based upon those women who craved the power and prestige that was Marie's . . . and who would do whatever was necessary to prove themselves her worthy successor.

Dear Reader:

As part of their 1872 Mardi Gras festivities, the people of New Orleans played host to the dashing Russian grand duke, Alexis Romanoff Alexandrovitch. His visit reputedly was prompted by his amorous pursuit of Lydia Thompson, a musical-comedy star whose schedule of performances had paralleled a portion of Alexis's own American tour.

Though their scandalous romance proved short-lived, the duke's visit inspired Carnival traditions that continue to this day. Among them were the selection of purple, green and gold as the regulation Carnival colors, and the impromptu choice of Lydia's whimsical ballad, "If Ever I Cease to Love," as the unofficial theme song of Mardi Gras.

But if the 19th century Orleanians thrilled to this brush with genuine royalty, Alexis seemed less than impressed with his hosts. By all accounts, he proved a disappointingly aloof observer of the Mardi Gras proceedings—hardly the sort of behavior one might expect from a flamboyant young man with a well-documented taste for adventure and romance.

It was from this paradox and my own fascination with New Orleans that Tark and Isabeau's story first sprang. You see, I preferred to think that Alexis found his own way to enjoy the magic of the "City that Care Forgot" . . . and who better to share his adventures than a feisty Creole heroine and a rugged American hero? I hope that, in telling their tale, I have captured for you something of the warm heart and passionate soul that is New Orleans.

Alexa Smart

DENISE LITTLE PRESENTS
ROMANCES THAT YOU'LL WANT TO READ
OVER AND OVER AGAIN!

LAWLESS (0017, $4.99)
by Alexandra Thorne

Determined to save her ranch, Caitlan must confront former lover, Comanche Killian. But the minute they lock eyes, she longs for his kiss. Frustrated by her feelings, she exchanges hard-hitting words with the rugged foreman; but underneath the anger lie two hearts in need of love. Beset by crooked Texas bankers, dishonest politicians, and greedy Japanese bankers, they fight for their heritage and each other.

DANGEROUS ILLUSIONS (0018, $4.99)
by Amanda Scott

After the bloody battle of Waterloo, Lord Gideon Deverill visits Lady Daintry Tarrett to break the news of the death of her fiance. His duty to his friend becomes a pleasure when lovely Lady Daintry turns to him for comfort.

TO SPITE THE DEVIL (0030, $4.99)
by Paula Jonas

Patience Hendley is having it rough. Her English nobleman husband has abandoned her after one month of marriage. Her father is a Tory, her brother is a patriot, and her handsome bondservant Tom, an outright rebel! And now she is torn between her loyalist upbringing and the revolution sweeping the American colonies. Her only salvation is the forbidden love that she shares with Tom, which frees her from the shackles of the past!

GLORY (0031, $4.99)
by Anna Hudson

When Faith, a beautiful "country mouse", goes to St. Louis to claim her inheritance, she comes face to face with the Seatons, a wealthy big city family. As Faith tries to turn these stuffed shirts around, the Seatons are trying to change her as well. Young Jason Seaton is sure he can civilize Faith, who is a threat to the family fortune. Then after many hilarious misunderstandings Jason and Faith fall madly in love, and she manages to thaw even the stuffiest Seaton!

Available wherever paperbacks are sold, or order direct from the Publisher. Send cover price plus 50¢ per copy for mailing and handling to Penguin USA, P.O. Box 999, c/o Dept. 17109, Bergenfield, NJ 07621. Residents of New York and Tennessee must include sales tax. DO NOT SEND CASH.

ROMANCES ABOUT AFRICAN-AMERICANS!
YOU'LL FALL IN LOVE
WITH ARABESQUE BOOKS FROM PINNACLE

SERENADE (0024, $4.99)
by Sandra Kitt

Alexandra Morrow was too young and naive when she first fell in love with musician, Parker Harrison—and vowed never to be so vulnerable again. Now Parker is back and although she tries to resist him, he strolls back into her life as smoothly as the jazz rhapsodies for which he is known. Though not the dreamy innocent she was before, Alexandra finds her defenses quickly crumbling and her mind, body and soul slowly opening up to her one and only love, who shows her that dreams do come true.

FOREVER YOURS (0025, $4.99)
by Francis Ray

Victoria Chandler must find a husband quickly or her grandparents will call in the loans that support her chain of lingerie boutiques. She arranges a mock marriage to tall, dark and handsome ranch owner Kane Taggart. The marriage will only last one year, and her business will be secure, and Kane will be able to walk away with no strings attached. The only problem is that Kane has other plans for Victoria. He'll cast a spell that will make her his forever after.

A SWEET REFRAIN (0041, $4.99)
by Margie Walker

Fifteen years before, jazz musician Nathaniel Padell walked out on Jenine to seek fame and fortune in New York City. But now the handsome widower is back with a baby girl in tow. Jenine is still irresistibly attracted to Nat and enchanted by his daughter. Yet even as love is rekindled, an unexpected danger threatens Nat's child. Now, Jenine must fight for Nat before someone stops the music forever!

Available wherever paperbacks are sold, or order direct from the Publisher. Send cover price plus 50¢ per copy for mailing and handling to Penguin USA, P.O. Box 999, c/o Dept. 17109, Bergenfield, NJ 07621. Residents of New York and Tennessee must include sales tax. DO NOT SEND CASH.

PUT SOME FANTASY IN YOUR LIFE—
FANTASTIC ROMANCES FROM PINNACLE

TIME STORM   (728, $4.99)
by Rosalyn Alsobrook
Modern-day Pennsylvanian physician JoAnn Griffin only believed
what she could feel with her five senses. But when, during a freak
storm, a blinding flash of lightning sent her back in time to 1889,
JoAnn realized she had somehow crossed the threshold into another century and was now gazing into the smoldering eyes of a
startlingly handsome stranger. JoAnn had stumbled through a rip
in time . . . and into a love affair so intense, it carried her to a point
of no return!

SEA TREASURE   (790, $4.50)
by Johanna Hailey
When Michael, a dashing sea captain, is rescued from drowning by
a beautiful sea siren—he does not know yet that she's actually a
mermaid. But her breathtaking beauty stirred irresistible yearnings
in Michael. And soon fate would drive them across the treacherous
Caribbean, tossing them on surging tides of passion that tran-
scended two worlds!

ONCE UPON FOREVER   (883, $4.99)
by Becky Lee Weyrich
A moonstone necklace and a mysterious diary written over a century ago were Clair Summerland's only clues to her true identity.
Two men loved her—one, a dashing civil war hero . . . the other, a
daring jet pilot. Now Clair must risk her past and future for a passion that spans two worlds—and a love that is stronger than time
itself.

SHADOWS IN TIME   (892, $4.50)
by Cherlyn Jac
Driving through the sultry New Orleans night, one moment Tori's
car spins out of control; the next she is in a horse-drawn carriage
with the handsomest man she has ever seen—who calls her wife—-
but whose eyes blaze with fury. Sent back in time one hundred
years, Tori is falling in love with the man she is apparently trying to
kill. Now she must race against time to change the tragic past and
claim her future with the man she will love through all eternity!

*Available wherever paperbacks are sold, or order direct from the
Publisher. Send cover price plus 50¢ per copy for mailing and handling to Penguin USA, P.O. Box 999, c/o Dept. 17109, Bergenfield, NJ 07621. Residents of New York and Tennessee must
include sales tax. DO NOT SEND CASH.*

IF ROMANCE BE THE FRUIT OF LIFE—
READ ON—
BREATH-QUICKENING HISTORICALS FROM PINNACLE

WILDCAT (772, $4.99)
by Rochelle Wayne
No man alive could break Diana Preston's fiery spirit . . . until seductive Vince Gannon galloped onto Diana's sprawling family ranch. Vince, a man with dark secrets, would sweep her into his world of danger and desire. And Diana couldn't deny the powerful yearnings that branded her as his own, for all time!

THE HIGHWAY MAN (765, $4.50)
by Nadine Crenshaw
When a trumped-up murder charge forced beautiful Jane Fitzpatrick to flee her home, she was found and sheltered by the highwayman—a man as dark and dangerous as the secrets that haunted him. As their hiding place became a place of shared dreams—and soaring desires—Jane knew she'd found the love she'd been yearning for!

SILKEN SPURS (756, $4.99)
by Jane Archer
Beautiful Harmony Harper, leader of a notorious outlaw gang, rode the desert plains of New Mexico in search of justice and vengeance. Now she has captured powerful and privileged Thor Clarke-Jargon, who is everything Harmony has ever hated—and all she will ever want. And after Harmony has taken the handsome adventurer hostage, she herself has become a captive—of her own desires!

WYOMING ECSTASY (740, $4.50)
by Gina Robins
Feisty criminal investigator, July MacKenzie, solicits the partnership of the legendary half-breed gunslinger-detective Nacona Blue. After being turned down, July—never one to accept the meaning of the word no—finds a way to convince Nacona to be her partner . . . first in business—then in passion. Across the wilds of Wyoming, and always one step ahead of trouble, July surrenders to passion's searing demands!

Available wherever paperbacks are sold, or order direct from the Publisher. Send cover price plus 50¢ per copy for mailing and handling to Penguin USA, P.O. Box 999, c/o Dept. 17109, Bergenfield, NJ 07621. Residents of New York and Tennessee must include sales tax. DO NOT SEND CASH.